BEWARE
THE
Raven

TM ROCHE

Library of Congress Control Number: 2025919682

Publisher's Cataloging-in-Publication Data

Names: Roche, T. M., author.

Title: Beware the Raven / T. M. Roche.

Series: The Hollow Prison Series

Description: Calhan, CO: Drag & Fly Press, LLC, 2025.

Identifiers: LCCN: 2025919682 | ISBN: 979-8-9931369-0-5 (hardcover) | 979-8-9931369-1-2 (paperback) | 979-8-9931369-2-9 (ebook) Subjects: LCSH Death--Fiction. | Family--Fiction. | Horror fiction. | Fantasy fiction. | BISAC FICTION / Fantasy / Dark Fantasy | FICTION / Horror Classification: LCC PS3618. O34 B49 2025 | DDC 813.6--dc23

Published by Drag & Fly Press
Calhan, Colorado, USA
www.dragandflypress.com

Cover design & Formatting by Tamara Cribley, The Deliberate Page

Printed in the United States of America

For those who walk through shadows and still reach for light,
May you hear your own echoes in these pages.

Whispers Before the Hollow

There is a door deep within the Hollow. It does not open out—only in.

(Some say it opens inward forever.

Daniel knows better. It opens to what waits.)

No one remembers who built it. No one claims to guard it.

But the mist hangs heavy there, like it knows.

Sometimes Daniel passes by, and the door stays quiet.

Other times, it hums—low and steady.

Behind it, stories collect.

Not written. Not told. Just waiting.

Names too old for memory.

Cries that never reached the surface.

Once, Daniel thought he heard his own voice beyond it.

Calling. Pleading.

Maybe to be let in.

Maybe to be let out.

Maybe both.

He did not open it.

Not yet.

What the Hollow Remembers

Before the boy. Before the key.
There were others.

The Hollow has seen many rulers rise and fall, each leaving marks in its mist. These were not heroes or villains, but echoes—the Hollow's first experiments in memory.

It remembers them as stories more than souls, for nothing stays whole here for long.

The Hollow remembers them all.

Its form was never fixed. Its rivers shift like veins beneath translucent skin. Its walls reshape to mirror the will of those who lingered too long. It has always been a place that learns from those who enter it, changing as they change.

The Hollow remembers the girl who came first, in the time when the boundaries were still soft. The girl who stitched a wolf's name into her sleeve because memory here was currency, and forgetting meant erasure. Her needle moved in careful spirals, thread catching moonlight that had never touched living skin. *Fenris*, she whispered with each stitch—the name of the creature that had torn her throat in another life, another world. No living creature answers to that name now; only the Hollow remembers it.

The wound she carried from another life had healed in silver threads, raised like embroidery across her throat. Here, she wore the scars like jewelry.

The Hollow had not yet learned to be cruel in those early days. It simply was—a pocket of existence where the lost could linger, where stories too broken for any other ending might find rest. The girl wandered through its mists for decades, teaching others how to anchor themselves with small rituals. How to hold onto the taste of their first kiss, the sound of their mother's laugh, the weight of their child's hand in theirs.

She taught them that memory was survival.

The Hollow learned. And grew hungry.

The Hollow remembers the fighter, broad-shouldered and grim-faced, whose hands had known the weight of a thousand swords in the world above. Here, he carried only a spade. He dug graves in ground that had never known seasons, marking each mound with stones carved from his own knuckles. At first, he etched names deep into the rock.

But the names faded. The stone remembered what he could no longer bear to recall.

By the hundredth grave, he carved only dates. By the thousandth, only marks. Tallies in a language of loss that no living tongue could speak.

The fighter never stopped digging. Even now, if you listen carefully on the nights when the mist runs thin, you can hear the scrape of metal against stone. The rhythm never changes. Never hurries. Never stops.

The Hollow has learned patience from him.

The sound endures, but the man is long gone. Only the Hollow keeps his rhythm.

The Hollow remembers the scholar, ink-stained and desperate, clutching parchments that crumbled at his touch. He had been writing the rules of the world when death found him—equations of light and shadow, theorems of soul and substance. Here, he tried to continue his work.

But the Hollow's mathematics were different. For every law he defined, two exceptions emerged. For every truth he carved in stone, the stone itself would lie. His papers filled with contradictions until ink wept from his eyes instead of tears. His fingers bled from writing words that unraveled as soon as they dried.

Still, he could not stop. Even as his flesh grew thin and his voice became a whisper, he wrote. He rewrote. He crossed out and began again, convinced that somewhere in the endless permutations of ink and intention lay the secret of escape.

The pages now blow through the Hollow like autumn leaves, covered in equations that solve for nothing, theorems that prove only their own impossibility. But sometimes a soul will find one of his fragments and understand something new about the nature of this place.

The Hollow had learned from his obsession how to make hope into torment.

His name has vanished from even the Hollow's memory; only the contradictions remain.

From these, the Hollow learned form and hunger. But what it became under the next soul was something new entirely.

Last came the one who would call himself Grim, though the name was not yet his own.

He had been a healer once, in the world of blood and breath. Elias, his name had been. Elias Blackthorne, whose hands could draw poison from wounds, whose voice could call the dying back from distant shores. But when plague swept through his city like wildfire, his skills proved worthless against such scale.

He watched them die. His patients. His assistants. His students. Those who had trusted him to hold the line between life and whatever lay beyond.

In his rage and grief, he had tried to follow them. To breach the wall between living and dead, to tear his loved ones back from whatever realm had claimed them. He succeeded, after a fashion. But what he pulled from the void were not his wife, nor his daughter, nor the bright-eyed apprentices who had called him Master.

What returned wore their faces, spoke their words, carried their memories. But underneath, they were hollow. Puppets of flesh animated by his desperate will, reflecting only what he needed to see.

When he realized his mistake, the horror drove him deeper into forbidden arts. If he could not restore them, perhaps he could join them. If he could not heal death, perhaps he could master it.

He succeeded in that, too.

As he studied death, The Hollow studied him in turn, its mists thickening around his thoughts, shaping themselves to the contours of his grief. When his heart stopped, the realm claimed him, but unlike them, he did not arrive as supplicant or refugee. He came as conqueror. His knowledge of death's machinery, fused with unending rage at its inevitability, made him something the Hollow had never encountered before.

A soul that refused to be digested.

The realm tried to break him as it had broken the others— with forgetting, with endless repetition, with the slow erosion of hope. But unlike them, his defiance became architecture. His will seeded walls and towers, corridors of penance that rose in answer to his hunger for control. The Hollow bent to him as it had bent for others before. Only this time, it did not stop bending. He began to reshape the Hollow to his vision. Where once it had been merely indifferent, he made it cruel. Where it had offered the mercy of forgetting, he created ledgers that remembered every transgression.

Where lost souls had once found strange comfort in shared exile, he built hierarchies of suffering.

Under Grim's rule, the Hollow learned its most terrible lesson: that some kinds of pain could be made eternal.

But the Hollow is older than any single soul, older than any single vision of what it should be. It remembers states of being that existed before Grim's iron certainty, and it carries within its mists the seeds of other possibilities.

It does not hope—hope is a living thing, and the Hollow is decidedly not alive. But it remembers what balance felt like, in the time before one soul became dominant over all others.

And lately, it has begun to stir.

There are rumors of a sound on the wind, something that carries neither rage nor meaning, yet threatens everything. The old ones—those few who remember the time before Grim—whisper that it sounds like calling. Like a voice reaching across impossible distances, seeking not conquest but connection.

The chains that bind the ledger in Grim's Sanctum have begun to sing in harmonies born of hope rather than bondage. Stone itself seems to listen, walls leaning inward as if straining to hear something just beyond the range of perception.

A raven has been seen circling the spires—black wings cutting through gray mist, eyes reflecting depths that should not exist in any living creature. It does not call as ravens should. It watches with ancient eyes, bearing witness to the first cracks in Grim's forged dominion.

The Hollow does not hope. But it remembers what happened the last time a key found its lock, the last time someone arrived who carried light instead of shadow, love instead of rage.

It remembers how Grim's certainty had wavered when faced with something he could not control through fear or force.

The realm holds its breath, waiting to see if the pattern will repeat. If another soul will arrive carrying questions instead of answers, compassion instead of judgment.

If someone will finally challenge not just Grim's rule, but the very foundations of what the Hollow has become.

The mist swirls in new patterns. The stones hum with frequencies they have not known for centuries.

Something is coming.

And for the first time in longer than memory, the Hollow wonders if it might yet become something other than a monument to one soul's eternal grief.

The raven calls once, sharp and clear and strangely hopeful. The silence that follows carries weight, pregnant with possibility. And through that silence comes the sound of footsteps on paths made of starlight and stubborn hope, moving toward a confrontation that has been centuries in the making.

The boy is coming.

The key is coming.

And the Hollow pauses on the edge of transformation, ready to remember what it felt like to be more than a prison.

Ready to discover what it might become when its long dream finally ends.

1

Where the Road Ends

*"Get in, get out. Don't overthink it.
Overthinking gets you caught. You've
done this a dozen times before."*

Daniel repeated the mantra under his breath as he stepped into the liquor store, blending into the slow-moving current of customers. With his eighteenth birthday only a couple of months away, he looked nowhere near old enough to buy liquor. But no one paid any attention to him. The disheveled man at the register was thumbing through his crumpled bills. The tired clerk rang up cheap vodka and whiskey without so much as a glance at the buyers. Everyone was too busy hiding their own shame to notice him.

He moved toward the cases stocked with mid-shelf liquor, where bottles gleamed under fluorescent light. Standing near a man already juggling a few selections, he kept his posture relaxed. Casual.

"Could you pass me one of those while you're in there?" Daniel asked, his voice polite, practiced.

The man barely looked up, already reaching for another bottle. "This one?"

"Yeah, thanks," Daniel said, taking the vodka from the stranger's hand.

It was too easy. The guy didn't even pause to wonder if Daniel was old enough to buy it. His mind was somewhere else, just another person lost in the fog of their own voices. That was the trick, really. Disappear into the rhythm of the store, let people assume you belong.

Daniel followed the man toward the checkout, trailing behind. As the man stepped into line, Daniel moved smoothly, tucking the bottle into the inner pocket of his jacket. His hands slid into his coat pockets. Posture easy, unbothered. Just a kid standing behind his dad, waiting to leave the store.

By the time the man grabbed his bag and walked out, no one remembered that Daniel had been holding anything at all. No one questioned why his hands were empty. No one spared him a glance as he strolled right out the door behind his unwitting accomplice.

"Aw, man! You did it!" One of his friends whooped, throwing the passenger door open. "Knew you would. Get in, we're about to have some fun."

Daniel slid into the back seat, the stolen bottle pressing against his ribs. It was nothing. A cheap bottle of vodka, a drop in the bucket for the shop owner, something easily written off as a loss. No one got hurt. No one even noticed. That was the way he had to think of it.

So why did his stomach still twist with unease?

It was a stupid reaction. The guilt would fade, like it always did. That was why the others sent him in. He was still getting used to it, still "toughening up." They told him it would get easier with time. Maybe they were right. After all, what did he have to lose? Everything that mattered was already gone.

The boys had skipped school and driven to the next town over, where no one knew their names or their parents. No nosy neighbors. No teachers to catch them loitering in the streets. It was easier to breathe here, easier to disappear into the noise of a bigger city.

And Daniel thought about disappearing a lot.

His fingers traced the curve of the bottle through his jacket as he stared out the window. If he vanished, who would even care? Would anyone notice?

The scream of sirens intruded on his thoughts.

His head snapped up. Police. They were close.

Instinct told him to stay still, to keep his hands steady, his face blank. It was just another chase, someone else's problem. They weren't doing anything. They hadn't even cracked the bottle open yet.

Then the sirens swelled, growing louder.

Two police cruisers roared into the shopping center parking lot, red and blue lights flashing in the dusk. Tires screeched against pavement as they skidded into position, boxing in the boys' car before anyone had a chance to react.

"Aw, shit," someone breathed.

Daniel's pulse slammed against his ribs.

Doors flung open. Officers moved fast, shouting commands.

Arms went up. His friends froze, too stunned to move.

Daniel barely registered the bottle slipping from his pocket, hitting the floorboard with a dull, final thud.

"Aw, shit," he whispered.

Elizabeth clenched her fists, fighting back the tears she knew would come. There were too many things to do before she could allow herself to drown in grief. Too many preparations, too many responsibilities. Her chest tightened with overwhelming dread. It built and built until she thought she might explode.

She needed to scream.

"It's not fair!" The words tore from her throat, raw and ragged. "What have I done to deserve this? How could you let this happen, God?" She lifted her face to the sky, tears blurring the edges of the world. "I've tried! I've done my best! And You just let the world shit all over me!" Her voice cracked. "Why?"

Silence.

Her throat burned from the force of her screams, her vocal cords raw and aching. The wind whispered, indifferent as ever.

Her knees buckled. A sob shuddered through her, then another. The fight left her all at once, and she sank to the floor, trembling. She knew there would be no answers. There never were. Life was cruel and unfair. It always had been. And yet, she had tried. She had stayed positive, done what was right. And this? This was how God repaid her? His final fuck you, Elizabeth?

Shame curled inside her, cold and bitter. She shouldn't think that way. She knew she shouldn't.

But deep down, she had known the truth long before the words left the doctor's lips. She had clung to hope, convinced herself it was just some passing illness. Something she could fight with vitamins, rest, and sheer determination. She would have done whatever it took. Anything so she could stay. Stay for the ones who needed her. For the ones she loved.

Her fingers curled into the fabric of her jeans as she drew in a shaky breath. "Please, God," she prayed, her voice barely more than a whisper. "Just give me enough time to take care of them first. Please. That's all I ask."

She wiped her tears away with trembling hands, sniffled, and forced herself to look in the mirror. Her mascara had smudged into dark circles smeared beneath her eyes. She grabbed a tissue, dabbing carefully beneath each one before blowing her nose.

First things first.

She had to get home.

Her mother would be expecting her soon. Dinner needed to be made. She had already been gone too long.

Elizabeth's stomach twisted as she thought of the last time she had left her mother alone for too long. The memory still made her throat tighten. The acrid scent of smoke, the flickering orange glow that had filled the kitchen, the panic in her mother's eyes as she stood frozen before the stove.

She hadn't meant to leave the burner on. She had only wanted to make Krissy something to eat after school, knowing Elizabeth was holed up in her office, writing.

Elizabeth had been lucky that time. Next time, though, who knows what might happen.

Her mother tried so hard to cling to her independence, but dementia was a cruel thief. And the hardest part wasn't the forgetting. It was watching her become someone Elizabeth barely recognized.

Her grip tightened around the steering wheel as she pulled onto the winding mountain road that led home. The late afternoon light filtered through the trees, casting long shadows across the pavement.

She had thought moving back to her hometown would bring comfort. A sense of familiarity, a fresh start for her and the kids after losing Marcus.

It hadn't.

It was struggle after struggle. A never-ending list of responsibilities and no one to share the burden. She had spent years dependent on her husband, his steady income, his presence as a protector, a provider. Without him, she had been left scrambling, desperate to stay afloat.

There were always offices to clean, churches in need of a caretaker. Small, thankless jobs that most people around here wouldn't lower themselves to do. But Elizabeth had no room for pride. With four mouths to feed and bills piling up, pride was a luxury she couldn't afford.

And then there was her writing.

Once, it had been a hobby, a passion she indulged in between deployments. A few short stories published in literary magazines. A couple of contests won. Not enough to make a career out of, but enough to spark something inside her. A world of her own making, an escape from reality's harsh grip.

Lately, though, it had become more than just a distraction.

It was survival.

Because when everything else felt impossible, when life closed in on her from every direction, writing was the one thing that still made sense. The only thing that was hers.

And God help her; she wasn't ready to let it go.

The drive home was easy enough. There was never any real traffic out there. The sun hung low in the autumn sky, casting long shadows across the road, but the brilliant red and gold leaves of the trees blocked most of the glare of the setting sun. Elizabeth let out a slow breath, willing the tension from her shoulders.

Thirty minutes. That was all the time she had to come up with a plan before she pulled into her driveway.

She would make some calls on Monday, but until then, there wasn't much she could do. This weekend would be for organizing, making lists, and weighing options. But mostly, she just wanted to be with her family. To sit at the kitchen table with Krissy, help her with homework, and maybe watch a movie together. Something simple. Something normal.

When she arrived home, the warmth of the tiny kitchen was a welcome contrast to the iciness outside. Krissy sat at the small table, books spread out in front of her, brow furrowed in concentration. Beside her, Elizabeth's mother sipped her tea, offering quiet suggestions where she could.

Elizabeth lingered in the doorway for a moment, watching them. Mom had been a math whiz in her day, adding long columns of numbers in her head faster than most people could punch them into a calculator. These days, elementary math sometimes stumped her. Elizabeth recognized the look on her mother's face. The way her brows knitted, her lips pressed together in frustration. Reaching for something she knew should be there, but grasping only wisps of smoke.

"Have you two eaten anything yet?" Elizabeth stepped further inside and set her purse down.

"Grandma made me ants on a log after school." Krissy kept her focus on her work. "But that was hours ago."

Elizabeth smiled, glancing at her mother. "And what about you?"

Her mother waved a hand dismissively. "Oh, I'll have whatever everyone else is having." She paused, then straightened. "Can I help with anything?"

Elizabeth hesitated. She knew how much her mother needed to feel useful.

"Sure, Mom. How about making some garlic butter for the bread?"

Her mother's face lit up, and she pushed back from the table eagerly. "Of course! I'll get started."

Elizabeth turned toward the stove, pulling out a pot to start dinner. Behind her, Krissy put her pencil down and stretched.

"What about spaghetti?" Krissy's voice lifted with hope.

"Spaghetti it is." Elizabeth pulled out a larger pot.

She had just set the pot of water on the burner when a flicker of movement caught her attention.

"Grandma?" Krissy's voice was uncertain.

Elizabeth turned to find her mother at the counter, pouring milk into a glass. Beside her sat a package of cookies, one already unwrapped and resting on a napkin.

"What are you doing, Grandma?" Krissy's voice carried that gentleness she had learned to use.

Her mother hesitated, looking around in mild confusion before setting the milk down.

"Making you cookies and milk, like you asked." Her mother's tone turned defensive.

Krissy and Elizabeth exchanged a glance.

Elizabeth moved to her mother's side, gently taking the milk from her hand and guiding her back toward the table. "That was very thoughtful, Mom. Why don't you sit down and relax for a little bit?"

Krissy caught on quickly. "Thanks, Grammy." Krissy's voice brightened as she grabbed the cookie and dunked it into the milk.

"These are my favorite." She popped it into her mouth, grinning as she chewed.

Her grandmother smiled, pleased, and Elizabeth let out a quiet breath of relief.

She turned back to the stove, stirring the noodles absently. "Has anyone seen Daniel today?"

Silence.

Of course, no one had.

Lately, Daniel came and went as he pleased, slipping in and out of the house like a ghost. He never offered explanations. When she asked where he had been, it usually ended in an argument— one loud enough to get the neighbors' attention, sometimes loud enough to bring the wrong kind of attention.

Lately, she had stopped asking.

She knew he was hurting. He had been closer to his father than anyone, and Marcus's death had gutted him. Elizabeth had tried to reach him, to get him to open up, but Daniel had shut her out at every turn.

Later, she thought. I'll figure it out later.

When dinner was finished, when her mother and Krissy were tucked into bed, Elizabeth finally allowed herself a moment to breathe.

She curled up on the couch, a book in her lap, fingers brushing over the well-worn pages. It was a historical fantasy novel. A story of forbidden love, of ancient wars, of a heroine on the verge of discovering her destiny.

Elizabeth lost herself in it, in the richness of the world, the depth of the characters. The heroine stood on the edge of the battlefield, heart pounding, knowing that one wrong move would seal her fate...

Her phone rang, cutting through the moment.

Elizabeth blinked, pulling herself back to reality. She frowned at the unknown number flashing on the screen.

Hesitating for only a moment, she answered, "Hello?"

"Mrs. Donnelly?"

The voice was unfamiliar. Steady, professional.

"Yes, this is Mrs. Donnelly. Who is this?"

"This is Sergeant Dean. We have your son with us."

Elizabeth's heart nearly stopped.

"We need you to come to the station, please."

2

Strangers in the Dust

aniel sat in the interrogation room, arms crossed, his foot bouncing impatiently against the cold tile floor. The dim overhead light hummed, casting a sickly glow over the dull gray walls. He stared at the one-way mirror across from him, knowing someone was watching from the other side. Assessing. Probably already labeling him as just another punk kid caught up in stupid rebellion.

His mother was on her way.

She was going to be furious.

He told himself he didn't care. Why should he?

But the knot tightening in his stomach suggested otherwise.

Disappointing her had never been his intention. Not really. But he had stopped trying to make things easier for her a long time ago. What was the point? Nothing he did made a difference. What happened to their family? What happened to him? None of it was her fault. But it wasn't fair either.

Everything had been fine before his father was killed. No, more than fine. Good. Great, even. His dad had been his hero, the unshakable presence who had held their world together. And when he was gone, everything fell apart. His mom tried to hold on. She tried to keep them moving forward. Daniel saw the exhaustion in her eyes, burdened by responsibilities she never asked for.

And what had he done to help her? Nothing. He had made it harder for her. Had blamed her, as if she were somehow responsible for his father's death.

Guilt twisted in his chest, but he shoved it down, replacing it with anger, an easier emotion to manage.

His thoughts drifted to the ones who had landed him here— his so-called friends.

They had voted, and he had pulled the short straw. Simple as that.

"It builds character," Bud had laughed, clapping Daniel on the shoulder as if they were brothers-in-arms. "Besides, you need the practice."

The memory made Daniel's hands curl into fists. Practice? What the hell was that supposed to mean? Was he expected to take the fall? Was this his sole purpose in their group? To do the dirty work while they skate free?

They were supposed to be like family, and didn't families look out for each other? Didn't they stick together?

But wasn't that exactly what he was failing to do for his own mother?

No. It wasn't the same thing.

He hadn't chosen to be part of his biological family. They were forced on him, bound by blood and circumstance. But his friends? Chosen family should have been different. They were supposed to be closer. Stronger. A family built by choice, not obligation.

Instead, he had been recruited for a role he hadn't agreed to—a scapegoat.

The realization burned, but it also deepened his determination.

Daniel hated being used.

He had a new goal now. Revenge.

A slow smile crept across his lips as he considered what he would do when he saw them next. They had left him to take the fall. Meaning, they believed he was weak. Disposable.

They were wrong.

They would pay for abandoning him. They would regret leaving him behind.

They would never forget his name.

The door creaked open, breaking his thoughts.

Daniel forced the smirk from his face just in time to see the officer step inside.

"Daniel, your mom is here." The officer motioned toward the hallway.

Perfect.

He sat straighter, schooling his expression into one of indifference. He could already picture the scene about to unfold: his mother's voice ringing through the station, the officers exchanging glances, the lingering judgment in their eyes.

Yes, this should be entertaining.

He cracked his knuckles and rose to his feet.

Time to face the music.

"In here, please, Mrs. Donnelly."

The officer stepped aside, motioning for Elizabeth to enter the room.

"Wait here. Someone will be in to speak with both of you shortly."

"Thank you," she murmured, though the words were hollow.

The moment she stepped inside, her stomach tensed. Daniel sat in handcuffs, looking smaller and more fragile than she had ever seen him. How had things come to this? Where had she gone wrong?

A silent prayer formed in her mind.

God, please give me the time and wisdom to help my son.

She forced herself to swallow the knot in her throat and stepped closer.

"Are you okay, Daniel?"

He shrugged. At least it was a response.

"Are you hurt? Do you need anything?"

Guilt flickered across his face. The hard shell he had built around himself cracked for a short moment.

"I'm okay, I guess," he mumbled, his voice barely above a whisper.

Elizabeth saw it, the way his eyes watered, the way his face flushed as he tried to hold everything in. He was still so young, trying so hard to be tough. He shouldn't have to carry this kind of burden on his shoulders.

"I'm sorry," she muttered.

Daniel's eyes snapped to hers, confusion flashing across his face. "Why are you sorry? You didn't do anything."

Elizabeth let out a slow breath. "I wasn't there for you when you needed me. It's my fault it's come to this."

Misery flickered in his expression, and for a long moment, he said nothing. At last, his shoulders slumped.

"It's not your fault, Mom. It's mine. I made the choice to skip school. I made the choice to go joyriding. And I made the choice to steal."

The word stopped her cold. Stealing. They hadn't told her why he was here.

"You skipped school, huh?" she said, feigning a stern expression.

Daniel blinked at her and let out a nervous bark of laughter.

"That's what you're worried about right now?" his voice cracked, and the next thing she knew, tears spilled down his cheeks. But he was laughing, and she let herself laugh with him.

For a brief moment, the world was right again.

At that moment, the door swung open.

"I'm glad you both find this amusing," came a dry voice. "So happy to be your source of entertainment."

The sergeant stood in the doorway, arms crossed. The laughter died in an instant.

"You two are in hot water," he said, looking between them.

Elizabeth's stomach clenched. Surely this was a scare tactic for the kid. But Daniel frowned. "Both of us? What did Mom do?"

The sergeant let out a short sigh. "You're a minor, son. Your mother is legally responsible for you. That means she's on the hook for any damage you cause, any fines the judge imposes, and any costs related to this little stunt of yours. Do you understand that?"

Daniel paled. It was clear he hadn't even considered it.

"I…" He hesitated, his jaw tightening. "I thought I was the one responsible. That it was my mess to deal with."

"Well, now you know," the sergeant said with a note of impatience. He turned to Elizabeth. "Mrs. Donnelly, I have to inform you that you could be held liable for restitution to the shop owner for the stolen merchandise and any other costs the court deems necessary. This includes court fees, legal processing, and, if applicable, incarceration costs should the judge rule accordingly."

Elizabeth's head spun.

"Additionally," the sergeant continued, his tone softening a bit, "you are entitled to legal representation if you cannot afford a private attorney. Do you understand?"

Her mouth was dry. She could barely breathe, but she managed to nod once.

"Yes," she rasped. "I understand."

"Good. There will be paperwork for you to sign, and your son will be released into your custody tonight. You'll receive a court summons in the mail. Don't miss it."

"I won't," her voice cracked.

The officer left them alone again, but Elizabeth barely noticed. The room was suffocating. Her world was caving in around her, the pressure of responsibility crushing her chest.

Daniel leaned away from her, looking utterly wrecked.

She should have been furious. She should have lectured him, demanded to know what he had been thinking. But she couldn't. Not now.

Not when she was barely holding it together herself.

She could fall apart later when she was alone, when no one was watching.

Right now, her immediate concern was to get them both out of this place.

To figure out how the hell she was going to fix this.

Elizabeth counted to ten and let her breath out. She gripped the steering wheel as she struggled to gather her thoughts. She needed to reach Daniel, but if he felt attacked, he would shut her out without listening to a word she had to say. She knew her son too well.

Without being aware of it, she ran her teeth over her lower lip, trying to compartmentalize the chaotic storm in her mind. There were so many battles to fight, so many crises demanding her attention. But right now, only one mattered, and that was the boy sulking in the passenger seat beside her.

Daniel sat rigid, arms crossed, leaning into the door, and putting as much distance between them as possible in the cramped space. The car rattled beneath them, ancient and worn, yet filled with memories, ones that were almost foreign now. Memories of Daniel's father behind the wheel, of family road trips filled with laughter, of simpler times before their world shattered. It was hard to believe those moments had ever existed.

She glanced at him, her voice gentle as she broke the silence. "Are you sure you're okay?"

He huffed, still staring out the window. "I'm good. It's not like they beat me up or anything. I didn't even get to go into a cell." His voice cracked, the bravado faltering.

Elizabeth seized the crack in his armor. "Didn't get to? Were you hoping to see the inside of a jail cell?" She tightened her grip on the wheel. "I hope to God not. This isn't a game, Daniel. This is serious. You might think it was just a stupid prank, but it's so much more than that. You're throwing your whole future away. Doesn't that concern you at all?"

He scoffed, "What future?" He glared at her, not even trying to rein in his anger. "You dumped us in this godforsaken town that you love so much. Without even asking us what we wanted. It wasn't fair. And life has sucked ever since. What do you even care about my future, Mom? What kind of future do I even have here?"

Elizabeth kept her voice steady, though she chose every word carefully. "Your future isn't here, Daniel. Your present is here. And you don't get a better future handed to you. You work for it. We all do." She glanced at him, gauging whether he was still listening. "But you can't do that from a jail cell. And that's exactly where you're headed. Skipping school. The bad attitude. Poor grades. Stealing. And those..." she clenched her jaw, inhaling to keep her frustration at bay, "... those damn hoodlums you call friends. You keep this up, and you'll be stuck here forever in a town you hate, with no way out. You want to be treated like an adult? Be included in decisions? Then stop acting like a spoiled child."

Daniel sat straighter, his shoulders squaring. His anger sparked, igniting resentment deep inside him. He leaned toward her, closing the distance between them, his face twisted in fury.

Elizabeth flinched.

For the first time, she was afraid of him.

"Me?" he spat, voice rising. "I'm acting like a child? You treat me like one! You want respect, but you don't respect me enough to include me in decisions that affect my life! You didn't even warn us. You just packed us up, and we were supposed to blindly follow whatever hair-brained idea you pulled out of your ass!"

Elizabeth's grip on the wheel tightened, her knuckles white. The road ahead blurred, the spectral fingers of the fog thickened, twisting through the mountain pass. She could barely see the dividing lines; the headlights lit a few feet ahead. Her body was so tense, she jerked the wheel when the wiper blades skidded across the damp glass. If a deer darted into the road, she would never see it in time.

She needed to focus. But Daniel's voice was hammering at her temples.

"Watch your tone," she snapped.

Daniel sneered. "See? You're still telling me what to do! You tell me to act like an adult, but you treat me like a kid. Pretty hypocritical of you, isn't it, Mother dear?"

Elizabeth's chest constricted. The venom in his voice was foreign, unrecognizable.

Where had this hate come from?

The rain thickened, hammering against the windshield. Her pulse pounded in her ears as she switched the wipers to full speed. The air in the car suffocated her, Daniel's words forming a noose that wrapped around her throat.

"Are you done yet?" she bit out. "Or do you have more hate to spill?"

Daniel didn't answer. He slumped against the door, arms crossed, his breath fogging the window.

Elizabeth swiped the back of her hand across her damp cheeks, wiping it dry against her jeans. She was beyond caring about feelings. She was done walking on eggshells.

"You want the truth?" she said, voice unemotional. "Fine. Here it is. We're broke, Daniel. There was nothing left of your father's benefits. Our choices were to live in this damned car on the streets or move somewhere we could afford to survive."

Daniel stared at her, the words sinking in.

"You think this town is miserable?" she continued. "Try living in this car during the winter."

Daniel's mouth opened, but no words came.

She pressed on. "And what about Grandma? What do we do with her? You think she belongs in a home?"

"Maybe," he muttered. "At least they could take care of her."

"Would they?" she shot back. "Do you know anything about those places? Have you done any research?"

His expression faltered. "No. But I can."

"Good. Do your research. Find out the cost. Then come back and tell me what we give up to afford it. Your phone? Gas? Food?" She glanced at him without turning her head away from the road, her tone edged in steel. "Nothing is free, Daniel. Nothing."

He groaned, rubbing his hands over his face. "So now everything is my fault?"

Elizabeth let out a humorless laugh. "Why do you think I picked you up? You are my responsibility. I didn't have a choice. Don't you think adults have to follow rules? That we get to do whatever we want? You're wrong."

Daniel snapped.

"Well, you won't have to worry about me anymore!" he shouted. "I'll find my own way! I don't need anything from you!"

Elizabeth let out a bitter laugh. "Oh, really? That's why we're sitting here, in this fucking weather, having this fucking conversation?"

His jaw clenched. His breath fogged the glass, and his voice dropped into a vicious whisper.

"I hate you."

Elizabeth felt nothing.

The words should have crushed her. But she was already numb.

"I hate you," he spat. "And I hope you die."

Her hands trembled.

Her foot pressed the gas pedal.

The car surged forward.

"Mom! Slow down!"

She spoke as though she couldn't hear him.

"I'm dying," she whispered. "I'm dying, and my whole world is shit. I don't fucking care anymore."

The car crossed the centerline, swerving into the oncoming lane. Wind howled through the mountain pass, battering the car like invisible fists. Headlights burst through the fog and darkness, twin blazes cutting through the rain-soaked night, close enough to illuminate the terror in the other driver's face.

Elizabeth jerked the wheel at the last second, missing the other vehicle by inches. But the road was slick with rain, treacherous in the mountain cold. The tires lost traction, sliding sideways as the wind caught the car. The guardrail exploded in a shower of sparks that lit the darkness, twisted metal shrieking as the storm swallowed the sound.

A wall of water slammed over the windshield as they broke through. The night swallowed them whole. For a moment, weightlessness engulfed them. The car hung suspended in black space while rain turned to a deafening roar. Wind rushed through the shattered windows, carrying the sharp scent of pine and mountain cold. Elizabeth's stomach lurched into that terrifying free-fall sensation, her hands still gripping the wheel as they plummeted into the void.

Time stretched through the black tumble of metal and breaking glass. The storm claimed them. Rain, wind, and night converged into something less like weather and more like the mountain's judgment. Then, as if the darkness itself had extinguished the storm, everything went silent.

In the shattered silence that followed, a raven landed on the twisted guardrail, its oily feathers gleaming in the moonlight. It cocked its head, studying the wreckage below with eyes too knowing for a mere bird. It opened its beak, and the emerging sound was neither caw nor cry, but a single word that echoed through the empty air.

"Come."

And from his lair deep in the Hollow, Grim raised his head, sensing the arrival of souls that didn't belong to him—yet.

3

Rules of the Dead

Elizabeth was free-falling. Arms and legs flailed as the world spun in a disorienting blur. The impact came fast and hard—face-first into wet, sucking mud. The force of it knocked the wind from her lungs, leaving her stunned, gasping. She lay there for a moment, the cool sludge seeping into her clothes, rain pattering against her back. The night tilted around her, distorted and unreal.

Instinct kicked in. She forced herself to move, fingers digging into the slick ground, checking for pain, for broken bones. Nothing. Just the dull ache of bruises that would make themselves known soon enough.

With a groan, she pushed herself upright, hands trembling as she wiped at the muck coating her face. But the effort was useless. Her palm smeared the filth deeper. She angled her body, trying to find a solid footing, but her knee slid into a freezing puddle. A shiver racked her body as she clenched her teeth, her lungs too tight to draw in air.

This wasn't where she was supposed to be.

She tugged her gritty lashes apart, blinking against the murky dark. Nothing looked familiar.

"Where am I?" she murmured, her voice hoarse and lost beneath the whisper of the rain.

She strained to listen, hoping for the hum of passing cars, for headlights piercing through the night. What she heard instead was nothing. Complete, unnatural silence. The kind that didn't belong anywhere near a roadside crash.

Too quiet.

Her skin prickled, and it had nothing to do with the rain soaking through her clothes.

Her breath came in short, sharp bursts as her mind scrambled to piece together fragments. The road. The car. Daniel sitting next to her in the passenger seat.

Where was he now?

Her eyes moved up the hillside, scanning the dark trees for crumpled metal caught in the branches, for headlights still burning. Nothing. Just bare branches reaching toward a starless sky. As if the car had simply... vanished.

Behind her, another path wound into the black void of the valley, disappearing into dense trees. Something about it made her stomach curdle, but she didn't have time to dwell on why.

"Daniel?" she called, her voice cracking, but the night swallowed her words.

She had to get to the road. Had to get to him.

Digging her fingers into the earth, she climbed. Rain slicked the mud beneath her palms, making every motion a battle. The slope was steep, and the loose soil gave way beneath her weight. She grasped at saplings, gripping their thin trunks, using them to haul herself higher. Her muscles screamed in protest, but she ignored them.

Higher.

She had to go higher.

Her pulse pounded in her ears, drowning out everything else. She wheezed as she reached for another hold—and the ground crumbled beneath her feet.

With a startled cry, she slid backward, hands clawing at the sliding earth. Rocks and roots scraped against her arms, her legs. The hill tilted at a steep angle, and gravity yanked her back toward the ground.

Then she was tumbling.

Down, down, down.

She landed hard, skidding through the mud before coming to a jolting stop on the lower path. Pain shot up her arms, her ribs throbbing with the impact. Blood mixed with rain as she tasted iron on her lips.

A strangled sound escaped her throat, half frustration, half fear.

She couldn't even climb a damned hill.

Tears burned in her eyes, but she forced them back. She had to try again. Had to get to Daniel.

Her limbs were like lead. Her soaked clothes turned icy against her skin, stealing what little warmth she had left. Her body had limits, and it was reaching them fast.

Teeth chattering, she turned her attention to the only other option—the trees.

She forced herself upright, every muscle protesting. If she couldn't go up, she had to move forward.

With slow, stumbling steps, she trudged toward the thick line of pines, their heavy branches stretching outward. The canopy was dense enough to block out most of the rain, giving her a momentary reprieve.

She collapsed beneath the shelter of the largest one, pressing her back against its rough bark. The scent of damp earth and pine needles surrounded her, grounding her in the moment.

For now, this was all she could do.

Elizabeth curled her arms around herself, drawing her knees close to her chest. She pulled loose needles over her lap in a feeble attempt to trap warmth, but the cold burrowed in deep. She couldn't stop shaking. Couldn't stop thinking.

Daniel was out there. Somewhere.

Her eyelids grew heavy, exhaustion dragging her limbs. But sleep wouldn't come.

Her mind refused to quiet, whispering the worst possibilities in the dark.

At some point, exhaustion must have claimed her, because without warning, she was in another place, standing in a hazy field of swaying grass. A figure stood with his back to her in the distance.

"Daniel?" she called, her voice sounding strange to her own ears.

The figure turned, but it wasn't her son. A man in dark clothing, his face obscured by shadow despite the brightness all around. A bird perched on his shoulder: a raven, its black feathers gleaming in the strange light.

"He's not yours anymore," the man said in a gravelly voice.

"The boy belongs to the Hollow now."

The raven spread its wings, and Elizabeth jolted awake with a gasp, heart pounding against her ribs. Dawn was breaking through the branches above her.

Just a dream. Little more than a nightmare born from fear and cold.

Yet the words lingered in her mind. *He belongs to the Hollow now.*

A ray of light filtered through the pine branches, coaxing Elizabeth from her restless sleep. She stirred, stretching cautiously, wincing as stiffness crept into her aching limbs. Blinking against the soft orange glow of the rising sun, she took a slow, deep breath. The night's bitterness had faded at long last, leaving only the damp earth and the lingering ache in her muscles as proof of her ordeal.

Pulling herself from beneath the tree's shelter, she stepped into the sunlight, feeling its weak warmth against her skin. Her body protested with every movement. Her legs hurt, her hands were scraped and raw from her desperate climb the night before. But as she took in her surroundings with fresh eyes, the morning light did little to ease her anxiety. The valley stretched before her, vast and untouched, the golden hues of autumn masking the reality of her predicament.

She turned back toward the hill where she believed the crash had happened, her pulse quickening. Daniel. The car. She had to find them.

Bracing herself, she forced her legs into motion and limped toward the slope. Now, in daylight, she could make out the details of her surroundings, and what she saw drained the last of her hope. The landscape was unblemished. No car. No snapped branches, no tire tracks, no shattered glass. Just unbroken sandstone where she had expected to see wreckage.

Her throat tightened as she took a step back, scanning the area with growing panic. This isn't possible. She had fallen. The car had been there. It had to be. But there was no sign of it, as if the accident had never happened at all.

"Daniel!" she called, her voice echoing in the still morning air. There was no answer. Even the birds ignored her cry. She tried again, louder. "DANIEL!"

The silence that followed sent ice through her veins. Last night. She remembered it with vivid clarity: the argument, her confession, his cruel words. Then the headlights, the swerve, the guardrail giving way. The car had tumbled down this very hillside. She was sure of it.

So where was the wreckage? Where was her son?

A terrible thought seized her. What if they had found him but stopped looking for her? What if rescue workers had come in the night, taking Daniel but missing her in the darkness? Or worse, what if he had been thrown from the car, injured where she couldn't see, couldn't reach?

No. She couldn't think like that. She had to focus.

Elizabeth looked down at herself. Her clothes were torn and mud-caked, but they were still her clothes. The same jeans and sweater she wore yesterday. This was real. She wasn't dreaming.

But this couldn't be real, either. The light was softer, more golden than the harsh clarity she was used to. And the air smelled cleaner, but with unfamiliar undertones. Woodsmoke. Herbs. Mustiness.

Frustration welled inside her. She turned toward the valley below, searching for a sign. A road. A house. Anything that could lead her to help. In the distance, faint plumes of smoke curled into the sky from what must have been a hidden settlement. Farmhouses, maybe.

With no road in sight and no other option, she set her focus on the winding path that descended behind the hill. The only direction she hadn't yet tried.

The narrow trail curved downward, edged by jagged rock and dry underbrush. It was smoother than she expected, as if it had been traveled in the not-too-distant past. Small tracks marred the dirt. Narrow, parallel marks, maybe from a wagon. Against all logic, the idea reassured her. At least she wasn't alone here.

She moved forward, her steps slow and deliberate, every muscle in her body protesting the descent. The deep silence of the valley was broken only by the occasional rustle of wind through the trees. No distant hum of traffic, no birdsong. Just an unnatural stillness that made her skin crawl.

It still didn't feel right.

She forced herself forward, gripping her arms around her torso against the morning crispness. There has to be someone. Somewhere.

As the path leveled off, a well-kept shed, with thick plumes of smoke curling from a stone chimney, sat nestled between the trees. The scent of cooked cured meat drifted toward her, rich and mouthwatering. Her stomach clenched. She hadn't realized how hungry she was.

Relief surged through her, and she hurried forward, stumbling in her eagerness. She reached the door and knocked hard, her fist rattling the wood.

"Hello?" she called, breathless. "Please, I need help! I just need to use your phone!"

All was quiet until she heard a sudden thump inside, followed by the startled cry of a child.

Elizabeth stepped back as hurried footsteps approached. A second later, the door swung open, revealing a large, barefoot woman blocking the threshold.

The woman's piercing gaze swept over her, lingering on her mud-streaked pants and torn jacket. Her mouth tightened into a thin line of disapproval.

"Lost yer cart, have yuh?" she muttered, shaking her head.

"Strange woman, dressed like a man." She huffed. "It ain't proper, a lady wearin' britches like that."

Elizabeth blinked, her mind struggling to catch up. Cart? Dressed like a man? What was she even talking about?

A small-faced child with dirt-smudged cheeks and wide, curious eyes peered around the woman's skirts. The woman shooed the child back inside with a firm hand.

"Go on now, Ellie. Mind the porridge."

The child vanished, but not before Elizabeth caught a glimpse of her clothing, a rough-spun dress that looked like it was from a historical museum or a period film. Not a T-shirt or jeans in sight.

"I don't have a cart," Elizabeth said with hesitation, trying to make sense of the situation. "I was in a car accident. My son..." her voice strained with pent-up emotion. "My son might be hurt. Please, I need to find a phone to call for help."

The woman's brow furrowed deeper, eyes narrowing with suspicion and perhaps confusion.

"Phone?" she repeated, the word strange in her mouth, like she was testing out a foreign language. "What manner of thing is that?"

The world tilted beneath Elizabeth's feet. A sweat broke across her forehead as understanding dawned. The clothing. The language. The lack of power lines or paved roads. The absence of any modern sounds, no distant highway, no airplanes overhead.

"What..." Elizabeth swallowed hard, her mouth going dry. "What year is it?"

The woman eyed her as if she had sprouted a second head. "Year? It's the harvest season." She paused, then added with obvious suspicion, "Eighteen and ninety-three, as any God-fearin' soul would know."

Elizabeth's knees threatened to buckle. Eighteen ninety-three? That was impossible. She had just been in 2023, hadn't she? The woman spoke with such certainty, as if she truly believed it was still 1893. But how could that be? This wasn't her world, Elizabeth realized with growing unease. This place followed different rules entirely.

"I..." she stammered. "Look, if you don't have a phone, I just need directions to someone who does. Please. Can you tell me where the nearest house is? Anyone who can help?"

The woman squinted at her, considering. Then, after a pause, she jerked her chin toward the trail.

"Parson's stead," she said without kindness. "'Bout an hour that way." She hesitated, then added, "But he don't have none o' them... them phones."

Elizabeth's stomach dropped. An hour? In her condition, that might as well have been a lifetime. And even if she made it there, what then? No phones. No hospitals. No way to find Daniel.

Her mind went numb. She nodded without thinking and backed away. "Thank you."

Turning on unsteady legs, she pushed back at her growing despair. An hour. *I can do this*, she thought. *I have to.*

As she was about to take her first step down the path, the sound of rattling wheels caught her attention.

Elizabeth's head snapped up. A wooden cart creaked around the bend, pulled by two tired-looking horses. A man and woman sat on the bench at the front, their clothes simple and well-worn. Their presence sent a jolt of relief through her veins.

The man pulled on the reins, slowing the horses as they approached. "Need help, ma'am?" he called out. "Where yuh headin'?"

Exhausted but grateful for a friendly face, Elizabeth managed a nod, her legs threatening to give out.

"Please," she rasped. "I just... I just need to get somewhere safe."

The woman in the cart patted the seat beside her. "Come on, then. Ain't safe to be wanderin' alone."

Elizabeth wasted no time. She hauled herself into the back, collapsing onto the wooden planks. The cart lurched forward, and she grabbed the wooden rail as they rolled down the path.

The couple didn't speak much at first, exchanging occasional glances between them. The man handled the reins with calloused hands, while the woman clutched a small bundle in her lap. As they traveled, Elizabeth studied their clothing. The man wore rough wool pants and a homespun shirt. The woman was in a long dress with a shawl wrapped around her shoulders. No synthetic fabrics. No modern fasteners. Just simple, hand-made garments that belonged to another century.

"Where you from?" The woman looked over her shoulder at Elizabeth. "Don't recall seein' you 'round here before."

"I'm… not from around here," Elizabeth managed, unsure how to explain what she didn't understand herself. "I'm looking for my son. We were separated."

The woman's face softened with sympathy. "How old's your boy?"

"Seventeen," Elizabeth said, and suddenly the reality of Daniel being lost here—wherever, whenever "here" was—hit her with fresh fear. Her teenage boy was alone in an unfamiliar place, possibly injured.

"We're headed to Grim's Hollow," the man offered without turning to look at her. "Small settlement just past the crossroads. If he's wandered that way, someone might've seen him."

Grim's Hollow. Elizabeth's skin crawled at the name. Something about it sounded ominous.

"Thank you," she said anyway, because what choice did she have?

As the cart creaked along, the landscape transformed with each mile. The wild forest gave way to scattered clearings, some with crude fences marking boundaries of small farm plots. In the distance, she could see what appeared to be a small village nestled in the valley. A cluster of buildings with smoke rising from chimneys.

No electrical lines. No paved roads. No vehicles.

Elizabeth clutched the edge of the cart, knuckles white. This couldn't be real. Time travel wasn't possible. And yet, everything around her insisted otherwise. Had the crash thrown her backward in time? Or was this all a hallucination, just her mind's way of coping with trauma?

But it was too real. The wooden cart beneath her, the smell of horses and hay, the bite of the morning breeze against her skin, all of it was too vivid, too consistent to be a dream.

If she were truly in 1893, what did that mean for Daniel? Was he here too? Or was he still in their time, perhaps lying injured in a hospital while doctors tried to explain to him that his mother was missing?

The image made her stomach clench. She had to find a way back. Had to find Daniel.

"You alright back there?" the woman called, noticing Elizabeth's distress. "You look pale as death."

"I'm fine," Elizabeth lied, straightening her shoulders. "Just worried about my son."

The woman nodded, her eyes kind but tired. "We'll be there before midday. Parson can help you. He helps all the lost souls that find their way to the Hollow."

"What year is it?" Elizabeth didn't know what she expected as an answer, but the answer she received left her mind reeling more than before.

"Depends," said the man. "On whom you ask. Time is different here. There are no laws to bind it."

She would need to process this when her head wasn't pounding, and she had a good meal in her belly.

As they rounded a bend in the path, Elizabeth noticed a cluster of stone markers in a clearing to her right. Too uniform to be natural, too rough to be modern gravestones. They formed a perfect circle, and in the center stood a single post with what looked like a bird carved at its top.

"What is that?" She pointed at the stones.

The man glanced over, then looked away, his shoulders tensing. The woman made a small sign with her hand.

"Best not to ask about such things," the woman murmured. "Some places in the Hollow ain't meant for discussion."

"The Hollow has its ways," the man added cryptically. "Keeps what it wants. Returns what it don't."

Elizabeth's skin prickled despite the strengthening sun. "What do you mean by that?"

Neither answered. The man snapped the reins, urging the horses to a faster pace, as if eager to leave the strange monument behind.

Lost souls. The phrase echoed in Elizabeth's mind as the cart continued its slow journey toward the settlement. That's exactly what she was now… lost… in every sense of the word.

Her heart pounded in her chest, hope flickering despite everything. She might not understand what had happened or how to get back, but she wasn't giving up. Daniel was out there. And she would find him.

Even if it meant searching through time itself.

Elsewhere, in a place neither here nor there, a boy opened his eyes to darkness.

He couldn't remember his name.

Couldn't remember how he had gotten here.

All he knew was the hunger gnawing at his insides and the strange sense that something important had been taken from him.

Something was coming for him in the dark.

And he needed to be ready when it did.

4

The Quiet Threat

The chamber was silent, save for the soft scrape of metal against stone. The air itself felt weighted with centuries— thick with the ghost-scent of dried herbs gone bitter with age, old parchment crumbling to dust, and something metallic that coated the back of the throat like copper pennies. An unnatural chill seeped from the onyx throne, making each breath visible in thin wisps that dissipated into the pressing darkness.

Grim sat hunched on his jagged throne—gleaming like black ice, its surface smooth as glass but cold enough to burn. Hairline fractures mapped its surface, the stone splintering slowly beneath centuries of weight and buried remorse. An ancient tool balanced across his knees, its blade gleaming faintly, catching light that didn't exist in the shadowed expanse around him. His skeletal fingers traced the edge, a slow, deliberate motion, as though the act alone tethered him to some shred of memory. The blade hummed faintly under his touch, metal vibrating with an almost-living resonance. Even through bone, he could feel the weapon's patient hunger—ancient, eternal, waiting.

A faint sound stirred—a whisper, no louder than a soft breeze. Grim's hollow eyes turned toward the noise, but there was no one. Only the souls. They always murmured, a tapestry of voices frayed and tangled.

One voice rose above the others, its clarity cutting through the din.

"Elias."

Grim flinched, the blade nicking his bony hand. A single drop of dark ichor welled up, then vanished into the void. He hadn't heard that name spoken in centuries.

His grip tightened on the tool's handle. It seemed heavier now, pressing against his thighs, dragging him back to a moment he had buried deep.

He closed his eyes, and the shadows of his domain altered, giving way to a memory.

The firelight flickered, casting wild shadows against the stone walls of the cavern. Elias knelt before the altar, his trembling hands outstretched. The ancient symbols carved into the rock pulsed with an eerie glow, responding to the chant he murmured under his breath.

Around him, the bodies of the lost lay still, their lifeless faces turned toward him as though waiting. Waiting for him to succeed.

"I can bring them back," he whispered, his voice breaking. "I just need more time."

But the ritual demanded a price he hadn't anticipated. The atmosphere grew thick, the warmth of the fire replaced by a bone-deep frost. The glow of the symbols flared, blinding, and when Elias opened his eyes again, he was no longer alone.

A figure loomed before him, cloaked in shadow, its voice as cold and final as the grave.

"You dare to claim the power of death?" it hissed. "Then bear the burden."

The scythe appeared in his hands, the weight of it driving him to his knees. Elias screamed as the cavern dissolved around him, the faces of the lost morphing into hollow-eyed wraiths.

Grim's eyes snapped open. The chamber was still. Silent.

The instrument of death rested across his knees, its blade faintly aglow. He stared at it, his empty gaze reflecting the hollowness in his chest.

"They deserved to live," he murmured, his voice brittle. "But I... I deserve this."

The shadows curled tighter around him, and the whispers resumed, louder now, accusing. He gripped the reaper's tool harder, silencing them with a thought.

Far away, in the purgatory he ruled, a faint ripple spread, a sign of disturbance. A new soul had entered his domain. One whose light burned brighter than most. One that could spell trouble for Grim.

Grim rose from his throne, the scythe scraping against the stone floor as he moved. His hollow eyes narrowed.

"They always try," he muttered, stepping into the darkness. As he moved, the shadows seemed to part before him and close behind, the very air shifting to accommodate his passage. His footsteps rang against stone with the finality of a closing tomb. "And they always fail."

In another part of the Hollow, a kaleidoscope burst open, scattering vivid pigments across the darkness: sparkling hues of purple and intense blues. The boy flinched instinctively from the brightness, a dull pain shooting across his temples. He thrust his head beneath his arms, trying to shield his eyes. His head throbbed with agony.

Eventually, the lights dimmed again. Soft grays replaced the painful glare, and his mind relaxed back into its dreaming. He dreamed of happy things. Of soft caresses and warm hugs, fresh-baked bread slathered in sweet, creamy butter.

Loud and obnoxious laughter crashed into his dreams. He tugged at the blankets to pull them over his head, hoping to muffle the sound, but they didn't budge. The scratch of rough wool against his skin was unfamiliar.

"Oh my God. Shut up!" he yelled.

To his surprise, everything went silent.

Sleep loosened its grip on his mind. His mouth felt cotton-dry, tongue thick and foreign against his teeth. Every muscle ached with a bone-deep stiffness. When he let one eyelid flutter open, at least a dozen wide eyes stared back at him in disbelief, some with jaws hanging open.

The scent of musty straw and unwashed bodies hit him with unexpected force, making his nose wrinkle. His skin prickled with awareness—the rough scratch of unfamiliar wool, air heavy with moisture clinging to his lungs. Sounds filtered in gradually: the creak of wooden floors, murmured voices with unfamiliar cadences, the rhythmic drip of water from somewhere nearby. Even the temperature felt strangely neutral.

"Um... thank you?" he offered, unsure. He had no idea who these people were, but they looked like they could eat him for breakfast and not think twice about it.

A large black dog lay stretched across the floor, its teeth rotted, its body giving off the stink of something dug up and only half buried again. The boy dared not move, afraid the beast might attack.

"Come 'ere, Wolfie," someone called. The dog sprang up from the cot and trotted over to the voice without a glance back. "Wolfie, here, comes and goes as he pleases. Never stays 'round long. He's the one showed us where you was."

The boy peeled the rough wool blanket off and sat on the edge of the cot, facing the strangers.

"Who are you? How did I get here?" he asked the room.

His head pounded, and the space spun around him when he tried to rise. He settled for sitting. Rolling his shoulders, he tried to loosen the stiffness in his muscles. Apparently, he had been hit by a truck, flipped in the air, slammed into the ground, and flattened by a steamroller. Yeah, it felt that bad.

Someone stood and shuffled toward him, dragging a rickety, three-legged stool. Planting it in front of the boy, the old man straddled it with his legs splayed wide and sat down. His cheek bulged with something tucked inside. He turned his head and spat a dark, nasty glob toward the corner of the room.

"We're the ones pulled you outta the creek," the man grunted. One eye was set in a permanent wink, while the other squinted with a glare. "You ain't none too 'preeshative, are you? Might be we shoulda let you be."

"Uh—no, sir," the boy stammered. "I do appreciate it. Honest. I'm just a little confused, is all. I don't remember the creek. I don't remember being saved. I don't even remember seeing any of you before."

"Leave 'em be, Tate," a voice called from behind. "He ain't got no memory o' what happened. Got a purdy good bump on 'is head. Might be a bit before he remembers."

A kind-eyed woman stepped forward, gently moving the old man aside. She knelt beside the cot and leaned in to examine the boy's face.

"You'll be all right, lad. Just some bumps an' bruises. 'Side from your head, an' stiff and sore a bit, you'll be fine," she assured him.

The others slowly returned to their game of cards, casting only the occasional glance his way. The woman sat on the cot, while the old man leaned forward again on his stool.

"So, what's your name, lad?" he asked, his breath sour enough to peel paint.

The boy leaned back instinctively, trying to escape the stench. He opened his mouth to respond, but the oddest thing happened. He thought he knew his name. Should have known it without question, but when he searched his memory, nothing came. He turned to the woman beside him, looking for answers.

She shrugged. "Don't look at me, love. You're as strange to me as I am to you. Never saw you before yesterday."

Yesterday? He tried to focus, tried to drag something... anything out of the haze in his mind. But there was no name. No family. No home. No sense of who he was or where he belonged.

A dizzying wave of vertigo overtook him, but this wasn't the simple spinning of a dizzy spell. It was the complete absence of anchor. His pulse hammered against his ribs as panic clawed up his throat. It felt like flying. Or falling through empty sky with nothing solid to catch him, nothing familiar to ground him to the world. The very concept of "self" seemed to slip through his fingers like water.

The edges of his vision began to blur, darkness creeping in from the corners. His limbs felt impossibly heavy, as though gravity had suddenly remembered he existed and decided to reclaim him. He collapsed back onto the cot, unconscious.

Betsy and Tate exchanged a look and moved together with practiced ease. They pulled the blanket up over the boy once more, their hands slow and careful, moving with the instinct of people who had done this before.

The warmth of the blanket settled around him like a promise of rest. Of silence. And for now, safety.

The young man shivered from the sudden biting cold, the ache of loneliness settling like a weight in his chest. His voice cracked as he called out for his mother, but no one answered. Wrapping his arms tightly around himself, he curled up on the cold, unforgiving ground, seeking comfort in the darkness.

Heated broth trickled down his sore throat. At first, a thousand shards of glass, then easing into soothing relief. The salty liquid warmed him from the inside, and finally, he slept.

"I hate you."

He heard the words echo through his mind.

"I hate you. I hate you. Just die."

The words, invoked with such venom, made his stomach lurch. The awful meaning behind them clawed at his conscience. He had the horrible feeling he had done something unspeakable, that he had caused someone's death. He looked down to find blood on his hands, frantically searching the shadows around him for the body he must have slain.

He was running. From what, he couldn't say. But he knew it was a matter of life or death. He had to hurry. Someone needed saving.

But who?

He stopped running, panting to catch some air, and looked around. Flashing lights.

Someone shouted, "Stop!"

He ran again. His chest burned with the effort. His lungs tightened.
He was suffocating.

He was dying.

"Shh. Just relax. It'll be fine. Just hush. Shh."

And he slept.

The world spun around him. Dizzy from the movement, he clutched at the sides of the box he was trapped in, trying to steady himself. But the spinning only got faster. Faster. Suddenly, it launched. He was flying now, soaring through space, suspended in the Milky Way, floating among the moon and stars.

"Daniel," someone whispered.

And he fell.

He flailed wildly, trying to slow the descent. The ground rushed toward him, faster, faster—

Something caught him. He stopped before hitting the earth.

"Sonny!"

Someone was shaking him.

"Wake up, boy. You're dreaming."

He jolted upright, heart hammering. His clothes clung to his body, soaked through. Sweat dampened his hair. The crisp air kissed his skin, and he shivered, his teeth chattering.

"Here. Let's git you outta those wet things. Put this dry shirt on. You'll be warm in no time."

The woman helped him change, wiping his face and neck with a rag. She brought over a dirty, hefty quilt and laid it gently over him.

"How long have I been out this time?" Daniel swallowed, easing his hoarse throat.

"Jest a bit over a day. Day an' a half, maybe. Could you drink some broth? You need it."

He nodded and took the bowl she handed to him. The warmth spread through his chest, and the shivering subsided. His brain fog lifted a little, his mind clearing.

"Why are you helping me?" He glanced around at the others. "This lot doesn't exactly give the impression of being the charitable kind. What's stopping them from robbing me and slitting my throat?"

The woman snorted so hard her face flushed red. At first, he believed she was choking. She sucked in a great gulp of air and burst into loud, gasping laughter, tears pouring from her eyes. He blinked, stunned.

At last, she wiped her face with her sleeve and cleared her throat with a couple of coughs.

"First off, lad, you ain't got nothin' to steal. What do you think you got that's worth anythin'?" She didn't wait for an answer. "Second, we don't slit no one's throat less they deserve it. You ain't done nothin' to us yet. We got no reason to do you harm, less you plannin' to stab us in the backs or some such."

A flutter of relief stirred in him.

"No, ma'am. I'm not planning anything like that. I do appreciate everything you've done for me. I just... I hope I can repay you somehow."

"I'm sure you'll show your 'preeshiation." She winked.

He finished the broth and set the bowl on the floor. Wolfie trotted over and licked it clean. The boy tried not to think too hard about what passed for dishwashing around here.

"Come on, son. Let's get some trousers on you and come meet the rest of us."

The one-eyed geezer shuffled over, holding out a pair of stiff jeans looped with a rough rope. The jeans were far too wide, though the legs stopped a few inches above his bare ankles. He slipped them on anyway and tied the makeshift belt. The man helped him stand and guided him toward the card table. The ground was strangely solid beneath his feet after so long in bed.

Once he was seated, the old man pointed to the others around the table and introduced them one by one. The boy was sure he would forget most of the names. All except the young man named Digger, who smiled and dipped his head, "hello," as though they had been friends forever.

"You know me, of course. I be Tate. An' this here's Betsy." He gestured to the woman who had cared for him since he woke.

"And now you, lad. What's your name?"

He looked down at his hands resting in his lap and shook his head.

"I don't know, sir. I still can't remember who I am."

A few of the strangers in the room exchanged knowing glances.

"Well, we thought you might say that," Tate said. "We got an idea, if you're willin' to hear it."

The boy looked up, curiosity piqued.

"Well," Tate continued, "we found you face-down in ol' Gobbler Creek. We're kinda partial to the name Gobbler. It's what we been callin' you amongst ourselves. It's fittin', don't you think?"

Gobbler, the boy thought, testing the name in his mind.

It felt strange on him, borrowed, like the oversized jeans he now wore. There was a shadowy sense another name should have answered when he reached into that blank space in his memory, something that fit him better than this crude nickname. For a fleeting second, he almost caught it. A whisper of who he had been before waking up here.

But it was gone again, slipping away like water through cupped hands. And what did it matter anyway? Without memories, without a past, he could be anyone. Gobbler was as good a name as any. At least it came with people who seemed to care whether he lived or died.

He smiled at the circle of faces around him.

"Hi," he said. "I'm Gobbler. Nice to meet you all."

The name tasted odd in his mouth, but he would get used to it. He had to start somewhere.

Laughter rippled around the table, easy and warm. Betsy smiled down at him and squeezed his arm.

"Nice to have you, Gobbler."

Gobbler sat on the edge of his cot, elbows propped on his knees, fingers pressed against his temples. The dreams still clung to him like cobwebs. Fragments he couldn't brush away.

The voice echoed through his mind. *I hate you. I hate you. Just die…* felt too real to be imagined. The blood on his hands, the desperate running, the name whispered in darkness… *Daniel.* Was that his real name? Someone he knew? Or just another phantom conjured by his injured mind?

He rubbed his eyes, trying to sort reality from dream. The harder he reached for memories, the faster they dissolved, leaving only impressions: the sensation of falling, a flash of headlights, the sickening lurch of weightlessness. And beneath it all, a crushing guilt he couldn't explain. Even the people around him felt disjointed. They seemed to come from across decades, maybe even centuries, as if this place collected souls from entirely different eras.

Voices and movement around the cabin pulled him from his musing. Unfamiliar faces moved through the dim light, moving furniture and clearing space.

"What's happening?" he asked, noticing Tate directing the others with animated gestures.

"Let's raise a glass to welcome Gobbler," Tate grinned, clapping Gobbler on the back hard enough to nearly knock him over. "We'll throw a little shindig. Bobby, get the word out. Tell the neighbors to bring what they got to share."

The others jumped up from the card table, scraping chairs and dragging furniture as they moved. Tin cups and plates clinked together, gathered up to be washed. The cabin bustled with more energy than Gobbler had seen since waking up here. It cleaned up quickly, and Gobbler barely had time to process what was happening before guests started to arrive.

Three women strolled in, each in frilly skirts and thick makeup, their ages spanning three decades. They made their way around the room, pairing off with the men as though they had done it a dozen times before.

More guests arrived. Some brought loaves of bread, salted meat, or wedges of cheese. A few carried crock jugs with liquid sloshing inside. Tate snagged a jug as it passed by, uncorking it to pour amber liquid into a pair of tin cups. He handed one to Gobbler and took a deep drink from the other. Betsy emerged with her own version of a cake, proudly placing it on the table like a centerpiece.

In one corner of the room, a makeshift band was set up. The banjo player had strings that looked one pluck away from snapping. The fiddler's bow wobbled with every stroke. A third man played spoons, clinking out a rhythm like a one-man percussion section. The sound was wild, offbeat, and oddly infectious.

Gobbler didn't recognize any of the songs they played, but he hadn't expected to. He didn't remember much of anything these days, but even without memories, he had a feeling this wasn't his kind of music. Still, he made up his mind to enjoy it. Why not?

A shy girl, maybe his age, approached him, her lengthy hair tied back in a loose braid and eyes that didn't match the chaos around them.

"Hello." She reached out with a shy smile. "I'm Alice."

"Hello, Alice. Do you, uh, live around here?" Gobbler asked and kicked himself mentally. Apparently, the ability to charm girls wasn't his strong suit either.

Alice smiled at his awkwardness. "Come on!" She grabbed his hand and tugged him toward the door.

They slipped out into the cool. The music and chatter faded behind them. It was the first time Gobbler had been outside since waking up. He still felt shaky, but he kept it to himself.

"Where are we going?" he asked.

"Just around," she replied. "It's stuffy inside. Easier to breathe out here with fewer prying eyes."

Her voice struck him. She didn't speak like the others. No thick accent, no strange phrasing. She sounded educated. Polished, even.

"Did you come in with someone?" he asked, watching how she walked slightly apart from the crowd, even out here.

Alice hesitated and looked out toward the dark hills beyond the trees. "No," she said softly. "I don't have anyone anymore."

She didn't elaborate. Her gaze stayed distant.

"I don't have parents," she continued after a moment. "The ladies took me in a few years ago when my parents were, um, killed." She paused. "They were just killed. That's all. Doesn't matter how."

Gobbler sensed there was more to the story, something deep and painful, but he didn't press. Maybe in time, she would tell him. For now, he appreciated her company.

"Are you cold?" he asked. "We can head back inside if you are."

Alice shook her head. "No. I'm fine for now."

He had a hundred questions he wanted to ask, but something about her presence warned him to wait. Now wasn't the time.

"Mind if we sit for a minute?" he asked. "I've sort of been bedridden the last few days. Still getting my strength back."

They found a dry patch of ground, and Gobbler sat down carefully. Alice waited until he was settled and sat beside him, snuggling close. Without thinking much of it, he draped his arm around her—more to shield her from the cold than anything else.

They said nothing and watched the stars drift slowly across the sky. Somewhere out in the trees, a raven called once and went quiet again.

The stillness that followed was unnatural.

Not as peaceful as before, but more like the world around them had paused its chaos.

A strange sensation crawled across Gobbler's skin. The hair on his arms stood up, though there was no breeze. The stars above flickered. Something had passed in front of them, just for a second.

Alice fidgeted beside him.

"Do you feel that?" She lowered her voice.

Gobbler nodded, not trusting his own.

After a beat, he muttered, "Yeah. Like someone just walked over my grave."

They were interrupted by stealthy, predatory footsteps, someone walking their way.

"There you both are." The voice made them jump. A boy stood at the edge of the clearing, arms crossed, trying to look casual, but unsuccessful at hiding the tension in his shoulders. "Tate's been lookin' for you. Says there's someone he wants you to meet."

Alice stood quickly, brushing dirt from her skirt. Gobbler rose more slowly, offering her his hand. She didn't speak, but her grip lingered for a second longer than necessary.

The boy didn't lead them back but pointed with his chin toward the light of the cabin.

"You'll see him when you get there," he muttered, before turning and disappearing into the trees.

They returned to a different party than the one they had left. The music still played, but it was quieter now, a little slurred around the edges. The laughter was thinner. And the air inside the cabin had cooled a few degrees.

All eyes turned when they entered.

Tate stood near the hearth, arms crossed over his chest, jaw set firm. His usual half-smile was gone. He kept his eyes on the room, posture rigid, doing his best not to look at the stranger at the center of it all—a man who somehow stood apart from the rest, not by action, but by presence alone.

"There you are, lad," Tate spoke louder than necessary. "Come meet our guest." Gobbler noticed the brief pause before the word *guest* and the way Tate's mouth tightened just enough to betray him.

The crowd shifted, and now Gobbler saw the man clearly.

He wasn't tall. Or broad. Or particularly striking in any way. His coat was passable but unmemorable, his hair dark and neat. Yet something about him pulled all the attention in the room toward him, like a drain sucking everything down.

His eyes were the only detail Gobbler couldn't look away from.

They were bright. Too bright. And far too intense. Pale gray, like ash or frost. And they saw him. Not looking at him, but into him. As if peeling back the layers of his soul with every second.

"Mr. Johnson," Tate said tightly. "This here's the lad. Goes by Gobbler, for now."

Mr. Johnson extended his hand.

Gobbler hesitated before shaking it. The man's grip was cool, dry, and a little too firm.

"Nice to meet you, sir," Gobbler kept his voice steady despite the roiling in his gut. "Are you—uh—the landlord or boss or something?"

Mr. Johnson smiled, but the smile didn't reach those cutting eyes.

"You could say that. I keep things... organized. And please, call me Grim. *Mr. Johnson* is so... reserved. And I prefer things more... personal."

Alice tensed beside him, and Gobbler suddenly sensed there was more to Mr. Johnson than met the eye.

"Do we all work for you, then?" Gobbler asked, glancing sideways at Tate.

Grim's smile widened a notch to show stained teeth.

"Work. Service. Allegiance. It all blends together. Eventually."

A heavy pause followed. Somewhere behind them, someone knocked over a cup. No one laughed.

"We could use a strong lad like you," Grim continued, releasing Gobbler's hand. "Seems you've got a bit of fire. That's hard to find these days."

"I'm still recovering." Gobbler tried to sound diplomatic without sounding defensive. "I don't even know what kind of work you do."

"Oh, we all find our place eventually." Grim's eyes gleamed. "The Hollow provides clarity."

His gaze swept the room, lingering on the others. "A curious collection you've gathered here, Tate. Strays and castoffs. Real misfits." He said it lightly, but the word slithered through the silence like a curse.

No one answered. Even the fire seemed to hesitate before crackling again.

Grim tipped his hat, nodded once to Tate, and exited through the rear door. After his exit, the mood in the cabin became slightly less tense. The celebration had toned down. More subdued and careful.

Gobbler turned to Tate, expecting an explanation.

But Tate only clapped a hand on his shoulder and walked away, joining a group of men near the hearth who were passing around a jug and avoiding eye contact.

Alice came to stand beside Gobbler, her brow furrowed.

"What was that?" Gobbler's voice dropped to a whisper.

"I think that was a warning." Alice watched Tate's back as he walked through the crowd.

The door creaked shut behind Grim, leaving the cabin hollow and still. For a long moment, no one spoke.

The young man called Roan gave a low whistle, his rough hands still smudged with ash. "Misfits, huh." He tried for humor, but it came out thin.

"He meant it as an insult," said the woman by the fire, reaching for a cup that wasn't hers. The firelight caught the edge of a blade strapped to her thigh. A quiet reminder that she was never truly at rest. "Figures he'd see us that way."

Tate turned from the hearth, eyes hard. "Then let him." He nodded toward the woman. "Ain't that right, Kess?"

Betsy snorted softly. "Misfit just means we ain't chained to his will. Still wild cards in his eyes."

The tension broke, just a little. Someone laughed—half relief, half defiance. The music picked up again, offbeat and rebellious.

Gobbler stood near the wall, watching the flicker of lamplight on their faces. The word still echoed in his head, sharp as flint, but now it glowed with something warmer--a pride of belonging.

5

The Meadow Knows

Gobbler lay awake long after the party ended, Alice's words echoing in his mind. *A warning.*

Grim's gaze still haunted him. Like something had burrowed its way into his spine, twitching every time he remembered those ash-gray eyes.

Fear. He recognized it immediately. But he didn't understand it. Not yet.

The cabin had fallen silent around him, the revelry fading to soft snores and the occasional creak of the wooden floor. But sleep wouldn't come. Every time he closed his eyes, he saw Grim's too-wide smile and heard the subtle threat beneath his polished words.

Work, service, allegiance. It all blends together eventually.

Only when the first faint light of dawn crept through the cracks in the walls did exhaustion take him. And when he did sleep, his dreams were filled with darting shadows and ravens speaking with human voices.

Gobbler woke with a killer headache and the foul, sour film of morning breath still coating his tongue. He would've traded his soul for a toothbrush and an aspirin. Around him, the others were already up, moving about the cabin as though they hadn't spent the night drinking and stomping holes in the floorboards.

The pounding in his skull made him want to crawl under the blanket and vanish from existence. But Tate had other plans.

"Rise an' shine, lad!" Tate swatted him across the hip with his hat.

Groaning, Gobbler pulled the gritty blanket over his head. "Just let me die in peace."

"Not today. We're headed to town. Best get yourself dressed or you'll be skippin' breakfast."

Gobbler peeled the blanket back and squinted into the dusty light. "I thought you had work today."

"We do. And you're comin'. Might as well learn somethin' while your bones mend."

Curiosity beat out the headache. He swung his legs over the cot. "Where are my shoes?"

"You ain't got none," Tate called back. "Now hurry up."

He was pretty sure he had owned shoes once. His feet didn't feel tough enough to have gone barefoot for long. But the others were already filing out the door. He yanked on his oversized trousers, grabbed two biscuits from the table, and ran after them.

"Shotgun!" he shouted, falling into step beside one of the younger men.

The boy blinked at him. "We don't need a shotgun today."

Gobbler laughed and winced at the sudden pain. "It's a figure of speech."

The boy grinned. "Well, whatever kinda speech it is, you'll jest be watchin'."

The cabin sat on the ragged outskirts of what the Misfits called "town," a crooked cluster of shacks pressed up against the Hollow's endless gray. The forest between them was thick and unfriendly, dense enough that no one but the Misfits dared to cross it, not with the things that wandered there after dark.

As they set out, Gobbler realized how exposed bare feet were in this world. The path wasn't like the smooth asphalt or concrete his feet still remembered. This was rough-cut earth, scattered with jagged stones and roots snaking up to snare his toes.

Each step was a negotiation with terrain that felt alien beneath his feet. Loose gravel bit into his soft soles, while the gnarled roots snagged at him from below. The earth itself felt different here— harder, older. It had never known the smooth comfort of pavement. Every stride was a painful reminder that he didn't belong.

"You get used to it," Digger said, noticing his grimace. "Feet toughen up after a while. Skin gets like leather."

Gobbler studied the boy's feet. Calloused, dirt-embedded, but sure-footed over the torturous terrain. Another reminder of the gap between who he was and who these people were.

Before an hour had passed, Gobbler regretted not pressing harder about the transportation. His bare feet were sliced and bruised from the rocky trail. He hissed and glared at the boy beside him.

"You could've warned me we were walking."

"How else we s'posed to get here? On broomsticks?"

"Digger!" Tate called from up ahead.

The young man snapped to attention.

"Stick with Gobbler today. Keep him outta trouble. We don't need your talents here."

Gobbler didn't ask what talents meant.

The town sprawling out before them looked like an image from a history book. Dirt roads cut across each other like the stitched seams of an old, dusty quilt. Wooden storefronts creaked in the breeze.

At the square's center rose an old courthouse, its clock frozen at high noon. Or midnight. Black iron plates sealed most of the windows, yet thin seams of light leaked through the cracks, as if something alive were inside. A weather-worn sign above the door still read "TOWN HALL," but someone had carved new words beneath it. CONVOCATION HALL. The townsfolk gave the building a wide berth, crossing themselves as they passed.

People in long coats and layered dresses tied their horses to posts and cast wary glances as the group passed.

Gone were the cars, the power lines, the rumble of engines. Hoofbeats and the low buzz of voices filled the void.

It was like walking into a dream—or maybe a nightmare. Everything felt wrong in ways he couldn't put into words. The world around him seemed filtered through sepia tones, muted and strange. His mind kept expecting different sights, different sounds: the hum of electricity, the digital chime of phones, the whoosh of passing vehicles. The absence of these things created a tension that made his head spin.

More troubling was how familiar it all seemed to the others. They moved through this antiquated world with practiced ease, as if they had never known anything different. Had he somehow traveled back in time? Or was this some isolated community, cut off from modern life?

Either way, he knew with bone-deep certainty he didn't belong here.

Digger led Gobbler onto the main street while the others scattered. The townspeople watched them with a wariness that went beyond mere suspicion. Women pulled their shawls tighter, whispering prayers under their breath. Men's hands drifted instinctively to their pockets, their eyes tracking the group's movement like prey sensing predators. A few folks crossed the street without breaking stride. Children were pulled closer to their mothers' skirts.

Something about it unsettled him.

On the far side of the road, one of their group brushed past a gentleman in a fine coat, knocking him sideways. The man apologized profusely, helped the gentleman back to his feet, and dusted him off.

"No harm done," the dandy replied, though his voice trembled.

But Gobbler saw it. The flick of the wrist, the vanishing wallet. His stomach twisted. No one else seemed to notice, or care.

The casual theft stirred something in his memory. A flicker of shame. A whispered voice. *That's not who you are.* But how could he know what kind of person he had been? The idea he might have lived this way before—taking things that didn't belong to him— made his skin crawl. Yet the action seemed almost familiar, like his hands remembered skills his mind had forgotten.

Half an hour later, the group reconvened at the town's main crossing, appearing casual, as if they had arrived there by accident. Tate stepped out of a corner shop, tucking a brown-wrapped parcel under his arm and tipping his hat to passersby.

They drifted away, slipping back toward the edge of town. Shouting erupted behind them.

"Stop! Thief!"

Two townsfolk tackled someone near the saloon. A Misfit from their group lay beneath the pile of good Samaritans.

A giant, rough-looking man strode over to the commotion. A permanent scowl etched on his brow. His badge glinted like a brand of power.

"Come on, lads," Tate muttered. "Time we headed home."

Gobbler stopped in his tracks, staring.

"We're just leaving him? Seriously?"

Tate didn't look back. "Nothin' to be done 'cept get caught yourself. Best to let the dust settle and get gone."

One by one, the group slipped away, their presence evaporating like smoke. Gobbler hesitated a moment longer and turned and followed, questions trailing him like ghosts.

"What the hell was that all about?" Gobbler's voice cracked as he backed away from the others, heart hammering. His breath came fast, uneven. "You're nothing but a bunch of thieves. Common criminals! Is this what you call work?"

The Misfits didn't flinch. No one looked ashamed. They stared without fidgeting. Just still, quiet indifference.

It hit him like a punch to the gut—they didn't care. Not one of them.

The idea of stealing, of becoming like them, coiled in his stomach like barbed wire. These weren't simply outcasts; they were criminals. And now, he was in the middle of it. Trapped. Alone.

But what choice did he have? Starve in the woods? Freeze to death under the trees?

He closed his eyes, trying to calm the storm in his chest. There was something fundamentally wrong with this, about all of it. A persistent voice inside him insisted this wasn't him. He hoped he had been someone different before, someone who wouldn't hesitate to walk away from thieves and liars.

But that someone had a home to go back to. Family, maybe. Friends. People who cared whether he lived or died. That someone had choices.

Gobbler had none.

A heavy arm landed across his shoulders. Digger's voice came low, almost kind.

"Look, Gob, I get it. You think we're all monsters. But we're just surviving." He guided him away from the others, steps slow and deliberate. "The world out here—" Digger pointed toward nowhere in particular, "—don't give a damn about us. We got each other. That's it. That's all."

He stopped walking and looked Gobbler dead in the eye. "But if you don't grow some thicker skin, you're gonna get us all killed. Grim's minions are all over that town. And they enforce his laws. Punish those who get caught breaking them."

Gobbler bristled but said nothing. What risk could he possibly pose? He kept the question to himself. He was sure he would find out sooner or later.

"We're Misfits," Digger continued. "Unwanted. Orphans. Mr. Johnson—Grim—he makes sure we have what we need. But nothing's free. We all owe a debt. One way or another."

Nothing's free. Gobbler knew the line from somewhere. It stirred something in the back of his mind.

As if Digger sensed his doubt, he pressed on. "You don't gotta like it. Hell, most of us don't. But ask too many questions too fast, you'll make it harder on yourself. Just give it time. Play the game."

Gobbler didn't respond. He folded the words up and tucked them away to be pulled out later when the time was right. Digger seemed too at ease with this life, too accepting. Proud, even. His callousness told Gobbler all he needed to know. Digger was a valuable source of information.

He would learn everything he could from him.

In the trees nearby, a group of ravens gathered on thick branches, muttering to one another in low, guttural clicks. Betsy tossed a bucket of scraps onto a pile near the garden, and the birds exploded into motion. Wings flapping, shrill cries filling the air as they dove onto the offering.

Digger watched them with something like reverence.

"Those ravens? They're like us," he said. "Scavengers, sure. But they protect their own. They know when to fly and when to huddle together. That's all we're doing here. Trying to survive."

He dipped his head toward the Misfits as they returned to their business, laughter and clinking tin drifting through the trees.

"That's what family is. A conspiracy of ravens, just holding on till the world makes sense again."

Gobbler swallowed hard, throat tight. The words made sense. Too much sense. But it didn't make him feel any better.

Everything inside him screamed to run. To get out now, before he got dragged in too deep.

But where would he go?

He had no name. No past. No recall of who he was or where he came from. He had fragments of memory. Sensations of darkness and cold.

And now he had this family that took him in without question.

For now, this would have to be enough.

He didn't have to belong. He had to survive long enough to figure out what came next.

A rustle on the path caught his attention. Gobbler turned, and his heart stumbled.

Alice was walking toward him, the light catching on her dark hair, her eyes fixed on his with a quiet intensity.

He let out a slow breath.

On the other hand, it's not all bad, he thought.

Alice walked by him, brushing his arm as she passed. "Take a stroll with me later," she whispered without breaking stride. "There's something you should know."

Before he could respond, she was already heading toward the cabin, her figure silhouetted against the afternoon light. Gobbler watched her go, wondering what secrets she held, and whether they might help him understand this strange new world.

Days passed, settling into a rhythm Gobbler didn't want to accept but couldn't escape. He watched the others, learning their ways, memorizing their habits. Waited for Alice to fulfill her promise of revelations. But she remained distant, throwing him occasional glances that seemed to say *not yet, not here.*

And so, Gobbler didn't ask questions. Not when someone from their own group failed to return, and no one dared to ask why. Not when the others came back in tense silence, bruised and rattled, their eyes avoiding his. Not when Tate muttered something about "keeping our heads down" and "laying low until Grim cools off."

The whole shack had gone quiet as night fell. Even Betsy's usual chatter dried up like someone had clamped her throat shut. They played cards without looking at each other, and Gobbler felt like an outsider all over again.

He could have asked. Someone might have told him what happened in town, what led to the shouting and the arrest, but he didn't. He didn't want to know. Knowing meant making choices, and he wasn't ready to make decisions, yet.

So, when Tate slapped a rough leather satchel into his chest the next morning and said, "You're up," Gobbler tipped his head once in agreement.

"Time to pull your weight, lad. Follow me."

They didn't speak as they hiked away from the clearing and down a narrow, muddy path winding deeper into the Hollow. The air grew denser, colder, and quieter as though even the trees were holding their breath. Gobbler adjusted the strap on his shoulder and glanced sideways at Tate, but the older man kept his eyes forward.

"You said something about a job?"

"Aye," Tate said without looking back. "Small task. Simple. In and out. Just a delivery."

"That's it?"

"That's it."

Gobbler wasn't convinced. Nothing was simple in this place. The Hollow had its own rules, and he hadn't learned half of them yet. But the idea of doing something was better than waiting around, pretending things were normal.

They stopped in front of a crooked shed half-swallowed by vines. Tate knocked once, hard, and stepped aside.

"You go in. Deliver the pouch. Don't ask questions. Don't touch anything. Don't stay long."

Gobbler raised an eyebrow. "Sounds easy."

"Looks can deceive."

Inside the shed stood a man who didn't seem quite human. His skin looked like wax pulled tight over brittle bones. His eyes were the color of aged parchment. He didn't speak but held out a skeletal hand. Gobbler placed the satchel in it and leapt back, resisting the urge to look at the contents.

"Good," the man croaked, his voice like dried leaves. "He watches you now, you know."

Gobbler blinked. "What?"

The man's dull eyes drifted down to Gobbler's bare, filthy feet.

"Payment," he rasped.

He reached behind a stack of warped crates and produced a pair of battered leather boots. Scuffed, mismatched laces, but sturdy. He shoved them into Gobbler's hands with surprising force.

"The Hollow provides for those who serve."

Gobbler stared, thrown off kilter. "For the delivery?"

The man smiled, showing black, rotting teeth. "For now."

Before Gobbler could ask anything else, the man turned away, the conversation apparently over.

Gobbler didn't wait to be dismissed. He slipped out of the oppressive shed and into the exposed clearing.

Tate was already walking. Gobbler jogged to catch up.

As they walked away from the vine-choked shed, Gobbler couldn't stop thinking about the pouch. The brown paper. The rough twine.

It was the same kind Tate brought back from town a few days ago.

Back then, it hadn't seemed important. But now, something twisted in his gut.

The package hadn't been for them. It had been for this.

Gobbler wasn't sure who Tate was delivering for.

The strangeness weighed on him. Every day in this place brought more questions and fewer answers. The more he saw, the less sense it made. And yet, a pattern was forming, connections taking shape if he could read them.

What had the man meant? *He watches you now.* Was he referring to Grim? Or something else? The way the words slithered from the man's throat suggested something darker, something Gobbler did not want to face.

"What was in that bag?" he asked, once they were back on the main path.

"I don't really know." Tate walked ahead of Gobbler. "And I never asked."

Gobbler frowned. "Then why, exactly, are we doing this?"

Tate exhaled through his nose. "It's not about the contents for us. It's about the exchange, and what it buys us."

Gobbler waited. Tate kept walking. Then finally...

"That man... thing... whatever he is, he's part of the Hollow. The old part. Back before Grim took rule.

Gobbler watched Tate for his reaction. "So why bring him anything?"

"Because as long as we do, we're not part of the cost." Tate's voice got quiet. Flat. "We play the game. We get some protection. We keep the target off our backs."

Gobbler didn't reply, but the boots felt heavier in his hands.

Back at the cabin, no one mentioned the job. No one asked how it went. The card game resumed, the laughter forced, the drinks passed around with exaggerated cheer. Gobbler played along. Smiled when they smiled. Laughed when someone cursed at their cards.

He didn't mention the man in the shed.

He didn't mention what he had said.

He noticed Alice watching him from across the room, her eyes carrying the same warning they held after meeting Grim. When their gazes met, the imperceptible shake of her head cautioned him to stay quiet. *Don't react. Don't give yourself away.* He wasn't sure how he understood her meaning, but he did.

As she passed him on her way to the sleeping area, she dropped something into his lap. A small, folded square of paper. He hid it with his hand, waiting until no one was looking before slipping it into his pocket.

Later, alone in the shadows on his cot, he unfolded it. A simple drawing: a raven perched on a branch, its beak open as if speaking. Beneath it, one word written in careful script. *Wait.*

Instead, he stayed up long after the others drifted to bed, sitting on the front stoop with Wolfie curled beside him and the stars heavy overhead. Somewhere in the trees, a raven called once and went quiet.

He didn't know what it meant. Why something so benign, so normal, could sound so ominous.

The night air carried whispers. Secrets traded between trees. Promises made in the night. Gobbler traced the outline of strange constellations overhead, searching for patterns he recognized. None came.

Wolfie stirred beside him, ears perking up at something beyond human hearing. The dog's yellow eyes reflected starlight as it stared into the forest.

"You see something, boy?" Gobbler murmured, following the animal's gaze.

He thought he saw movement—a tall, thin figure standing between distant trees. But when he blinked, there was nothing. Just shadows and mist and the persistent feeling he was being watched.

Wolfie rose and padded toward the trees, silent but for the creak of old bones. He paused once at the edge of the clearing, ears pricked toward some sound only he could hear, then slipped into the mist without a sound. The fog swallowed the hound whole.

Tomorrow, he decided. Tomorrow, he would find Alice. Tomorrow, he would ask the right questions.

But tonight, he would sit with the fear and the not-knowing, letting it wash over him like the cool night breeze. Sometimes, ignorance was the only comfort.

6

Beneath Her Silence

The note from Alice simply said, *Tomorrow. Dawn. Edge of the clearing.* He spent the day watching the others, searching their faces for any sign they knew, if they could see the tension humming between him and Alice.

Digger was sparring with a few of the younger Misfits, clearly uninterested in anything Gobbler was doing.

Betsy hung laundry on the line, humming a tune he didn't recognize.

Tate was nowhere to be found. He was usually off brooding somewhere and didn't mix much with the rest of them.

No one seemed to notice Gobbler's nervousness. Or if they did, they didn't care.

The hours crawled by, slow and shapeless, with nothing to occupy his time but his own thoughts and doubts.

As midnight crept closer, so did doubt. What if this was a trap?

A Misfit snored two cots over. Another shifted restlessly and muttered something Gobbler couldn't make out. What if they sensed his unease, his reluctance to fall in line with their dishonest ways?

What if Alice wasn't who she seemed?

So many questions. His mind was working overtime, keeping Gobbler awake.

The Hollow never truly slept, but tonight it pulsed with an energy that made his skin itch and his thoughts spiral. Shadows outside the barracks felt more threatening tonight. Less random. Somewhere in the distance, a scream rang out and died as quickly as it had come. Not unusual, but tonight it sounded human.

He rolled onto his side again, staring at the warped wooden wall inches from his face. Cold sweat clung to his neck despite the chill. He didn't dream; he just lay there, that same empty feeling pressing in from all sides.

Alice hadn't spoken to him much these past days. Not like before. No personal communication since her last note saying "*wait,*" which seemed like years ago.

She had been drifting lately, slipping away in small, unspoken ways. Sometimes, she would stare at the horizon long after the others had gone inside, hands folded like she was listening to something far off. Other times, she would stop mid-sentence and never finish her thought, like whatever she meant to say had evaporated before it reached her lips.

Even when she stood beside him, her eyes didn't focus on the present. They slid past him, past the trees, like they were searching for an opening to someplace else. Somewhere just beyond reach.

Her thoughts, he realized, were no longer tethered to this place. Not entirely. And he didn't know why, but it left him deeply unsettled. Like he was losing something he didn't even understand yet.

The night sky gradually gave way to a gray morning sky.

He sat up, boots thudding softly on the worn planks of the floor.

Outside, the air was thick and damp. The Hollow stretched before him in endless grays and creeping darkness; its trees hunched like sentries.

He caught a glimpse of something white. A sleeve. A shoulder. Moving through the trees, ghostlike. Alice.

She was waiting exactly where she said she would be, early morning light catching on her pale skin, making her seem almost ethereal. For a moment, Gobbler wondered if she was even real or just another fragment of this strange world.

But she turned, and the relief in her eyes was unmistakably human. Whatever else was happening here, whatever mysteries surrounded them, this connection was real.

She didn't look back. She glided through the narrow paths with the grace of a goddess.

Gobbler hesitated. Every instinct screamed that following her was a bad idea.

And yet.

He pulled his coat tighter around him and stepped into the trees.

They walked together, appearing like an ordinary couple on a lover's stroll. But nothing in the Hollow was ever ordinary. The woods pressed close around them, too quiet. Only the soft crunch of their footsteps broke the silence, each step swallowed quickly by the damp earth. The soft glow of the early morning sun lit their way.

Gobbler didn't speak. He hadn't meant to follow her. But once he saw her drifting between the trees like smoke, something inside him refused to let her go alone.

Alice didn't acknowledge him. But she didn't tell him to leave either.

The trees thinned and a soft mist wafted through the space between them. Sunlight filtered through the canopy in muted streaks, golden and gray. When they stepped into the clearing, the change was immediate—bracing, cold, biting, and sudden.

Gobbler pulled his coat tighter. The clearing stretched wide, wrapped in a veil of fog. Leaves lay scattered in rich hues of scarlet, pumpkin, and pine. There was something surreal about it, like a painting half-finished. Beautiful, yes, but incomplete—like the artist had forgotten what it was meant to be.

He turned to Alice.

She stood still, her expression unreadable. Her lips parted slightly, her eyes unfocused, as if seeing something far beyond the trees. A half-smile touched her mouth, but her shoulders tensed beneath her coat.

"Alice?" he asked softly.

She didn't answer, but stared into the mist as if it were calling her.

He gently wrapped an arm around her. "Should we turn back?"

She flinched at the sound of his voice but shook her head. "Not yet. In a minute, okay?"

She leaned into him slightly, but her eyes never left the mist. Her body went still. She held her breath, listening to something he couldn't hear.

Chaos broke their tranquil moment.

Her fingers twitched. She clenched her jaw. That half-smile vanished as her body tensed, recoiling from something only she could see. Whatever had held her in her daydream had curdled into a nightmare.

She shuddered, sharp and involuntary, then crumpled like a rag doll.

"Alice!" Gobbler caught her, gripping her shoulders. She blinked, dazed. Her breath came back in a slow, shaky draw.

"You ok?" He rubbed warmth into her arms.

She nodded weakly.

He helped her up and they stood together in silence. The clearing pressed around them, thick with the memory of those who passed this way before.

Alice shivered, and Daniel pulled her closer. Her teeth chattered, and her fingers, still in his grasp, had gone nearly blue.

"Okay. We're done here." He moved quickly, guiding her away from the mist. The deeper forest wasn't warm, but at least it didn't bite into their core.

She stumbled once. Gobbler caught her and led her to a mossy log. He brushed it off and sat her down gently.

Her hands were icy. He took them into his, rubbing fast, breathing warmth over them, ignoring the sting in his own fingers. Seeing her soaked shoes, he pulled them off and placed her wet feet in his lap to warm them.

"Thank you." The voice didn't sound like Alice's. Fragile and human in a way that startled him.

"You okay now?" He didn't trust his own voice.

She gave a slow nod, but her eyes were far away again.

"What happened out there?" He kept his voice low and gentle. "It was like… like your body was here, but your mind…"

"I was somewhere else," she said, lowering her voice.

He waited.

"Where?"

Her gaze flicked toward the clearing. "Home."

That hit him hard, a fist straight to the sternum. *Home.* He hadn't thought of that word in… well, ever. Not since arriving in the Hollow. Not since forgetting who he had been before.

"Tell me about it?" he asked, voice low.

"It wasn't real," she murmured. "Not really. Like watching someone else's memories. I could almost touch it. Almost."

"What was it like? Where you're from?"

She wrapped her arms around herself. "Different. The world was… quieter. Slower. People were still cruel, but at least the game wasn't rigged. We all played by the same rules. My family now— they're gone. All of them. Even if I could return…" Her voice trembled. "There would be nothing left for me."

He sat beside her, still rubbing warmth into her hands. "You don't have to be alone now."

She looked at him, her expression unreadable. "Don't be sorry. You can't change the past."

"But maybe we can change what comes next."

She didn't answer. She turned away, guarding something behind her silence.

Before he could speak again, the mist rolled in, thicker than before. They had company. Gobbler stopped, shoulders tight, listening.

A faceless form stepped from the white veil. Broad-shouldered. Tall. Unmistakably human. Its shape lacked definition.

"Who's there?" Gobbler called, but the fog muffled his voice.

Alice dug her fingers into his arm. "No one," she said too quickly. Her voice was steady, but her body trembled.

The figure moved forward, gliding through the fog as it curled around its limbs. Frost radiated from it in waves, seeping into their bones with the persistence of hunger.

Alice whispered, low as a ghost, "Father..."

Gobbler flinched, eyes locking on her. "Alice? What is that? Is it real?"

She shook her head. Slow at first, then with the urgency of someone trying to shake an image from their mind.

"No. No! It's not him. It can't be. He's not here."

But her eyes had already unraveled.

The figure raised its hand, nothing more than that.

Alice flinched, stumbling back, instinctively trying to put distance between them. She paled and slapped both hands over her mouth to stifle her uncontrolled whimpers.

Gobbler exploded, stepping between Alice and the figure. "Stay away from her!"

The shout burst from him, raw and loud. Pure animal rage. It ricocheted through the dying branches, bouncing from trunk to trunk.

The figure paused, tilting his head in confusion. He lowered his hand in surrender, fading backward as it tilted closer toward the ground. It came apart, then, mist unwinding in long threads, the Hollow reclaiming its illusion.

The silence that followed was absolute. They both struggled to steady their breathing, bodies still in fight-or-flight mode, and the air itself felt harder to draw into their lungs. Alice sagged against him, tears carving pale lines down her cheeks.

"I'm sorry." Her cheeks flushed as she tried to push away from him. "I didn't mean for you to see that."

Gobbler held her steady, his voice low, real. "You don't have to apologize. You're safe."

She looked away. Her jaw clenched. Her eyes still glistened. "Am I? You can't guarantee that. You're a fool if you believe it."

"I do," he said. He didn't even hesitate.

"It's getting late. Let's get back to the camp. I don't want anyone to start asking questions." With that, Alice stepped back onto the trail that led back to the cabins.

They didn't talk as they moved back beneath the trees. It grew warmer the further they moved from the clearing. It was quiet now, and empty. The memory of the apparition etched itself into the fog, a permanent reminder that the Hollow controls reality and can bend it to suit its will.

She walked beside him, only the rustle of her skirts to fill the silence. Her shoulders were tense, drawn inward. Her steps were unhurried as she dragged her toes through the fallen leaves.

"Do you want to talk about it?"

She shook her head. "Not now."

She didn't completely shut him out, but she left little room for discussion. Gobbler didn't push it. As they strode nearer to camp, he found himself walking closer to her, matching her pace deliberately.

He had seen more than fear in her eyes back there. He had seen recognition. Whatever history Alice had with the figure, it held influence over her. Someone or something she had tried to forget.

Still, they were here together. He felt a protectiveness he couldn't explain. And for the first time since arriving in this broken place, Gobbler understood someone mattered to him, and he would do anything to keep her safe.

The Hollow's shadows stretched ahead of them, thick and watchful. He was still aware of the danger pulsing in the roots, of the secrets carried on the breeze, drifting just out of reach before anyone could untangle them.

But Gobbler no longer wanted to run.

If the Hollow wanted her, it would have to go through him first.

The deeper they walked, the more the forest seemed to lean in. The trees were familiar, but the Hollow had redirected the path. The trees no longer spoke with the breeze's soft voice, settling instead into a sort of reverent silence usually reserved for someone important.

Alice drew closer to Daniel. Her hands warmed, but she held tight to his sleeve. Every so often, she glanced back over her shoulder as if expecting the shadow to reappear.

When they reached the edge of the tree line, the Hollow finally opened before them again. Faint trails twisted in all directions, dotted with movement. A pair of Misfits shuffled past in the distance, hunched and muttering, too preoccupied to notice them. To her left, Alice spotted her friend Lilith making her way toward the main camp.

Farther off, dark spires loomed like black teeth in the pale light. Twisted towers that could only belong to Grim.

They paused here, watching the bustle of the camp, just out of reach of the tower's shadow.

Gobbler broke the silence first. "Are you sure you're alright?"

Alice stared at a patch of moss, unmoving.

"I don't know what he was," she said at last. "But he wasn't supposed to find me."

She didn't sound scared anymore. She sounded pensive and held the look of one trying to solve an unsolvable puzzle.

"Was he really your father?" Gobbler asked, not wanting to interrupt her mental calculations, but too impatient to wait for her to finish, either by solving or giving up. Neither was likely to happen.

She gave the faintest shake of her head. "No. Not really. At least I don't think so. This has never happened quite like this before. My father, as far as I know, is gone from me. In another world. One that is inaccessible to me. Dead, in human terms."

He nodded, not really understanding, but giving her the space to work it out. The Hollow had its own rules, and it was up to its prisoners to figure them out, or be victim to their obscurity. It intentionally kept things buried, broken, and unfinished. Whatever Alice thought she had left behind, it wasn't ready to stay quiet.

"You don't have to tell me everything," he said. "Not yet. But if it comes back—if he does, I want you to know I'm not walking away."

She studied him, her eyes glassy with tears she was too tough to shed. She didn't say thank you. That wasn't her way. But he could tell, in the way she looked at him, and that was enough.

The trees behind them rustled. They turned in unison, ready to spring if the need was there.

But it was only a harmless crow, wings slicing through the branches before it disappeared into the mist.

Alice willed the tension away and found her voice again.

"I have chores to do, I better get back before it gets late," she said.

As they approached camp, voices drifted from the small glade where they usually held meetings on pleasant evenings. Alice perked up, a smile planted on her lips. "That's Lilith," she said, almost to herself. "Sounds like she's telling one of her stories again. You haven't met her yet. I'll introduce you when she's not so busy gossiping. She always has a tale to tell."

Before the path opened to the Misfit camp, Gobbler noticed something lying beside the mouth of it. A long black feather, deliberately placed for someone to find. A shadow moved across the path above. He looked up in time to see a raven gliding through the canopy. Silent, heavy-winged. It didn't slow. But its shadow passed over his feet and lingered, a few seconds too long. He knew it was a message meant for him, and he would have to understand it before someone got hurt.

And Gobbler realized he wasn't just a pawn to be played, he was a real player now. Someone with power. With presence. With purpose. For once, he belonged. The Hollow hadn't noticed him before. But after tonight, it would.

T.M. ROCHE

7

What the Hollow Takes

Lilith lay rigid in her dormitory bed, eyes wide and burning in absolute darkness. The air was dense and electric like the moment before lightning strikes.

Click, click, click.

She held her breath and froze, straining to hear past the frantic pulse hammering in her ears.

Click, click, click. Closer now.

She searched through the darkness for movement. A shift in the shadow, a deeper patch of black. Anything. But the moonless night had swallowed everything, leaving her blind and exposed. The room was in complete darkness.

A floorboard creaked somewhere in the dorm room. She slid her arms under the blankets, gripping the comforter under her chin. If her hands and feet stayed tucked under the covers, no monstrous claws could grab them. She would be safe until morning, when the sunlight would chase away the shadow demon.

She told herself she was letting her imagination get the best of her, and she tried to relax into the soft mattress.

Tap, tap, tap, came a sound from the foot of the bed. Lilith tensed, straining her ears, trying to dismiss the sounds as mere settling noises. She rolled onto her side and drew her knees closer to her chest, distancing her limbs from the edges of the bed. She wrapped the blanket tighter around her body.

She whimpered softly, barely making a sound. It could sense she was there, but it didn't know exactly where she was. Not yet. She steadied her breathing. Silence was her shield.

A soft scratching came from the corner of the room. Claws shuffled along the floor. One of the other girls must be awake, she thought. Again, she listened for more sounds.

Something struck the bed frame, and it shuddered in protest. Lilith's breath caught in her throat. She held back a scream. Any sound would mean the end for her.

This was a game of willpower. Of cat and mouse. She had heard the stories of the dark moon monster, stalking and teasing to see how quickly it could catch its prey. It took great pleasure in the hunt, and fear fed its demonic soul.

There were no other sounds in the dormitory. No one else stirred. They all slept soundly. But "it" wasn't interested in anyone else. It had come for her and her alone. She knew this would be the case the moment the raven visited her that day.

Her back ached from being in the same balled-up position for so long. The muscles in her arms were stiff and sore. She mentally calculated the hours until sunrise, but she had no way of knowing what time it was now. If she could stay quiet until daybreak, she would be safe. It would need to go unfed until the next dark moon night.

The demon had gone silent. It didn't tap. It didn't scratch or shuffle along the floor now. Perhaps it had gone. Perhaps it slept. Maybe it was trying to lull her into a sense of security. The waiting was agonizing for Lilith. It was better when she knew it was still there, and her adrenaline kept her vigilant. Not knowing was so much worse.

The quiet was so absolute, a complete absence of sound. Lilith gradually became aware of a ringing in her ears. The only sound in the room came from her own head, increasing in decibels until it was deafening, driving her to near madness.

She clamped her hands over her ears, forcing herself to focus on her senses and compose herself. She listened to the calming sound of her own steady breathing, and the ringing finally subsided. She took another deep sigh of relief. Lilith was exhausted. The darkness played tricks on her mind. She needed sleep, but she had to stay alert.

A low growl came from beneath the bed, accompanied by a wave of icy air that chilled her to the bone. The warmth of her cocoon was no longer enough to keep her shivering at bay. She swore she could smell sulfur, like the acrid smoke of a dying fire. Her nose wrinkled at the scent, but she dared not move.

It sighed, a soft, guttural purr. Calming. Hypnotic. Lulling Lilith to relax and close her eyes. She couldn't fight the fatigue any longer. She would let herself rest for just a minute.

She drifted into a deeper slumber. The warmth of dreams drew her further into unconsciousness.

She dreamed of a dark, winged creature waiting for her, standing in a sunlit meadow. It was unlike the darkness of her waking fear—a soft glow surrounded him, and the scent of wildflowers filled the air. His wings, vast and feathered, seemed to stretch forever, offering shelter.

"Do not be afraid," he said in a voice both soothing and commanding. "Come to me. I will protect you. You don't have to fight anymore."

Behind him, the silhouette of someone she recognized. Her sister, alive, whole, and smiling as she had been before.

Lilith hesitated, stepping forward. "How…?"

"I can reunite you," the creature said, holding out a hand. "All it takes is one step, and you will never be alone again."

The warmth tempted her, but as she reached for his hand, the glow dimmed. The wildflowers wilted, and the creature's eyes darkened like endless voids. She stumbled back, the Meadow crumbling into a cold, black forest.

"No," her voice shook with terror.

The creature's feathers rustled like a thousand whispers. His beak twisted into something resembling a grin. "You can't run forever."

Lilith turned to flee, but the forest shifted around her, and massive wings blocked her escape. The unexpected obstacle caused her to lose her footing on the slippery leaves and tumble backwards. Instinctively, she threw her arms behind her to catch herself, but she met no resistance to stop her fall. Arms flailing, heart pounding, the weightlessness went on until Lilith feared she could take the horror no longer.

Her screams finally caught up to her ears, her downward momentum slowed, and she landed hard on something firm, but yielding at the same time. The plummet startled her from her sleep, and for a moment, she wondered where she was.

She soon remembered, as out of the darkness came a low, menacing chuckle.

Finally. The word hissed through the darkness.

It knew where she was, now. It had found her.

The blankets slipped from Lilith's body. She grabbed them with both fists, cocooning herself within them, shielding herself from this beast.

"No," she whispered, her voice barely audible but steady. "You won't take me."

Her hand groped the bedside table for a weapon. Anything to fight with. Her fingers curled around the edge of a broken ceramic shard, leftover from a forgotten knick-knack. She raised it, her heart pounding in her chest.

The blankets slid away despite her grip, exposing her to the cold air that now reeked of decay and sulfur. Her trembling fingers still clutched the ceramic shard, raising it in pathetic defense.

A low, guttural chuckle reverberated through the room. "How amusing." The creature's voice slithered through the shadows as it loomed closer.

Cold, clammy fingers with too many joints wrapped around her ankle. Claws pierced skin, drawing hot trickles of blood.

She tried to scream. Her throat constricted, allowing only a strangled whimper. It wouldn't matter. No one could help her now.

"Your sister sends her regards," it said.

The ceramic shard fell from her nerveless fingers. The darkness lunged.

And Lilith... was gone.

The dawn broke over the horizon with a pale, hesitant light, casting long shadows across the encampment. The stillness of the dormitory was suffocating.

The beds in this wing stood in perfect, untouched order, sheets pulled tight with military precision. All except one. Lilith's bed was a nest of violence. Her sheets were shredded to ribbons. The mattress torn open as if by massive claws. Dark stains soaked through to the frame below. The wall beside it bore scratch marks. Not the desperate scratches of human fingernails, but deeper and broader. Sharp talons had dragged across the surface with deliberate slowness.

No one spoke of what they heard in the night. No one mentioned the screams that had begun as human but ended in pathetic, tortured howls. The sounds had carried through the dense woods like a warning, and the message had been received. Heads stayed down. Eyes averted.

Alice stood in the doorway of the dormitory, her arms folded tightly across her chest, fingernails digging crescents into her skin. The metallic taste of fear coated her tongue. She didn't need to look inside to know Lilith was gone. She had seen it happen before, smelled the lingering sulfur on the wind, felt the unnatural cold that persisted for days afterward.

Her death fed the Hollow, and Grim's shadow deepened. His strength was never static. It grew with obedience, shrank with defiance. That was the law down here: the Hollow bent for whoever held the most power and commanded the most souls.

"They'll say she's been released," whispered a voice behind her. One of the newer girls, still naive enough to speak of such things. "That's what they always say."

Alice's jaw tightened. Release. Such a gentle word for such a violent end. Grim's euphemism for punishment, for example-making, for erasure. She was one of the few in this hellhole privileged enough to know the gory details of what "release" truly meant. A privilege she would have gladly forfeited.

It was knowledge, nonetheless. And in the Hollow, knowledge was as valuable as it was dangerous. Understanding the patterns, recognizing the signs. These things might not save her, but they could buy time. Time to plan. Time to wait for an opportunity.

Hope was a dangerous luxury in a place like this. Alice had seen hope crushed too many times to trust it. But determination was different. Determination kept her playing Grim's games, kept her watching, waiting for the moment when she might finally save those she had come to love as family. For when she might finally escape this eternal hell.

She turned away from the dormitory, from the evidence of Lilith's final moments, steeling herself against the grief that threatened to overwhelm her. Crying for the dead attracted unwanted attention. Mourning was a private thing, to be hidden away like treasure.

"Clean it up," came the cold command from behind her. One of Grim's minions, already working to erase Lilith's existence. "All of it. By midday."

Grim's forces took many forms. Some still wore the faces they had died with, tasked with keeping the Misfits in line. Others were stripped of humanity entirely, monstrous things he summoned when lessons needed to be taught. And beneath them all, the mindless skeletons, animated husks that did his bidding without thought or mercy.

Alice bowed her head without turning, her face a careful mask of obedience. But her hands trembled with silent rage as she walked away.

By sunset, there would be no sign Lilith ever existed. No belongings. No memories shared. Her name would never be spoken again.

That was the cruelest part of "release". Not just the taking of life, but the erasure of it. As if it never mattered at all.

Gobbler sat on the edge of the Misfit encampment, where the trees hadn't yet decided if they belonged to the Hollow or the woods beyond. The sun overhead was a weak, dishwater yellow, barely cutting through the mist curling along the ground.

He dragged a stick through the dirt, drawing circles. Every shape was incomplete. Just like him.

He wasn't worried about who he used to be. That version of him—the boy before the Hollow—was slipping further into abstraction, like a story someone else started telling him but never finished.

What haunted him now was the way everyone around here moved like they were being watched. Like they had a role to play. Like there were rules he had yet to learn.

Digger sat nearby, pretending not to notice the tension in Gobbler's shoulders or the fact that he kept glancing toward the ridge where the scream had echoed the night before.

"So." Gobbler dragged his stick through another unfinished loop. "That thing I heard last night. Was it real?"

Digger didn't answer right away. His knife cut deeper. He whittled a little faster.

"What you heard was a 'release.' It's what happens when you're done here." His voice pitched low enough that it wouldn't carry beyond the two of them. "Or when Grim is done with you," he added, lowering his voice.

"Done with what?"

"Everything." Digger flicked a sliver of wood toward Gobbler's feet, his expression carefully blank. "Working for Grim. Surviving. Existing."

A shadow fell across them. Alice stood behind the bench, her face drawn and pale. Her eyes were rimmed with red, though whether from tears or lack of sleep, Gobbler couldn't tell. She had been absent from breakfast, and now he understood why.

"It's not as simple as that," she said, her voice barely above a whisper. "You don't just get released. You get taken."

Gobbler slid sideways on the bench, making room for her, but Alice remained standing, her fingers gripping the weathered back of the bench until her knuckles bleached white.

"Taken where?" Gobbler pressed, studying her face.

Alice's gaze darted around the camp, checking for eavesdroppers before she leaned closer. "No one knows for sure. But every time someone's released, there's... a presence." Her voice faltered. "Something dark. You hear it. You feel it. And then they're gone. Until Grim summons it again."

Digger snorted, his knife digging too deep into the wood, splitting it. He tossed the ruined stick aside with barely contained violence. "It's not a presence. It's a damn beast." He turned to Gobbler, his usual sardonic expression replaced by steel and ice. "Wings like a nightmare, eyes like the abyss. It hunts them down, and when it's done, there's nothing left."

His voice had an edge of desperate conviction, as if needing Gobbler to understand the horror lurking at the edges of their existence.

Alice's eyes flickered toward the spires, visible just beyond the trees. "He calls it when he wants to remind us who's in charge in the Hollow," she murmured. "Every scream is a sermon meant for our ears."

A cold knot formed in Gobbler's stomach as Digger's words sank in. The hair on his arms stood on end despite the warmth of the morning sun. "And Grim just lets this happen?"

Alice made a sound—half laugh, half choke—her eyes darting toward the main camp where several of Grim's trusted lieutenants were now watching them with thinly veiled interest.

"Lets it happen?" she echoed, her voice dropping even lower. She moved to sit beside Gobbler, her body angled away from prying eyes. "He orchestrates it."

Her fingers worked nervously at a frayed thread on her sleeve, twisting it until it snapped. "The ones who question him?" Her voice cracked. "They're the ones who get released. In the most nightmarish way possible."

Her gaze met Gobbler's, unflinching despite the fear evident in her trembling hands. "It's his way of keeping us in line."

A heavy silence fell between them. Somewhere in the camp, someone was chopping wood, the steady thunk-thunk-thunk like a heartbeat measuring out the moments.

Gobbler's mind raced as pieces of the Hollow's puzzle fit together: the way people lowered their voices when Grim's name was mentioned, how tasks were completed without question, the strange deference shown to even his most minor requests. It wasn't respect. It was terror.

He remembered the faces he had seen since arriving. Those who moved through their days with mechanical precision, and those who had quietly disappeared, mentioned only in hushed whispers before their names were never spoken again.

"What about her?" He kept his voice steady despite the dread pooling in his stomach. "Your friend. Lilith. Did she…?"

Alice's composure cracked. Her eyes welled with tears, and she blinked them away furiously, her jaw clenching hard enough that Gobbler could see the muscle jumping beneath her skin.

"She didn't deserve what happened to her," she said, each word measured and precise despite the emotion behind them.

"She was defiant, sure. She didn't follow every order. But she wasn't a bad person." Her voice broke on the last word, and she fell silent, swallowing hard.

Digger glanced toward the camp, his posture tense. He stepped closer, using his body to shield their conversation from view.

"Being good or bad doesn't matter here," he said, his voice rough. "Survival does. And if you want to survive, you do what Grim says. No questions. No hesitation."

He gave Gobbler a hard look.

"You've been asking a lot of questions since you got here. Watching things you shouldn't. That kind of attention isn't healthy."

The warning was clear, and for the first time since waking in this strange place, Gobbler was truly afraid. Not just confused or wary, but genuinely terrified. There was no authority to appeal to, no rules except Grim's, and the punishment for breaking them was a fate worse than death.

Somewhere deep in the Hollow, the air shivered. Just enough to make him wonder if another sermon had begun.

The sound of boots crunching on gravel sliced through their conversation. Deliberate, unhurried steps instantly straightened Digger's posture and wiped all expression from Alice's face. The change was immediate, like watching masks slide into place.

Gobbler looked up and saw Grim approaching, his tall figure absorbing rather than blocking the sunlight. The unnaturally long shadows at his feet stretched toward them, threatening.

"Beautiful morning," Grim's voice was smooth as polished stone. His smile didn't reflect in his eyes, which remained cold and assessing as they moved from Digger to Alice before settling on Gobbler. There was something almost hungry in his gaze, and it made Gobbler's skin prickle with instinctive warning.

Digger mumbled an agreement; his eyes fixed on the ground. Alice had gone completely still, her breathing so shallow she might not have been breathing at all.

Grim stepped closer, breaching the invisible boundary of their small circle with casual dominance.

"I trust you're ready for today's tasks?" The question was directed at Gobbler, though Grim's gaze flicked briefly to the other two, a silent reminder they were all being addressed, all being judged.

Gobbler nodded, fighting to keep his expression neutral despite the rapid drumming of his heart.

"Yes," he managed, hating the way his voice sounded smaller in Grim's presence.

"Good." Grim's fingers toyed with something he pulled from his pocket. A small metallic object caught the light as he turned it over and over. "Because in this world, loyalty is everything." He paused, the silence stretching uncomfortably before he continued. "And those who forget that. Well, it seems you've heard the stories."

He said it lightly, almost amused, but the threat hung in the air like the ozone before a storm. His gaze settled on Alice, whose fingers had gone white where they gripped the edge of the bench.

"I would hate to lose any more of you," Grim added softly. "Especially those with... potential."

Without waiting for a response, he turned and walked away, his movements too fluid, too precise. Graceful for a man of his stature.

Only when he was well out of earshot did Digger exhale, running a trembling hand over his face.

"He knows," he muttered. "He always fucking knows."

Gobbler glanced at Alice, who had finally started acting normal again, the color slowly returning to her face. "Knows what?"

"That we were talking about her. About Lilith." Alice looked around like she expected to be struck for speaking the words.

The knot in Gobbler's stomach tightened painfully. He stared after Grim's retreating figure, trying to understand what kind of power could inspire such immediate, visceral fear. What kind of creature could command not only obedience, but this bone-deep terror?

And why, despite everything, did something about Grim feel strangely familiar?

Across the desolate expanse of the Hollow, Elizabeth lay awake in her makeshift shelter, counting the hours until dawn. The canvas walls fluttered in the night breeze, too thin to provide real shelter from the elements, or from the sounds carried across the darkness.

The distant scream tore through the night, raw and filled with such terror it made her stomach drop.

She pressed her hands to her ears, but it had been no use; the sound could have pierced bone and mind alike, leaving a permanent echo.

Around her, the other "Visitors" stirred in their sleep, some whimpering, others praying in quiet voices. No one spoke of what they heard, but their eyes in the morning would tell the same story: another one taken, another soul lost to the darkness that prowled the Hollow's edges.

Rumors spread through the encampment like a fever. Tales of things taking people in the night. Of shadows moving against the wind, of creatures with too many limbs and eyes that reflected no light. Elizabeth had dismissed most of it as fear talking, stories passed between the broken and the lost to explain the inexplicable.

But tonight, the scream sounded too real. Too close.

She reached into the darkness, her fingers curling around the hilt of the short blade she kept nearby. The metal was cold and familiar beneath her touch, a poor weapon against nightmares but better than nothing. She hoped it would be enough. She hoped she would never have to find out.

The camp settled into uneasy silence again, a false peace heavy with collective dread. No one would speak of it come morning. No one ever did.

The first gray light of dawn found Elizabeth sitting up in her tent, her back rigid from too many nights on uneven ground. The air inside was thick with the scent of damp earth and woodsmoke that had appeared overnight. Sulfur and the smell of burned flesh permeated the camp.

She clutched the locket around her neck, her thumb tracing its worn edge as it had a thousand times before. The small silver shape was the only tangible piece of Daniel she had left—this and the unwavering certainty that he was here, somewhere in this fractured place. The hope of finding him was the only reason she hadn't let despair take root, hadn't surrendered to the hollow-eyed resignation she saw in so many others.

Outside, the camp was stirring to life. The Visitors moved with the efficiency of those who knew their welcome was conditional, their safety temporary. Elizabeth had learned their rhythms quickly. The morning water collection, the gathering of firewood, the careful rationing of supplies. Tasks assigned by the "settlement council," those who had been here longest and wielded authority with cryptic references to "the rules."

But the camp murmured of others. Those who had wandered out and never returned. Of places that pulled people in and didn't let go. Of decisions that couldn't be undone.

"Are you ready to move on?"

The voice pulled her from her thoughts. A man, Parson, stood at the tent's entrance, his face half-shadowed by the early light. Graying hair, sunken eyes, skin weathered beyond his years. He looked like he had been here too long and knew it.

"Move on?" she repeated, frowning.

He nodded, adjusting his weight from one foot to the other. "That's what we do here. We don't stay long. We can't. When the time comes, you either go back to where you came from or…"

His words trailed off, his gaze drifting toward the dark tree line at the camp's edge.

"Or what?" Elizabeth asked, her voice low.

The man's eyes dropped to the ground, his shoulders curving inward as if carrying an invisible weight. "Or you don't." He shrugged as if forcing the words out.

The words hung between them, heavy with meaning Elizabeth couldn't fully grasp but instinctively feared.

"My son is out there," she said, her fingers tightening around the locket. "I'm not leaving without him."

Pity crossed the man's face. "Then I hope you find him soon," he said, turning to go. "Before the Hollow decides for you."

Dusk crept across the camp like a black stain, lengthening shadows and merging until the boundaries between objects blurred. Gobbler sat alone on the steps of the supply shed, watching as the others went about their evening tasks with the quiet efficiency of the truly afraid.

Their movements were wary, each gesture measured to avoid notice. Gobbler watched a woman carry a stack of firewood with her elbows pinned to her ribs, shrinking into herself as if it could make her invisible. Another paused before crossing an open stretch between cabins, scanning the shadows first, then slipping through with her head lowered. No one spoke above a murmur. No one risked a sudden motion. The whole camp seemed to move on a single, trembling instinct, like creatures who sensed the predator nearby but had no idea where it waited.

Except there was nowhere to run to.

Gobbler's mind kept returning to the morning's conversations, to Alice's grief over Lilith, to Digger's warning, to Grim's veiled threat. The pieces didn't quite fit together yet, but the outline was taking shape, a puzzle with death at its center.

He studied the faces around him, searching for resistance, anger, anything beyond the hollow-eyed compliance he saw everywhere. Most avoided his gaze. A few stared back with empty looks that spoke of surrender, of spirits broken long ago.

Across the clearing, Grim emerged from the shadows, and the camp's rhythm faltered for a heartbeat before resuming with even more careful precision. He moved through the space as if he owned it. Like he owned them. His eyes missed nothing.

For a moment, Grim's eyes locked with Gobbler's. A challenge passed between them. Anger stirred deep in Gobbler's chest.

"Don't stare too long," Alice murmured, appearing beside him with two tin cups of steaming liquid. She handed one to him and sat, her movements deliberately casual despite the tension in her shoulders. "He notices things like that."

Gobbler accepted the cup, grateful for its warmth against his palms. "I can't just pretend everything's normal after what you told me today."

"You can... and you will," she said softly, her voice barely audible. "If you want to survive long enough to do anything about it."

The liquid in the cup tasted bitter and earthy, but Gobbler drank it anyway, letting the warmth spread through him.

"And is that what you're doing? Surviving long enough to do something about it?"

Alice's expression remained carefully neutral, but determination sparked in her eyes. Or hope.

"I've been here longer than most," she said after a pause. "I've seen things. Learned things. There are patterns in this place, in what Grim does. In how the releases happen."

She stopped talking as one of Grim's lieutenants passed nearby, resuming only when they were alone again. "There are ways to navigate this place without drawing attention. Ways to bend without breaking."

Gobbler studied her face, noting the careful way she chose her words, the deliberate vagueness. "You're planning something."

It wasn't a question, and Alice didn't treat it as one. She simply held his gaze, a silent communication passing between them. She stood, taking his empty cup.

"Rest tonight," she said, loud enough for anyone nearby to hear. "First day of real work tomorrow. You'll need your strength."

As she walked away, resolve snapped inside Gobbler, forming where confusion had been. He knew, with sudden clarity, that he was walking a fine line in this place, balancing between survival and defiance. The stakes had never been higher.

Night settled fully over the camp, bringing with it an unnatural stillness. No cricket song, no rustling leaves, just the occasional crackle of the central fire and the soft murmur of subdued conversations.

Gobbler made his way to his assigned sleeping quarters, lying down on the thin pallet serving as his bed. But sleep remained distant; his mind was too full of the day's revelations.

Deep in the darkness, he made a silent vow to himself. He would survive this place. He would understand its secrets, its rules, its weaknesses. And he would find a way out not only for himself, but for Alice and the others who hadn't surrendered completely.

As he finally drifted toward uneasy sleep, a sound came from the distant woods. A raven's call, echoing once before falling silent. Gobbler's eyes flew open, his heart racing though he wasn't sure why.

It had happened before, he realized. Always when a decision settled inside him. As if the raven were listening. As if it understood.

8

You're Closer Than You Think

Elizabeth stepped out of her makeshift shelter and brushed the pine needles from her hair and clothes. The crisp morning air carried the aroma of strong coffee from a nearby campfire, stirring memories of her old life. She closed her eyes and sucked in long, deep breaths, letting the bittersweet scent transport her to a time when a steaming cup of coffee was a mundane part of her routine. A luxury she hadn't appreciated until it was gone.

Breakfast had become a relic of her past. Mornings now were spent foraging for her next meal. She wandered through the forest, searching for whatever nature had to offer: late-season mushrooms, crabapples, wild grapes, acorns, pine needles, and rose hips. If luck were on her side, she would find a rabbit or squirrel caught in one of her snares. These she learned to clean, cut into strips, and smoke over a fire, a skill taught by the kindness of others in this transient community.

Without their help, she would never have survived. Yet even with their guidance, the toll of this new life was clear. She lost more weight than she could afford, and her oversized, hand-me-down dress now hung on her frame like a sack. It wasn't important, though. Survival left no room for vanity.

As she moved, Elizabeth plucked a twig from a teaberry bush, chewing the end until it frayed. The minty taste offered a hint of comfort and doubled as a makeshift toothbrush. She popped a teaberry into her mouth, savoring the burst of flavor as she scanned the ground for mushrooms. At the base of an old oak, she spotted a cluster of "hen of the woods." The mushrooms were past their prime, starting to dry, but beggars couldn't be choosers. She sliced the stems, careful to leave the base, and tucked them into her apron pocket.

Her morning haul was a meager handful of wild grapes, a few rose hips, and some pine needles for tea. She sighed, resigning herself to another sparse meal. Hunger was her constant companion, but it was the thought of Daniel that kept her going. The hope of finding her son kept her alive. For him, she endured the ache in her belly, the cold nights, and the uncertainty of every day.

Back at her shelter, she rummaged through her few belongings, pulling out a tin can she had repurposed as a cooking pot. She half-filled it with water and set it on a flat rock beside her fire. Rose-hip tea would have to suffice for breakfast. She dropped half the small red fruit into the can, saving the rest for later.

The smell of food wafting from neighboring camps made her stomach growl. She reached into her pocket for a grape, popped it into her mouth, and savored the sweetness of the fruit. By the time her tea was ready, the grapes were gone, but at least she had something warm to drink.

Pouring the tea through a scrap of cloth into a second tin, Elizabeth sipped it, careful not to burn herself as she watched her neighbors. Most were travelers, stopping here for a short time before moving on to destinations unknown. They respected each other's privacy, sharing an unspoken understanding that judgment had no place here. It was a small comfort in an otherwise harsh existence.

Her mind drifted to the day she arrived, expecting to find a phone, make a call, and return to her life. Instead, she found herself in an entirely different world. One where she was a stranger not only to the people but to the time itself. How she had ended up here was a mystery, one she had learned to guard with care. Admitting she was from a different time would invite suspicion or worse.

Her musing was interrupted by a cheerful voice. "Miss Elizabeth!"

A little girl with rosy cheeks came running up, clutching a cloth-wrapped parcel with pride. "Mamma told me to bring this to you."

Elizabeth took the bundle, warmth seeping through the fabric.

"Thank you, sweetheart. And thank your mamma for me." She knelt. "Would you like to sit with me for a bit?"

The girl grinned and plopped onto the ground. Inside the cloth were two fresh biscuits. Tears pricked Elizabeth's eyes at the generosity of her neighbors. Sniffling, she offered one to the child.

"No, thank you." The girl set her hands in her lap, making no move to take the biscuit. "Those are for you."

Elizabeth smiled, touched by the gesture. She nibbled the biscuits, savoring every bite, while the girl kept her company. They chatted comfortably until the child's mother called her back to their camp, leaving Elizabeth alone once more, but her spirits were lifted.

With her hunger eased, she prepared for the day ahead. Tidying her few belongings, she daydreamed, imagining herself manifesting her perfect day.

Today will be the day I find answers. Someone here knows something. Daniel is near. I can feel it as strongly as my own heartbeat. Is he hurt? Is he safe? This world is harsh, and I pray wherever he is, God is keeping him safe until I find him.

She paused, letting the thought settle, and added, *Together, we will find a way home.*

As the warm tea settled in her belly and the camp quieted into its morning rhythms, Elizabeth packed her bag with practiced motions: scraps of food, her knife, a handful of pine needles for later. Her fingers lingered on the locket around her neck, the metal warm against her skin. Inside was a tiny photograph of Daniel, his smile frozen in time. The image was fading now, worn from countless openings, endless moments when she needed to remember his face.

The idea of forgetting what he looked like terrified her more than starvation.

She tucked the locket back under her dress and let her gaze drift toward the inconspicuous path beyond the ridge. The town. The mere mention caused goosebumps.

The Hollow behaved strangely around newcomers, as if testing where they belonged. Sometimes it shifted streets or folded time, blurring the line between memory and dream. Elizabeth didn't know that, of course. She only knew the world kept changing shape every time she tried to reach town.

She had tried once before. Maybe twice. The memories blurred like dreams. Each time, something had stopped her. A storm coming out of nowhere. A wrong turn bringing her back to where she started. The sense she was being tracked by unseen predators.

Each attempt had ended with her stumbling back to camp, empty-handed, bruised in body and spirit, with gaps in her memory she couldn't explain.

It wasn't just the path that resisted her. It was the people.

"Not for us." They spoke in quiet tones, their eyes darting toward the ridge and away again. "The town isn't meant for folks like us."

No one could say what happened to those who made it in, mainly because it was rare for anyone ever to come back. The stories changed from person to person. Some claimed it shimmered like a mirage; others believed it swallowed time whole. A few spoke of people returning changed. Speaking in riddles, aging years in days, or forgetting their own names.

Whatever the truth, the message was the same. Don't go.

But Elizabeth had never been good at following rules she didn't understand. And every night she dreamt of Daniel, and every morning she woke with his name in her heart. The town might be cursed. Or empty. Or worse. But it also might hold answers.

She adjusted the strap of her bag and squared her shoulders. Her breath curled in the cold air.

Today, she would try again.

She didn't expect the road to welcome her. But this time, she wouldn't turn back.

This time, she would find her son or die trying.

Elizabeth stood at the edge of the old trail, where the worn trees thinned into open space. Beyond the ridge, peeking through the morning haze, sat the town. The one everyone whispered about but no one dared enter.

The Hollow wasn't consistent. Sometimes the way to town vanished entirely, but today the path was open, quiet, waiting, almost inviting.

Which was the problem.

The rules were simple. *Don't go to town.* Some swore the town wasn't real at all, but that it was a trick of the Hollow meant to lure desperate souls deeper until they disappeared. But Elizabeth wasn't desperate. She was determined.

With each step, she reminded herself, *Daniel might be there. A clue. A trace. Anything.*

She crested the rise and spotted a cluster of buildings slouched together, as if they were holding each other up. Wooden sidewalks buckled with age. Faded signs dangled from rusted brackets. Despite its appearance, it was welcoming and familiar.

The post office. The general store. Even the crooked awning over what might have once been a bakery.

Realization stopped Elizabeth cold.

I've never been here before, she thought. But she had. Or a place like it. Buried deep in memory. It was every small town from her childhood road trips. The places with dusty shelves and hand-painted window signs. The scent of coffee and tobacco. The sense of refuge.

Except this wasn't safe. She knew it wasn't. The silence here was muffled. Like sound under water.

A woman passed her without a glance, walking as though on a tightrope. Her dress was clean. Her face calm. Elizabeth offered a polite nod, but the woman responded by whispering to herself, "It's almost my turn. I'm ready. I can't be late," and disappeared into a side alley.

Elizabeth turned to look back the way she had come. The path was still visible behind her, the trees parting enough to remind her she could leave, if she wanted to.

But she didn't.

She walked on.

Inside the general store, the bell above the door made a faint "tinkle" sound as she entered. A man stood behind the counter; his face weathered like cracked leather. He looked up, eyes squinting, deciding if she belonged or not.

"Not often we get new ones in town." He slid a jar across the counter to an unseen customer.

Elizabeth straightened. "I'm… just… passing through."

"Mmm." He didn't press further and gestured at the shelves. "Don't touch what isn't yours."

How odd, she thought, confused by his instructions.

The floorboards creaked under her boots as she walked the aisles. Canned goods. Blank journals. Jars of candy that looked like they hadn't moved in years. Every item was coated in a thin film of dust and memories.

In the back corner, a cracked mirror hung on the wall. She caught her reflection.

And blinked.

The face staring back at her wasn't her own.

Or it was, but younger. Softer. The version of herself from ten years ago, before her husband was taken away from her. Before the worry lines. She reached out. The mirror flickered, and the image reset back to her normal reflection.

Her face again. Hollow-cheeked. Tired. Real.

All an illusion. A trick of the mind to confuse her.

Elizabeth pulled her hand back, holding it tight to her chest, and left the store. There was nothing here meant for her.

Outside, the tumbleweeds chased each other across the street. She didn't remember the wind picking up, but the dust stirred at her feet. Soft and strange. The sun hung in the same position it had when she entered the store, though she was certain she had spent at least twenty minutes inside. Time behaved strangely here, stretching and contracting according to rules she couldn't understand.

It wasn't just wind. It was the hush again. The one always following her, just out of sight, as if the Hollow were secretly rearranging its streets behind her. People passed her on the sidewalk. Men in weathered hats. Women in faded dresses. But no one acknowledged her now. They moved with odd, deliberate steps, like actors hitting their marks on stage. They mumbled incoherent words to themselves on repeat like they were memorizing a script.

"I think I'm ready." A woman carrying an empty basket.

"It's time." A man checking a pocket watch with no hands.

"He said I could go soon." A child bouncing a ball that made no sound when it hit the ground.

Elizabeth's heartbeat spiked. The town wasn't merely strange. These souls were trapped in repetition. The same performance over and over. Never moving toward resolution.

A trial? A trap? A ritual?

Whatever it was, she needed to leave.

But when she turned back toward the path, it was gone. Where trees had stood at the edge of town, there was now another row of buildings, their shadows stretching long despite the high sun.

She spun around once, twice, looking for her way out. Her pulse roared in her ears. Buildings warped, struggling to hold their forms. Signs were gone. Doors changed color. She walked in one direction, then doubled back, only to find the general store facing the opposite way, its sign now in a language she couldn't read.

Panic clawed at her throat. The town was closing around her like a fist.

A hand gripped her shoulder.

She turned, and a boy, maybe ten, stood there. He looked tired; ancient wisdom momentarily sparkled in his youthful eyes.

He didn't say a word but pointed toward a narrow alley behind the telegraph building. Her way out. She ran without a backward glance. Without so much as a thank you to the boy.

The path reappeared as she passed through the shadows—trees returning, the smell of earth rising. Her lungs burned. Her chest ached.

But she was out.

When she reached her camp again, she dropped to her knees in the dirt, the biscuit from earlier still heavy in her stomach.

The town hadn't tried to keep her.

Not yet.

Much later, Elizabeth would swear she hadn't meant to return.

She remembered sleeping. The fire crackled low. Her breath fogged in the night air. The Hollow tugged at her even in her dreams.

Without realizing she moved, she shifted in her sleep. In her dreams, she took a step, leaving the camp behind. Her second step landed on a gritty sidewalk. And before her, the Hollow appeared once again.

Elizabeth didn't walk out of camp this time.

One moment, she was asleep and dreaming of the Hollow, shifting and distorting like a funhouse mirror. The next, she was standing at the edge of town, blinking at the warped signs and leaning buildings as though they had materialized from the mist.

The path hadn't hurt this time.

No blisters, no dragging exhaustion, no branches clawing at her arms. Just one step. Then another. And then the town, waiting.

It should have unsettled her more than it did.

She walked down the grimy road, peering into alleys and through curtainless windows, watching for signs of life. The streets looked the same as before, dusty, half-abandoned, too quiet. But the buildings now stood straighter. The glass in the windows was cleaner. The wind was warmer here, almost sweet.

She turned a corner she hadn't noticed on her last visit.

It led to a narrow street lined with tiny shops. There were no signs, no names above the doors, but one window caught her eye.

There was nothing special about the window itself, but what sat behind the glass caught her attention.

A green ceramic pitcher.

It was cracked near the handle, like the one that used to sit on her mother's kitchen table. The same uneven paint, the same little chip at the rim. She had broken it once, years ago, trying to help with dinner. Her mother had glued it back together and told her, "Now it's ours."

She hadn't seen the pitcher in decades. And yet... There it was.

Elizabeth stepped closer, heart pounding.

The door to the shop creaked open before she touched it. A little bell chimed overhead, a soft, single note.

Inside, the shop was dim and smelled of dust and lavender. Shelves lined the walls, filled with mismatched objects: a child's shoe, a broken typewriter, a wedding veil, a melted candle shaped like a horse.

At the counter stood what appeared to be a man.

He wore a waistcoat far too neat for this place, his hair slicked back with precision. His eyes were pale, almost colorless. He didn't speak, but nodded once, as if she were expected.

"I..." she started. Her voice came out wrong. "Do you sell things here?"

The man gestured to the shelves without a word.

Elizabeth wandered deeper, drawn toward the pitcher. But when she looked for it again, it was gone, and in its place sat a book bound in soft green leather, with no title.

Curious, she opened it.

Inside were sketches. *Her* sketches.

The ones she used to draw on scraps of paper while Daniel napped. Little moments captured in pencil, his tiny hand curled around her finger, the way his hair stood up after sleep, his first wobbly steps across their kitchen floor. She flipped pages faster. There was the little cartoon of a rabbit in a top hat she had drawn to make him laugh when he had chicken pox. There was the sketch of her grandmother's garden, the place she had told him stories about, but he had never seen.

These were more than mere sketches. They were memories. Her memories. Intimate details she alone could know.

Her hands trembled as she turned to the final page.

There she found a drawing she didn't remember making.

It was Daniel, her child, but older. Gaunt. Hollow-eyed. Wearing a coat she had never seen and standing in a forest of twisted trees. His face was thinner. Marked by hardship. But his eyes were the same. They held the same defiant spark, even in the midst of whatever darkness surrounded him.

He was here, somewhere in this place. And he was alive.

She slammed the book shut, a sob catching in her throat.

When she looked up, the man was gone.

The shop was darker now. Colder. The dust motes floated where there had been none moments before, as if years passed in the seconds she had spent looking at the book.

Elizabeth clutched the book to her chest, unwilling to let go of this one tangible connection to her son.

"Where is he?" she called out, her voice a dull echo in the empty shop. "Please, I just want to find my son!"

A voice whispered, quiet, right beside her ear.

"You're closer than you realize."

She turned, heart pounding. No one was there.

The bell above the door chimed again as she bolted outside, back into the strange street.

Only now… it wasn't a street.

It was forest again. The shop behind her vanished.

Elizabeth stood alone in the trees, clutching the book. No, wait. The book was gone. Her hands were empty, fingers gripping nothing but air.

Yet the drawing of Daniel still haunted her. Older, changed, but alive. The image burned in her mind like an afterimage from staring at the sun.

You're closer than you realize.

The words repeated in her head, becoming clearer and more insistent. She circled, scanning the shadows between trees.

"Where? Where is he?" she called out, her voice breaking—the sound absorbed by the trees.

She turned in place, confusion giving way to frustration. The shadows looked familiar, like a photograph out of focus. The Hollow had brought her back, but to where? The camp should be visible, people should be within earshot, yet all she could see were trees stretching in all directions.

She sank to her knees on the damp earth in defeat. Tears of rage and helplessness spilled down her cheeks. So close. She had been so close to proving Daniel was here. And now it was gone, slipped through her fingers like everything else in this cursed place.

Elizabeth pressed her palms against her eyes, trying to hold onto the image from the book. Daniel's face. The coat he wore. The trees behind him. Anything might help her find him.

When she looked up again, a sliver of light appeared between the trees. The scent of smoke. Voices.

The camp.

She stumbled toward it, exhaustion settling into her bones. As she emerged from the tree line, faces turned toward her. Surprised. Relieved. They told her she had been gone for three days. They told her they searched but found no trace of her.

Three days? It seemed like only hours.

Huddled by her evening fire, Elizabeth took out a scrap of paper and her pencil stub. She drew what she had seen in the book. Daniel's older face, the strange coat, the gnarled trees. She folded it with care and tucked it into her pocket.

Next time the Hollow called, she would be ready.

Three days passed before Elizabeth trusted herself near the camp's borders again. Awake, at least. She wasn't entirely sure what the Hollow might try when she slept.

She was not looking for the path toward town this time. She wasn't ready to go back yet. She went with the other women to the small creek where they did laundry, grateful for something ordinary that didn't slip and warp beneath her feet.

The creek bubbled over smooth stones, the water icy but clear. Elizabeth knelt on the bank, using a flat rock to scrub at her threadbare dress. The rhythmic motion soothed her frayed nerves. For a few precious moments, she could almost pretend Daniel was nearby, and she was doing regular, everyday chores.

"You went to town."

Elizabeth jumped at the sound of the voice, dropping the small cake of lye soap in the water. She looked up to see an older woman she hadn't noticed before, sitting on a fallen log a few feet away. Her hair was silver, pulled back in a severe bun, and her eyes were intense despite the lines framing them.

"I…" Elizabeth hesitated, unsure how to respond. She hadn't told anyone about her journey. Wasn't sure herself what had been real and what had been a dream.

"No need to deny it. I can see the mark on you." The older woman gestured toward Elizabeth's face. "Town leaves a trace. Like dust you can't wash off."

Elizabeth abandoned her washing and stood, water dripping from her hands.

"What do you know about the town? About what's there?"

The older woman studied her for a long moment.

"Sit." She patted the log beside her. "You're looking for someone."

It wasn't a question. Elizabeth sat, keeping a cautious distance. "My son. Daniel."

"Ah." The woman nodded. "And you believe he's in town."

"I saw him. Or a drawing of him. In a shop behind the clock tower."

The older woman's expression didn't change, but her eyes told a different story. Recognition, perhaps. Or concern.

"The Hollow shows us what we want most. Doesn't mean it's real."

"It felt real."

"Of course it did." The woman sighed, her breath visible in the cool air. "That's how it works. The Hollow… it feeds on hope. On desire. On the things we can't let go."

A shiver, having nothing to do with the creek's icy water, ran through Elizabeth. "Then tell me the truth. What is the Hollow?"

The older woman looked away, her gaze fixed on the far tree line. "There are those who call it purgatory. Others think of it as a test. I've heard it called the in-between, the waiting place, the land of almost." She shrugged. "Names don't matter much here."

"But my son…"

"Names matter to the living," the woman continued as if Elizabeth hadn't spoken, "to those still trying to hold onto who they were. The longer you stay, the less important they become."

"I'm not staying." Elizabeth tightened her grip on the locket. "I'm finding my son and going home."

The older woman turned back to her, pity clear in her weathered face.

"Child, don't you understand? The Hollow doesn't let most people go. Not once it claims them. It keeps what it wants."

"Then why am I here? Why is Daniel here?"

"That," said the woman, as she struggled to stand, "is the question, isn't it? Why are any of us here? What unfinished business holds us?"

She shuffled away, undeterred by the uneven ground.

"Wait!" Elizabeth called after her. "You didn't tell me how to find him!"

The older woman paused but didn't turn around.

"The town is a mirror, child. It shows you what you bring to it. If you want to find your son, you need to understand what brought him here in the first place. What tethers him."

With that, she disappeared into the trees, leaving Elizabeth alone with her half-washed clothes and a growing sense that the Hollow knew far more about all of them than she could have imagined.

As she gathered her things to return to camp, Elizabeth noticed something gleaming in the shallow water. A small silver key, bright against the dark stones of the creek bed. She reached for it, fingers closing around cold metal. It hummed with hidden energy.

She slipped it into her pocket, unsure why the urge to keep it was so strong, but knew leaving it behind would have been a mistake.

9

I Know Who You Are

Elizabeth woke with ash in her hair and a coppery taste on her tongue. Her body felt hollow, scraped out from the inside, as though she had lost something of herself during the night, losing more than just sleep.

The fire beside her was cold, gray coals dusted with frost despite the season. Her blanket lay half-kicked off, twisted around her ankles like she had been fighting it. Her satchel was still tucked under her arm, clutched even in unconsciousness.

She blinked at the dusky sky, uncertain how long she had been out. Hours? Days? It was impossible to tell in the Hollow-light— unfixed, hovering between dusk and dawn. Time here felt elastic, stretching and contracting. Not bound by the rules of an every-day world.

Her fingers shook as she touched her face, finding dried tracks of tears she hadn't remembered crying. Her throat felt raw, as if she had been screaming in her sleep. The other campers kept their distance, casting wary glances her way. They had learned that newcomers who talked to the Hollow in their dreams were rarely around for long.

She sat up slowly, joints stiff as ancient hinges, muscles protesting each movement. Had she dreamt it all? The pitcher. The house. The shadowed man. The book with the sketch she had never made. It all felt so vivid, so real... but now it was smoke. Wisps of memory slipping away.

Did the Hollow bring me back? Or did I run?

No one around her seemed to notice her confusion. Campfires crackled. People murmured and moved about their routines as usual, as if she had always been there, just another lost soul waiting for an exit that might never appear.

She stood, brushed herself off, and scanned the edge of the woods, searching for any sign of the path that had led her to that strange street. To that shop. To that book.

Nothing. Just trees and shadows, still and silent.

But the pull remained. Stronger now, insistent. Not from the trees this time, but from the town. A memory. A face.

Daniel. She whispered into the breeze.

And a path appeared.

She didn't hesitate. She turned toward the trail that led back into town, her heart suddenly beating with renewed purpose. The woods didn't resist this time, either. They simply opened, like a door swinging wide for an expected guest.

Or a trap waiting to spring.

The dim morning light filtered through the mist that clung to the Hollow like a shroud, diffusing into a sickly gray that made shadows seem deeper, more alive. Gobbler adjusted the fraying scarf around his neck. The gesture itself felt like an echo, a muscle memory that belonged to someone else. The cold didn't bother him anymore. But he clung to the ritual, to the small humanity in it.

Frost crunched beneath his boots as he walked, the sound too loud in the unnatural quiet of dawn. The other Misfits were already moving about their tasks. Heads down, voices low, eyes darting— another day of survival in Grim's world.

Digger's voice cut through the silence, startling a crow from a nearby branch.

"This one's ready to snap," he muttered, gesturing toward a traveler slumped near a dying fire. The man's face was gaunt, cheeks hollow, eyes jittery like those of a trapped animal. His fingers constantly working the frayed edges of his coat.

"He's been here too long. Either he cracks or he starves. Grim wins either way."

Gobbler gave a slight nod, though a familiar nausea curled in his stomach, acid rising in his throat. This was the job. Identify the cracks. Nudge them wider. Plant the seeds of desperation and watch them bloom into actions that severed souls from their last shreds of decency. Soften the soul until Grim could harvest what was left.

He hated this part. The taste of it was bitter, metallic, like blood on his tongue. But hesitation was dangerous. He had learned that early, had seen the consequences. Misfits were punished for their failures, beaten by Grim's minions. But never by Grim himself. The act of corporal punishment was beneath him.

Gobbler approached the man slowly, boots crunching over frostbitten ground. The traveler's breath formed small clouds that dissipated too quickly, the Hollow drinking them in.

"Rough night?" he asked, his tone casual, almost kind. The words tasted like stones in his mouth.

The man startled, blinking up at him with bloodshot eyes. His lips were chapped, cracking at the corners. "Huh... who are you?"

"Friend," Gobbler lied, the word leaving an oily residue. "Looks like you could use one."

He crouched by the fire, letting the dying heat lick at his gloves. The flames were too low to offer genuine warmth, just enough to remind you of what you were missing. The man tensed but didn't pull away. His shoulders hunched, his body coiled like a spring.

"This place doesn't play fair," Gobbler said softly, each syllable carefully measured. "You either learn the rules or... someone else makes the rules for you."

The man's eyes flicked toward a nearby pack—unguarded, half-open. A loaf of bread peeked out, wrapped in faded cloth. Hunger made his lips tremble, his gaze lingering a heartbeat too long.

"Sometimes surviving means taking what you need," Gobbler continued, each word burning his throat like acid. "It doesn't make you a bad man. It just means you're still alive."

The man hesitated, torn. His fingers twitched against his knee—reaching, then pulling back, and then reaching again.

Gobbler stood. He didn't stop him. He didn't look back.

Behind him, he heard the rustle. A theft. A cry of outrage. The spark of conflict Grim needed. Souls fracturing against each other, creating the hairline cracks through which doubt and despair could seep.

Gobbler walked away, fists clenched so tight his nails bit into his palms. In his pocket, he turned over a small button—brass, worn smooth, unremarkable. He had taken it from the traveler's coat while they spoke, a minor theft of his own.

A reminder of the cost. Of what this place was turning him into. Of whom he might have been before.

The square was little more than packed earth and ash, the kind of place where words disappeared into the air before they could echo. Buildings leaned inward around the edges, their windows like watchful eyes, their doorways dark mouths. Elizabeth stood at the edge of it, her hands trembling inside her threadbare sleeves. The cold bit through her clothing, but she barely noticed it. Her heart hammered against her ribs with such force she thought it might crack bone.

The town was different this time. More real. The people were more present. The buildings were more solid.

She hadn't come here to find him—not today. She had only meant to look around, to listen for his name, to hope. To gather her courage for when the moment finally came.

But there he was.

Across the open space, loading a wagon with hollow-eyed efficiency, was her son.

Her knees buckled and she sucked in a sharp breath. The world narrowed to a single point, everything else blurring at the edges.

Daniel.

He was taller. Older. His hair was longer, darker, and falling across his forehead in a way that made her fingers itch to brush it back, as she had done a thousand times before. His jaw was more defined, his shoulders broader, but it was him. It was him. She knew it like she knew her own name. Even with the weight he carried, the exhaustion in his stance, the hollowness in his face. He was hers. The curve of his cheek. The set of his shoulders. The way his fingers gripped the edge of the wagon, so deliberate and careful.

Her body moved before her mind could catch up. One step, then another.

"Daniel?" Her voice barely made it past her lips.

But he heard it.

His hand stilled mid-motion, a burlap sack half-hoisted. Something in his posture changed—a sudden stillness, like a deer scenting danger. He turned slowly, his eyes sweeping the square, landing on her. For a moment, he just stared without recognition.

He tensed, drawing his shoulders up slightly and clenching his jaw.

He took a small step back. His face shuttered, closing like a door.

"Do I know you?" His voice was lower than she remembered. Rougher. The voice of a man, not the boy she had last held.

Elizabeth's chest tightened, a pain so acute it stole her breath. "It's me." Her voice cracked. Her fingers pressed against her breastbone as if she could physically hold herself together. "Daniel. It's Mom."

There was something. A muscle in his jaw jumped. His brows twitched. His eyes searched hers, and for just a heartbeat, something like confusion passed over his features. A shadow of recognition, there and gone too quickly to grasp.

He looked away before anyone noticed. Shaking his head, his expression hardened into something practiced: a mask he was forced to wear.

"You've got the wrong person," he said flatly. "I'm not Daniel."

"Yes, you are," she whispered, stepping closer, hand outstretched as if she could bridge the distance with touch alone. "You are. I know you might not remember, but you're my son. I've been looking for you, Daniel. Please."

Around them, those in the square stopped what they were doing and stared. Watching the boy's response. Listening to their words. Gathering anything they could use for currency. The air itself seemed to stop moving.

"I don't know who you think I am." He took another step back. His eyes darted around. People were beginning to notice. A few figures gathered along the edges of the square. A door creaked open somewhere. A crowd was gathering, their stares prickling his skin.

He kept his voice low, urgent now. "You shouldn't be here. It's not safe."

Elizabeth's voice broke, splintering on the jagged edges of her hope. "I don't care. You don't understand. I've come so far. I've... I've nearly died trying to find you. I thought I had lost you forever."

His face flickered again. A shadow of something—pain? Fear?— washed over his features. But he forced it still, muscle by muscle, until it was a mask again. "I can't help you," he said. "You need to leave. Now."

She reached out for him, desperate. Her fingers almost grazed his sleeve. "Daniel, please. Just listen. Just let me explain."

He stepped out of reach with practiced precision. "I'm sorry, ma'am," he said, with a formality that crushed her confidence. "You're mistaken."

And then he turned his back on her.

He picked up the sack he had dropped. His hands shook slightly, but he didn't look back. He continued loading the wagon as if she weren't there, as if she hadn't just shattered into a thousand pieces onto the ground behind him.

Elizabeth was stunned. Her body shivered, a sudden chill burrowing deep into her core. Words and breath abandoned her. Something inside her shattered.

She didn't move. Couldn't.

Someone passed behind her, muttering something about "visitors who don't know the rules." She didn't hear it. Her entire world had narrowed to the space where her son had stood. Where he had looked at her and seen a stranger.

Her knees gave. She sank slowly to the ground, her hands buried in her skirts, her breath ragged and shallow. A burning sensation spread behind her eyes, but no tears came. She was too empty for tears.

"I found you." She lowered her eyes and her voice. "But I lost you anyway."

The square went on without her. Misfits passed by, indifferent to her collapse. The Hollow swallowed her heartbreak like it did everything else. Another meal, another soul cracking open.

And from a nearby alley, a man watched with quiet satisfaction, his lips curved in what might have been a smile.

Alice had seen a lot of desperation in the Hollow. It clung to people like fog, muffling their senses, blurring their judgment. It was the currency Grim traded in, the fuel that kept his machine running. But this was different.

She had been halfway through earning her rations, the kind of favor that didn't come without gritted teeth and a bitten tongue, when she noticed the commotion in the square. Her client, a merchant with sausage fingers and too many rings that caught the light as he gestured, had been mid-complaint about her services when she turned on her heel and walked away. She knew she would pay for it later.

"You've got terrible timing, sweetheart," Alice muttered to herself, adjusting the collar of her worn coat as she strode toward the square. The leather was cracked at the edges, but it was still the warmest thing she owned.

The woman—Elizabeth—stood frozen, her arms limp at her sides, eyes glued to Gobbler's retreating form. She looked gutted, like someone had reached in and crushed everything that had been holding her together. Her face had gone pale beneath the dirt and wear, her lips bloodless, her hands trembling visibly even from several paces away.

Alice scanned the square, noting the too-casual postures of Grim's watchers. They were always there, in the shadows, at the edges, in plain sight but easy to miss if you didn't know what to look for. They would be reporting this. All of it. The name. The recognition. The rejection.

Alice didn't speak at first. She just stood beside Elizabeth, silent as the void between them. The woman smelled of smoke and pine, of earth and too many nights sleeping rough. Her breathing was shallow and quick, like she might collapse at any moment.

Then, quieter than her usual swagger, Alice said, "You shouldn't have done that."

Elizabeth blinked, startled out of her daze. She turned to Alice, eyes bright with desperation. "What do you mean? He's my son. I had to try."

"Your what?" Alice's eyebrows lifted, then lowered just as quickly. She dragged a hand through her tangled hair, dark strands catching on her chipped nails. Across the square, one of Grim's watchers leaned forward slightly. Listening. "Lady, I don't know what your deal is, but that?" She gestured toward where Gobbler had been. "That was reckless."

Elizabeth turned on her. Her spine straightened, some of the muted distress in her eyes hardening into determination. "He's Daniel. My Daniel. I know it's him."

Alice opened her mouth, nearly laughing out loud, but clamped it shut again. The insanity of this woman standing here, speaking a name like that out loud, as if she had a right. As if the words themselves weren't dangerous. She looked around instead, scanning for ears in the shadows, for the telltale stillness of those who served Grim.

"You say that name around here, you're going to get someone killed. Probably you. Maybe him."

"Who's going to kill me?" Elizabeth snapped, her voice cracking. A spark of anger flared in her eyes, burning through the fog of grief. "Grim?" She didn't know who Grim was, but she had heard the rumors.

Alice flinched at the mention of his name. Just saying it carried power here, like he might appear when called.

"You don't get it," she hissed, grabbing Elizabeth's arm and pulling her toward the edge of the square, away from the most obvious observers. "You think this place is just cruel? It's worse than that. It listens. It watches. And Grim? He doesn't like people poking at what he's already claimed."

Elizabeth's lip trembled, but her spine straightened further, something stubborn and fierce replacing the brokenness from moments before. "I'm not afraid of him."

"You should be." Alice leaned in closer, her voice dropping to a murmur. The scent of something bitter and herbal clung to her— remedies for pains she never spoke about. "He sees everything. Especially weakness and most especially desperation."

Elizabeth shook her head, a strand of gray-streaked hair falling across her face. "I don't care. He's my son. I'll remind him if I have to. And love isn't weakness. It's strength!"

Alice's expression changed ever so slightly. A flicker of something almost tender beneath the hard-edged survival she wore like armor. Pain, maybe. Memory. Her eyes softened, just for a heartbeat.

"That boy you remember?" she said, voice rough now. "He's not here. What's left... It's someone else. Grim's got his claws in him deep."

"But he hesitated," Elizabeth held the locket around her neck without thinking. "When I said his name. He felt it. I saw it in his face."

Alice didn't deny it. Couldn't. She had known Gobbler longer than most here and had watched the careful way he held himself apart. She had noticed the times when he had made a gesture, used a phrase, shown a moment of kindness that should have been beaten out of him by now.

"Then you've got a harder fight ahead than you can imagine. Just don't be stupid about it."

Elizabeth exhaled, her shoulders sagging. The brief fire dimmed but didn't go out. "I'm not giving up on him."

Alice looked away, her jaw tense. There was danger in hope here. Danger in attachment. She had seen what happened to those who clung too tightly to the past.

"You better not. But if you want to have a shot, you keep your mouth shut for now. Stay invisible. Because if Grim catches wind of what you're doing—"

She didn't finish the sentence. Didn't need to. The threat hung between them like a storm cloud.

Instead, Alice gave a faint nod toward the alley where the greasy merchant was probably fuming. There would be consequences later. There always were.

"I gotta go before my lack of professionalism gets me whipped."

Elizabeth looked like she wanted to say more, to beg for answers, for help, for anything that might lead her back to her son. But Alice had already turned, slipping back into the smoke and whispers of the Hollow, her steps quick and light, leaving no trace.

And just before she vanished into the crowd, Alice tossed over her shoulder, "Don't say the name again. Not unless you're ready to lose what little of him is left."

The man's boots struck the dusty path with more force than necessary, each step fueled by wounded pride and the hot burn of rejection. Alice had humiliated him. Walked out mid-service like he was beneath her notice, like his coin wasn't good enough. He would have her punished. Ruined, if he could.

His face still felt hot, his expensive coat too tight across his shoulders. The other patrons had witnessed his humiliation. Had smirked behind their hands and whispered behind his back. It was intolerable.

But fate, in its cruel kindness, handed him something better.

He spotted her not far from the square, slipping away from a scene that had caught his eye: a pale woman who had been clinging to the arm of one of Grim's favored Misfits. Gobbler, they called him. A strange name for a strange man. The name meant nothing to the merchant. What mattered was the name the woman had used. The one that rippled through the square like a stone dropped in still water.

"Daniel," she had said, soft and raw like she believed it.

The Misfit froze. For one beat, maybe two, something cracked in his expression. Recognition? Fear? The moment passed, but not before the merchant saw it.

Interesting.

He turned on his heel and made for Grim's fortress, the hunger for vengeance momentarily overridden by a different appetite. Information was currency here. And this, he sensed, was valuable indeed.

The path to the Keep narrowed as he approached, the buildings leaning closer together, blocking out the meager sunlight. The air grew colder with each step, the sounds of the town fading into an unnatural silence. The hair on the back of his neck stood up, but he pushed forward.

Grim's fortress sat at the edge of town, its shape warping the moment one tried to pin it down. Sometimes a grand building with columns, sometimes a humble shack, sometimes something that defied description altogether. Today it appeared as a modest stone building, unadorned except for a single lantern burning beside the door, its flame steady and blue.

The merchant hesitated at the threshold, suddenly aware of the significance of what he was about to expose. But it was too late to turn back.

Grim sat behind a desk that looked carved from shadow itself, his fingers idly turning the pages of a ledger. He didn't look up as the merchant entered, as if he had been expected. The room was cold and still, the air tasting faintly of mildew.

"She called him Daniel," the merchant blurted, the words escaping before he could frame them more carefully. "Said she was his mother."

Grim didn't blink. Didn't look surprised. His eyes, when they finally lifted from the ledger, were the color of ashes.

"And what did he say?"

"Said she had the wrong man. But..." The merchant licked his lips, which had suddenly gone dry. "He hesitated. Like he wasn't sure."

Grim steepled his fingers, his expression unreadable. The shadows in the room seemed to lean closer, listening. "And you're sure she said 'Daniel'?"

"Clear as anything, sir. Like she meant it. Like she knew him."

Silence pooled in the space between them. The merchant fought the urge to fidget under that steady gaze.

Finally, Grim nodded once. "You've done well to bring this to me." The words were simple, but they carried a weight that settled into the merchant's bones like cold satisfaction.

The man puffed his chest with pride. Perhaps his trip to the Hollow wouldn't be wasted after all. Maybe there would be compensation for his troubles.

"Leave," Grim added, already turning his attention elsewhere, voice dismissive.

The merchant blinked, momentarily thrown by the abrupt dismissal. But he knew better than to protest. He backed toward the door, offering a small bow that Grim didn't acknowledge.

Grim didn't watch the man go. Didn't need to.

He stared instead at the flickering candle on the edge of his desk, the flame dancing nervously as if sensing his attention. The shadows stretched longer, darker.

Then, ever-so-softly, almost to himself, as the door closed behind the merchant...

"A mother," Grim murmured, rolling the word on his tongue like testing an unfamiliar wine. His lips curved into a sneer. "How quaint."

Alice was late.

That, in itself, wasn't unusual. She had a way of slipping between spaces, letting time bend around her like a cat weaving through obstacles. But this time... she wasn't just late. She was summoned.

The message had come with the dawn. A raven feather on her pillow, its edge crusted with something that might have been rust or dried blood. She knew what it meant.

Gobbler stood just outside the Hall's courtyard, flanked by Digger with his perpetually filthy nails, and Tate with his rheumy eyes that missed nothing. The stone beneath Gobbler's boots felt colder than it should have.

The air tasted of frost and anticipation. The gathering wasn't announced, but word traveled fast in the Hollow. By the time Grim appeared, stepping from the shadows of the Convocation Hall, a small crowd had already formed in the courtyard. Curious. Cautious. Hungry for someone else's misfortune.

And then Alice arrived—escorted.

She didn't walk so much as she was herded forward, two of Grim's more human-looking minions flanking her, their hands not touching her arms but close enough that she couldn't break away. Her steps were steady, her back straight, but Gobbler saw the effort it cost her. Saw the calculation in her eyes as she scanned the crowd, the positions, the mood.

Her lip was split, a thin line of blood tracing the curve of her mouth. Her cheek was turning red, the edges of the bruise already purple. She held her back straight and her head high as she walked, tight-lipped and determined not to show emotion. Gobbler knew she had learned that lesson well before today's summoning.

His chest tightened. This wasn't the first time she had been dragged before them. But it was the first time Grim made such a spectacle of her punishment. Grim was sending a special message to someone. But to whom? Gobbler suspected he knew the answer.

The merchant from before—the one with the too-many rings and nowhere near enough patience—stood beside Grim like a loyal pet, smirking behind one manicured hand. His grand attire looked out of place in the Hollow, too clean, too new. His satisfaction radiated from him in waves.

"This one," Grim's voice slid like silk over gravel, carrying across the courtyard without effort, "has forgotten her place."

Gobbler felt his jaw tighten, his teeth grinding together. Around him, the other Misfits shuffled back a step, eyes down, shoulders hunched. They knew the dance. They had seen it before: keep your head down, don't draw attention, and survive another day.

The punishment was ritual more than rage: public theatrics, a performance for those who might be wavering. Alice was forced to kneel for display. The cobblestones were uneven, their edges cutting her knees. A thin stream of sunlight caught in her tangled hair, turning it briefly to ember before cloud cover returned.

Grim circled her like a wolf stalking its prey; his movements were fluid and precise. His shadow stretched long and dark behind him, as if trying to crawl away from the firelight.

"She thinks herself clever." He smiled faintly, addressing the crowd more than Alice herself. "She thinks kindness is a shield. That we won't notice when her attention strays… or when her loyalties wander."

The words weren't just for Alice. They were for anyone watching. Anyone slipping. Anyone who might feel the tug of something they used to be.

Gobbler balled his hands into fists. He forced them into his pockets, out of sight. The other Misfits around him watched in silence, faces carefully blank. This was survival. Silence was survival. To speak now would only mean stepping forward and joining her on the stones.

Alice didn't baulk when Grim lifted her chin with one long finger. She met his eyes, unflinching. Her defiance wasn't loud—but it was there, humming under the bruises, a current that hadn't yet been grounded.

And then his voice dropped. Quiet. Just for her. But in the unnatural stillness of the courtyard, it carried to those closest.

"You're fond of him, aren't you?"

She didn't reply. Didn't need to. The answer was there in the way her eyes flashed, just for a heartbeat, toward Gobbler before returning to Grim's face.

Grim's smile widened, cold and predatory. "Then you'll be careful next time." The words were gentle, almost tender, like a lover's caress. All the more terrifying for their softness.

He turned away. The show was over.

But before she was dragged off, Alice's eyes found Gobbler in the crowd. Pleading.

Don't. Please.

Gobbler didn't move. Didn't blink. His face remained a mask of careful indifference, the expression he had perfected in his time here. But inside, a knot twisted tighter with each passing moment.

She had bled for his mistake.

For the woman who had called him Daniel. For the name that had stirred something deep inside him. For the moment, he hesitated instead of immediately rejecting the claim.

And now Grim knew exactly what buttons to push.

Elizabeth stood just beyond the square, half-shadowed by a sagging porch beam, her heart pounding so hard it muffled the voices around her. The world had narrowed to a single point of focus, then exploded outward again, leaving her dizzy and unmoored.

She had seen him. The boy she raised. The boy who once cried when he scraped his knees, who had clung to her shirt hem during thunderstorms, who had fallen asleep against her shoulder during long car rides. Only now, he was older. Harder. A stranger in his own skin.

"Daniel," she had called—barely a whisper, but it had cracked something in her chest when he turned. When his eyes met hers, she knew something had flickered there, like dying embers.

And then he turned away.

She wrapped her arms around her ribs, as if to hold herself together. Her legs trembled beneath her, muscles weak from the sustained tension of hope and despair warring inside her.

He hadn't known her.

Or worse, he had and chose not to acknowledge her.

That thought undid her. She stepped backward until her spine met a wall, fingers curling against the cracked wood. She could feel splinters catching on her skin, tiny points of pain that anchored her to the moment when she might otherwise have floated away entirely.

Around her, the town pulsed with strange energy. Cold wind snaked through the square, stirring ash from the fire pits. Grim's voice echoed from behind the old Town Hall, a distant, controlled reprimand that made her skin crawl. A crowd had gathered there. In the center, a woman knelt. Alice, the one who had warned her. Her defiance was visible even from this distance.

Elizabeth couldn't look. Not yet. Not when the reality of what she had caused made her stomach clench with shame.

The name had done it. The moment she spoke it, she realized the crowd had gone still. Heads had turned. She caught the hint of recognition in the boy's face. A flicker. Like a match almost catching, then dying in the wind.

It had been enough to draw the wrong kind of attention. Enough to put others in danger.

She should have stayed quiet, should have heeded the warnings. Should have been more careful with the one thing she had left. The truth of who her son was.

But how could she?

She closed her eyes, her senses overloaded. The Hollow was too loud or too quiet. Too focused and then too fluid. Every whisper behind her back sounded like an accusation. Every footstep was like a countdown. Her body still ached from the walk. Her stomach churned with hunger. But nothing hurt as much as the look on her son's face. That blank, practiced emptiness. Like she was nothing. Like she had never existed.

She had come here for him. Had endured for him. She hadn't even told anyone what the doctor had said back home. There hadn't been time. The headaches, the bloodwork, the way she had stared at her phone screen in the sterile clinic waiting for her name to be called…

All of it felt so far away now. Another life. Another time.

But the ticking inside her hadn't stopped. The disease still crawled through her, cell by cell. The clock was still running down.

And now? She was running out of time.

Elizabeth turned away from the square, forcing her feet to move, though her body protested every step. Her eyes burned with tears she refused to shed. Her body screamed for rest. But her heart had clenched around one stubborn truth: he's here, and he's real.

She reached her camp after dusk, bones aching from the grueling walk back. The fire was low, the tea she managed to brew weak and bitter, but the ritual helped. She cradled the tin cup in trembling hands and stared into the embers like they held answers.

Tomorrow, she would try again.

To remind him of who he had been. Who he still was, beneath Grim's influence and the Hollow's memory-stealing fog.

Even if he didn't remember her, she would remember enough for the both of them.

Because this place? This Hollow? It would not keep him.

She would find the cracks. And she would find the way through.

And if Grim thought a mother's love was a weakness, then he had clearly never met a woman who had lost everything and still refused to give up. A woman with nothing left to lose and a terminal diagnosis that made fear irrelevant.

Elizabeth wrapped the threadbare blanket tighter around her shoulders. The wind whistled low through the trees, carrying the scent of smoke. Somewhere in the dark, a raven called—shrill and solitary.

"I'll find you," she spoke into the night. "I'll bring you back."

The locket around her neck suddenly seemed heavier, warmer against her skin. Inside, the tiny photograph was more faded than the day before. Daniel, his smile crooked, his eyes bright with a future that still seemed endless.

She didn't need to open it to see his face. She carried it in her heart, etched there through years of love. Through life and death and whatever strange existence this was between.

And now, she had seen him again. Different, yes. Changed, yes. But alive.

It was enough to keep her going. It had to be.

10

The Price of Defiance

ong before the Hollow and the throne, Elias Blackthorne
had lived by candlelight and plague smoke in a world
where whispered prayers collided with the stench
of death.

*The dim flicker of candlelight illuminated the crude operating room, a
sanctuary of desperation where whispered prayers collided with the stench
of death. Shadows danced across blood-slicked walls as Elias Blackthorne,
gaunt and driven, leaned over a plague-stricken patient. The room reeked
of copper and rot, of burning herbs meant to ward off miasma, of sweat
and fear no incense could mask. Around him, assistants moved with
muted urgency, their breath rasping behind damp cloth masks, more
talismans than true protection.*

*The patient's chest rose and fell in erratic patterns, black buboes vis-
ible at his neck and armpits, skin mottled and feverish. His eyes were
yellowed and unfocused, and his gaze darted around the room as if tracking invisible terrors.*

*"Hold him still," Elias ordered, his voice cutting through the heavy air.
A young assistant hesitated, hands trembling, slipping off the patient's
fever-slick skin. Elias's eyes snapped to him, dark and unforgiving. "Do
you want him to die? Hold. Him."*

Outside, church bells tolled the hour, each strike a reminder of how many souls had already been lost. Elias had stopped counting days ago. Had stopped praying weeks before.

The assistant obeyed, bearing down, his face turning away from the stench of imminent death. The man on the table gasped, his lips pale and cracked, eyes rolling wild. Elias didn't flinch. His hands, once gentle with healing, now moved with mechanical precision, devoid of his former compassion. He injected a murky liquid into the patient's arm, a viscous, iridescent substance shimmering under the flickering light. A creation of alchemy. Of desperation. Of something not quite medicine but akin to sorcery.

For a moment, the room was still.

The patient arched, a hoarse scream erupting from his throat as foam bubbled from his mouth. Limbs thrashed against the restraints, the leather straps cut into wasted flesh. The wooden table groaned beneath him, the legs scraping against stone floors worn smooth by too many similar sessions. Gasps and murmurs rippled through the crowd gathered at the doorway, their faces pale with a blend of horror and morbid fascination. A woman crossed herself, lips moving in silent prayer. A man turned away, unable to watch.

Elias's jaw clenched, but he did not move. Where once he might have rushed to ease suffering, now he stepped back, clasping his hands behind his back, watching with a pretense of calculated detachment that disturbed even his most loyal assistants. His eyes gleamed with a passion beyond scientific interest. Hunger fed by each failure, each corpse, each step closer to his impossible goal.

"You see?" Elias announced, voice calm, almost triumphant, as though addressing students rather than witnesses to horror. "The body resists, but it will heal. This is progress."

The convulsions ceased.

The room fell silent save for the sputtering candles and the distant wails of mourners in the street below. Elias leaned forward, two fingers against the patient's neck, feeling for a pulse he already knew was gone. A pause. He drew back, expression unreadable, though his eyes flickered, calculating. He reached for his leather-bound journal *and began writing, the quill scratching across the page with relentless precision.*

"He was already dead," he muttered. "We'll adjust the dosage."

An older assistant stepped forward, eyes wide beneath his soot-streaked mask. This man had been with Elias from the beginning, had witnessed his transformation from healer to something else entirely. "Dr. Blackthorne... this isn't medicine," he whispered, voice tight with barely contained horror. "It's desecration! The devil's craft!"

Elias didn't look up. "Medicine is what we make it," he said, each word precise as a scalpel. "God has abandoned these people. Someone must take His place." The blasphemy rolled off his tongue without hesitation, as if daring divine retribution.

The assistant flinched, stepping back into silence, but his hands shook as he returned to his place. Around him, the others stared at the floor, afraid to meet each other's gaze, afraid to acknowledge what they had become part of.

The plague bell tolled faintly through the streets beyond the cracked window. A low, hollow sound resonated deep within the bones. It was both warning and lament, a rhythmic countdown to despair. But Elias had come to hear it differently. To him, it was the sound of a challenge.

Elias set down the quill and turned to the body. For a moment, regret darkened his features. Or maybe a memory. A flash of the man he had once been, the healer who had sworn to do no harm. But it vanished, devoured by resolve hardened through months of watching death win again and again.

"Take him to the lower chamber," he said. "Record his progression. There may still be answers to glean from his final moments."

As they moved to comply, wrapping the corpse in stained linen, Elias crossed to the window. Fires flickered in the distance, consuming homes abandoned to grief. The wind carried the cries of the dying like ash. In the glass, he could see his own reflection: gaunt, hollow-eyed, and barely recognizable as the respected physician he had once been.

In the glass, his reflection stretched long and crooked across the wall, as if an invisible thing had stepped in behind him. Watching. Waiting.

Elias stared into the darkened city. His smile was faint, but certain. In his eyes burned the light of a terrible purpose. He had become a man who had stopped seeing patients and started seeing vessels for his ambition.

Death was not a master to fear. It was an adversary to defeat.

And he was so very close to winning.

The memory faded, leaving only the echo of bells tolling in the dark, and the faint scent of smoke that never seemed to leave him.

Centuries later, the same hunger lingered behind another pair of eyes. Grim surveyed the Misfits gathered before him, no longer a healer who defied death, but its emissary, its keeper of souls. The obsession remained, transformed but undiminished.

Grim's voice sliced through the hall, every word deliberate, smooth, and soaked in venom. He didn't shout. He didn't need to. The authority of his presence and his control settled over the Misfits gathered before him.

"You think you're clever?" Grim asked, his voice coiling around the room like smoke, wrapping tight around their necks. "You think you can outwit me?" He took a step forward, his boots echoing ominously against the stone floor. "Every breath you take here belongs to me. Every act of rebellion is an invitation to a personal... consultation with me." He drew out the word "consultation," his lips curling into a cold smile.

The great hall itself bent toward him. Shadows elongated, light dimming wherever he stepped. The stone walls, ancient and pitted, had been witness to countless similar gatherings. How many had stood where they stood now, only to disappear days later?

Gobbler hung near the back, trying to make himself as inconspicuous as possible, leaning against the rough stone wall. His heart pounded in his chest, the sound of it almost deafening in his ears. Sweat traced his spine despite the cold sting in the Hall. Grim's essence filled the room, taking up more space than his physical presence, making the large Hall feel close.

Something peculiar about Grim's voice tugged at Gobbler's mind. A half-remembered nightmare. An echo beyond memory's grasp. Each word scraped against his consciousness like nails on a chalkboard.

Grim scanned the room like a spotlight, finally settling on Alice. Her defiance held in check, replaced with a stiff, rigid stance hinting at the punishment she had endured. The bruises on her face had faded to a sickly purple-green, but the cut on her lip remained. Gobbler's stomach churned at the sight of her pale face, her clenched fists. His own hands itched with the desire to step forward, to place himself between her and Grim's penetrating stare.

Gobbler maintained his practiced neutral expression, self-preservation battling with the unfamiliar urge to protect. The struggle made his chest ache with shame.

"You," Grim said, his voice soft but no less deadly as he addressed Alice. "Do not mistake my mercy for weakness."

He took another step toward Alice, his fiery eyes narrowing to fiery red slits. "You will find my patience is not infinite."

Alice didn't flinch, but Gobbler saw the strain behind her stillness. There was an almost imperceptible tremor in her jaw. The way her throat worked as she swallowed. After yesterday's punishment, she knew better than to show weakness. She glanced at Gobbler for the briefest moment, a silent warning. *Stay quiet. Don't interfere. This isn't the time.*

Grim turned away, his dark cloak swirling around him like a living thing, the edges dissolving into the shadows. "Get out," he commanded, his hand slicing the air in a dismissive gesture.

The Misfits moved as one, shuffling toward the door with bowed heads and hushed whispers. No one dared meet another's eyes. No one dared speak above a murmur. Gobbler felt the collective relief as bodies crowded toward the exit, eager to escape Grim's attention.

Alice passed him, her face unreadable, but her eyes lingered on him for a fraction of a second longer than the others'. A message passed between them. Concern, warning, and something else. His heart skipped a beat. He knew he was falling hopelessly in love with

Alice, against his better judgment. In this purgatory, there was no room for such indulgent emotions as love.

As the last of the Misfits filed out, Gobbler turned to follow, his muscles tense with the instinct to flee. He had almost made it to the threshold when Grim's voice rang out behind him.

"Not you, lad."

Gobbler's blood ran cold, a surge of dread washing through him so powerful he staggered. He knew instinctively which "lad" Grim meant. All at once, the door appeared far away. He turned back, finding Grim standing in the center of the hall, his fiery gaze locked onto him. The doors creaked shut behind the last departing Misfit, sealing them in. The sound was final, like a coffin lid closing.

For a moment, neither of them spoke. Grim's presence grew larger, if that were possible. The air grew thick, difficult to breathe, carrying the acrid bite of sulfur and caustic heat.

"Still so quiet," Grim said, his tone almost conversational, though the underlying menace was unmistakable. "I had hoped our last discussion taught you something."

He stepped closer, his movements slow, deliberate, a predator who knows its prey has nowhere to run. "I've been watching you, Gobbler. You've proven yourself unexpectedly valuable. Too valuable to waste on something as trivial as looming death."

His mouth went dry. Gobbler's mind raced through options, finding no exit, no defense. "Just trying to do my job, sir," he said, his voice steadier than he expected, though fear clawed at his insides.

Grim's unsettling chuckle sounded like bones grinding together. "Your job. Yes, of course. But tell me." He took another step closer, his towering figure casting Gobbler in his shadow. The temperature dropped around them, frost forming in Gobbler's lungs. "Are you distracted?"

The question puzzled him, fear giving way to confusion. "Distracted?"

Grim narrowed his eyes, the hint of a smile playing at his lips. "Alice." The single word hung between them like a dagger. "She's quite the distraction, isn't she?"

His tongue swept across parched lips as invisible hands tightened around his chest. The image of Alice flashed through Gobbler's mind, her quiet strength, the way her rare smiles pushed back the Hollow's gloom. He opened his mouth to respond, but Grim raised a hand, silencing him.

"Affection," Grim whispered, tasting the word like something foreign. "A curious indulgence in a place that devours such things." His gaze drifted, as though watching old memories burn in the air.

"It's almost sweet," he went on, the faintest curl of amusement set at his mouth. "A spark of warmth in all this cold." His eyes brightened, molten and merciless. But sparks become flames, and flames…"

He tapped a finger against Gobbler's chest.

"Flames need only fuel to spread."

"I don't know what you mean," Gobbler kept his voice level, though his pulse pounded in his ears, a desperate rhythm saying *run, run, run.*

Grim's smile widened, hungry with predatory anticipation.

"Oh, I think you do. Let me make myself clear." He leaned in, his voice dropping to a deadly whisper. His breath rancid. "Alice is mine. Her loyalty, her service, her very existence. All of it belongs to me. Just as yours does."

Gobbler almost spoke before the sense of danger caught up with him. He shifted his weight; muscles braced for a fight he knew he wouldn't win.

Instead, he clenched his jaw so hard his teeth ached. Anger flared without warning, hot and bright in his chest, burning through the fear. The possessiveness in Grim's voice sparked a defiance he didn't know he had—Protectiveness, both foreign and deeply familiar.

"I'm trying to follow orders."

Grim straightened, his expression cold and unreadable, though his eyes flashed with curiosity, perhaps. Or satisfaction, as if he had confirmed suspicion.

"Good. Then let me give you one." He stepped back, his cloak brushing the floor like the rustle of dead leaves. "Stay away from her. Focus on your duties. You have potential, Gobbler. Don't waste it on foolish attachments."

The threat was unmistakable, even if it was cloaked in rational words. Gobbler's hands curled into fists at his sides, fingernails biting into his palms, but he forced himself to keep his voice calm, to keep his face a mask, revealing nothing of the storm beneath.

"Understood," he said through gritted teeth.

Grim studied him for a long moment, his eyes gleaming with amusement. With a wave of his hand, he turned and strode toward the far end of the hall.

"Remember," Grim called over his shoulder, his voice echoing in the cavernous space, "disobedience is death. And in your case, unbearable suffering that will leave you begging for death's release."

The room lightened again as Grim disappeared into the shadows and with him, the oppressive atmosphere of his presence. Gobbler stood frozen for a moment, his mind racing, heart still hammering against his ribs.

He turned to leave, his hand finding the wall to steady himself. Grim's warning was clear, but it wasn't merely the threat lingering in Gobbler's mind. It was the way Grim had spoken of Alice with such jealousy. And that, in Gobbler's mind, made Grim far more dangerous.

As Gobbler stormed away, heart pounding, the shadows closed in. He felt Grim's warning like a brand on his skin. Each step away from the hall felt both like escape and like he was being herded toward the inevitable.

Somewhere, a creak echoed in the darkness. It could have been the old wood settling. Or it could have been a soul gathering information for their own advantage.

A metallic glint sparked by the light, tucked into the inky blackness near the edge of the corridor. A single sigh broke the silence before fading into nothing. Gobbler froze for a moment but shook it off, too consumed by his own reflections to investigate further.

Unseen, the figure remained motionless, their eyes narrowed as they watched him go. The game had changed to their advantage, and they intended to make their next move count.

The courtyard outside the Convocation Hall was too quiet.

The Misfits gathered in a loose circle, their eyes locked on the trembling man forced onto the raised platform. He was no one important. A new soul. Nervous. Chatty. Always asking questions. Maybe too many questions. A few days ago, he had been someone with a name, with habits and quirks recognized by others. Now he stood swaying under the Hollow's stagnant sky, his name already dissolving from memory, as if the Hollow had begun erasing him before the sentence was even passed.

Some in the crowd looked away, unable to watch. Others stared with morbid fascination, and relief hidden behind their eyes. Relieved it wasn't them on the platform. A few were almost eager, their expressions hungry for the spectacle. They all wore the same threadbare clothes, the same hollow eyes, but their reactions revealed the layers of humanity they still clung to or had surrendered.

Grim stepped forward.

The crowd's murmurs died instantly. He commanded stillness with his presence alone, a void consuming sound and warmth. His footfalls fell with unnatural precision, each step soundless against the wooden platform. His silhouette was angled in places, impossibly soft in others, wavering like a ghost. Those closest to the platform tensed in collective fear, an instinctive recognition of a predator no rational notions could dismiss.

"You chose to curry favor you didn't deserve," Grim said, his voice calm and cold, carrying effortlessly to every corner of the space. "You scurried to me like a rat with scraps and dared to call it loyalty."

He stepped in close, shadow swallowing the trembling soul. "But what you ultimately did," he murmured, "was insult my judgment."

His words glided across the stone. Several Misfits flinched, though Grim hadn't raised his voice. One woman pressed a hand to her mouth, stifling a sound.

A few glances slid toward Alice, standing to the side with her chin lifted, and her hands clenched in the folds of her skirt. Her face was a careful mask, but her knuckles were white with tension. Gobbler stood farther back, still as stone, his face unreadable though a muscle jumped in his jaw. Elizabeth lingered behind a crooked fence post, close enough to feel the tension. Close enough to know an awful thing was coming.

She'd heard whispers of "release" since arriving. Always spoken in hushed tones, always with averted eyes. She had imagined it meant freedom. Now, watching the terror on the condemned man's face, she understood it meant something else entirely.

"I didn't mean…" the man's voice cracked, hands trembling as he stretched in supplication. "I thought it was wrong. What she— what Alice—"

Grim's mouth curved into a cold, predatory grin. "You thought," he repeated, each syllable precise. "How generous."

The air thinned.

Elizabeth felt it first as pressure in her ears, like descending a mountain too quickly. It manifested into heaviness in her lungs, each breath harder to draw than the last. Around her, others felt it too. A woman clutched her throat. A man staggered and steadied himself on a nearby shoulder.

Somewhere in the trees, the fog stirred.

It moved with purpose, like a predator scenting prey. Tendrils slithered toward the courtyard, testing. Tasting.

Alice watched it, recognition and horror flashing across her face. Gobbler's hand twitched at his side, his body tensing with the instinct to flee, but he anchored himself, holding his ground. He had seen 'release' only once before, but it had been mild compared to this.

Elizabeth didn't know what was coming, but the terror on every face told her enough.

Grim turned his back on the man and raised a pale hand, the gesture almost elegant, like a conductor summoning a single, terrible note.

From the mist, the thing answered.

It slithered out of the Hollow's rocks and crevices, viscous and deliberate. A ravenous, sentient being from humanity's darkest nightmares. A shape with too many limbs. Its outline refused to hold, slick and shifting, like an amoeba under a microscope. Where it touched the ground, frost bloomed in delicate patterns. Where it passed through the air, sound disappeared. Its groan clawed its way under the skin. A creature wrought from the nightmares of gods.

Elizabeth covered her mouth, bile rising in her throat. This wasn't a simple execution. It was a torturous erasure. Fundamentally wrong and a violation of the natural order of death itself.

The creature didn't snarl. Its thoughts whispered in the minds of the onlookers. "Re-leeea-ssssse," it hissed.

The sound invaded one's own mental voice. Unwanted whispers took root, burrowing deep and breeding madness.

"No," the man whimpered, stepping back until he hit the platform's edge, nowhere left to retreat.

"No, please, I—I was trying to help…"

The fog came for him with purpose, as though it had all the time in the world, knowing he couldn't escape. A tendril curled around his ankle, leaving no mark but drawing a choked gasp from his throat.

Grim watched, expressionless, as the fog wound tighter around the man's legs, lifting him without force, without struggle. It might have been merciful, almost beautiful, if not for the scream ripping through the air the moment the mist touched his spine.

Terror. Pure and ragged, from the throat of a soul who knew this wasn't going to be a benevolent death. It was a lesson, and he was the teaching aid.

His back arched. His body convulsed. His mouth opened in a silent scream as the fog climbed his spine, invading his body. His eyes met Elizabeth's for a brief moment, pleading, before they rolled back, showing the whites.

The sound stopped, his voice fading before his body did.

His body stilled, frozen in a grotesque, contorted shape. His outline blurred, edges softening, and details dissolving like a chalk outline washed away by rain.

A blink later, there was nothing.

Nobody. Just absence. He had been unwritten.

A long, strained silence followed. A woman in the crowd sobbed once and fell silent again. A child buried her face in a woman's skirts. Most stood motionless, afraid to draw attention.

Elizabeth felt the world tilt beneath her feet. Her stomach heaved, though there was nothing in it to expel. The enormity of what she had seen—of what this place was capable of—crashed over her like a wave. If the Hollow could do this to a soul, what was it doing to Daniel? To her son?

Grim lowered his hand.

"That," he said, turning to face the crowd, "is release." He spread his arms wide; his chin lifted like an actor taking a bow.

No one made a sound. No one moved. They all stood frozen, a tableau of subjugation painted in pallid faces and downcast eyes.

The fog retreated, curling back into the cracks between worlds, into the places where reality thinned. It appeared almost satisfied, if such a thing could experience satisfaction.

Alice tensed, her fists trembling at her sides. She didn't look at Gobbler, but he heard her voice anyway. Low, hoarse, and deadly calm.

"That's not mercy," she said.

Gobbler turned his head.

She met his gaze.

"It's torture at its worst."

In the words lay all the horror of the Hollow. Not simple death, but oblivion. Not a mere ending but never having been.

Elizabeth sank to her knees behind the fence post, hand against her heart. The locket around her neck felt heavy, the only proof Daniel had existed at all before this place claimed him.

She knew she would fight until her last breath to save him from this fate. From being forgotten. From being erased.

Gobbler couldn't get the image out of his head. The way the man had simply... stopped existing. Not died. Erased.

He should have done something. Should have—what? Stepped forward? Challenged Grim? Ended up on that platform himself, becoming another lesson for the crowd?

His hands still trembled. He shoved them into his pockets, grinding his teeth against the nausea churning in his gut.

Alice had been right. This wasn't mercy. It was torture at its worst.

And he had stood there and done nothing. Again.

The fog churned thicker near the edge of the Hollow, sinking low and swirling in a confused mass. It made a faint, crawling rasp, like insects crawling across the decaying leaves. The trees here grew twisted, branches bending toward each other like greedy hands, creating a canopy where the weakened light filtered into ghostly patterns on the ground below.

From his perch beneath the broken arch of an old gatepost, Tate watched the most recent addition to their dwindling ranks. The stone was cold beneath him, seeping through his clothes, but he had long since stopped noticing such discomforts. Time in the Hollow had a way of dulling certain sensations while sharpening others.

Gobbler sat alone on a fallen tree a few yards away, his shoulders hunched, hands dangling uselessly between his knees. The posture of a man carrying a weight too heavy to bear. A man who had choices to make. Tate knew the look too well. Had seen it in too many faces, all of them since disappeared.

He had been watching the kid for weeks.

There was a unique deference about this one. A resistance far beyond the usual rebellion of new arrivals. A core not yet void of hope by the Hollow's patient grinding. It showed in small things. A hesitation before obeying orders, a glance of concern when others suffered, the way he often stared at his own hands as if they belonged to another person.

Grim had started circling, like he always did when a soul showed promise. Or defiance. Or both. The pattern was familiar, almost ritualistic. First isolation. Followed by temptation. And finally, the inevitable fall.

Tate lit a short match, cupping the flame against the cutting wind. He let it burn low, watching the fire crawl toward his fingers before shaking it out and slipping the scorched tip between his teeth—something to chew on while he debated whether this was the right moment. Whether Gobbler was ready.

He watched the younger man drag a hand across his face and exhale like he had been holding his breath for hours. The gesture was so human, so vulnerable, it made Tate's decision for him.

Yeah. This was the moment.

Tate pushed off the gatepost with a grunt and started down the slope, boots crunching on frostbitten moss. The sound carried in the stillness, but Gobbler didn't look at him until Tate was close enough to speak.

"Nice view," Tate said, his voice easy, his posture even easier. He gestured toward the mist-shrouded valley below, where distant shapes moved in unnatural patterns.

Gobbler glanced sideways. There was wariness in his eyes, but also questions, desperate for answers. Anything to help make sense of this place.

"Didn't think anyone came out here."

Tate smirked, tucking his hands in his coat pockets of a coat too large for him. It had belonged to someone bigger, someone long gone.

"Not many do. Not unless they're lookin' for quiet."

He paused. His mouth curled into an evil grin, leaving his eyes cold and flat. "Or trouble."

Gobbler turned away from the fog, resting his elbows on his knees. His fingers were red with cold, but he didn't take notice. "You always talk like that? In riddles?"

Tate chuckled and dropped onto a nearby rock. The sound was rusty, unused. "Only when I'm sayin' something dangerous." That got Gobbler's attention.

A pause stretched between them, filled with the damp hush of the Hollow. The place was never truly silent. There was always a low hum, as if the world were whispering behind a locked door.

In the distance, a conspiracy of ravens took flight, their dark wings stark against the colorless sky. They circled once, twice, and at last disappeared into the mist. Watching, always watching.

"You got questions." Tate brushed frost from his coat sleeve with gnarled fingers. It wasn't a question. "You wouldn't be out 'ere if you didn't."

Gobbler said nothing. He didn't have to. His silence was its own kind of confession, heavy with unspoken doubts.

"I been 'ere longer 'an most," Tate continued, his voice taking on a gravelly weight, as if each word had to be dragged from a deep and painful place.

"Long enough to know what Grim does when his subject stops playing the part he gave 'em."

"I'm not trying to cause trouble." There was a defiance in the set of Gobbler's jaw contradicting his words.

"That's the thing, kid." Tate leaned forward, his tone darkening, eyes vigilant beneath his weathered brows. "You don't have to try. All it takes is a flicker of mem'ry. A moment o' doubt. A name like Daniel, maybe."

Gobbler stiffened, eyes wide with a mixture of fear and dread. "You heard?"

"Didn't need to," Tate said, tapping the side of his nose. "Grim's dogs are howlin'. He's circlin'. That means you're either dangerous or disposable."

A cold knot tightened in Gobbler's chest.

The wind carried the sweet, earthy scent of decay. The branches overhead creaked in protest.

"And which do you think I am?"

"Don't matter what I think." Tate flicked an invisible thread from his sleeve. "It matters what he decides. And right now, you're under the microscope."

Gobbler clenched his fists, knuckles going white. "What do you want from me?"

"I want you to wake up." The playful edge vanished from Tate's voice, replaced by urgency, making Gobbler sit straighter. "You're bein' groomed. Polished like silver. Grim sees somethin' in you. Somethin' useful. And that should scare the hell outta you."

Gobbler frowned. "Why are you telling me this?"

Tate's voice dropped, quieter now, as if the very fog might carry his words to the wrong ears.

"Because I seen too many like you. Bright eyes. Sharp mind. Brave enough to ask questions, dumb enough to believe they'll get answers." Gobbler imagined he should be insulted, but he didn't have the energy to be offended.

Tate stood, adjusting the collar of his coat. A practiced, almost ritualistic gesture. A remnant of who he had been before.

"There's a game bein' played in the Hollow, Gobbler. And Grim wrote the rules."

"Then maybe it's time someone rewrote them."

Tate paused, almost smiling, though the expression held more sadness than amusement. "Careful, kid. That kind of thinkin' gets you in trouble."

He turned and disappeared into the mist, his silhouette swallowed by the gray. One moment there, the next gone. No warning. No goodbye.

Gobbler remained, his pulse thrumming like a warning bell. Above him, a single raven alighted on a branch, its black eyes gleaming with intelligence far beyond any ordinary bird.

Tate hadn't meant to return, but halfway down the path, he felt he hadn't said enough. He owed the kid more than empty warnings.

He didn't come back right away.

When he finally did, his stride had changed. No casual swagger. No teasing smirk. His steps were more measured, his eyes scanning the tree line. He moved like an animal being hunted.

Gobbler sat where he had been, elbows on knees, staring into the mist clinging to the Hollow's edge. He didn't turn. "Thought you were done talking to me."

"I was." Tate settled beside him again. But he didn't lean back this time. He leaned forward, elbows on his knees, watching the mist. The usual edge in him had gone dull.

"You alright?" Gobbler did not expect Tate to answer.

Tate rubbed his jaw. "I've been watchin' you. Tryin' to figure when I'd have to say something. Reckon that time's now."

"You're gonna hate me for it," Tate added. "Might as well get it out in the open."

Out in the fog, an animal let out a cry that started as a howl and ended like a scream. It echoed, and it didn't stop.

Tate's shoulders sagged, eyes still fixed ahead. "Grim had a name once. Elias."

Gobbler flinched. He knew the name, like a word on the tip of his tongue. Important. Loaded. It stirred his memory, a flicker of recognition, there and gone before he could grasp its meaning.

"He was a healer. Brilliant, cold, obsessed. Believed he could cure death. Not delay it. Cure it." Tate's voice took on a distant quality, as if reciting a tale learned long ago.

"When the world started crumblin' with war, plague, and famine, he didn't grieve. He got to work."

"What happened?" Gobbler asked, drawn in despite himself.

"He crossed a line." Tate's jaw clenched, a muscle jumping beneath the weathered skin. "And then he kept crossin'. Until there was no line left."

He rubbed his hands together. His fingers were gnarled with old breaks never properly set, nails cracked and yellowed.

"They begged him to stop. His assistants. His patients. But he wanted control. Immortality. And when his 'miracles' started failin', when people started dyin' in new ways, he called it evolution."

Gobbler's stomach twisted. A memory surfaced. Not his own, but more of a short reel in his mind. A wooden table. Candles. The smell of death.

"So, he made a deal."

Tate glanced over, surprised. "You're smarter than you look."

"I've heard enough riddles," Gobbler muttered. "You, Alice, Digger. Even Grim."

Tate chuckled, a bitterness devoid of humor.

"Yeah. Well, the deal he made? It gave him power, but not peace. Not control. Just command."

"What's the difference?"

"Command is external. It's force. Threat. Fear." Tate looked away, his eyes fixed on some middle distance where memory lived. "Control is knowin' who you are. Grim lost his identity long before the Hollow found 'im."

A wind stirred the trees, bringing with it the scent of pine mixed with burning wood.

Tate's voice grew softer. "He believes this place is his kingdom. But it's not. It's his cage. He just learned how to make the bars invisible."

Gobbler sat in silence, absorbing this. The pieces were beginning to fit together: Grim's obsession with obedience, with ownership, with proving his power through fear. The man who had tried to conquer death had become its servant, wielding erasure as his ultimate weapon.

"And you? Where do you fit into this?"

Tate's answer was a whisper, almost lost in the wind. "I helped build the lock."

The words landed like a blow to the chest. "You worked for him?"

"I believed in 'im." Tate's smile was haunted, revealing teeth worn by years of grinding. "I thought he could fix everythin'. I believed his vision was salvation. We were both wrong."

Gobbler squirmed. "So why help me?"

"Because you ain't him." Tate rose, brushing his hands on his coat. "And because if someone don't break the cycle, it'll keep repeatin'."

He looked back one last time. "You're running out of time, son. So, make it count."

He vanished into the grayness, leaving Gobbler alone with a name, a truth, and a burden he hadn't asked for. The responsibility of it settled on his shoulders like a mantle.

In the tree above, the raven watched, head cocked to one side. It spread its wings and took flight, disappearing into the fog. Carrying secrets. Carrying warnings.

In the meantime…

Grim watched the exchange from a distance, a slow smile spreading across his face. He couldn't hear the words, but body language was enough. The furtive glances, the tension in Tate's shoulders, the way Gobbler leaned in to listen. It all spoke of conspiracy. Of rebellion brewing.

Gobbler was slipping, aligning himself with the wrong influences. It was time to apply pressure, to remind him who held the strings.

Let him make a friend, Grim thought, his smile spreading wide, revealing teeth too sharp for a human mouth. *It'll hurt more when I take it away.*

Elizabeth sat in the corner of a dusty inn, the worn wooden table before her a stark reminder of how far she had fallen. Once, she'd had a home with polished countertops and soft chairs. Once, she'd had security, comfort, a future. Now she had splinters digging into her palms and the constant gnawing of hunger in her belly.

Her fingers traced the rim of a chipped mug as the fire crackled low in the hearth. The tea inside had gone cold; a film formed on its surface. Most of the patrons had turned in. A few stragglers lingered in the gloom, murmuring over half-drunk cups and fading candlelight.

She had been so close to him.

Daniel had stood a mere yard away. And when she called his name, his eyes registered brief recognition. Not much. But a spark in the darkness too real to deny.

Her heart wrenched at the memory of his vacant expression afterward, and the way he had turned away like she was a mere stranger. Another lost soul in a place full of them.

He didn't fully remember her. But part of him had. She was sure of it.

The room buzzed with faint conversation, but Elizabeth's attention kept drifting toward the shadows. A presence waited in the darkness beyond ordinary night creatures. She couldn't shake the sense she was being watched. Evaluated.

After what she had seen in the courtyard—the horrible "release"—she understood the stakes with painful clarity. If Grim knew she was there, if he understood who she really was and what Daniel meant to her, it wouldn't be her life alone on the line. It would be his. He would be unmade, erased from existence itself.

She couldn't let that happen.

Not while she still drew breath. Not while her heart still beat. Not while she had time left.

Her trembling hand found the scattered scraps of paper, their edges creased and stained from weeks of use. She hadn't written in days, too consumed by the chaos, by hunger, by fear. By the growing pain radiating from her core in waves, often leaving her gasping for breath.

She held her ribs, willing the pain to fade. It didn't. It never did anymore. The disease had turned her world upside down so long ago. It plagued her even in this liminal place, relentless, feeding on her desperation like a parasite.

"Not yet," she whispered, voice low, a plea to a body betraying her day by day. "I can't leave him. Not like this."

The candle on her table sputtered, casting flickering shadows on the wall like ghosts dancing beyond the flames. She stared at the page, her vision blurring and refocusing. She picked up the stub of a pencil, the wood worn smooth from weeks of use, and pressed it onto the paper. The words came slowly and unevenly, each one an effort.

If you're still there, Daniel, hold on. I'm not leaving without you.

She gathered the torn pages into a rough stack, pressing her palm over them as if she could will her determination directly into the pages. Her free hand went to her locket, fingers tracing its familiar shape.

Outside, the wind swept across the abandoned streets. A quiet, lonely movement. Soft and slow and endless. The easy exhale of gods. Or something darker. Patiently waiting for its moment.

In the darkness beyond her window, a raven perched on a broken signpost. Its eyes gleamed with reflected light as it watched the woman hunched over her makeshift journal. It spread its wings, stretching them wide, and settled back to continue its vigil.

11

Echoes from the Grave

The Convocation Hall had emptied, the echoes of Grim's booming voice fading like dying cinders in the oppressive gloom. The gathered Misfits shuffled out, their murmurs and footsteps dissolving into the cold corridors.

But someone lingered.

Near the arched doorway, hidden in the shadows where the dim light barely reached, a figure stood motionless. The stone was cold against their back, the ancient grit rough beneath their fingertips. The breeze carried the scent of brimstone and decay, Grim's signature perfume, tainting everything he touched. It used to amuse the figure, how mortals believed such scents were the trappings of power. In truth, it was merely the stench of a creature trying very hard to be feared.

The others passed by without noticing the shadow, eager to escape Grim's severe presence, their faces drawn with the particular relief of prey avoiding the predator's notice. The figure watched, breathing slow and shallow, eyes fixed on the scene unfolding in the heart of the chamber.

Grim loomed over Gobbler, his voice low but severe, the words cutting through the silence like a knife.

"Stay away from Alice."

The command, laced with venom, sent a chill through the room. Even from this distance, the figure could feel its potency—how it froze the air, how it carried authority no mortal voice should possess.

Gobbler stiffened, defiance sparking beneath the weight of that command. The figure observed him the way one watches a seed split its shell. Quietly. Patiently. With interest older than the carved stone surrounding them.

Grim's shadow stretched across the floor, unnaturally long, impossibly dark, a predator's warning before the strike. But shadows lied. This one most of all.

The figure remained unmoved.

For a moment, the chamber was still, the tension coiled like a serpent ready to strike. Grim swept from the chamber, his robes trailing like a dark tide, each step leaving a momentary coldness on the stone floor. Gobbler remained, his hands clenched into fists, staring at the ground. Finally, he turned and left, his steps heavy with dread.

The figure in the shadows stayed perfectly still, even as the last echoes of Gobbler's footsteps faded. Only when the silence was absolute did they move, a nearly imperceptible stir of darkness separating itself from the cold stone wall. Their gaze followed the corridor where Gobbler had disappeared, the boy's scent still fresh—fear, defiance, a spark of something untampered and bright. It pulsed faintly in the Hollow's fabric.

Interesting. Their thoughts racing behind eyes calculating every possibility, weighing every advantage.

So, the figure thought. *There's much more to this than meets the eye.*

The dim light obscured the figure's expression, but there was no mistaking the calculating glint in their eyes. Grim's warning had not gone unnoticed, nor had the tension between Gobbler and Alice. There was more here—personal, potentially useful. Pieces of a larger puzzle were forming, and the figure intended to put them together.

With one last glance at the now empty hall, they slipped into the darkness, their footsteps silent as they disappeared into the labyrinth of corridors. Unlike the others, they moved with purpose, with knowledge of pathways few remembered. What they had seen, what they now knew, wouldn't stay hidden for long.

Knowledge was currency in the Hollow. And some were richer than others.

The first rays of pale light filtered through the cracks in the cabin walls, casting faint lines across the rough wooden floor. Gobbler stirred on his cot, the events of the Convocation replaying in his mind like a bad dream. His muscles were tense from Grim's warning. Sleep had offered no reprieve, only fragmented dreams of shadows with too many reaching inky tendrils and voices whispering his name. Not Gobbler. The other name. The one that stirred something inside him he couldn't quite grasp. Maybe it was Daniel, but there was the tiniest nudge of doubt.

A creak broke the morning silence, wood protesting against careful weight. Gobbler opened his eyes in time to see a shadow slipping through the door. Digger. His silhouette was unmistakable, slightly hunched, head always tilted as if listening for someone to sneak up on him.

Frowning, Gobbler pushed off his thin blanket and quietly followed, the floorboards cold beneath his bare feet. He grabbed his boots and carried them outside to avoid making noise. The night was cool, holding the faint tang of rot ever-present in the Hollow, a reminder that nothing here was truly alive, but merely existing in some in-between state. Mist clung to the ground. It curled around Gobbler's ankles, grasping like smokey fingers as he pulled on his boots.

Ahead, Digger moved with practiced ease, his silhouette blending with the mist as he navigated the maze of jagged trees and crumbling stone paths. He walked with the confidence of someone who had made this journey many times before, never hesitating at forks in the path, never slowing to get his bearings.

Gobbler kept his distance, slipping from one shadow to the next. The light here was strange. Not the waxing light of dawn. Not the waning light of dusk, but a filtered brightness casting everything in shades of gray. Digger didn't look back, his steps purposeful, his shoulders tense with the mission driving him out before the others woke.

It wasn't long before they reached an old graveyard, tucked away at the edge of the Hollow. Weathered headstones jutted from the earth at odd angles, many of them cracked or toppled entirely. Names had been worn away by time and the elements, leaving only faint impressions of who might have been buried here, if anyone. Gobbler had long suspected the Hollow created places like this as mockeries of the living world.

Gobbler froze, crouching behind a leaning headstone as he watched Digger approach a freshly dug mound of earth. It stood out against the ancient graves. A rusted shovel leaned against a cracked monument, and without hesitation, Digger grabbed it and started digging.

The sound of the shovel biting into the dirt was jarring in the quiet morning, sending a shiver along Gobbler's spine. Each thrust into the earth felt like a violation. He squinted, trying to make sense of the scene. Why would Digger be digging a grave here?

After several minutes, Digger paused, wiping sweat from his brow despite the morning chill. The hole was deep now, and the shape of it made Gobbler's stomach churn. It wasn't large enough for a whole body. It looked like... a hiding place.

"Looking for treasure?" Gobbler stepped out from his hiding spot, his voice cutting through the stillness.

Digger froze, the shovel poised mid-air. He turned, his expression unreadable. His eyes twitched with wariness.

"Thought you'd still be snoring away back at the cabin," Digger said, his tone casual, but his eyes betrayed a hint of irritation. He tightened his grip on the shovel.

Gobbler crossed his arms. "Not when you're sneaking off before dawn like this. What are you doing out here?"

Digger leaned on the shovel, studying Gobbler for a long moment. His gaze was calculating, measuring. He shrugged, a crooked smile tugging at his lips. "Call it a hobby."

"Hobby?" Gobbler looked at the hole. "That doesn't look like a hobby. That looks like... something Grim would have an issue with." The words hung between them, both a question and a warning.

Digger snorted. "Grim has an issue with just about everything. Doesn't mean it's his business." There was bitterness in his voice, old and worn like a well-used tool.

Digger stabbed the shovel back into the earth with a grunt, his jaw tight. "There are places even Grim doesn't touch. The crypts." Digger lifted his hand and gestured vaguely toward the old stone shapes crouched at the graveyard's edge. "Bastions."

Gobbler blinked. "What are—?"

"Strongholds," Digger said, not meeting his eyes. "Old bones of the Hollow. Built before Grim staked his claim. He can twist the land all he wants, but those places? He doesn't own them."

A gust of wind stirred the mist, curling around the worn gravestones like smoke searching for a way in. Digger's voice dropped. "He uses them anyway. Not to hide from others. To hide things from himself. From whatever still listens down here."

Gobbler felt a cold prickle on the back of his neck.

"If he locks something in a Bastion," Digger added, lowering his voice, "it's because even he's afraid of what it might become if it got out."

"Betsy says the Hollow isn't all bad," Gobbler offered cautiously, still not stepping closer. "That there are... patterns. Safe paths. Grim doesn't see everything."

Digger snorted. "Betsy's been here too long. She's made peace with being a ghost."

"She just wants to help," Gobbler said, though the words were thinner now.

Digger leaned on the shovel and dropped his voice to a low rasp. "Yeah, help you die a little slower, maybe." He jabbed the blade into the dirt for emphasis. "The Hollow isn't some haunted house with rules and riddles. It's a trap. And it evolves. The second you think you've mapped it, it rewrites itself. That's Grim's genius. He doesn't need to kill you. He just lets the place hollow you out."

Gobbler swallowed, eyes flicking back to the open grave.

"So, what's in the hole?" Gobbler inched closer, the damp earth soft beneath his boots.

Digger's smile faltered. For a moment, he looked as though he might try to deflect again, but he sighed. He gestured toward the grave.

"Go on, have a look," Digger said, his tone serious. "Been wanting to show someone anyway."

Gobbler hesitated and peered into the pit. His stomach turned as his eyes landed on the small bundle at the bottom—a worn satchel, its leather faded and cracked with age. So ordinary for an object buried with such secrecy.

"What is it?" Gobbler asked.

"Memories," Digger said, his voice low. "Things I should've buried a long time ago." The way he said it sounded like a confession. Gobbler waited for him to explain.

He stared at Digger, trying to decipher the meaning behind his words. The older boy's face was unreadable, his usual jovial demeanor replaced by contempt. Lines Gobbler had never noticed before were etched into his skin, making him look older than his years.

"Why now?" Gobbler asked.

Digger's jaw tightened. "Because I've been reminded secrets don't stay buried forever."

The gravity of the statement hung between them, and Gobbler sensed this was about more than the satchel. It was about Grim. About Alice. About the game being played in the shadows of the Hollow.

"What are you really hiding, Digger?" Gobbler's voice was steady, but inside, unease churned like a storm gathering strength.

Digger didn't answer right away. He leaned on the shovel again, staring into the hole as though it held the answer. His eyes were distant, focused on something Gobbler couldn't see—memories, perhaps, or regrets.

"Some things are better left buried, kid," Digger said. "But sometimes… sometimes those things remind us how we were once human. They remind us we once had hopes. Dreams." There was a haunted quality to his voice, a man who had seen too much and remembered it all.

Gobbler's eyes remained fixed on the satchel, the unease in his gut coiling tighter. He crouched by the edge of the hole, his curiosity warring with caution. "What were your dreams, Digger?"

Digger didn't answer right away. His gaze remained on the satchel, a storm of emotions flickering across his face—guilt, anger, and broken hope.

Digger sighed and stepped into the grave, his boots crunching against the loose dirt. He crouched, lifting the satchel with care, as though it might crumble in his hands. When he climbed out, he held it out toward Gobbler, his movements deliberate.

"Go on," Digger said, his voice flat. "You wanted to know. So, know."

Gobbler hesitated, taking the satchel. It was heavier than it looked, the leather cool and worn under his fingers. It smelled of earth and age. He unbuckled the clasp and flipped it open.

Inside was a collection of innocuous items: a stack of faded letters, their edges crumbling; a tarnished pocket watch, its face cracked; a thin silver chain, tangled and dull; and a small journal bound in black leather, its pages swollen with damp.

"What is this?" Gobbler pulled out the journal.

Digger's expression darkened. "That's a piece of who I used to be. Back when I thought I could play by Grim's rules and come out ahead." His voice was bitter, edged with self-loathing.

Gobbler flipped open the journal. The pages were filled with cramped, angular writing, the ink smudging in places. Diagrams and symbols covered the margins, alongside what looked like maps of the Hollow—not just the parts he knew, but deeper regions, places he had never seen or heard mentioned.

"You were mapping this place?" Gobbler stared at him, a spark of excitement cutting through the unease.

"Not just mapping. I was trying to find a way out. My, um, partner and I were. It was our hope, our dream to escape this place."

Gobbler's heart skipped a beat. "And did you find a way out?" The possibility of escape—of freedom—was almost too much to comprehend.

"I thought I did." Digger took the journal from Gobbler's hands, turning to a page near the back. A detailed map spread across the parchment, lines and notations marking paths through unknown territories. "But Grim's grip is tighter than you think. Every path I found circled back. Every shortcut led to another dead end. He's got this place locked down like a fortress."

Gobbler frowned, thumbing through the journal.

"So why keep this? Why bury it?"

Digger's jaw clenched. "Because it's not just a record of my failures. It's a record of my betrayal."

"Betrayal?" Gobbler watched Digger's reaction.

Digger met his gaze, his eyes dark with regret.

"You think Grim lets anyone get close to him without a price? Back then, I was one of his trusted men. I did his dirty work, kept the Misfits in line. And when someone like you showed up, someone with potential, I was the one who handed them over. Every time."

Digger's confession hit Gobbler like a punch to the gut. The implications sank in.

"You sold them out." His voice thickened with disbelief.

Digger's demeanor didn't change. "I thought I didn't have a choice. I thought it was the only way to survive. But the more I did it, the more I realized I was just another pawn in his game. And the loyalty definitely only went one way. Grim is loyal only to himself."

Gobbler stared at the journal, the pages trembling in his hands. "Why are you sharing all of this with me now?" The question was loaded with unspoken accusations.

Digger leaned closer, his voice low and urgent.

"Because you're not like the others. Grim's got his eye on you, and if you're not careful, you'll end up just like I did. A puppet with strings too tangled to cut. If you show any emotion, any connection to anyone else, Grim will rip them away from you, just to prove he can. He'll use them to control you."

The words settled in Gobbler's chest like a stone. He wanted to hate Digger for what he had done, for the lives he had traded away. But he couldn't ignore the sincerity in his voice, the raw regret etched into each word.

"Are you talking from experience? Did Grim use someone you loved to get to you?" Gobbler asked.

Digger, looking at the grave as though contemplating crawling in, said nothing. But his silence was answer enough. His eyes held the haunted look of a man who had lost everything worth holding onto.

"What's in the letters?" Gobbler softened his voice.

Digger hesitated, then tilted his head toward the satchel. "See for yourself."

Gobbler pulled out the stack of letters, the paper brittle and yellowed with age. He unfolded one and read it.

The words were a mix of pleading and desperation, written by a man named Renzo. The writer begged for mercy, for forgiveness, for a way to escape the torment of the Hollow. The handwriting grew increasingly erratic as the letter continued, desperation clear in every stroke.

"Renzo?" Gobbler was surprised he had never heard the name before.

Digger's face was grim. "That was his name before Grim took him and turned him into a dark and vile thing. Back when he was still one of us. Back when he was the closest thing I ever had to happiness."

A heavy, unwelcome truth dawned inside Gobbler. Renzo. Digger had known him, had a history with him. And whatever that history was, it had left scars deep enough to twist Digger into the broken soul he was now. And Grim had taken him away as punishment for Digger.

"Why do you still have these?" Gobbler asked, his voice shaking.

Digger's gaze drifted to the grave. "Because they're a reminder. Of better times. Of what we were. Of what we both became."

In the gray light of the Hollow's eternal twilight, surrounded by weathered graves and secrets unearthed, Gobbler felt the first stirrings of what might have been resolve. He knew when the time came, he would fight. He knew he had something to fight for, and he would rather cease to exist than go on in any world without Alice.

Gobbler sat on the porch of the cabin; his gaze fixed on the shifting mist in the distance. Digger's journal was tucked safely inside his coat, its weight a constant reminder of the truths he had learned that morning. The sun—or whatever passed for it in the Hollow—cast a dim, pallid light over the landscape, giving it a washed-out, lifeless hue. The mist pulsed to its own rhythm, advancing and retreating in a slow, hypnotic dance that made it hard to look away.

The others had left hours ago, whispering among themselves as they prepared for another mission. Their glances slid over Gobbler like he was invisible. Not one of them had so much as looked in his direction, their conversations faltering whenever he came near.

The isolation was suffocating. He had never been popular among the Misfits. He had always been the newcomer, the one still finding his place. But they had accepted him as part of the family. Or so he thought. Now, even they avoided him, giving him a wide berth as if proximity alone might mark them for Grim's attention. Gobbler suspected it had everything to do with Grim's sudden interest in him. No one wanted to be collateral damage when Grim's wrath fell.

He ran his fingers along the weathered wood of the porch, the splinters catching against his skin. The physical sensation anchored him, kept his mind from spiraling into darker thoughts. His stomach had been empty for hours, but hunger was a distant concern compared to the gnawing feeling of abandonment.

The cabin door creaked open behind him, hinges protesting through layers of rust. Betsy stepped out, a chipped mug in her hand, steam rising from whatever brew she had concocted. Her face was lined with years, but her eyes remained alert beneath the weathered exterior.

"You look like you been kicked by a horse," she said, plopping onto the step beside him. The wooden stairs groaned beneath her weight, a sound so ordinary and domestic it made the strangeness of the Hollow momentarily recede.

Gobbler managed a half-smile. "Feels like it too."

Betsy chuckled and sipped her tea, the steam curling like miniature versions of the mist beyond. The liquid smelled of herbs he didn't recognize, bitter with a bite, but comforting.

"They'll come 'round, you know. Always do. Misfits don't stay mad for long. Well, except for Alice, but that's just part of her charm."

She casually said Alice's name; it struck Gobbler as odd. The memory of Grim's warning echoed in his mind. *Stay away from her.*

"Don't think it's anger," Gobbler muttered, picking at a loose thread on his sleeve. "More like fear. I know they think Grim's watching me, and now they're keeping their distance like I've got a target on my back."

Betsy's smile faltered, her gaze softening to sympathy. She suddenly looked older; weariness carved into the slope of her shoulders.

"It ain't personal, son. It's survival. Grim's attention don't come cheap, and none of us can afford to be in his spotlight."

Gobbler nodded, though it didn't make the rejection sting any less. The knowledge sat heavy in his chest—in this place, even bonds of friendship were conditional, tenuous things that could snap at the first sign of danger.

Betsy leaned back, setting her mug on the step. The ceramic made a soft clink against the wood.

"You know, when I first got 'ere, I thought I would stick it out alone. Thought that was the only way to keep my head down. But it ain't no way to live, even if this ain't real livin'. Took me a while

to figure out we're stronger together. Even if together means dealin'
with Grim breathin' down our necks."

He glanced at her, surprised by the rare seriousness in her tone.
There was wisdom in her words, hard-won and genuine.

"'Sides," she continued, brightening a little. "You'd be amazed
at how many cracks there are in Grim's perfect little world. I mean,
did you know Digger once managed to swipe a shipment right out
from under them minions' noses? Took it straight to the old crypts
before anyone noticed. You know, those half-buried vaults in the
old graveyard past the ravine? The ones he's always pokin' 'round in.
Nobody goes there unless they got a death wish. Not even Grim
saw it coming."

The mention of Digger made Gobbler's hand instinctively press
against the journal hidden inside his coat.

"The crypts? Why would he take it there?"

Betsy waved a hand dismissively, but her eyes missed nothing.

"Who knows? Digger got his secrets. But I'll tell you this much.
Those crypts are older than anything else here. Some say they were
here before Grim even showed up." Her voice dropped so no unseen
ears could hear.

"Creepy place, but Digger swears by them. Says they got...
potential."

"Potential for what?" The question came out more eagerly than
Gobbler intended.

Betsy shrugged, lifting her mug again. Her fingers traced the
chip on its rim.

"No idea. But if you're feelin' bold, you might want to ask him
yourself. Or, on second thought, stay clear. Trouble sticks to him
like glue, and it got a way of spreadin'."

She made it sound like casual advice, but there was a message
hidden behind her words. A nudge in a direction she pretended to
know nothing about.

Gobbler stared out at the mist again, his mind racing.
Digger's secrets. The crypts. Cracks in Grim's world. The strange
maps in the journal, showing passages he had never known

existed. It all connected in a way he hadn't figured out, yet. A possibility that had never been real before. A potential way out of this hellhole?

For the first time in days, a determination stirred within him, cutting through the haze of doubt and frustration. He wasn't just going to sit here, waiting for Grim to decide his fate. If there were a way to push back, to find those cracks and pry them open, he would take it... whatever it took.

"Thanks, Betsy." The words meant more than she could know.

Before she could respond, he leaned in and kissed her weathered cheek. The gesture surprised them both, a small moment of genuine connection in a place designed to destroy such things.

She blinked, startled, the faintest blush creeping across her face. Her fingers touched the spot, as if checking whether the affection had left a physical mark.

"Goodness," she mumbled, brushing at her cheek as if the kiss lingered there. "This tea must be hotter than I thought. Brings color to the cheeks."

Gobbler chuckled low and soft, the sound unfamiliar even to himself after days of tension. It felt good to laugh, even for a minute. A small rebellion against the Hollow's oppressiveness.

"I think I'm going to go exploring for a bit." Gobbler stood and stretched. A new energy hummed in his veins, a purpose where before there had only been reaction.

"Mind if I grab a couple of supplies to take along?"

Betsy waved a hand absently toward the cabin entrance. "Help yourself. Just... be careful, alright?" There was genuine concern in her voice, motherly in a way that stirred something half-forgotten in his chest.

"I will," Gobbler replied, a spark of resolve in his voice. He turned toward the cabin, the faint ghost of a smile on his face. He didn't have a plan yet, but what he had was better... a purpose.

And in the Hollow, purpose was as rare as hope.

He didn't know where it would lead, only that he was done playing it safe. He was ready to make a difference.

The air was cool and crisp as it whispered through the towering pines. Their rustling needles created a soothing symphony that carried across the Meadow, a stark contrast to the oppressive silence that pervaded most of the Hollow. The morning sun broke through the canopy, casting golden beams that danced along the forest floor, illuminating particles of dust and pollen suspended in the air like tiny constellations.

Gobbler tilted his head back, letting the warmth of the light seep through his clothes and onto his skin. The chill of the Hollow's ever-present mist retreated under its touch, and for a fleeting moment, he felt a peace he hadn't felt in a long time. It settled over him, loosening the knots of tension that had been his constant companions.

This place was different. The Meadow existed in contradiction to everything he knew about the Hollow. Too bright. Too alive. Too... real.

Birdsong filled the air, delicate and lively. Sparrows flitted between branches, their tiny wings a blur as they chased each other through the copse. A pair of finches landed nearby, pecking at the ground with quick, precise movements. The scent of pine sap and damp earth grounded him, pulling him into the present like an anchor. It was a sharp contrast to the oppressive gloom he had grown accustomed to. Here, the shadows seemed reluctant to intrude, hovering just at the edges of the Meadow as if they, too, were wary of breaking this fragile serenity.

He took a deep breath, savoring the air, untainted by decay or despair. It almost felt alive. Alive in a way he wasn't sure he could be anymore. A light breeze stirred the tall grasses, carrying with it the faintest trace of sweetness, like the memory of wildflowers long gone. He knelt and ran his fingers through the blades, marveling at their softness. They swayed in unison, bowing to the wind's gentle insistence.

For a moment, he let himself believe he was somewhere else, anywhere else. A place other than purgatory. A place that didn't feel like a perpetual balancing act on the edge of oblivion. Here, he wasn't Gobbler or anyone else who felt heavy and broken. Here, he simply was.

It reminded him of something. A brief memory. Gone again before he could latch onto it. The feel of grass beneath bare feet. The sound of laughter, carefree and genuine. The warmth of sunlight on skin that hadn't yet known real pain.

A raven's caw pierced the stillness, stark and jarring. Gobbler flinched, his shoulders tensing as the sound shattered his reverie. He looked up, scanning the sky for the source. The bird was perched high above, a solitary sentinel on the otherwise perfect morning. Its black eyes glinted, watching, waiting. A reminder that, in the Hollow, there were no secrets.

Because nothing in the Hollow was ever safe, just a short distance away, unseen and ignored in this fleeting reprieve, there was suffering. It twisted souls into unrecognizable shells. Perpetual hunger gnawed at those left to wander, brutal punishments crushed what little spirit remained, and an all-consuming loneliness festered in every shadow.

Gobbler exhaled slowly, willing his shoulders to relax. This moment was an illusion, he knew. But illusions were all he had. He closed his eyes and tipped his face to the sun again, letting its rays trickle down like a balm on his weary soul.

For now, he could let the breeze carry his troubles far away. For now, the Meadow held its peace. And for now, he was safe.

But the raven cawed again, and the safety felt thinner than before.

A movement in the distance caught Gobbler's attention.

At first, he thought it was a trick of the light—wisps of mist wafting against the golden backdrop. But no, they were figures, hazy yet distinct, drifting through the tall grass like specters untethered by gravity. Their forms were wrapped in an ethereal glow, neither fully solid nor entirely transparent. They moved with an impossible grace, feet brushing across the ground. They walked in a slow, deliberate procession, their gazes fixed ahead on a point not yet visible to Gobbler.

Visitors.

They were rare in the Hollow. Souls who didn't belong here, who had stumbled through by accident or design. And these souls… they weren't lingering. They weren't lost. They were leaving.

Gobbler straightened and a stitch tugged between his ribs. He had seen souls pass before—torn away, dragged down, or simply disappearing—but this was different. There was no struggle, no forceful hand pulling them forward. They were walking of their own volition, toward a place beyond the Meadow, toward an unknown destination, but clearly beckoning.

The Visitors themselves were varied. Men and women of different ages, some in ancient clothes, others in more modern dress. But they shared the same manner: peaceful, expectant, as if heading toward a promise. Their edges blurred against the golden light, making them appear as if they were dissolving into it, becoming one with the radiance ahead.

Instinct stirred in his gut, a pull inside him recognized what lay ahead. He took a step forward, and another, following the silent procession, his heart pounding with a strange mix of curiosity and longing.

The Visitors passed through the Meadow's far edge, toward a thinning in the mist. It wasn't a doorway. Not exactly. But there was something there, something more than just empty space. It shimmered, vibrating with an energy he didn't understand, an opening in the world pulsing with life.

What's beyond this? What was it they saw that he couldn't?

Gobbler picked up his pace, breaking into long strides—only for the world to wobble around him.

A cold gust slammed into him, the golden light fracturing like a mirror struck by stone. The ground beneath him lurched, the peaceful Meadow blurring like an unraveling dream. He stumbled, arms windmilling for balance, blinking as the trees around him twisted, warping into more jagged versions of themselves.

When he steadied himself, the Meadow was gone.

The Visitors were gone.

And he was somewhere else entirely.

The air was thicker here, the oppressive darkness of the Hollow pushing in around him. Trees stood like broken sentinels, their bark peeling away to reveal nothing beneath. Shadows looped between them, watching, waiting. The illusion had shattered, and the truth had swallowed him whole.

A raven's caw pierced the silence, stark and jarring.

Gobbler exhaled slowly, his hands clenching into fists. It figures. He should've known he couldn't leave. He should've expected it. The Hollow wasn't done with him.

Not yet.

It was more than eerie. It was outright terrifying.

The fog was dense enough to feel like a living thing closing in around him. Nothing else stirred within it. No rustling leaves, no distant howls, no whispers of unseen creatures. Just a ringing in his ears.

Every noise he made, every leaf brushed aside, every stick cracking beneath his feet—was swallowed instantly, reduced to dull and lifeless thuds. Even his own voice, muttered to keep his nerves from fraying, was clipped short, cut off before it could properly exist. No echo bouncing around the trees. Just words going nowhere, as if the fog buffered and blocked them from being heard.

But there were the whispers. The only thing that echoed in the fog.

Hushed. Ominous. Surrounding him. Closing in.

Words he couldn't make out, spoken by disembodied voices. Some sounded pleading, others angry, and many were simply lost. They seemed to move with the fog, circling him, always just beyond understanding.

The air grew still, heavy with an unnatural silence. Gobbler had followed the faint pull of curiosity and desperation through the desolate expanse of skeletal trees. His breath clouded in the unnatural cold, and the brittle grass crunched underfoot like the dry hollow bones of tiny birds.

At the heart of the field stood a single gnarled tree, blackened and ancient. Its twisted branches clawed at the darkened sky, each one dotted with shadowy forms. Ravens. Dozens of them. Their glossy feathers gleamed in the dim light, their beady eyes tracking his every move with an intelligence well beyond animal instinct. They didn't caw or flutter, but sat perfectly still, watching him approach with eerie collective patience.

A chill ran along Gobbler's spine as he stepped closer. At the base of the tree lay an ancient, weathered chest, half-buried in the dead earth. It was made of dark wood, banded with tarnished metal, its surface covered in symbols he couldn't read but assumed were a message of some kind. It called to him—a faint voice in his head, urging him forward. A compulsion beyond curiosity, beyond reason.

The makeshift weapon he always carried—a jagged piece of metal he had scavenged from the ruins—felt heavy in his hand as he approached. It was woefully inadequate against whatever power dwelled here, but it was a comfort nonetheless, solid in a place where one never knew what to expect.

"You're not supposed to be here."

The voice came from above, grating and raspy. Gobbler froze, his eyes scouring the haze above him. The most enormous raven perched at the highest point of the tree; its head cocked unnaturally to the side. Its eyes locked onto his, unblinking. They weren't the eyes of a bird, but a primordial being. Knowing. Patient.

"Turn back," the raven warned, its voice scraping like rusted hinges. The words emerged from its beak without it opening, as if projected into Gobbler's mind. "While you still can."

Gobbler clenched his jaw and took another step forward. Fear battled with determination inside him.

"I'm not leaving until I get some answers." The words came out steadier than he felt.

The raven let out a low, guttural caw, and the others joined in, their cries swelling into a cacophony filling the air. Before he could react, they exploded into motion, a storm of black feathers and sharp talons descending toward him.

Gobbler swung his weapon wide, the wind from their wings battering him. It was like fighting shadows—no matter where he struck, they reformed and attacked again. Claws raked his skin, drawing thin lines of blood, exciting them further. Their wings beat against his face, blinding him, their bodies impossibly solid one moment and insubstantial the next.

"Stop!" he shouted, his voice cracking. Desperation fueled his words. "I'm here to help!"

The flurry of wings ceased all at once, and silence fell, so suddenly and completely it felt like he was being plunged underwater. The largest raven landed in front of him, its form shifting unnaturally. Feathers rippled and twisted, growing into a tall, humanoid figure cloaked in black. Shadows obscured its face, but its eyes gleamed, bright and piercing—the same eyes that had watched him from the tree. Not red like Grim's, but a deep, bottomless black reflecting nothing.

"Help?" The figure's voice was calm, almost amused. "There is no help here. Only death. And it watches you closely, boy."

Gobbler straightened, trying to hide his fear.

"I'm not afraid of death. I've already seen worse." The words were bravado, but they held a kernel of truth. After what he had witnessed in the Hollow, after the "release," death was almost merciful by comparison.

The figure tilted its head, the motion too smooth, too deliberate to be human.

"Brave words for one so small." It gestured to the chest behind it, the ancient wood creaking under the attention. "Do you think that will save you? Or doom you?"

Gobbler hesitated but forced himself to step forward. The figure didn't move to stop him, merely watched with an air of detached curiosity. Its presence was cold, but not hostile—not like Grim's burning malice. This was wiser, and it watched him without judgment.

As he approached the chest, the figure's gaze bore into him. His fingers brushed the lid, and he gasped from the shock of cold running up his arm. It wasn't painful, but it was uncomfortable—like plunging his hand into ice water. The chest creaked open without him having to lift it, revealing its contents: an artifact, small and unassuming, but pulsating with an otherworldly energy.

It was a curved metal object, talon-shaped and jagged, roughly the length of his palm. Made of a material he had never seen before. It wasn't silver or gold or any metal he recognized. It wavered between states, appearing solid, then almost liquid, its surface etched with symbols similar to those on the chest. But at its center was a symbol he did recognize—a raven in flight, rendered in exquisite detail.

"What is it?" Gobbler asked.

The figure's mouth turned upward in a jack-o'-lantern grin, an unsettling exhibition that raised the hair on the back of his neck.

"A key," it said. "To what, even I cannot say. But beware, boy. Every key unlocks a door, and some doors should never be opened."

Before Gobbler could respond, the figure dissolved into a flurry of feathers, leaving him alone with the Talon. The ravens in the tree remained motionless now, watching like an audience at a play. Waiting for the final act, when they might flap their wings in applause and slip out of the theater.

He stared at the Talon, heart pounding. It felt significant, powerful. He didn't know what it was or how it would help, but one thing was clear. This was the beginning of a journey far greater than he had imagined.

With a steadying breath, he secured the Talon in a makeshift sheath at his belt and turned back toward the misty horizon, the ravens' cries echoing behind him as he made his way back to the relative safety of the cabin. The Talon grew heavier with each step, both a burden and a promise.

He had made an important discovery—but whether it would lead to salvation or destruction remained to be seen.

12

A Mother's Cry

The Misfits trickled back to camp in the pale gray of dawn; their faces etched with weariness. Gobbler sat perched on a cracked stone near the cabin, idly tossing a shard of broken tile between his hands. The Talon from the raven tree rested secure in its sheath at his hip, its weight a constant reminder of the secrets yet to be revealed in this world. He watched the group return, each member filing into the cramped space they called home. Betsy caught his eye and gave him a tight, knowing smile, but no one else acknowledged him.

They've been avoiding me since the Convocation, he thought. Grim's warning had worked like a poison, spreading distrust and unease among the Misfits. Gobbler couldn't blame them; keeping a low profile in the Hollow was a survival tactic. Being noticed by Grim marked you, and no one wanted to share that target.

He didn't mind the isolation… much. It gave him time to think, to turn over Digger's cryptic warnings and the things Betsy had let slip. *Cracks in Grim's world*, she had told him. The idea of a way out had rooted itself deep in Gobbler's mind, though he hadn't figured out how to act on it yet.

"You should've seen it," said Della, the youngest of the group, her voice pulling him back to the present. She was talking to Roan, the sharp-eyed scout who always returned from missions with stories to tell.

"A Visitor woman. First one I've seen here in years. She looked—"

"Out of place," Roan finished, his tone dismissive. "Not our concern. Minions had her. She's Grim's problem now."

Gobbler froze. The tile shard slipped from his fingers and shattered against the stone. A few heads turned at the sound, but he paid them no mind, his focus entirely on what he had just heard.

"A visitor woman?" he interrupted, standing abruptly. The Misfits turned to look at him, Della curious and Roan guarded.

"Yeah." Della lifted her shoulders with indifference. "Didn't get a close look. She had dark hair, though. And the way she was yelling, I don't think she's been here long enough to know who she's dealing with."

Heat crawled up his throat, a sudden urgency he couldn't explain coursing through him.

"Did you hear her name? Anything else?"

"Nope," Roan replied, his tone flat. "Didn't stick around to chat. Like I said. Not our problem."

But it was Gobbler's problem. He knew it deep in his gut. A Visitor woman in the Hollow, shouting loud enough to draw attention, and escorted by Grim's minions. How many Visitors could there be down here? The Visitors typically stayed on the other side of the grimy town until they moved on.

He had to see for himself who this woman was.

The perpetual fog shrouded the misshapen trees and jagged outcroppings of stone. Gobbler stood at the edge of the camp, his chest tight with a growing sense of unease. Elizabeth had been taken; he was sure of it.

He tried to tell himself she would be fine, that Grim doesn't take much interest in the Visitors. But something deeper instinctually gnawed at him. It was the same feeling that had pushed him to track Digger to the graveyard, the voice in the back of his mind telling him she's in danger. Only this time, the voice had grown into a roar.

A sudden shout pierced the stillness. Gobbler stilled, the shout slicing straight through him. It was unmistakably Elizabeth's voice, raw with fear.

Without a second thought, he bolted toward the sound, his feet pounding the uneven ground. The fog swirled around him as he ran, the oppressive air burning his lungs. Branches whipped at his face, leaving thin scratches across his cheeks. Roots threatened to trip him with every step, but some instinct kept him moving forward, guided by a thread of memory just out of grasp, but impossible to ignore.

He came to a clearing and skidded to a halt, his heart plummeting.

Elizabeth was there, surrounded by three figures cloaked in shadows. Minions. Their skeletal forms flickered with a supernatural glow, their claws glinting as they closed in on her. One of them hissed, sounding like nails dragging across slate.

She looked different than when he had seen her before. Thinner, more haggard, her clothes torn, and her face smudged with dirt. But there was a defiance in her stance that stirred something deep within him. Even cornered, she wasn't giving up.

Elizabeth's back was against a crumbling stone wall, her eyes wide and frantic as she clutched a jagged branch—a pathetic weapon against the predators circling her.

"Stay back!" she warned, her voice trembling but determined. "I'm not afraid of you!"

A noise sounding like bones rattling against each other escaped the minions' mouths. Chittering laughter. The largest one grabbed for her, its elongated fingers flexing in anticipation.

Gobbler didn't hesitate. He grabbed the nearest rock and hurled it with surprising accuracy. It struck the closest minion's shoulder with a sickening crack, and it spun toward him with a guttural snarl. The creature wore the insignia of Grim's lieutenant—one of his chosen.

"Hey! Over here, you ugly son of a…" Gobbler's taunt was cut off as the minion lunged with inhuman speed. He ducked just in time, its claws swiping inches from his face, severing a lock of his hair. The creature's breath washed over him—heated from the depths of hell. He rolled to his feet, grabbing a fallen branch to swing at his attacker.

The branch connected with a dull crack. He hadn't aimed; his body had simply moved, faster than thought. For a heartbeat, he stared, shocked by his own strength behind it.

"Get away from her!" he shouted, rage building in his chest. The emotion came out of nowhere, a protectiveness he couldn't explain but couldn't deny.

"Daniel!" Elizabeth's voice cut through the chaos. "Be careful!"

The name froze him in place. Daniel. It wasn't just the sound of it. It was the way she said it, filled with desperation and familiarity and a mother's love. Something in his chest cracked open—a hairline fracture in whatever spell had been holding his memories at bay.

A second minion took advantage of his distraction, rushing him with a shriek that pierced his eardrums. Gobbler swung his improvised weapon, catching it across the head with a force surprising even him. The creature screeched, stumbling back, but the impact jarred the branch from his grip, splintering it into useless fragments. Before he could recover, the first minion was on him again, its claws tearing into his arm. Pain lanced through him, white-hot and blinding.

"Daniel!" Elizabeth's scream cut through the haze of pain. He looked up to see the third minion closing in on her, its jaws opening impossibly wide, revealing rows of needle-like teeth. Its form expanded, growing larger as it prepared to engulf her.

Something inside him snapped. It wasn't anger or fear. It was something more profound, primal. *Protect her. Protect her at all costs.*

A flood of images crashed over him all at once, overwhelming in their intensity: a warm kitchen filled with laughter, the smell of cookies baking. The soft lull of a bedtime story, words he could almost recite from memory. A woman's voice humming a tune he couldn't name but knew by heart. A car ride through the mountains, his head resting against the window as he dozed. Elizabeth's face, younger but unmistakable, smiling at him as she tucked him into bed, her hand smoothing his hair back.

"Sweet dreams, Danny," she whispered.

Mom.

The word hit him like a lightning strike, shattering the fog that had clouded his mind. The memories flooded back. Who he was, who she was, what they meant to each other. Elizabeth wasn't just another lost soul. She was his mother.

Somewhere deep in the Hollow, something responded, quiet but unmistakable. A shift in the balance neither Daniel nor Grim had foreseen; something in Hollow's order slipped, and Grim felt it move through his grasp.

With a guttural roar that shook the very air, he threw himself at the minion closest to Elizabeth. His fist connected and the creature staggered. From there, his body moved on instinct, every strike and dodge fueled by a newfound clarity and purpose. He wasn't just fighting for survival anymore. He was fighting for her.

The minion facing him hesitated, its glowing eyes flickering as if sensing the change in him. The awakening of something out of place in the Hollow. Defiance. Strength. A brightness that threatened their darkened souls.

Daniel didn't give it a chance to regroup. He feinted left and drove his shoulder into the creature's midsection. It howled as it stumbled backward, its form momentarily destabilizing like static on an old television. Daniel pressed his advantage, grabbing a jagged rock from the ground and smashing it into the minion's face. The creature's head caved inward with a sound like glass shattering, before it disintegrated into ash, scattering on the wind.

The remaining two minions hissed and circled, suddenly cautious. One lunged at Elizabeth, hoping to use her as leverage.

"No!" Daniel's voice carried a power he didn't recognize, making the very shadows of the Hollow recoil. He moved faster than he imagined possible, placing himself between his mother and the threat. The minion's claws raked across his back, tearing through cloth and skin, but he barely felt it. His blood sang with purpose, with memory, with identity.

Elizabeth had managed to grab a branch again, and as the minion overextended itself, she drove the sharpened end into its eye. It shrieked, flailing backward.

"Daniel, behind you!" she warned.

He spun in time to catch the last minion as it leapt for his throat. Its momentum carried them both to the ground, rolling through dirt and ash. The creature was strong, unnaturally so, its limbs bending at impossible angles as it fought to pin him down. Its face, if it could be called that, was inches from his, a mockery of human features contorted with rage.

"Not... my... family," Daniel ground out, forcing the words through clenched teeth as he struggled against the creature's strength.

With a surge of effort born of desperation and love, he twisted his body and managed to throw the minion off. Before it could recover, he was on his feet, stomping on its throat with all his weight. The creature thrashed, its form beginning to dissolve.

Elizabeth had finished off the other minion, her makeshift spear embedded in what passed for its chest. She stood panting, dirty and bloodied but alive.

Daniel turned to her, recognition flooded through him, almost bringing him to his knees.

"Mom..." The word was both foreign and achingly familiar on his tongue.

The last minion gave a final, desperate hiss before it too dissolved into ash, leaving them alone in the sudden stillness of the clearing.

Silence fell, interrupted only by their ragged breaths. Elizabeth stared at him, her eyes shimmering with unshed tears.

"Daniel." Her voice broke. "You remember me."

"Mom... I..." The rest of the words jammed in his throat. The enormity of it all flooded him. The memories, the recognition, the sheer impossibility of her being here crashed over him at once. His legs gave out and he sank to his knees, dazed by the overwhelming enormity of finally knowing. Of being himself again after so long lost.

But more memories surfaced. New memories. He clutched his head as they came crashing back: the argument in the car, the accident that had torn them apart, how they had ended up here. The moment everything went wrong.

And then, the darkness. The Hollow.

Elizabeth dropped to her knees beside him, pulling him into a fierce embrace. He clung to her, his body shaking with silent sobs. For a moment, the world around them disappeared, the horrors of the Hollow eclipsed by the sheer relief of being together again.

She smelled like home—like safety and comfort and everything he had forgotten he was missing. Her arms around him felt like the first real thing he had experienced since waking in this place.

"I knew it was you," she whispered against his hair. "I knew it the moment I saw you. They tried to tell me you were gone, but I knew better."

But the reunion was short-lived. A slow clap echoed through the clearing, deliberate and mocking. Daniel started and scanned around for the source, but he already had a sinking feeling.

Grim stood at the edge of the clearing, his figure shrouded in the ever-present mist. His smile was thin, his eyes glinting with satisfaction.

"Touching," Grim drawled, his voice like velvet over steel. "Truly. But family reunions are such fleeting things."

Daniel rose to his feet, positioning himself between Elizabeth and Grim. His back stung from the minion's claws, but adrenaline kept the pain at bay. His grip tightened on the branch Elizabeth had been using, though he knew it was a pitiful defense against the entity before them.

"What do you want?" Daniel demanded, his voice steady despite the fear coiling in his gut.

Grim's smile widened, revealing teeth too pointy to be human. "Why, Daniel, I want exactly what you want. For you to remember. To embrace who you are and who you're meant to be."

He gestured to the ashes scattered across the clearing.

"But perhaps you need more persuasion. You've tasted what it means to protect. Now let's see how far you're willing to go to keep her safe."

With a snap of his fingers, the fog thickened, enveloping Grim as he disappeared. His parting words lingered, loaded with threat.

"The game has only just begun."

Daniel turned back to his mother, a new fear settling in his bones. Not for himself, but for her. Whatever Grim wanted from him, he now had the perfect leverage.

He didn't know what would happen from this point on, but he knew that blind obedience to Grim was no longer an option.

Daniel sat near the edge of the tower's reach, where the flickering torchlight gave way to mist and memory. His hands were filthy, clenched tight around a knot of fabric he hadn't realized he was still holding. His mother's shawl, frayed and soot stained. He brought it to his face, inhaling the scent of her. A tenuous connection to a life both impossibly distant and achingly present.

The voice she had used when she called out his name echoed inside him, still ringing even as the world tried to drown it out.

He was Daniel. And she had come for him. Crossed worlds, defied death, refused to give up. All for him. The realization left him raw, exposed, as if his skin had been peeled back to reveal the person he had been all along.

Word spread fast in the camp. Names mattered here, and once his was spoken aloud, everyone picked it up easily. No more Gobbler. No more boy. Just Daniel, returned, remembered, and unmistakenly himself.

A soft rustle of underbrush behind him didn't startle him this time. He felt the presence before the voice came. Another sense recovered along with his name.

"Well, hell. Look at you. All dramatic-like with your back to the world, starin' into the fog like some gothic novel." Tate's voice was half teasing, half warning. It didn't carry the smirk it usually did.

Daniel's eyes remained fixed on the shifting patterns of the mist.

"Did you follow me?"

"Yeah. And you knew I would, so don't act surprised." Tate eased onto a rock nearby, legs stretched out like he owned the place. "Kid, the whole camp could feel you spiraling."

Daniel scoffed but still didn't meet his eyes.

"Tate." He paused, the name tasting different now that he had recovered his own. "Or is that even your name?"

Tate sucked his teeth, a contemplative sound.

"Tate's what they call me now. It used to be Renwick. Back before all this..." He gestured vaguely at the Hollow, the movement encompassing everything around them. "...back when the sky still looked like somethin' worth wakin' up under."

Daniel sat quietly for a long stretch, listening to the wind tug at the trees. The fire back at camp was a dull glow behind them now.

He glanced at Tate. "You said you knew him. Grim. Elias. Whatever name he's wearing now."

Tate didn't answer right away. He rocked on his heels, cracking a twig beneath. His eyes had gone hard.

"Better than anyone," he said finally. "'Cause I was the one who followed him into the dark."

Daniel blinked. "You said you were his apprentice."

Tate gave a small, humorless laugh. "Yeah. That, too. At least it's what he called it."

He leaned forward, forearms on his knees, staring into the fog. "But we were friends once. Before all this. Before he forgot how to be human."

They sat in silence for a beat. The wind sighed through the crooked trees, and the distant sound of dripping water echoed like the ticking of a too-slow clock. A raven cawed somewhere beyond view, the sound carrying unnaturally in the still air.

Daniel broke the silence, his voice low but firm.

"Tell me the truth. All of it."

Tate stared into the dark, jaw tight with memories he would clearly rather forget.

"Elias…" He stopped, shook his head. Started again. "He was brilliant. Too damn brilliant for his own good. Thought he could fix everything, save everyone." His voice dropped. "Thought he was supposed to."

Daniel swallowed hard. "So, what happened?"

"Lost a kid first. Eight years old, fever wouldn't break." Tate's hands clenched. "And this woman. Pregnant. She and the babe both gone before he could…" He trailed off, eyes unfocused.

"And then what happened?" Daniel prompted gently.

Tate's voice cracked. "He lost someone he loved." He wiped his mouth with the back of his hand. "That's when he… when he decided death wasn't gonna win anymore. Not on his watch."

"So, he made a deal."

Tate nodded once, slow and heavy.

"It started with books. Old ones. And…" Tate gestured vaguely, trying to find the right words. "Alchemy, sure, but then the things you don't come back from. Rituals. Blood. I helped him, God help me. Didn't know what we were doing until it was too late."

Cold vapor curled from Daniel's mouth when he spoke.

"So, he made a deal. With who?"

Tate didn't answer at first. He stared through the trees as if the dark might overhear.

Finally, quietly: "He didn't bargain with a person, Daniel. He bargained with a place."

Daniel felt the Hollow lean in around them.

Tate continued, voice rough. "The Hollow listens when you're desperate enough. It answers. It offers. And Elias… he answered back. Carved the circles. Lit the candles. Read the words. He needed a sacrifice to bind the deal. Human.

"Let me guess," Daniel said, connecting the pieces. "You were the sacrifice."

Tate snorted, but there was no humor in it.

"Not at first. I helped him. I held the knife. I drew the symbols. Thought it was just another desperate swing at immortality."

"But it worked." The implications settled in Daniel's gut like stones.

"Oh, it worked. But not the way he wanted." Tate leaned back against the crooked tree behind him, his eyes reflecting the distant firelight. "The man I knew died that night. And what took his place wasn't him. Not anymore."

Daniel's thoughts tumbled, scattered by what he was hearing, by the terrible parallels to his own situation.

"And you believe I should know all of this now. Why? How does this help any of us?"

"Because you're next." Tate didn't sugarcoat it; his tone was as blunt as a hammer blow. "You've got the same glint in your eye. The one he used to have. The spark of rebellion. And Grim's gonna try to shape it into a weapon. Or break it entirely."

Daniel looked at the fog, realizing for the first time it wasn't simply weather but something sentient, patient. Hungry.

Daniel shook his head, a reflexive denial. "I'm not like him."

"Not yet," Tate agreed. "But you could be. He's countin' on it. He's watchin' you closer than you know. And worse? The Hollow's watchin' too."

Daniel looked at the trees, at the fog that never lifted, sensing for the first time the mist wasn't simply weather but a sentient, patient, hungry entity.

"So Grim made a deal with the Hollow," Daniel said slowly.

Tate's eyes grew distant, looking at something beyond the physical realm."

"With somethin' ancient that lived here. I don't know its name. Don't want to know." Tate shuddered. "It gives you what you think you want, but the price..." He trailed off, then forced himself to continue. "You never leave this place. You become part of it."

Daniel's voice dropped to a whisper, the words coming from beyond conscious thought.

"The Reaper."

Tate glanced around instinctively, as if saying the words might summon unwanted attention.

"Grim is the Reaper now. But he's not free. He's just the hand that swings the blade. And every time he collects a soul, that thing tightens its grip."

Daniel looked at his hands. They didn't shake, but they were heavier than before. Like they belonged to someone else now, and he needed permission to use them.

"He wants you to take his place," Tate said, the words falling between them like stones in still water.

Daniel flinched. "How do you know that?"

"'Cause I was supposed to." Tate's voice was barely audible now, weighted with decades of regret. "He offered me the mantle when it started wearin' him thin. Told me it would be an honor. A release." He spat into the dirt.

"I told him to rot. And I've been on borrowed time ever since."

Daniel's chest rose and fell with shallow breaths as the implications settled fully.

"So, if I say no, what happens?"

Tate looked at him, eyes hollow but fierce with a survivor's determination.

"Then you fight like I did. But if you say yes, if you take what he offers? You'll lose yourself. Piece by piece, until the only thing left in you is a mirror image of him."

They were quiet for a long time. The wind rustled through the grass. A low creak echoed too close.

A velvety voice tickled Daniel's ear.

You already know how this ends.

Daniel jolted upright. "Did you hear that?"

Tate went rigid, suddenly alert. "No. But I felt it."

Daniel stood, clearly shaken by the disembodied voice. "It's not just him anymore, is it?"

"No," Tate said grimly. "It's the Hollow. It listens."

Daniel clutched his mother's shawl tighter.

"Then I need to get her out of here. Before it's too late."

Tate's expression was pained, skeptical. "No one leaves the Hollow, boy. You know that."

"But they do leave the Hollow. I saw them. Visitors walked through the Meadow and just... left."

"Them that are meant to go, I suppose." Tate rubbed his chin in reflection.

"She didn't belong here in the first place," Daniel insisted. "She still has unfinished business back in our world. She's a Visitor. There has to be a way."

"There might be a way," Tate conceded. "But the price..."

He trailed off, leaving the warning unspoken.

Daniel squared his shoulders, his jaw set with the same determination that had brought his mother to this place.

"Whatever it costs, I'll pay it. But not her. She goes home."

Daniel lay in bed, staring out the window at the full moon, its light breaking through the mist in flashes of electric blue. Wisps of fog clung to the cabin walls. He had insisted his mother stay here, in the Misfits' cabin where he could keep watch, close enough to hear her breathing in the next room.

Images of old horror movies came to mind—*The Blob* specifically. That formless, hungry mass wasn't so different from the fog here, drifting in soupy droplets that swallowed anything unlucky enough to meet them.

Once again, Daniel had the feeling he was missing something important. A purpose, maybe. Something he should be doing. When he tried to dig into the back of his mind for the memories still returning in fragments, it was as if a door slammed shut, locking away crucial pieces. A strange tingle crept along his neck, as if the universe was trying to get him to notice that whatever it was, it was pivotal. He had to figure it out. And soon.

But he was tired. Numb. His mind was wrapped in a fog thicker than the one outside. He needed rest. Maybe tomorrow he would remember whatever it was he was supposed to.

He fluffed his saggy pillow, pulled the dirty quilt to his chin, and snuggled into the relative warmth of the cot. His arms were ice-cold, despite the bandages covering the wounds from the minions' claws. He briefly considered getting up to fetch a long-sleeved shirt, but the idea of crawling back out of the covers into the chilly air made him hesitate just enough. Before another thought crossed his mind, he was asleep.

And he dreamed.

He dreamed of ravens, perched in the gnarly branches of bare trees, their raspy "kraa, kraa" echoing in the stillness of the night. They shared secrets he couldn't comprehend. Warnings, maybe. Omens, definitely. Except he couldn't figure them out.

He dreamed of faceless, robed figures, drifting toward him on mist-covered boats, floating on a dark, endless sea. They beckoned him to join them, their arms outstretched, their forms flickering between solid and vapor.

And he dreamed of sorrow. Of loneliness. Of pain. Of his mother's face, illuminated by headlights, her eyes wide with fear in the moment before weightlessness carried him through the starlit sky.

He dreamed of the moon. Massive and full, like polished silver in the sky. A symbol of completion. Of intention. A moon hanging so close he could almost reach out and pluck it from the sky.

There was meaning in his dreams. Clues to the answers he was seeking. A mystery to solve. And he studied each scene, each shadow, as though his life depended on it. He had to decipher them to return to some semblance of normalcy, whatever normal was.

He stood in a corridor lined with doors. Each one pulsed faintly with light behind the seams, and from each, a whisper leaked through: laughter, weeping, screams. All too familiar.

The door nearest to him creaked open.

Inside: a kitchen. Warm light. His mother hummed as she stirred something on the stove. He stepped toward her, drawn like a child to comfort.

But when she turned, her eyes were empty. No whites, no irises. Only vacant black sockets, and her mouth moved without sound. The warmth vanished. Her face flickered. Her figure warped.

He stumbled back.

The kitchen dissolved.

Another door opened. A boy, much younger, sat in a hospital bed, clutching a stuffed animal. He watched this Daniel with a pleading expression, lips moving silently. *Don't forget me.*

He reached for the boy, but the bed burst into flames. Smoke filled the hallway, choking and thick. The walls warped. The doors shrank. The hallway stretched on forever.

Daniel ran.

The corridor narrowed, the floor slick beneath his feet, his reflection warping in the walls around him. He saw himself as Gobbler, cold-eyed, unfeeling. Then as Daniel, frightened and bleeding. Then as a creature with a crown of bone and eyes like Grim's.

"No!" he shouted. "That's not me!"

But the Hollow disagreed.

A final door stood before him, larger than the rest. Blackened, rusted. It opened slowly on its own.

And inside was the Meadow.

But not like he remembered it.

The grass was dead. The stream ran black. A figure stood with its back to him, tall and still. Not Grim, but similar.

The figure turned.

Daniel looked at himself, clad in a black robe, eyes empty of emotion. Worn and beaten. His eyes shone with the same fire that lived in Grim's. And in his hand, he held the scythe.

The two Daniels stared at each other.

The second one—the Reaper—tilted his head. "There is no version of you that walks away," he said.

Daniel screamed.

He bolted upright in the dark, drenched in sweat. His cry caught in his throat, his ears ringing with the sound of the Hollow. The cabin was dark, its fire having long since died. It was quiet, the others seemingly asleep, and the woods unnervingly still.

But his heart kept racing. And he knew. Something had changed. Something had woken up.

The night stretched on, a restless blur of dreams and wakefulness. He drifted in and out of fitful sleep, caught in an endless cycle of exhaustion. When he finally stirred again, the first pale hints of morning crept through the window, though the light did little to chase away the heavy gloom. Another day in the Hollow, as bleak and unrelenting as all the others.

He threw the covers back and sat up. Might as well start the day.

There was change in the air. He could feel it. The fog. The dreams. The warnings.

They hadn't left him.

One, especially, rang louder than the rest. A child's voice, strange and clear as glass:

"Your mom is very, very sick, Daniel. If she doesn't get well soon, she will die. It's not her time yet. You have to help her find her way back to the world. Your family still needs her."

The words echoed in his mind, taking root, blooming into comprehension. It wasn't just about him anymore. It wasn't even just about his mother being in danger here. She was sick—dying—in the real world. Her body was failing while her spirit wandered the Hollow, searching for him.

She had come here to save him. Now it was his turn to save her.

Daniel rose and moved to the window, looking out at the dawn breaking over the Hollow. His mother slept only a few steps away, but something in the air told him she was slipping farther away from him all the same. Slipping beyond the mist and shadows. Beyond the Hollow itself, a world waited. Their world, where they both belonged.

Grim wanted him to stay. To become something monstrous. To take his place.

But Daniel had found something stronger than Grim's will, stronger than the Hollow's pull. He had found his name. His memory. His purpose.

The Talon from the raven tree sat on the small table beside his bed. He picked it up, feeling its weight, its strange power. A key, the raven had called it. Every key unlocks a door.

Daniel closed his fingers around it, determination hardening within him like steel being forged. The Talon pulsed faintly in his grip, warm against his skin. A reminder that answers existed, if only he could find them.

He looked toward where his mother slept, her breathing finally steady among the Misfits who had agreed to watch over her. The faint rise and fall of her chest steadied something in him. She was safe, for now. But safety wasn't enough. Every moment they stayed in the Hollow was another moment closer to losing her forever. Here and in the world beyond.

The dreams had shown him the truth; time was running out. She was dying while her spirit searched for him in this place. And Grim's game was only beginning.

Outside, the Misfits moved quietly around the dying fires. Kess had only just returned from a perimeter sweep, her face pale and jaw tight as she reported that two more had been taken by the shadows along the trail.

The message was loud and clear.

Grim was growing tired of playing with his Misfit toys. He was preparing to create new ones. Puppets that would bend to his will instead of biting back.

Daniel secured the Talon in its sheath at his hip and rose. The Hollow held secrets. Doors could be unlocked, paths led home. He couldn't find them by sitting still.

"*I'll take care of you, Mom,*" he promised. "*I'll get you home.*"

But first, he had to find the way.

13

Whispers in the Mist

Kess's voice lingered from earlier: "We lost two more. The shadows pulled them right off the trail."

His arms still throbbed from the fight, the ghost of impact pulsing through muscle and bone. The ache was worse for what it meant—he had learned he could harm another and feel no fear or remorse in doing so. The Talon burned against his palm. A key, the raven had said. Every key unlocks a door. But which door? And where?

He tried to stay close, to keep watch as he had promised. But the restlessness had grown unbearable, clawing at him until he had to move. He had to search, to find the way out before it was too late. His mother was dying in the real world while her spirit wandered here. He couldn't save her by sitting still.

The Talon grew hot against Daniel's hip, pulsing with unfamiliar energy. He pulled it from its sheath. It vibrated in his palm, responding to something unseen, causing his teeth to ache and his vision to blur at the edges.

Daniel moved through the Hollow, barely disturbing the mist around him. The moss gave way underfoot, damp and spongy, muffling his steps in a silence that felt unnatural. He had been walking toward the Misfit camp, certain of the leaning gate with its rusty iron teeth, the broken gravestones, the guttering blue lanterns. But now, there was nothing. No gate. No lights. No sound.

It was a different version of the Hollow.

The Talon went silent, and Daniel slipped it back into its sheath with a mental note to figure out what the hell that was about later. Behind him, something rustled. A wet, sliding sound like fabric being dragged through mud. When he turned, there was nothing, only the impression of movement dissolving into shadows.

The silence thickened, clinging to his skin like damp cloth. Even the air had changed, dense and clinging, tasting of copper and decay. The Hollow's usual symphony of rattling chains and wind through cracked branches had vanished, replaced by something worse: the sound of his own pulse, magnified, echoing back from invisible walls that seemed to close in with each heartbeat.

Daniel slowed. His hand brushed against blackened bark, startlingly brittle and cold. Yet it was soft underneath, like rotting flesh barely held together by charred skin.

He whispered without meaning to, "Where is everyone?"

The question fell dead, but somewhere in the distance, something giggled, high and broken, the sound a child might make while pulling wings off flies.

The Hollow was cruel, yes. It lied and stalked and lured you with memory before tearing you open. But it had never been hungry like this. Never this patient. As though the entire place had gone dormant, crouching just beyond sight, savoring the anticipation.

Waiting to feed.

He turned slowly, eyes tracing the monochrome landscape. Ash, bark, stone. Pale thorns veining the dirt like exposed nerves. Nothing moved, but the shadows were all wrong, falling upward in places, bending toward him like fingers reaching from underground graves.

Yet the hair on the back of his neck stood. He was being watched. Not the way Grim watched, or even the Misfits when they thought he didn't notice.

This presence was older. More patient. It moved against him like mist curling through a locked door—curious, hungry, tasting him with invisible tongues that left trails of ice along his spine.

His fingers curled around the Talon in his pocket. Still silent. Just cold metal, as if it had gone deaf to the Hollow's voice.

From the corner of his eye, he caught a flash of movement.

A shadow skimming above the ground. Low, sinuous, gone the moment he turned to follow it. But not before he glimpsed what might have been teeth, white and needle-sharp, grinning in the darkness.

His chest tightened, breath coming shorter.

"Okay," he said to himself, trying to act braver than he felt. "Not creepy at all."

But the words were muffled, swallowed up by the fog. And from somewhere behind the trees came an answering whisper. His own voice, echoing back what he said, *"Not creepy at all... not creepy... not..."*

The echo stretched, distorting, until it sounded like screaming.

He kept moving, each step felt like an invasion into a sleeping predator's mouth. The ground had warmed, heat rising from below like the sigh of a sleeping dragon. The Hollow, though still and silent, had begun to burn inwardly with septic heat.

A ridge rose ahead, veiled in leafless trees whose branches moved with no wind, gesturing him forward like bone-white fingers. He climbed, one hand trailing across bark that crumbled under his fingers. At the crest, he stopped, stunned by what he saw.

Below lay a clearing, eerily still. The half-fallen trees bent inward, and in the center bloomed a ring of pale, delicate flowers. Even as he watched, their petals opened and closed like tiny mouths gasping for air.

Nestled within them lay a small, shallow pool, silver and smooth as glass. Something moved beneath the surface, a restless tension just below the stillness. Ripples moved across in delicate patterns that resembled script. The ghost of a face or a hand appeared in the wavelets and faded away again.

Daniel frowned. Clear water in the Hollow was rare. It normally trickled with blood-warm sludge, twisted reflections into snarling teeth or sobbing children. But this was clean and still, unnerving in its purity—too clean.

He stepped forward, drawn by compulsion that felt like invisible hands pulling his strings. The pool did not stir.

Neither did the Hollow.

But somewhere, something began to hum. A low, subsonic vibration that made his skin itch.

The moment Daniel stepped into the clearing, the air changed.

The pressure in the clearing lightened, releasing the smell of roses and grave dirt. The flowers around the pool turned toward him, their pale faces tracking his movement with predatory focus.

He paused, skin prickling with the sense that he didn't belong here in this moment, as if he had stumbled into a scene written before he was born. A trap set before time began, and he would soon be expelled. Spat back to his own reality.

The pool sat at the center, unnaturally round, its edges too perfect.

He took a step forward. The humming grew louder. Another step, and he heard not one voice, but dozens, harmonizing in frequencies that made his teeth ache and his vision swim.

The moss here was softer. Dense and cool, with strange depth beneath. The scent deepened, smoke and crushed herbs laced with the sweetness of flowers left too long on a grave.

The Hollow did not hold onto warmth, yet this place hoarded it like a treasure.

He knelt at the water's edge, shallow breaths misting in air that had suddenly gone cold. His reflection rose to meet him—familiar features, same unruly hair. But the eyes held a knowing quality that made his stomach clench.

The reflection blinked a fraction of a second after he did.

Daniel pulled back, unease prickling along his spine. A trick of the light, maybe. Or his mind playing games in this strange place.

The pool's surface rippled and blurred, distorting the world behind him. The trees wavered as though an infinite presence was adjusting its vision to see him more clearly. Everything bent subtly, distances stretching and contracting with each blink. Daniel's vision tunneled, the edges softening and graying while the center sharpened to painful clarity.

A high, thin ringing began in his ears, growing louder. The world's frequency shifting off-key, sliding toward pitches that made his skull ache. The clearing grew incredibly large, then shrank impossibly small. His own hands looked far away, then too close, filling his sight with details he had never noticed: every pore, every line, every hair standing on end with electric terror.

The ground beneath him tilted, though his feet never moved. The clearing warped around him, and through the cracks, something else was looking in. And it had his face.

Daniel blinked again, squeezing his eyes shut and counting to three.

When he opened them, the alternate version of the Hollow was gone.

In its place stood the Meadow. The air shimmered with golden motes that, when he looked closely, weren't dust at all but tiny winged things, their faces too small to see but their screams audible as high, sweet music.

The grass undulated in waves, long blades brushing against each other with whispers that almost formed words in a language he had never heard but somehow understood. Words that spoke of hunger and longing and the price of staying.

The pool remained. But around it, the world had transformed into something both beautiful and terrifying.

Blue flowers bloomed where none had before, their petals opening and closing with the rhythm of breathing. A tree stood at the far end, sparkling faintly at the edges as though summoned by fairy dust, its trunk split open to reveal a hollow interior that pulsed with wet, organic sounds.

Daniel turned slowly, taking it in. His pulse had steadied, but his stomach remained tight with the instinctive knowledge that he was looking at a trap. A trap designed specifically for him.

It didn't smell like a meadow at all. It smelled of fresh bread and summer rain. The worn cotton of his mother's sleeve when he buried his face in it to hide. But underneath, always underneath, the smell of rot and decay seeped through. The scent of a life that had been loved so much it had been loved to death.

Daniel longed to stay in this place, to become a part of it. It wanted him to stay. He could feel it.

He felt the embrace of its invisible arms. He felt it in the curve of the path that led nowhere, in the shape of sunlight that warmed but carried no source, in the way the flowers turned toward him, an invitation written in quiet perfection. And in the small bones hidden among the grass roots, the remains of others who had accepted similar invitations.

All thoughts of the Misfits or his mom left his mind, pushed out by drowsiness thick as cotton soaked in honey, sweet and suffocating. It was just him, and the lure of eternal peace, and the growing certainty that if he stayed much longer, he would never want to leave.

Would never be able to leave.

"Daniel?"

The woman's voice wasn't loud, but it landed inside him with the force of a physical blow, shattering the creeping lethargy. He recognized it with a shock that felt like ice water.

This was his mother. The woman he had recently discovered was still alive. The memories that had only just returned. The revelation was still fresh, raw, making every fiber of his being ache with confusion and desperation. Was this a trick? His mom was safe, back at camp.

"Daniel... wake up."

Closer now. Still without a visible source, but carrying an undertone of urgency, of barely controlled panic, as though she were trying to draw him from danger.

His feet moved on their own accord, pulled forward by invisible strings. The grass parted gently, trailing fingers against his calves, the Meadow itself touching him with a thousand tiny hands.

A figure stood beneath a willow that hadn't been there a moment ago or perhaps had always been there, and he had simply failed to see it until this moment. She stood with her back to him, still and centered, hands folded at her waist in a gesture he remembered from childhood, from times when she waited for him to confess some minor transgression.

Her hair caught the sourceless wind—long, brown, exactly as he remembered it. Unaged. Unchanged. Perfect.

Too perfect.

"Mom?" he whispered, the word scraping his throat raw with grief and the fresh wound of knowing she was alive but perhaps lost to him all the same.

She did not turn. But her shoulders tensed slightly, and he heard her draw a slow, careful breath as though she were gathering the courage to show her face to him.

Behind him, the water rippled with a sound like barely suppressed laughter, and Daniel instinctively turned.

The pool had gone black as the inside of a closed coffin. And in that blackness, there was movement.

The murky image of him had changed.

Now it stood upright within the reflective pool, no longer crouched beside him, no longer pretending to be a simple replication. It stared at him with eyes that glowed faint gold. They held too much knowledge, too much awareness of things Daniel had never learned, never experienced. They were the eyes of a stranger that had watched him from birth, that knew every secret thought, every shameful moment, every fear he had never dared to voice.

It tilted its head in a perfectly familiar way, as Daniel sometimes did when working through a complex problem. However, the gesture gave the mirror Daniel a more predatory appearance. Calculating.

"You're not alone," it said, and Daniel felt the words burrow into his skull like parasites, taking root in the soft places behind his thoughts. "You never were. We've been with you since the beginning, waiting for you to see us. Waiting for you to understand what you really are."

The words slithered through the soupy sludge dripping from the swampy reflection. The voice was his, but more articulate, stripped of uncertainty. It was the voice he might have had in another life, in another world, where he had never learned to fear or self-doubt.

It was the voice of a soul that had never been human.

Daniel stepped back, now trapped between two terrifying creatures. His heel landed on an object that crunched like a fragile skull of a small animal. The sound rang out like a gunshot in the emptiness.

The ghostly woman by the tree turned just then, and Daniel saw her face clearly. It was perfect. Every line exactly as he remembered, every freckle in its proper place, every expression precisely copied to trigger his deepest memories of love and safety and home.

She was as beautiful as he remembered. But her eyes...

Her eyes were wild. Frantic. Mad with hunger.

"Daniel," she said, and her voice was exactly right, exactly as it should be, exactly as it had been in life. "Come to me, sweetheart. Come home."

She held out her arms, and he saw her fingers—unnaturally long, bone-pale, ending in needle points. Her smile widened, revealing rows of perfect white teeth that belonged in no human mouth.

Despite every instinct screaming danger, he felt himself taking a step toward her. Because she was his mother, and the part of him that was still a little boy and afraid of the dark needed her to be real.

Even if she wasn't.

Even if she was a thing that had crawled up from the deepest places of the Hollow and learned to wear his mother's face like a mask.

"That's right," she whispered, voice warm as honey and twice as sweet. "Come to Mama. Let me take care of you. Let me make everything all right."

Behind her, the tree split open with a wet, tearing sound, revealing a hollow interior that pulsed with organic rhythm. Inside, Daniel caught glimpses of other faces; perhaps they were other mothers, other lovers, other figures from the deepest memories of the lost and desperate souls who had wandered into this place seeking comfort.

All of them were smiling. All of them were hungry.

All of them waited.

"Wake up, Daniel. Wake up before it's too late."

The Hollow returned like a curtain being yanked away. Heavy and cruel and dank, yes, but also honest in its malevolence. At least here, the things that wanted to hurt him didn't pretend to love him first.

And he knew, with the certainty of absolute terror, that something waited for him in the deeper places—watching, learning, growing stronger with each step he took into its domain.

Awareness prickled along his arms. He could sense the shape he cast in unseen dimensions, shadows that moved independently of his body, reality warping around him like water disturbed by predators circling beneath.

He did not know if what he had seen was memory, illusion, or warning. But a truth had been spoken in that place of beautiful lies.

And he had heard it.

The question was, what was he going to do about it?

Far from the Meadow's faded whispers, something darker stirred in the Hollow's depths.

The Keep groaned, its spires clawing upward in steep, unnatural spirals that hurt to look at directly—bone-white and streaked with rusted crimson that pulsed like exposed arteries. These were towers grown from fossilized grief, from the cruel despair of lives that had ended badly and been forgotten. Every inch of stone remembered something—screams soaked into mortar until they became part of the structure itself, names forgotten by the world but etched into the floor beneath a thousand silent footfalls, the echo of final prayers that had gone unanswered.

Inside, the air writhed, thick with whispers in languages that predated human speech. The walls trembled with subtle, living rhythm while veins pulsed just beneath the surface, carrying something that might have been blood if blood could think, could desire, could remember every atrocity it had witnessed.

At the center of the fortress, beneath the highest arch of the tallest spire, Grim stood in his Sanctum.

The chamber murmured around him like a living thing, but his presence filled the space with a heaviness born of suggestion, reality itself bent slightly inward toward him. The folds of his long, black coat hung, untouched by the subtle wind that stirred everything else, the fabric woven from compressed shadows and the threads of forgotten souls.

His eyes were fixed on the mirror floating before him, suspended by an invisible force, held in place by will alone.

Its shape shifted subtly in his peripheral vision, edges flowing like mercury. The mirror's surface rippled with spectral faces, their mouths open in silent screams. The glass itself was crafted from the remnants of Grim's tortured souls.

Grim raised one hand. The muscles in his forearm tightened, stifling his impatience; his movements were slow and deliberate. Each finger moved across the surface of the mirror in a controlled sequence.

The glass convulsed. A straight fracture split down the center. The crack pushed past the surface, opening a thin seam in the air beyond.

The sound tore through the Sanctum in a sharp, unnatural ripple, the walls and floor vibrating from the impact. Below, in the buried oubliettes, the souls answered at once. Their voices rose in a thin, piercing chorus that cut upward through the stone.

Grim heard them as he always did, and he didn't flinch. His hand hung over the fracture, fingers splayed in a steady, controlling hold. He held the screams and the silence beneath, managing both without effort.

"He's in the Meadow again," he said, his voice low and even. There was no hostility, only cold curiosity.

The mirror darkened at the edges. The black pushed inward, erasing the surface as it went, until the glass showed nothing at all.

The glass collapsed inward as it darkened, shedding thin fragments that drifted to the floor.

Beneath the black surface, shapes began to form. They distorted into faces that flickered and faded—a girl with hollow eyes who had died calling for her mother, a soldier with no mouth who had choked on his own blood, a child who had forgotten how to breathe in the moments before the water closed over his head. Each surfaced on the edge of recognition, then broke apart and sank back into the dark.

Footsteps approached behind him. Stone on stone. Measured and precise.

Grim did not turn. He never did. Turning suggested uncertainty, and uncertainty was a luxury he could not afford.

Digger stood at the chamber's edge, hands folded behind his back, the picture of practiced patience. Always watching. Always quiet. His outline sifted in the fractured light of the darkening mirror—not from uncertainty, but from the weight of the knowledge he carried.

He had been standing there for longer than Grim had acknowledged—hours, perhaps, or days. Time in the Sanctum stretched to fit Grim's will.

Grim spoke without raising his voice. "Find out what he saw."

A brief pause followed. Then, as if it were a minor detail, Grim added, "And if Alice was with him."

Digger hesitated for a moment too long. It meant complications. And answers Grim would not welcome.

He answered in the same low drawl he had used for years. "Of course."

Grim turned now. Just enough to let Digger know he had noticed the hesitation. The gesture alone was sufficient reminder of the imbalance of power between them.

His gaze was stern and cold, carrying within it the promise of consequences for those who failed to meet expectations.

"Daniel is no longer wandering," Grim said. "He's already changing."

Digger tilted his head—acknowledgement without agreement.

"That's dangerous," Grim added, and there was something in his tone now that hadn't been there before. Not fear—Grim had moved beyond such simple emotions long ago—but recognition. The acknowledgment of a threat he couldn't fully control.

There was no malice in his voice. Only certainty.

Digger let the silence stretch, weighing the implications. Then he asked, soft but steady, "To him? Or to you?"

The question hung in the air between them longer than it should have, heavier than mere words had any right to be. No weight to it in terms of challenge or accusation—Digger was far too careful for that—nonetheless, a probe designed to test the boundaries of what could be safely discussed.

Grim's lips pulled into an expression of no clear intent. A memory of a face he had once worn when he had been human, when the concepts of amusement and contempt had held meaning for him.

"To everything," he said, and the words carried with them the gravity of prophecy, of endings that had been set in motion long before Daniel had ever set foot in the Hollow.

He turned back to the mirror. It was still breaking, the cracks spreading outward from the first fracture. Hairline splits webbed across the surface, each one widening the damage.

Every new split hummed faintly, singing in waves that made the air vibrate, glass tuning itself to frequencies that existed only in the spaces between time.

Behind the growing web of cracks, darker shapes stirred. Closer now than they had been before. More distinct. They gathered at the surface as if sensing a barrier thinning.

Grim's smile vanished. His hand dropped to his side, fingers curling once before settling into stillness. Controlled and deliberate as always.

"Let's see how far he gets," he said, his eyes still on the mirror. "Before the Hollow decides to take him back."

The Sanctum answered with a low hum, the stone reacting to the mirror's collapse. Cracks widened, revealing more of what was waiting behind the glass.

And far below, so far that their voices were barely whispers carried on wind that had forgotten how to be gentle, the souls screamed again.

This time, Grim did smile.

Daniel stood at the edge of where the Meadow had been, lungs tight, the reflection's words still trailing behind his thoughts.

"A little far from home, aren't you?"

Her voice melded into the silence, as if it had always been a part of this place.

He turned to her.

Alice stood a few feet behind him, one hand relaxed at her side, the other curled slightly near her hip, where no weapon rested. There had been no sound. No rustling of her skirt. No brushing through the dry grass. One moment, he had been alone; the next, she was there, as if she had stepped from behind time's curtain.

Something was different about her. The shape of her remained the same—dark hair falling over her shoulder in familiar waves, black lace sleeves frayed just above the elbow, boots worn soft with use—but the air around her shimmered with a faint distortion. Her edges wavered, uncertain.

Daniel studied her face, usually alive with sarcasm, now guarded. Her eyes seemed darker, burdened with hidden knowledge.

"I see you found your way here," she said.

He inhaled, buying himself some time before responding. "What is this place? I mean, beyond it being a way out for worthy souls. What is it, really? There are secrets here."

Alice's gaze slipped past him to the pond. Her arms crossed instinctively, shielding herself from something in the reflection.

"A scar. A wound." Her voice was quieter now. "Ancient beyond memory. It was here before the Hollow, before us."

Daniel heard the tension in her tone but pressed on. "You knew it was here?"

"I've walked it more times than I can count." There was no pride in her voice, just dogged weariness.

Daniel narrowed his eyes.

"You're different here."

Alice didn't respond. He stepped closer, hoping she would tell him he was wrong.

"What are you?" he asked.

Her mouth twitched with resignation. Or fear.

She turned to him fully. When she spoke, her voice was raw at the edges.

"I'm not what Grim tried to make me." The words came too fast, too desperate. She took a deep breath and steadied herself. "But I've changed. I'm not what I was, either."

"What does that mean?"

"It means you're not the only one who doesn't belong here."

They stood together in silence. The pond glinted behind them, its surface obsidian black.

Daniel turned to the water.

His reflection stared back. His own face, calm and ordinary. No supernatural glow. No strange expressions. Just Daniel, breathing and blinking like any normal person.

He looked for Alice's reflection beside his own. Nothing appeared in the water where her image should have been.

He turned to her slowly, pulse quickening.

"Alice," he said. "You're not reflected."

She didn't flinch. "I know."

"Why?"

"I stopped being mirrored a long time ago. Reflections only belong to the living," she said quietly. "And I've spent too long here to count as that anymore."

Her voice was strong and steady, filled with a wisdom that no one so young should have known.

Daniel went rigid.

And then her image flickered—a crack in the illusion.

Her skin dimmed to translucent. Her eyes went flat and lightless. Her face shifted, bones and shadow beneath the surface. Features rearranged themselves. For that instance, she didn't look like Alice.

She looked like something pretending to be Alice.

The moment passed. Alice stood before him again—whole, familiar, composed. But Daniel had seen the truth, and he couldn't unsee it.

He staggered back half a step, every instinct screaming danger, eyes jumping from her face to the water and back again. The reflection, the mouth, the voice, the knowledge—branded itself behind his eyes.

Unnatural. Deformed.

"I saw something in you." Daniel hesitated, looking for the right words. "Just now. The same kind of... I don't know how to explain it. Like something was moving under your skin."

Alice clenched her teeth but didn't deny it. She only watched him, refusing to speak. The tension grew heavier between them.

"You're changing, too, Daniel." Alice's voice took on a prophetic tone. "And the Hollow is changing with you."

She stepped closer. Her voice dropped to a whisper.

"It's watching you closely. The Hollow itself, not just Grim. You'll have to make a choice soon—one we hoped you could avoid. But it's happening, and there's no stopping it now."

Daniel's mind raced with questions, but no words came.

Daniel stepped back from the pool. Everything had changed—his understanding of the Hollow, of Alice, of what was real.

Alice stood nearby, no longer flickering. Her eyes held their familiar guarded look, though Daniel was still processing what she had revealed.

He looked down at the water, hoping the reflection would show him something that made sense. His own face stared back, paler than it once had been. He blinked, and the reflection blinked with him. But the water still showed no trace of Alice's image. He looked away, jaw tightening.

The air had grown colder. Daniel exhaled, watching the mist from his breath disappear.

"I need to go." He directed the words toward the space between them, avoiding her eyes.

She didn't move.

"Then go," she said. "But you'll have to decide soon—what you are. Who you're with."

Daniel flinched.

"That's what this is now?"

"It always was." Her voice was calm, but there was a brittle undertone to it. "You just didn't see it yet."

He couldn't look at her. "Everything's different now."

"Yes," she said. "And it will keep getting worse."

He stepped forward, leaving the pool behind. The path beneath him wasn't the one he had taken in. Nothing in the Hollow ever allowed for symmetry. Still, he recognized pieces. Shadows he had passed before.

He passed beneath an arch of mangled roots and stepped through. The Meadow was gone.

Reality knitted itself back together around him, the Hollow seeping back into place.

Mist uncoiled from the trees. The earth beneath him changed with each step. Daniel pressed on, boots crunching through ash-laced bracken, and didn't look back.

Behind him, where Meadow had met Hollow, the space did not close cleanly. A thin shimmer held in the breach, a silver line, barely there. It flickered once or twice, then vanished.

High above the winding paths and gnarled trees, Grim watched.

He stood on the edge of his high spire, the stone beneath his boots untouched by the decay that claimed everything else in the Hollow. The mirror no longer floated before him. It had shattered hours ago, its purpose served, its fragments scattered to dimensions that existed parallel to sight.

But he didn't need it anymore.

He had Daniel.

Grim's eyes tracked the place where the seam had flickered, where the boundary between what was real and what was possible had failed to seal. A hairline crack left behind when something had not closed as it should.

His expression did not change as he murmured, "He doesn't even realize what he's becoming."

The words carried something colder than curiosity, something that partook of anticipation but was not quite that either. The satisfaction of a plan unfolding exactly as it had been set in motion. Pieces moving across a board in the patterns he had predicted from the start.

The slow, beautiful destruction of something precious, one choice at a time.

Somewhere deeper in the Hollow, after the echoes of Grim's voice had faded, two figures crouched beneath the jagged edge of a ruined wall. The mist churned at their ankles. Their breath smoked in the cold.

"We're not asking him," one said. "He'll say no."

"We need him, whether he likes it or not."

"And if Grim catches us?"

"Then maybe we finally stop running."

Their shapes vanished into shadow a moment later. They didn't look back.

14

Bastion Battle

er footsteps didn't echo through the halls of the Keep. They were muffled, swallowed by the fleshy walls that lined the hallways like bumpers.

Alice stood at the threshold, her pulse thrumming hard beneath her breast. She hadn't been called into the Convocation Hall since her public thrashing. Today felt different. It was too quiet. No guards were posted at the door to announce her arrival.

She hesitated for only a minute and stepped inside. One never knew the mood Grim might be in, so it was best not to keep him waiting, regardless of circumstances.

Grim's voice floated from somewhere deeper in the fortress. Alice sighed with relief. He didn't sound angry. His tone was almost pleasant. Careful. Measured. A glimpse of what he might have been before the Hollow recast him into a villain.

"…They believe they can wound me," he said, his tone tainted with boredom. "The Bastion is weakened. Hollowed from the inside. All it would take is one well-placed strike. Our only defense is fear—to keep them away from the decaying stronghold."

There was a pause. Footsteps shuffling. The rustle of paper, or wings.

One of the minions spoke, voice flat, "Should we reinforce?"

"No," Grim said. "It's too late. The damage is already done."

Another pause. A low sound—perhaps a chuckle, though it sounded rehearsed.

"Let them act on what they think they know."

A beat.

"Let them come," he said, to someone she couldn't see. "The Bastion won't hold. But it will open."

Alice's brows drew together. The phrasing was elegant. Too clear. Too practiced.

Another pause. A nervous shuffling of cloaks and boots.

"And the vault beneath it?" A minion's voice, low and clipped.

"Will break," Grim replied. "Just as we've always known it would. It was never meant to last through eternity."

Alice froze near the entrance arch, one foot still in shadow.

She knew that phrase. *The vault beneath it.* A feared thing whispered in code by older Misfits, only half-believed. She didn't know what was inside. But if Grim meant what he said, it wouldn't matter for long.

"If the boy is with them, though, it could be the end of us."

Something rustled to her left. A servant glided past without acknowledging her. No one looked surprised to see her. No one flinched or reported her presence. And Grim never turned. He just kept speaking as if she were part of the furniture.

That was what unsettled her most.

She backed away, step by step, into the cold of the outer hall. Her heart was pounding now, but not with fear.

With doubt.

Had she just overheard a crack in his defenses?

Or a script he meant her to witness?

She never heard the rest.

She never saw the look he gave the wall where she had been standing a moment before.

By the time she returned to the Misfit camp, dusk had fallen like a curse, swift and merciless, turning the sky the pale blue of corpse skin. The fog sat lower, clinging to the ground. The air smelled faintly of stone and static, like the scent of the Keep had followed her home.

The Misfits all sat around the fire, Kess honing a blade already razor-sharp. Tate leaned against a crumbling log, tracing lines on a map like a man memorizing his own escape route. They looked up when Alice arrived, but didn't ask where she had been.

She sat. Picked at the edge of her coat. The fabric still held the Keep scent. Cold, chemical, strangely sweet. She scratched at it like she could scrub the memory from the weave.

Two more Misfits were missing. No one talked about it. Not tonight.

Say nothing, she told herself. *He wanted you to hear it. Which means it isn't true. You know that.*

But what if it was?

What if, this time, the intel wasn't a manipulation? What if it was a mistake? A thread slipped by accident?

What if they finally had a chance to be freed?

It was Roan who finally broke the silence. "We should hit back. Catch him by surprise."

"We're running out of time," Kess cut in. "Shadows are stalking the borders. They've never done that before."

"No," said Tate. "Not yet."

"Why the hell not? We've waited long enough!"

"Because we don't know what we're walking into. Kess found someone near the dry creek," Tate murmured. "Looked like Tommy. Moved like him. But when he turned... "

No one asked him to finish. No one wanted to hear the rest.

"The Bastion should be our target," Alice's voice was quiet but certain. "He said the structure won't hold. It's now or never."

The group went still.

She felt it. The moment all their weight shifted toward her.

Tate turned slowly. "What?"

She didn't look at him. She wished she hadn't spoken, but she couldn't unsay the words. "I heard it. Today. Grim said... If we struck now, we would breach it. He doesn't think we're ready."

Kess narrowed her eyes. "You were with him?"

Alice gave a small nod. "Summoned. Just… routine. But he didn't know I overheard them."

Roan slammed a fist against the stone. "Then we move now. Before he takes more of us. If we hit the Bastion, we don't just hurt him. We cut off his control."

Tate hesitated. "Or it's a trap."

"Everything's a trap," Kess said. "But that doesn't mean we wait to be picked off like flies." Her gaze slid back to Alice. "Assuming the rot's real."

"It is," Tate said, too quickly. Then, more carefully, "Alice said she overheard some kind of breach. If we're ever gonna pull him off his throne, it starts there."

Alice didn't argue. Couldn't. The words had already left her mouth.

She watched them catch fire in Roan's eyes, settle into a grim purpose in Kess's jaw.

And Tate… Tate was already moving his weight from one foot to the other, the way he always did when preparing for a fight he didn't want but knew was coming.

Alice opened her mouth, then closed it again.

She wanted to call the words back. Wanted to say, *wait*. Wanted to say, *what if it's a lie?*

But part of her believed it, too.

And that part was louder.

The Misfits trudged through the thick fog.

Kess led them in a ragged line, her gauntlets black with soot, her breath misting in the bitter air. Behind her, Tate kept pace despite the stiffness in his stride, his joints protesting the cold. Bren stayed beside him—sharp-eyed, silent, her twin daggers catching what little light filtered through the gray—and the rest followed in a tight cluster.

Elwin brought up the rear, barely more than a boy, his pack clinking with improvised charges and a nervous hum under his breath.

Souls who had decided that going down fighting was better than dying on their knees begging for mercy.

The Bastion rose before them like a jagged, broken tooth. No lights burned in its hollow windows. No guards patrolled its walls. All that broke the silence was the drip of water, faintly smelling of sulfur.

"Too quiet," Kess whispered, raising her fist to halt the group.

Someone shifted behind Bren, a tiny sound in the blanket of fog. It wasn't nerves. It was the space where Daniel should have been. Even if no one said it out loud, the awareness settled over them like another layer of cold. The mood felt heavier without him.

Tate moved up beside her, favoring his right leg. "This is what we wanted. Let's not talk ourselves out of it."

Alice had been right. The intel she had overheard in the Keep: Grim had said the Bastion was hollowed out, weakened from within, a perfect target for a strike that might actually wound him.

Roan crouched near the base of the wall, fingers tracing the ancient stonework. "I can breach it here," he said, pulling out a cobbled-together charge. Old Misfit ingenuity, half-forgotten explosives wrapped in prayers. "Give me thirty seconds."

They had brought thirteen. It wasn't enough, and every one of them knew it. But it was all they had left who could still fight.

Roan pressed the charge against the wall and struck the fuse. A soft hiss, then silence.

Then the wall simply gave way.

Not an explosion. Not even much sound. The stones just crumbled inward as though they had been waiting centuries to fall, revealing a gap large enough for three people to walk through side by side.

"That was too easy," Digger muttered from the back of the group.

Bren slipped through first, moving like smoke, daggers ready. Her voice echoed back a moment later, "Clear. But something's wrong."

They filed in one by one, boots crunching over rubble and something that looked disturbingly like ground bone. The interior was vast. A cathedral of emptiness with pillars that reached too high and cast shadows that didn't follow the light.

Ancient chains hung from the ceiling like dead serpents. A row of desks stood along the far wall, draped in parchment that cracked. Everything was covered in thick dust.

"This was his stronghold?" Kess said, turning slowly in the center of the hall.

Tate ran his hand along the nearest pillar. The stone was cold, but underneath... underneath it pulsed with life. "Doesn't make sense. No guards. No resistance. No..."

His words died as Elwin, one of the younger Misfits, pointed at the floor.

A scorched ring seared into the stone, edges still faintly glowing.

"This is recent," Tate said, almost to himself.

Elwin stepped forward and touched it with the tip of his boot. Nothing happened.

He took another step, placing his full weight on the circle.

His shadow didn't follow.

It stayed behind him, frozen in the moment before he had moved, while his body continued forward. The disconnect was subtle at first, just a heartbeat's delay. Then it became obvious, wrong, like watching someone's reflection decide to live its own life.

"We shouldn't be here," Digger said, his voice holding the conviction of someone who had survived too long by trusting his instincts.

Kess moved to a desk and pulled open a drawer. Inside was a ledger, half-burned but somehow still intact. She opened it carefully. The pages were blank, but not clean. Soaked with something that smelled like ink and copper and regret. Faint, ghostlike impressions lingered where words should have been, washed out or waiting to come to the surface.

She hesitated, fingers trembling. "This shouldn't be here," she whispered. "He kept this in his Sanctum. How the hell did it end up here?"

When she tried to close it, the liquid had already stained her fingers black. She dropped the book, wiping her hands on her coat. But the stains wouldn't come off.

She looked back at the ledger lying on the dusty floor and instinctively snatched it up again. Tearing a scrap of frayed cloth from her coat, she wrapped the ledger and shoved it in her bag. If this place was a trap, she wasn't leaving Grim's secrets behind to feed it.

"It's a memory," Roan said quietly, staring at a cracked mirror propped against one of the pillars. His reflection showed in the glass, but it was older, more weathered, with eyes that had seen things his actual eyes never had. "This whole place. It's not real. It's what the Bastion used to be."

They all felt it, then. It started as pressure behind their eyes. Then a low humming that seemed to come from the stones themselves. The floor beneath their feet trembled, and the pillars leaned inward, like fingers closing around prey.

"Form up!" Kess shouted, but her voice sounded muffled, distant. Then the Bastion struck back.

Shadows bled from the cracks in the walls. They moved with purpose, reaching for the Misfits with tendrils that felt like ice and tasted like despair.

Elwin screamed as one of the shadows wrapped around his ankle. Where it touched, his leg began to fade. He could still move it, but it was more a memory of movement rather than the thing itself.

Bren lunged forward, slashing at the shadow with her daggers. The blades passed through it without resistance, but the shadow recoiled anyway, letting out a sound like wind through empty rooms.

More shapes emerged from the walls. Contorted things that might once have been human but had been stretched and folded by grief until they resembled abstract sculptures of pain. They moved jerkily, like marionettes operated by someone who had forgotten how limbs were supposed to work.

Roan threw a fire charge at the nearest cluster. It exploded in a burst of heat and light, but when the flames died, the creatures were still there, untouched. The fire had burned around them, through them, without ever reaching them.

"They're not really here!" Tate shouted, pressing his back against Kess's as shadows pressed in from all sides. "We're fighting ghosts!"

"Then how do we—" Kess's words were cut off as the floor beneath them turned to quicksand, and they began to sink.

Digger carved a desperate path toward what looked like a door, his sword trailing sparks as it scraped against stone that was becoming less solid by the moment. "There!" he called. "We need out!"

But the exit was already sealing itself, stone flowing like water to close the gap they had entered through.

Bren hurled one of her daggers at the closing wall. It struck true, embedding itself in the stone just as the gap sealed completely. Where the metal touched, cracks spread. Hairline fractures that leaked golden light where the Bastion was coming undone.

"The blade!" Tate yelled. "It's real iron. Forged in the real world! That's why they can't touch it!"

Kess understood immediately. She pulled her sword and drove it into the nearest shadow-creature. This time, when the metal connected, the thing let out a shriek that sounded almost like gratitude as it dissolved.

Working together, they carved a path through the manifestations of old grief and forgotten guilt. Each strike released a soul that had been trapped too long in this place of false memory. The creatures fell away like shed skin, revealing the truth beneath: The Bastion wasn't just empty. It was hungry.

It had been feeding on its own history, digesting and re-digesting the same moments of power and control until they had become a kind of spiritual vomit. A place that existed only to remember what it used to be.

They fought their way to the far wall, where Bren's embedded dagger still leaked cracks of real light into the false stone. Roan placed another charge against the weakened wall while the others held off the pressing shadows.

"This is it!" he called. "Everyone down!"

The explosion was small but precise. The wall unraveled, reality coming apart like old fabric to reveal gray sky beyond.

But getting out was worse than getting in.

Kess took three steps toward the breach before something invisible slammed into her chest. She went down hard, skull cracking against stone, blood streaming from her nose. Her eyes rolled back, showing only white.

"Kess!" Bren lunged for her, hauling her toward the exit as Kess's limbs twitched with unnatural spasms.

Tate tried to follow, but his boot came down on something that looked like ordinary stone. The moment his weight settled, the rock began to smoke. Acid. It ate through his boot, then his sock, then his skin, burning deeper with each heartbeat. He screamed and stumbled forward, leaving bloody footprints that sizzled on the floor.

Near the back, Digger caught a young Misfit as he staggered toward the exit. But the boy's face—half of it was gone. Not torn away, not burned. Just... absent. Like someone had carefully erased the left side of his features, leaving smooth, blank skin where his eye and cheek should have been. He was still conscious, still breathing, but when he tried to speak, only half the words came out.

Digger hefted the young Misfit's weight and pushed toward the breach, his own face grim with understanding. Some wounds couldn't be bandaged.

Behind them, Roan had stopped moving. He stood frozen in the center of the collapsing hall, head tilted at an unnatural angle, eyes wide with terror.

"No," he whispered, backing away from something invisible to everyone but him. "No, please, I didn't mean—I'm sorry. I'm sorry!"

He swung his sword at nothing, tears streaming down his face. Whatever he was seeing, it was worse than anything the rest of them could perceive.

"Roan!" Tate called, limping back despite the acid eating at his leg. "There's nothing there!"

But Roan kept backing away, kept apologizing to shadows only he could see. "I know what I did," he sobbed. "I know what I did to you. Please don't…"

Tate grabbed him, dragging him toward the exit even as Roan fought against invisible hands, screaming at phantoms that followed him from the false memory of the Bastion.

They tumbled through the breach one by one, Bren carrying Kess's unconscious form, Digger supporting the young, half-faced Misfit, Tate dragging the hysterical Roan while his own leg left a trail of blood and smoke.

Behind them, the Bastion sealed itself with deliberate satisfaction. Stone flowed like thick liquid, closing the wound they had torn in its side. The walls contracted, pulling inward with muscular precision, until the breach was gone and the structure looked exactly as it had before.

Like a mouth closing after a satisfying meal.

But they hadn't all made it out whole.

Elwin's shadow-touched leg continued to fade, becoming more transparent with each step until he could barely feel it touching the ground. The young Misfit's missing face showed no sign of returning. Kess remained unconscious, her breathing shallow and erratic.

Tate's acid burns ate deeper, the chemical reaction spreading up his calf despite Digger's attempts to wash it with precious water from their supplies. And Roan… Roan kept looking over his shoulder, flinching from things that weren't there, whispering apologies to the empty air.

And all of them bore the knowledge of what they had learned: they hadn't just failed to strike at Grim's power. They had been fed to it.

15

After the Fall

aniel smelled the blood before he saw the bodies.

The scent hit him as he crested the ridge—metallic and thick, mixed with smoke and ruin. He had been walking without purpose since leaving the Meadow, trying to outpace the silver seam's closure and the memory of what he had seen there. But his feet had carried him here anyway, to an old watch tower the Misfits called the Rook, where they sometimes sheltered.

What was left of it sat in the hills behind the Misfit camp.

The structure had partially collapsed, its north wall blown inward as if a fist had punched through the stone. Scorch marks blackened the remaining walls and rubble in branching patterns. Discarded bandages and debris were scattered across the rubble.

"Jesus," Daniel whispered.

Bodies lay everywhere. Some he recognized: Kess with her ruined gauntlets still strapped to her hands, Bren slumped against a broken beam, eyes staring at nothing. Others were harder to identify, torn apart by gods-only-know-what.

Movement caught his eye, and a figure stumbled from the wreckage, clutching a blood-soaked bandage to his ribs.

Tate.

"Daniel?" Tate's voice cracked on the name. "Where the hell were you?"

Daniel scrambled down the slope, boots sliding on loose stone. "What happened? Why aren't you at the camp?"

"The Bastion... was a trap." Tate swayed on his feet, face gray with blood loss. "We walked right into it. Alice said it was empty, weakened. We thought..." He laughed bitterly. "We thought we could hurt him."

Daniel reached him just as Tate's knees buckled. He caught the older man's weight, feeling how light he had become. "How many?"

"Dead? Five. Maybe six. I didn't count." Tate's breathing was shallow, ragged. "The rest scattered. Some might've made it deeper into the Hollow. Most... " He gestured weakly at the Misfits that were left.

Daniel eased him against a relatively intact piece of wall, scanning the devastation. As Tate settled, Daniel saw how nasty the wound really was. Too much blood. Too deep. The kind of injury that meant he was on borrowed time.

"This wasn't just a trap," Daniel said quietly. "It was an arena. He just set the stage, and ours was the blood he meant to spill."

"Message received." Tate's voice was getting weaker, his skin taking on a waxy pallor. "He's done playing with us."

Daniel turned at the sound of footsteps on stone. Three figures emerged from behind the collapsed wall: Digger, his coat singed and torn; a young woman Daniel recognized but couldn't name, her left arm hanging uselessly at her side; and an older man whose face was smeared with filth and streaked with tears.

They stopped when they saw Daniel. Relief flickered across their faces—quickly swallowed by anger and wounded disappointment.

"So, you came back," Digger said. His voice was flat, empty of its usual sardonic edge.

"I didn't know," Daniel said, defensive without meaning to be.

"Where were you?" The young woman stepped forward, her good hand resting on the hilt of a knife. "We waited as long as we could. You just... vanished."

Daniel's throat tightened. "The Meadow. I was..."

"The Meadow." Digger's laugh was sharp and humorless. "Of course. While we were dying, you were off playing in paradise."

"It wasn't like that."

"Wasn't it?" The older man spoke for the first time, his voice hoarse with smoke and grief. "We needed you. Counted on you. And you were nowhere."

The words hit him like a fist to the gut. Daniel looked around at what remained of the Misfits—six people, maybe seven if Tate lived through the night. A rebellion reduced to scattered survivors and bitter accusations.

"You think this is my fault," he said.

"I think," Digger growled, "that you've been playing both sides so long you forgot which one you're on."

Daniel's hands clenched into fists. "When did I become your leader? I'm nobody! I'm still trying to figure out how to save my mom. And myself."

"No. But you never turned it down, either. Grim's fight is with you. Because of you, we're all expendable to him." He stepped closer, and Daniel could see the exhaustion carved into the lines of his face. "You took the Talon. You walked through Grim's domain as if you owned it. You made him notice us."

"And then you disappeared when we needed you most," the young woman added. "Left us to face what you stirred up."

The accusation stung. Daniel wanted to deny it—tried to tell them about the Meadow, the silver seam, and the pressure of expectations he never asked for. But looking at the devastation around them, the words felt hollow.

"So, what now?" he asked instead.

Tate's breathing had grown more labored, each syllable an effort. "Now? We run. Hide in whatever holes we can find and hope Grim forgets we exist." He coughed, blood flecking his lips. "But you... You don't get to run anymore."

"Tate..."

"Listen to me." Tate's hand shot out, gripping Daniel's wrist with surprising strength. "This isn't over. Whatever you think you are, whatever you're becoming... it matters. Grim knows it, too. Don't let them... "

His grip slackened as a violent cough tore through him, blood trailing down his chin. His eyes clouded, cleared, then dulled again.

Tate moved his mouth to say more, but no words came out. Just a wet rattle from deep in his lungs. Until even the rattle ceased to come.

"Tate?" Daniel shook him gently. "Tate!"

But Tate was gone, his final breath slipped out in a wet, broken sigh. Daniel stared at the man who had been his first ally in this place, who had tried to teach him how to survive, how to fight, how to care about something beyond his own desperate need.

The silence stretched until Digger's tight voice cut through it.

"That's on you," he said quietly, reigning in his emotion. "He died because you weren't here."

"Like hell." The young woman's voice was defiant. "They died for nothing if we just crawl away."

"They died because we were stupid," Digger said. "Because we thought we could fight a god with sticks and stones."

"We thought we had a weapon." Her eyes were fixed on Daniel. "We still do. He just has to be willing to fight."

Daniel felt their stares. Desperate hope tangled with bitter resentment, and beneath it all, the raw grief of watching Tate die. His absence had cost them more than any battle ever could.

"I'm not your weapon," he said quietly, his voice hoarse.

"Then what are you?" Digger's question cut through the space between them. "Because right now, all I see is a liability."

Daniel looked at them all—broken, exhausted, mourning. He thought of Tate's final words, the faith that had died with him. He thought of Grim in his tower, playing games while good people bled. He thought of the Meadow and its impossible peace, purchased with the suffering of everyone he had left behind.

"I'm someone who got in too deep," he said finally. "Someone who made you believe I was more than I am."

The young woman stepped forward, tears cutting tracks through the ash on her face. "Tate believed in you. Even at the end. Are you really going to make his death meaningless?"

Daniel met her eyes, seeing the same desperate faith that had gotten Tate killed, that would get her killed too if he let it continue.

"His death is already meaningless," Daniel said, the words like glass in his throat. "They all are. Because I'm not who you think I am, and I never was."

Digger made a sound, half laughter, half sob. "So that's it? You're walking away?"

Daniel met his eyes. "I'm stopping this before more people die for my mistakes."

He turned toward the path leading deeper into the Hollow, away from the Rook and its ghosts, away from Tate's still body and the accusations in the survivors' eyes.

Behind him, the young woman called out, "If you leave now, you're as much of a coward as Grim is."

Daniel paused but didn't turn around. "Maybe. But at least I'll be an honest one."

The Hollow swallowed his footsteps as he walked away from the wreckage, leaving the survivors to their grief and their anger and their impossible choices. He carried Tate's final words with him—the dying man's faith, his belief that Daniel mattered, that this wasn't over.

But faith, Daniel had learned, was just another way of getting people killed.

Above, a raven circled once and disappeared into the gray sky, carrying news of another ending to whatever powers watched from the edges of this broken realm.

Daniel walked until he could no longer hear their voices, until their expectations finally released their grip on him. Only then did he stop, leaning against a twisted tree, and letting the truth settle with all its weight:

He wasn't their savior. He had never been their savior.

And Tate had died believing a lie.

16

The Shimmer and the Weight

They had hauled the injured back from the Rook in the dark, dragging and carrying whoever still breathed. The camp was quieter now, but the wounds remained raw. Daniel stepped away from the cabins, needing distance from the voices inside.

They weren't arguing anymore. Not exactly. Just frayed, exhausted voices planning war when they had nothing left but anger. He didn't go far, just far enough for their grief and fear to fade into a dull murmur behind him.

The cold bit deeper than usual. The Hollow was always cold, its wind dry and its shadows long, but this was different. This cold pressed inward, seeping through his skin and into his bones.

He pulled his coat tighter around his shoulders. The fabric had grown thin, frayed at the cuffs, and torn along one seam. It didn't matter when the chill wasn't coming from the air. It was coming from the world itself.

He stopped beside a ring of dead trees. Their blackened trunks, hollowed and split, rose from the cracked earth like old bones. Fire had touched them once, long ago, and nothing had grown back since. Nothing grew there anymore, not even the rot.

The ground here was dust-dry, grooved with deep scars. Still, the mist curled low across the ground, thin, white, moving too slow to be wind and too quick to be natural. It drifted around his boots like curious fingers before fading back into the cracks of the earth.

Daniel raised his left hand. The one he had touched the Meadow with. It shimmered.

The skin tingled—a sensation like the moment before pins and needles, but pleasant and warm. The pale luminescence pulsed with his heartbeat, visible one moment and gone the next as he rotated his wrist through a shaft of weak light. Not a glow—more like something alive under the skin trying to surface. Gossamer threads of silver traced his veins, making them visible in strange, asymmetrical patterns. Where the shimmer was strongest, the skin felt warmer, almost feverish. If he concentrated, he could hear a sound too high and faint for ordinary ears, like crystal struck from miles away.

He flexed his fingers, and the light retreated.

Alice's voice slid across his mind: *You're changing. And the Hollow is changing with you.*

He didn't understand what she meant. Not fully. But he could feel it, now. Moving under his skin like a presence burrowed deep. His body hummed in tune with its pulse.

He crouched and touched the earth.

Cold. Dry. Silent. Yet under the silence, his fingertips caught a faint vibration—a heartbeat migrating from somewhere beyond the dead forest.

He didn't need to look in that direction. He knew where it came from. The Meadow's presence lingered there, just out of sight. Whispering to him of possibilities.

He closed his eyes.

Listened.

No message came. No vision. Just a pressure in his chest, the sense of meaning waiting just beyond comprehension. The Meadow didn't give answers. It gave direction. Intention. And maybe that mattered more.

He rose slowly, brushing the dirt from his knees. The Hollow stretched before him again, gray fog swallowing the horizon, cabins sagging under the weight of too many rebuilds, shattered ruins slumped between bone-pale trees. Everywhere, remnants. Of bodies. Of ideas. Of rebellions that had burned out years before any of them had arrived.

Walls meant for safety. Weapons intended for war.

He wondered what the Hollow had been before Grim, before it became this unbearable prison, this maze of contracts and punishment. Was it always a ruin? Or had something broken it? The ground seemed to hold memories—not just of those lost here, but of what the place itself had lost, a grief older than the souls who wandered it.

Tate's face surfaced unbidden—ashen, unmoving, the last of his breath slipping out like a secret.

Daniel shut his eyes hard. He hadn't let himself feel the pain. Not then. Not yet. But guilt settled just below his ribs, cold and heavy.

So many were slipping away. And those who stayed behind were fraying at the seams. What if he couldn't hold them together? What if he wasn't meant to?

He didn't know. But he had begun to believe the Meadow wasn't part of this place. Not entirely. It felt older. Or newer. Or truer.

A remnant of before, perhaps. Or a fragment of what was meant to come after.

Either way, it didn't follow Grim's rules. And Daniel was tired of playing by them.

The Misfits only saw blood and smoke and vengeance. And who could blame them? They had lived too long with knives at their throats, waking every day in a cage that looked like freedom.

But they were looking a little too far into the dark.

The real battle wasn't in the Bastion or the fortress or in corpses stitched together and pressed back into war. Grim fed on loops of suffering. On predictable wounds.

But the Meadow whispered in a different language. Daniel just didn't know how to speak it yet.

A gust rose behind him, low and mournful. It swept across the ground and struck the nearest cabin with a hollow thud. The whole structure groaned, beams straining. Inside, the Misfits kept planning, counting supplies. Stitching wounds. Shaping grief into something useful.

He didn't turn back.

They believed they were ready and that they could finally make a difference.

But nothing would change unless *he* did.

Daniel looked at his hand again. Silver light pulsed under the surface of his skin like a second heartbeat.

This time, he didn't hide it. Tate was gone. There was no one left to shield him. Just this—whatever it was, whatever he was becoming.

17

The One He Fears

"You can't save them all." The words drifted in like mist, soft and inevitable.

Daniel didn't turn. He didn't need to. Alice never simply approached someone. She merely appeared, as if the world suddenly remembered it hadn't already placed her there. He felt her before he saw her, the Hollow hushing around her presence.

She stood a few paces behind him, arms folded, hair in elegant disarray, one boot dragging idly through grit: indecision, or the performance of it.

"I figured you would show up eventually." Daniel didn't bother to hide his annoyance.

"You make a habit of brooding dramatically in ominous landscapes." Her voice carried a hint of dry humor, but it fell flat tonight. "It's like ringing a bell." Neither of them smiled.

Daniel turned to face her. Her eyes had that familiar glassy sheen, but tonight they looked older. Already knowing how this would end.

"They're going to get themselves killed," he said.

Alice looked beyond the fog-blurred horizon. The Hollow stretched out like a dreamscape. A place that one only visits when one closes her eyes.

"They know." Her breath didn't fog in the cold. A detail Daniel hadn't noticed before. It dawned on him there was a lot he was learning about Alice that he hadn't noticed before.

Daniel shook his head. "They think they're being brave. But they're not. They're desperate. That plan? It's not a battle strategy. It's a suicide mission."

"And yet they built it together," she murmured. "You think you can come up with something better? On your own?"

"You don't know me as well as you think you do. I'm not trying to be a hero. I have my own selfish reasons for wanting to dethrone Grim."

"No, not a hero," Alice said, eyes narrowed. "You're trying to outsmart him. And you're right, it's not the same thing." Her voice dropped. "That's what makes you a danger to yourself, and to all of us. You think you have all the answers and that you can do this alone. What you don't realize is that's Grim's strategy. You might have knowledge and a little bit of power, but those weapons won't do you any good against him on your own."

Daniel frowned. "You think I'm a danger to you? You're one to talk. I'm not the one keeping secrets."

"Aren't you? I think the moment you believe you're not dangerous," she cut in, "is the moment you get us all released. And in the most brutal way you could ever imagine. You haven't begun to see Grim's wrath."

The space between them stretched like old wire. Daniel searched her face, but her mask was in place again—perfect and unreadable, worn for longer than he had been alive.

"You could help them," he said. "Help me. You know this place better than anyone. You've survived it."

"I know how it breaks people." Her shoulders sagged. She pushed the heels of her hands into her temples, rubbing the tension away as best she could. The icy bitterness had left her and she was so tired.

"I know what happens to the ones who try to hold it together for everyone else. I wouldn't call that survival."

"That's not a no."

"Daniel... you still think they're looking for truth. They're not. They want a martyr who will die for their mistakes. You offer insight, and they'll throw it on the fire and ask if it burns brighter."

He swallowed hard and looked away. She was right. Every word of it sank into him.

"They want revenge," she said softly. "And you—you want answers. You're not even playing the same game."

"Then help me change the game." His voice caught on his words. The fight had drained out of him, leaving only a hollow exhaustion that made his limbs feel like lead.

"Help me understand what the Meadow is really showing me. Why it's changing. Why I'm changing."

It was subtle, but Daniel caught the slight widening of her eyes, the minute stiffening of her shoulders.

"You've seen it too," he said, watching her closely. "The way it changes, the way it pulls at something inside you."

"It doesn't matter," she said. Too quickly. "I've seen many things, Daniel, but brooding on them won't help either of us."

"Alice, it matters to me."

Her composure slipped. The careful mask she had worn for decades cracked. Her eyes widened, her lips parted, and her posture folded in on itself. She looked at him like he was a secret she had once trusted with her whole heart—and the only part of her past that ever tried to love her back. Her fingers spread and then curled as she paced back and forth.

"I've helped you more than you know," she said, her voice dripping with irritation.

"Then help them." Daniel nodded toward the cabin a short distance off. The warm glow of its windows bloomed through the haze.

"They don't trust me after the Bastion incident." Alice's eyes sparkled with unshed tears. "They wouldn't listen to me now."

"They might. Is it that they don't trust you? Or that you don't trust yourself with them anymore?"

"No, Daniel." She stepped closer, close enough that her voice dropped to a whisper. "They'll follow you. They want to trust in you." She hesitated, the words catching in her throat. "That's what they're waiting for. They don't want your kindness or understanding. They want someone who'll take control. Someone who'll shoulder the responsibility if things go wrong."

Daniel's chest warmed. For a terrible heartbeat, he saw himself as they wanted him: standing before the Misfits, Talon gleaming, voice unyielding, a figure lit by flame. The vision carried a seductive gravity, a promise of purpose that excited him.

The vision faded, leaving him cold inside. His fingers bit into his palms, trying to break the spell the feeling cast on him.

"That's not me," he said, but his voice wavered just enough to reveal the lie beneath.

"I hope not." Her words carried the burden of a thousand disappointments.

"I won't become him," Daniel said at last, the words a promise he wasn't sure he could keep.

Alice looked at him for a long moment, tension growing in her jaw. When she finally spoke, her voice had hardened again, becoming the Alice he had known since coming to this place. The one who survived. The one who knew better than to hope.

"That's what makes you a wild card," she said. "And maybe..."

She looked off toward the horizon. "...maybe that's why HE'S afraid of you."

And with that, she turned and walked away until the fog swallowed her.

Daniel watched the space where she had disappeared long after she was gone. The cold wrapped tighter around him, seeping through his clothes to the skin beneath.

He wasn't any closer to the truth. But he wasn't the only one afraid of what the truth might cost.

The Hollow remained silent as Daniel crossed the threshold.

No heads turned. No greetings rose from the scattered figures beneath the cabin's low roof. The space felt smaller than before—walls closer, fire dimmer, shadows thick with unspoken grief. Kess sat near the hearth, cleaning a blade with mechanical precision. Digger rested against the far wall, eyes downcast, working a whetstone against steel in a steady rhythm that matched his breathing. Others paced restless circles, murmured to empty air, or stared at nothing with vacant eyes. None spoke his name.

Daniel stepped further inside, his boots silent on the worn planks. He didn't seek their eyes or forgiveness. Their grief was their own, their loss not his to heal. He carried his own sorrow openly now, the shimmer beneath his skin quiet but present.

Roan noticed first, his shoulders tensing as he shifted away without looking up from the pile of rope he had been absently coiling and uncoiling.

Kess slowly lifted her head, the blade going still in her hands. Her eyes held that wary look she got just before a fight.

"You came back." Her words carried no welcome, only tired observation.

Daniel sat on a cut log at the circle's edge, close enough to be a part of the group, but not so close as to intrude. "I didn't know where else to go."

Digger's whetstone paused mid-stroke. He looked up with amusement washing across his weathered features. "And here I thought you'd finally learned to disappear."

The attempted humor fell flat. The fire crackled, embers settling in the silence.

Daniel leaned closer to the half-circle gathered around the warmth of the hearth's fire, elbows on his knees, hands open between them. "I'm not here to be a leader of anyone."

"Good." Roan's voice pitched as he spoke, apparently recovering quite well from his experience in the Bastion. He wound the rope tighter around his fist until his knuckles went white. "We've had our fill of prophets."

"I never claimed to be a prophet." Daniel's voice stayed quiet, steady. "But the Hollow has shown me some things. And I think they mean something important."

His words rippled through the group. Even Digger's whetstone went still. Kess laid her blade across her lap, her focus now on Daniel. Even Roan stopped his restless fidgeting to look at Daniel for the first time since he had entered.

Kess leaned in, the firelight catching her eyes and casting sparks of their own. "You think you can decipher the Hollow's message?"

"I think I'm becoming part of it." Daniel's admission was filled with implications no one was ready to talk about.

From somewhere in the shadows—the rafters, the corner near a broken chair—came a faint sound. Something stirred, gentle and deliberate, like someone settling in to watch over him.

Daniel let the silence hold the truth he wasn't ready to acknowledge. Let them feel the possibility that everything they had been fighting for might require a sacrifice none of them had considered.

Kess touched the blade in her lap but didn't pick it up. She traced its edges like a talisman. "You have a plan?"

Daniel shook his head. "Not yet. But I know its shape. We've been fighting Grim on his terms, repeating cycles he feeds on. Exactly what he expects."

Digger set down his whetstone and crossed his arms; skepticism etched in every line of his face. "And you have a better way?"

Daniel opened his hands, palms up. The shimmer was invisible now, hidden beneath skin and scars. But it hummed beneath the surface, a current of potential that made the air around him taste of copper and lightning.

"I have something he won't see coming."

18

Rell's Crossing

Daniel sat alone on the ridge overlooking the Misfit camp. The stone beneath him was cold, and the emptiness below stretched endlessly.

The cabins lay scattered like broken tombstones across the clearing. Smoke curled weakly from a single chimney. No voices filled the camp. No laughter ringing through the air. Only the faint sound of someone coughing inside one of the shelters and the distant clatter of Digger sharpening steel again, because movement felt better than mourning.

Betsy wasn't by the fire pit. No one sat outside anymore. They lingered indoors, tending wounds or pretending to sleep, trying not to look at the empty bedrolls that would never be filled again.

Daniel pulled his coat tighter, though the cold biting through him had nothing to do with the air. It was the weight of choices—his, theirs, Grims—and the price they kept paying for all of them.

He hadn't asked about Elizabeth. He wasn't sure he could bear the answer.

He stared out toward the gray horizon, toward the faint pulse where the Meadow brushed the Hollow. He had avoided it since Alice's warning. But tonight, it tugged at him again. Quiet. Insistent. Patient.

"Should've been here," he said to the empty space. But the wind carried no judgment. Only cold.

Would his being here have saved anyone? Would one more body have changed anything, or would there simply be another body to gather?

He found no answers from the Hollow.

Footsteps behind him broke the silence. Daniel turned as Rell appeared at his side, pale and unsteady, one hand pressed against his ribs. The dried blood around his mouth stood stark against his skin.

"Jesus, Rell!" Daniel rushed to help him. "You shouldn't be walking."

Rell eased himself down next to Daniel. His face contorted in pain; one hand pressed against his ribs. Blood seeped between his fingers. "I couldn't stay down there," he whispered. "I don't want my last memory to be of that place."

They sat in silence for a while. Rell's breathing was shallow, each inhale catching wetly in his lungs.

Daniel studied him carefully. "How bad is it?"

"Bad enough." Rell gave a thin smile. "Whatever happened back there, it's spreading. Betsy tried to help, but…" He swallowed hard. "I don't think I'll see morning."

He looked out toward the shimmering horizon, the faint pulse of non-light where the gray ended and the Meadow began.

Daniel looked down. Rell had always kept to the edges. Quiet, reliable, unnoticed until now.

"Dammit, Rell. You should have stayed back." Daniel's voice softened with worry.

"Probably," Rell murmured. "But I wanted to help." His voice was so strained that Daniel had to lean closer to hear.

"I needed to do something," his voice was weak but steady. "That's what we do, right? Help each other."

They looked out toward the horizon. Rell's eyes were wet, trying to hold back the tears. "I keep thinking about before. You know? Before all this. I can't remember much, but… I remember being scared of dying. Like it was the worst thing that could happen."

"It is." Daniel looked out over the horizon.

"Is it?" Rell tilted his head. "Because right now, staying here feels worse. Listening to everyone blame themselves. Watching Betsy pretend she's not falling apart." His voice dropped. "Feeling pieces of myself just... letting go."

Daniel nodded slowly, unable to find words. They sat quietly, watching the distant shimmer.

"You saw the Meadow before," Rell said after a moment. "Is it true? Is it peaceful there?"

"Yes." Daniel's voice took on a dreamy tone as he stared at the Meadow's glow. "It's quiet, warm. Not like here. Untouched by the Hollow's poison."

Rell nodded, a small, relieved smile crossing his lips. "Will you take me there? I don't want to end here."

Daniel hesitated, looking back at the Meadow. "I'm not sure it works that way."

"It might." Tears rolled down Rell's face. He brushed them away before they had a chance to find their way to his chest. "Even close would be enough. I'm not asking you to save me. I just... I don't want to die here. In this place. I want to go somewhere that doesn't hurt."

Daniel stared at him, at a loss for words. Sixteen years old, maybe seventeen. Too young to be asking for a good place to die.

But Daniel was too young for a lot of things, too.

He stood, reached out, and helped Rell to his feet. They moved slowly, Rell leaning on Daniel. Gradually, the Hollow's landscape shifted around them. Dust gave way to grass, brittle breeze turned soft, and a warm scent filled the space. The Meadow opened gently, growing around them.

"It's so different from the hell we've been trapped in for so long," Rell said, tilting his face toward the warm light. "The air is so clean. So fresh. It feels like... home."

"I can't believe it," Rell whispered, reaching out to touch the grass as it rose around them. The Meadow welcomed them like expected guests.

They moved deeper, and Rell stumbled. Daniel carefully eased him down onto soft grass, and the Meadow welcomed them both.

"You okay to keep going?"

Rell nodded, though Daniel noticed the effort it cost him. "Yeah. It's just... I feel lighter. Like whatever's been eating at me is falling behind."

They crested a small hill, and Daniel stopped.

The Meadow spread before them, green and gold and impossible. Not vast—its edges visible in the distance—but infinite in the way of dreams. Grass moved in waves, though there was no wind. Flowers bloomed in clusters of white and yellow and soft blue, nonexistent colors in the Hollow's muted world.

Rell made a sound like a sob. "It's real."

"Yeah."

"It's beautiful."

Daniel helped him down the slope toward the grass. With each step, the gray fell away behind them. It grew warmer the further they walked. Welcoming.

When they reached the edge of the Meadow proper, the grass parted for them. Literally parted, creating a soft path of earth more comfortable than any bed Daniel had ever known.

"Can we stop here?" Rell asked faintly. "It's enough."

Daniel knelt quietly beside him. Rell looked up at the endless sky and let his eyes drift closed for a moment. "It's warm. I didn't expect that."

Daniel didn't answer. He sat beside Rell, offering silent company.

Rell lay back in the grass and closed his eyes. For the first time in days, his face relaxed. The lines of pain smoothed away.

"I can't feel it anymore," he whispered. "The hurt. It's just... gone."

"Do you think this place remembers us?" Rell asked.

Daniel looked around thoughtfully. "I think it remembers everything."

"That's good," Rell whispered, his voice fading. "I want to be remembered."

Daniel knelt beside him. "I'll remember you, Rell. I'm not going anywhere."

"Thank you." Rell's voice was getting softer. "For this. For bringing me somewhere good."

"Thank you for trusting me."

Rell's chest rose and fell more slowly. Deeper. His hand, which had been pressed against his wounded ribs, fell to his side. But he was smiling.

"I remember now," he said, so quietly Daniel had to lean in to hear. "I remember my name. My real name."

"What is it?"

"Michael." A breath. "My name was Michael."

He sighed and his eyelids closed. His chest rose once more, then was still.

The Meadow held him gently, as if cradling a child. Daniel sat there long after the light dimmed, knowing something had shifted. Not just for Rell, but for him, too.

And the Hollow, watching, knew it too.

Daniel remained beside the small flowers marking the spot where Rell had been, letting the peace of the Meadow wash over him. The golden light felt different here, surrounding him like a warm embrace.

A soft footstep made him look up.

A young woman stood at the edge of the clearing, her form more solid than the souls who had crossed over. She looked to be in her early twenties, with dark hair and eyes, holding the particular exhaustion of someone who had been fighting a long battle.

"You helped him find peace," she said, nodding toward where Rell had been.

Daniel stood slowly. "He was ready."

"I've been watching. Trying to figure things out." She took a hesitant step closer. "I think... I think I've been here too long. I can still feel it, you know. My heartbeat. Somewhere far away."

Understanding dawned. "You're not supposed to be here. You need to go back now."

She shook her head at first, then stopped, catching her own contradiction. "I got lost," she whispered. "There was an accident, and I was so worried about someone I left behind; I couldn't find my way back." Her voice grew smaller. "Someone who needed to know they were brave, even when I wasn't there to tell them."

Her story hit home for Daniel. "What's your name?"

"Ava." She touched her chest again, feeling for that distant heartbeat. "Someone's calling my name and crying. I think... I think they need me."

Daniel felt a familiar tug; the same one he had felt when helping Rell. But this was different. Not the gentle release of crossing over, but pulling, as though tracing a thread that hadn't broken. Of *returning*.

"If I get back home," Ava said, meeting his eyes, "and if you ever need someone to watch over the ones you love in that world... I won't forget what you've done for me here."

Daniel nodded, understanding passing between them. "Go home, Ava."

The golden haze gathered around her, weaving gently through her form. But instead of rising like Rell's, it pulled her back—toward warmth, toward pulse, toward breath.

She smiled as she faded. "Thank you."

And she was gone, not into the beyond, but toward life, toward a hospital bed and a voice that had never stopped calling her name.

Elsewhere—between waking and the place where breath forgets itself—Elizabeth drifted. Not asleep, not gone, but held in that thin, trembling space where the body falters, and the mind wanders—the place where nightmares walk in through unlocked doors.

Somewhere inside that fog, Elizabeth heard her son's voice. "Mom?"

Light bent. The world folded. And the nightmare answered.

The Reaper came for her.

He didn't bother wearing a gentler guise this time. No softened shadow. No distant silhouette. He arrived fully formed, a towering figure riding a great skeletal ox, each massive step shaking the false ground beneath her. A midnight raven perched on his right shoulder, its eyes ember-red. His wings spread behind him, swallowing the daylight whole.

The warm afternoon dimmed to a moonless night. The air turned arctic around them. His great beast snorted, leaving misty contrails around its massive bony head.

He sat there, watching her but saying nothing. Elizabeth tried to move but couldn't. Her limbs were stone. Her breath stilled.

The darkness closed in around her, thickening until the world narrowed to him alone. His presence pressed against her thoughts, gentle as a lullaby, terrible as surrender.

She felt the pull. Relief waited in the shadow under his wings. An end to pain. To worry. To the ache of fighting. She felt herself leaning toward it without meaning to.

His dark wings parted slightly, allowing a sliver of light to shine through the gap, illuminating his cloaked head. He looked less menacing, almost angelic in the light. She saw salvation in his face. Promise. Hope. Suddenly, she knew she didn't need to stay tethered to this world to take care of Daniel. He would be fine. Someone was watching over him, and she did not need to worry. A weight lifted from her shoulders. She felt lighter. Less burdened. It was enough. She could move on.

She had not crossed over. Not fully. She traveled through a realm where illusions and shadows converged around her, her perception a jumble of soft shades of gray. This place was a pause between heartbeats—between staying and letting go. It was soothing. Comforting. And she floated along on a lazy river of twilight clouds, swaddled in a warm velvety blanket of dusk.

Shots of blinding light jolted through her vision, pulling her out of her dream world. A voice broke through the fog. Her senses sharpened again, and blurry images became clearer.

"Mom!" came the voice, a second time.

Daniel

His voice didn't come from the shadow world. It came from a place where hearts still beat, and machines still hummed at bedside tables, pushing through the illusion, more powerful than the light that parted the Reaper's wings.

Black and white became clear.

The dark imposter standing before her was not salvation. It was a thief dressed in borrowed light. He meant to draw her into the world of the dead, and she was not ready to go.

She pushed back against the invisible force tugging her to this dark creature. She had no weapons to fight him with. None except her own willpower. He was closer, whether she moved toward him or he toward her, she didn't know. But he was so close she felt the breath of his beast on her cheek. The raven's eyes flared hot and red, hypnotic, pulling at the part of her that was so tired of fighting.

Her knees buckled and the world around her blurred, but she shook her head and refocused all her energy on fighting the Reaper's pull. So much was happening all at once.

The great beast snorted and stomped. The robes of the Reaper floated behind him like great black kites in the sky. The raven flapped its wings, and suddenly the sky was filled with dozens of large savage birds, inky even in this darkness. They kraa'd and screamed as they dove toward her, and she raised her arms to ward off their attack. She was swallowed in a cloud of flapping wings and biting beaks. Yanking her hair. Tearing her arms where they covered her eyes. They smelled of death and decay. Like an old, rotting, neglected graveyard. She was helpless to fight them off.

"STOP!" She heard the scream, but she didn't know if it was her own voice or if it came from someone else.

The world slowed. Muted. Sound dulled to a faraway hum. Her body moved as if it belonged to another person.

And then, she slipped free.

The sounds of the flapping wings and screaming birds began to fade to a low din. The beating wings softened to a light flutter against her face and arms. Drifting beyond the scene, she floated outside her body, watching the moment from somewhere beyond the battle—no longer an active participant—now a helpless observer.

She watched the shadows blur into nothing, then even that dissolved.

Darkness faded to silver. Noise faded to stillness. She drifted on a quiet pool of moonlight, suspended between staying and leaving.

Not dead.

Not awake.

Held in place by a will stronger than her own.

In the quiet that followed Ava's return and Michael's crossing, Daniel felt a shift. A tremor of warmth brushing the edge of his awareness.

Somewhere, just beyond the Hollow's reach, his mother had stirred.

He didn't know how he knew. Only that the Meadow, in its strange, impossible way, let him feel the thread that still tethered her to the world he had left behind.

Daniel stayed beside Rell—Michael—for a long time, his hand resting on the grass where the boy had lain. Small white flowers with golden centers pushed up through the grass like tiny stars, marking the place the Meadow had welcomed him home.

When Daniel finally stood, he wiped his eyes with the back of his hand. He looked once more toward the Meadow's heart, then turned back toward the Hollow, the gray already creeping back along the horizon.

In his tower, Grim stood before a wall of mirrors.

Most reflected what he expected—corridors of his domain, souls in various stages of processing, the ceaseless mechanics of his control over the dead and dying. But one mirror, the largest, showed nothing at all.

The glass was dark. Not black—dark. Like looking into deep water at night.

Grim pressed his palm against the surface. It was warm.

"Impossible," he whispered.

The Meadow had always been visible to him. Even if he couldn't enter it, it was part of his realm, technically. A locus of order he pretended was part of his design. A place he tolerated because it served its function.

But now it was hidden from him. Veiled behind warmth and light and something that tasted unnervingly like...

Hope.

The mirror cracked under his hand. A thin line split the glass from top to bottom, and through it seeped a golden light that made his eyes water.

"The Meadow. It's moved," he hissed.

Behind him, Digger stood with hands clasped behind his back, expression carved into neutrality.

"Or. Maybe it's always been able to move, but only for the one strong enough to influence it."

Digger grew tired of playing Grim's games. He secretly hoped Daniel could free them all soon.

A dangerous silence followed.

Grim's head turned just enough to catch Digger in his peripheral.

"Mind your footing, lad!" Grim warned. "Your loyalty is slipping dangerously close to the wrong side."

Grim turned back to the mirror, fists clenched. For the first time, he saw Daniel clearly as a threat. His voice lowered, filled with quiet menace.

Grim's reflection split along the crack in the mirror, showing two versions of himself—one pale and controlled, the other darker, hungrier. More like what he had been before he had learned to wear civilization like a mask.

"I won't allow it."

Digger said nothing.

"The Meadow belongs to me. Everything here belongs to me." Grim's voice was soft, reasonable. The tone he used when he was most dangerous. "Including him."

In the cracked mirror, golden light pulsed like a heartbeat.

And for the first time in centuries, Grim felt something he had almost forgotten.

Fear.

"This must stop," he said coldly. "Break the bridge."

The mirror flickered once, defiant, before turning dark again.

The fire had burned low. Most of the Misfits had drifted to their cabins or disappeared into the mist, leaving the camp hollow and still. Daniel lingered near the edge of the clearing, watching Wolfie pace the perimeter, his ears twitching, hackles up, sensing things no human ever could.

"Peaceful out there?" Digger's voice slid in behind him, easy as ever.

Daniel didn't turn. Wolfie growled low in his throat but didn't advance.

"Not really."

Then Digger stepped to Daniel's side, hands in his coat pockets, posture loose but eyes alert.

"Heard what you did. For the boy."

Daniel gave a slight nod. "It was the only thing I could do."

Digger bent, picked up a fallen twig, and rolled it between his fingers. "You ever wonder why it's you? Why Grim doesn't crush you outright like the rest?"

Daniel finally looked at him. "I have."

"Mmm." Digger didn't elaborate. He flicked the twig into the fire and watched it catch.

"Some say the Hollow bends around you. That the Meadow wakes up when you even breathe near it."

Daniel tensed. "You sound like Betsy."

"She's observant." Digger leaned in, his voice lower now. "So's Grim."

Daniel's pulse quickened. "Are you warning me or threatening me?"

Digger's smile didn't reach his eyes. "Wouldn't dream of threatening you. But I've been here a long time. Long enough to know that when Grim starts paying attention... things have already gone wrong."

Wolfie circled back toward them, nose to the ground, tail rigid. Something beyond the trees made him whine—a soft, uneasy sound Daniel had never heard from him.

Daniel's jaw tightened. "So, what are you saying, Digger?"

Digger lowered his voice. "If you're planning on walking between Grim's lines... make sure your footing's solid."

He flicked a matchstick he had been toying with. It sparked bright, then died before touching the ground.

Digger straightened. "Get some rest. You'll need it."

He walked into the mist without looking back.

Daniel stared after him, Wolfie pressed close to his leg, and wondered if he had just been warned...

Or quietly counted.

The camp was quieter now, if such a thing were possible. The few Misfits who remained moved like shadows between the cabins, checking supplies, tending wounds, speaking in hushed fragments.

No one had said a word about Rell. Maybe because they didn't know he was gone, yet. Perhaps because they did.

Daniel stayed on the ridge until the sun dipped low, then climbed down, shoulders tight with the weight of everything he carried. He walked past the leaning cabins, past cooking pots left cooling in the open, past gear piled where exhausted hands had dropped it.

He made his way to the fire pit at the center of camp.

Betsy was there. Same as before. Same posture. Same silence.

Wolfie lay beside her feet, head resting on his paws, eyes half-open but alert. His ears twitched at Daniel's approach. He didn't stand, but he watched him closely.

Daniel hesitated, then sat beside her.

For a long time, neither of them spoke.

The fire had nearly gone out, just a dull red glow under a crust of ash. She was poking at it absently with a broken stick, like she was trying to see if anything warm was left inside.

Her voice, when it came, was so quiet he almost missed it.

"You keep asking yourself what would've happened if you'd been there."

Daniel didn't respond. His hands were locked around his knees. His fingers were stiff, still marked with Rell's dried blood.

Betsy gave the embers a nudge. A wisp of smoke lifted, then faded.

"I used to think that way too," she murmured. "After each one we lost. If I'd said something sooner. If I'd taken the trail left instead of the right. If I'd fought harder. Or run."

A weary pause.

"Never changed a damn thing."

Daniel glanced at her.

"But the truth is..." she said, "things don't break because one person wasn't there. They break because the weight gets too heavy. You tried to bring something good into this place. And now you're sitting here, wondering if that made things worse."

He looked down. "It did make things worse. I should've been here. I should've stopped him."

"Maybe." Betsy tilted her head thoughtfully. "Or maybe he would've torn you in half just to prove he could."

Daniel didn't reply.

She finally turned to look at him, eyes red-rimmed but dry. "He's afraid of you."

Daniel blinked. "Grim?"

Betsy nodded. "He sees something in you he doesn't understand. And monsters like him? They fear what they can't name."

She leaned closer to the fire. Her voice dropped, like she was sharing something the Hollow itself wasn't supposed to hear.

"That's why he isn't tryin' to kill you. Not yet. He's carryin' out the people around you. Making you feel like a ghost in your own army. Like it's *you* who poisons everything you touch."

A quiet pause.

"But it's not your weakness," she said. "It's his."

Daniel stared into the ash. "What if I can't stop him?"

"You will," she said.

"How can you be sure?"

"Because you haven't run." She looked him in the eye. "Because you still care."

She stood then, brushing the soot from her hands, and reached for the large wooden spoon beside the cauldron of stew.

"You keep trying to protect us, Daniel." Betsy lifted the lid of the cauldron. She stirred the pot with slow, distracted movements. "But the only way to protect us now... is to become what he fears."

"You ain't asked about her," she added quietly. Daniel didn't answer right away. He knew she meant his mother.

"She's not here, not in the real sense," Betsy went on. "But she's not gone either." She paused, choosing her words carefully. "She's been close. Watching."

Daniel looked up. "Watching?"

Betsy nodded. "From the quiet places," she said. "The shadows where you think you're alone. Making sure you're safe." Her eyes softened. "A mother's love doesn't just stop because the world shifts."

The ache under Daniel's ribs tightened. He remembered those moments. The feeling of someone nearby, the air changing, the sense of protection.

"She was there," he whispered.

Betsy nodded. "Course she was. Question is whether she still needs to be."

Daniel's gaze drifted upward, scanning the broken beams above them, the dark corners where someone could watch unseen. How many times had he felt that gentle presence? How many moments when he had thought he was alone, but hadn't been?

Daniel stared into the fire, understanding blooming like dawn. "I tried to get her back to her world."

"Maybe you did," Betsy said. "Just not all the way. Maybe she's staying to see if you still need her."

Daniel stayed by the fire long after Betsy's footsteps faded. The wind stirred the ash, drawing faint trails through the coals like messages he couldn't read.

In the distance, he thought he heard something. A break in the silence, like the Hollow exhaling.

He stood slowly. Whatever was coming next had already begun.

T.M. ROCHE

19

The Retaliation

The clearing had grown too quiet.

The Hollow's usual wind had died. Even the fog stopped drifting. The last time their world had gone this still, Tate had died the next day.

Kess stood at the edge of the camp, arms crossed, watching the tree line, no longer trusting the shadows gathering there. Her sword hung loose at her hip, but her hand never strayed far from the hilt. Three days since the Bastion. Two days had passed since they had buried what remained of Tate. And still, Kess prepared for the fallout she knew was coming.

"Feels like there are eyes everywhere. Watching us."

"That's because there are," Digger said without looking up from the blade he sharpened. "We've stayed here too long. We should move somewhere safe."

"He has eyes everywhere. What could be safer than our own home base?" Kess asked.

"The town, maybe? He wouldn't risk destroying that."

Bren shifted where she sat, one hand pressed to the bandage on her thigh. "Town means more of Grim's minions. Means more eyes watching us."

Kess replied, not turning from her vigil. "At least in town, we might have warning."

Alice sat apart on a broken timber, head down, thumb absently tracing patterns in the dirt. Circles and half-circles that she wiped away the moment she realized she had made them. A leather-bound journal in her lap remained unopened, its pages heavy with secrets she wasn't ready to learn.

A ripple spread across the perpetual gray, like water disturbed by a massive beast moving beneath. In its wake, faint waves appeared, carved into the clouds themselves, twisting slowly before fading back to uniform emptiness.

"Did you see..." Bren leapt to her feet, crouched for action.

A hush rolled through the clearing so complete that Daniel looked up from cleaning his blade, unsure why his heart had started hammering.

Wolfie lifted his head from beside Bren, ears flattened, a low growl rumbling in his chest.

That was the first warning.

The second came when the fire guttered sideways, flames bending at an odd angle, unsupported by any breeze.

Kess's hand found her sword. "All right," she said, voice steady but tense, "everyone up. Now."

The Misfits rose at once, instinct overriding exhaustion: weapons drawn, packs pulled tight, wounded supported under both arms. Even Daniel felt the air shift, charged, sour, familiar in a way that made his stomach turn.

But they were too late.

The first figure lurched out of the tree line before anyone could shout a warning.

It moved too fast, joints bending in directions that would make a normal soul cringe instinctively. Its face proved even more horrifying. Human features stretched and spiraled, mouth torn wide, eyes hollow but still familiar.

"Marcus?" Bren whispered, her voice cracking on the name.

What had once been Marcus stared back, tilting its head at the sound, recognition flickering behind the emptiness. Its mouth worked soundlessly, trying to form words spurned by its deformed throat.

His skin was gray and sunken, his eyes clouded over, his mouth pulled into a rigid, unnatural snarl. Death had not been kind, nor had whatever dragged him back.

It screamed—a sound like metal tearing—and lunged.

Bren froze. Long enough for claws to rake across her shoulder, tearing fabric and flesh. She stumbled backward, blade rising too late, too slow.

More shapes poured from the trees. Dozens of them. All deliberately warped and contorted into nightmarish forms. All familiar.

Kess saw Jerrim, the scout who had died in the eastern raids, but his limbs were too long now, stretched like taffy, spirals carved deep into his exposed ribs. Digger faced something that might once have been Kira, her face split down the middle and rewired with silver thread pulsing with its own light.

"They're using our dead," someone screamed.

"FORM UP!" Kess shouted, but the clearing was already dissolving into chaos.

Wolfie lunged at one of the dead, teeth sinking into an already-rotting arm. The corpse didn't even flinch. It dragged Wolfie several feet before Kess slashed through its spine and sent it crumpling.

"Wolfie—GO!" she barked.

The dog tore free, bolting toward the rocks at the tree line, tail between his legs, yelping. Safe. Daniel exhaled a breath of relief before a corpse swung at his throat. Drawing his knife, he ducked, sliding his knife between its ribs. But the corpse pushed straight through the wound as if the knife were only a figment of Daniel's imagination.

Daniel staggered back. Weapons swung around him. Steel clashing uselessly against bone hard as granite.

Digger cursed as a dead man's fingers locked around his coat, nearly dragging him down. Bren fought one-handed, her injured arm limp at her side.

"That's Jerrim—JERRIM—" she sobbed. "God, stop—"

Kess cut down another corpse. "Don't look at their faces! Just MOVE!"

But the ground betrayed them, softening underfoot like loose shale, sending every stance off-balance, turning each dodge into a stumble.

Daniel ducked, a broken arm swinging like a club. He drove his shoulder into the corpse's chest and shoved it back far enough for Kess to take its head clean off.

Still, more kept coming. Dozens of them stepped from behind trees and boulders.

The clearing filled with the sound of boots slipping on dirt, steel striking dead flesh, and the hollow crack of bone.

"We can't hold!" Bren yelled, voice cracking as she blocked a blow with the flat of her blade.

"Fall BACK!" Kess shouted. "Toward the ridge! MOVE!"

The Misfits ran with the desperation of people who still wanted to live. They shoved wounded, dragged those who faltered, ducked and dodged, and kicked and swung.

Daniel covered their retreat, breath raw in his throat, muscles burning. A corpse grabbed his coat. He ripped free, barely keeping his feet.

Behind them, what had once been their home buckled. Cabins splintered as bodies crashed through walls.

Firepits overturned. Food stores spilled into the dirt.

The clearing was no longer a camp. It was a graveyard.

"GO!" Daniel shouted. "We have to GO!"

They ran. They didn't stop running until their lungs burned and their legs gave out.

The forest swallowed them quickly. Gnarled trunks, claw-like branches, roots jutting like ribs. The path they usually took was gone, churned to mud by too many storms and too little sunlight. Every step felt like a gamble.

Behind them, the dead crashed through underbrush, relentless.

"Left!" Kess barked, shoving Bren ahead of her.

A fallen pine blocked the way. Daniel vaulted it, then turned to help Digger pull one of the wounded over before the dead reached them. A hand, cold and stiff, snatched at Daniel's ankle.

He kicked hard, felt the grip loosen, and ran.

Bren stumbled and Daniel caught her elbow before she could fall. "I've got you," he said.

She nodded once, jaw clenched, face white with pain.

Up the ridge they climbed, the same ridge Daniel had stood on not so long ago, watching the Hollow breathe. Now it was a lifeline. The dead struggled on slopes. Gravity finally worked in the Misfits' favor.

"Keep moving!" Kess urged, though her own breath was ragged.

Daniel didn't let himself look back. He could hear the dead. Bones clacking. Breathless groans. The sound of bodies that didn't tire and wouldn't stop.

Wolfie appeared on the ridge above, barking sharply. Then he turned and ran ahead as if guiding them.

"Smart boy," Daniel muttered, pushing harder.

The trees thinned. A tower of stone appeared through the fog.

"There!" Bren gasped. "The Rook!"

The old lookout tower rose from the ridge like a broken tooth. Walls buckled from past fights, stairs mostly intact, roof half caved in. But it was shelter. Height. Visibility. A chance.

They stumbled into its shadow, boots slipping on shale. Kess turned, sword raised. "Inside! MOVE!"

The Misfits surged through what remained of the doorway. Daniel shoved a fallen beam aside and dragged the last wounded soul through just as three dead slammed into the threshold.

The impact shook dust from the rafters.

"Daniel!" Digger yelled.

Daniel caught the shattered doorframe and hauled himself inside, slamming a rusted metal sheet across the gap. Digger and Bren grabbed the edges with him as a corpse crashed against the outside.

Another hit, and then another.

The panel rattled but held.

"Up!" Kess commanded, pointing to the interior stairs. "Get higher. They can't climb as fast as they can run."

They scrambled up the spiraling steps. Daniel stayed below long enough to shove debris in front of the opening. Crates. Splintered table legs. Anything he could drag. Wolfie growled at the base of the steps, hackles raised, but obeyed when Daniel snapped his fingers.

The tower groaned like an old ship.

Daniel took the stairs two at a time, joining the others on the upper level.

The room was cramped, half-collapsed, but high enough to see the clearing below. It was a nightmare below.

Their camp, their home, was gone. Flames. Smoke. Bodies twisted in the dirt. The cabins they had built, the benches they had carved, the fire pit where they had told stories.

All of it trampled. Crushed. Consumed.

Bren covered her mouth with both hands.

Kess stood rigid, sword tip dragging the stone floor.

Digger sank to one knee; forehead pressed to the cool wall.

Daniel felt it hit him like a blow to the sternum. He hadn't been fast enough. He hadn't been enough, period.

The dead milled below, wandering the ruins, losing interest now that their purpose was complete. A few lingered at the base of the tower, hands clawing at stone.

But most drifted back toward the trees, as if returning to the hand that had sent them.

Daniel swallowed the rising bile. "He's not just killing us. He's showing us who he controls. That could be our fate."

Kess's voice cracked. "Our friends. Our dead."

"No," Daniel said, voice low, shaking. "Our warning."

Wolfie pressed against his leg, trembling. Daniel rested his hand on the dog's neck.

The Rook swayed in the wind, but it held firm. Around them, the Hollow stretched, quiet again. Too quiet.

Until Digger spoke, voice raw:

"We can't stay here. This was just a taste of what Grim has planned for us."

Daniel nodded.

"We move at dawn."

They barricaded the tower as best they could.

Broken beams wedged against the shattered doorframe. A rusted cabinet was dragged in front of the stairs. The survivors worked without speaking. Everything creaked with each gust of wind, but nothing moved. The dead had wandered off, leaving only silence and the echo of what had been destroyed.

Daniel sagged against the nearest wall, clutching his ribs. His coat was shredded, streaked with ash and someone's blood. Maybe his own. Wolfie pressed against his leg, whining softly, fur standing on end.

The fight had followed them all the way here, biting at their heels. But now, at least, the night held still.

Kess sat heavily on the floor, her destroyed gauntlets tossed aside. She held a strip of cloth to her temple where a claw had caught her. Bren crouched by a splintered crate, binding her own shoulder with shaking hands. Digger slumped against the wall.

Alice remained standing near the open section of the wall, staring out toward the direction they had fled. Her breath was controlled, but her hands kept flexing. Tiny spasms she couldn't stop. She was as shaken as any of them, though she would never say the words.

No one spoke until Daniel finally found his voice.

"...how many made it?" It came out raw and gravelly.

Kess looked up. "Six. Counting you."

Bren's eyes filled with tears, but they didn't spill. "I saw Marcus... what was left of him. And Jerrim. And—" Her voice broke. "They shouldn't have looked like that."

Digger scrubbed a hand through his hair. "Grim wanted us to see them. Wanted it to hurt."

Wolfie growled as though he agreed.

Daniel forced himself to sit upright, pain blooming under his ribs. "We couldn't have saved them."

Kess shook her head, jaw tight. "No. But he made sure it felt like we shouldn't be fighting back."

Alice didn't turn from the window. "That's what he does. The man who once healed became the monster that punishes and tortures."

Daniel stared down at his hands, blood-stained and shaking. He thought of Rell's final moments, that peaceful warmth. Could he ever hope to find that kind of peace? He thought of the Meadow stirring when Rell crossed its threshold. He thought of Grim watching them through the eyes of the dead.

"He's afraid," Daniel whispered.

"Of us? Or of you?" Kess asked sharply.

"Both, I suppose."

Wolfie crawled into Daniel's lap, shivering. Daniel wrapped an arm around the dog and held him close, grateful for something living, something real.

Bren rubbed her face with her uninjured hand. "What do we do now?"

Kess answered first. "We survived. That's the only win we get tonight."

"But it's not enough," Daniel said.

Alice finally turned to look at Daniel for the first time since they barricaded themselves in the tower. "What are you thinking?"

Daniel swallowed hard. His voice was steady, even if he wasn't. "We can't fight him the way we've been fighting. He rigs every battleground. He uses every loss."

Kess nodded slowly. "Then what do you propose?"

Daniel looked at each of them in turn. Tired. Wounded. Afraid, but alive.

"We stop playing his game."

Digger snorted. "And do what instead?"

Daniel exhaled, breath shaky but certain. "I don't know yet. But whatever it is, it starts here, with us still breathing."

Wolfie nudged his hand, grounding him.

"It starts with not letting him decide who we become next. It starts with us making the next move."

The Rook creaked in the wind. No one argued.

Finally, the Hollow seemed to hold its breath in recognition of the shift that Daniel's words had caused.

And Grim, wherever he lurked, would feel it soon enough, too.

20

The Walk Between Worlds

*D*aniel returned to the Misfit camp because he couldn't stand not knowing. He fled with the survivors, felt every scream at his back, heard the last of the corrupt dead falling behind them. But he needed to come back. Needed to see it. Needed proof of who was gone. And who wasn't.

The walk was too quiet. The air held the memory of violence from the previous night. It carried a bitter, metallic taste that settled heavy in his throat and a pungent smell of destruction and recent death.

He crested the ridge and halted, pulse hammering.

Below him, the Misfits' camp was gone. The simple cabins, the barricades of salvaged metal and timber—all reduced to shattered pieces and smoldering ash. Smoke curled slowly over the ruin, drifting like steam off cooling embers. Even from here, Daniel could make out broken weapons, charred fabric, and the unmoving shapes among the debris.

His chest tightened. They hadn't attacked. They hadn't even prepared for a fight. Grim had brought the battle to them—and it had torn through everything.

The silence was heavy, broken only by faint popping and crackling sounds from the burnt remains. Daniel forced himself forward, boots crunching through layers of ash and debris. Each step revealed more details he wished he hadn't seen: a snapped spear shaft, a torn coat sleeve, dark stains trailing across stones, and vanished beneath fallen timber.

He crouched, examining a warped and melted shield, its surface twisted beyond recognition. Beside it lay a fragment of fabric—familiar, pale cloth. Betsy's shawl. He swore out loud and jumped to his feet, pushing forward through the wreckage.

A soft whine, and Wolfie emerged from behind a toppled beam, limping slightly from the attack. The dog pressed his head against Daniel's thigh, trembling hard enough for Daniel to feel it through his clothes. Daniel dropped to one knee, burying his fingers in Wolfie's fur.

"Good boy," he whispered. "I'm right here. It's okay."

Wolfie's tremors didn't stop. His ears pinned back. His muscles tightened. His nose lifted, smelling something in the wind, and he froze.

Daniel felt it, too.

The dog growled at Daniel, low and warning.

He whined again, circled Daniel once in frantic hesitation, then bolted into the trees, running with the desperate certainty of an animal fleeing wildfire.

"Wolfie!" Daniel shouted, lunging forward.

But the dog didn't look back. Even the Hollow felt smaller without the dog as his constant companion. The only soul who had ever accepted him just as he was, expecting nothing in return except a scratch or two behind the ears.

A metallic creak cut through the silence, the sound of armor that wasn't there. Smoke shifted unnaturally, drawing toward a single point. A silhouette formed within it, tall and straight-backed.

Grim stepped forward through the haze, the smoke seeming to part for him as if repelled. He didn't bother hiding the satisfaction on his face.

Daniel drew himself up to face the Reaper.

"It seems your dog has better instincts than your people," Grim said.

Daniel held his tongue, positioning himself between Grim and the ruins.

"You should have expected this," Grim said, his voice calm, almost conversational. He glanced around the ruins with a distant interest, as though inspecting the aftermath of a minor inconvenience. "So much waste." He sighed, shaking his head as if disappointed.

Daniel kept his voice steady. "You slaughtered them. For your own entertainment."

"I culled them." Grim corrected, looking directly at Daniel now, eyes colder. "There's a difference. They've been chipping away at the edges of my patience for far too long. It was time they learned."

"You didn't need to do this." Daniel's fists tightened. He could feel the faint thrum of the Hollow beneath his boots, a slow, rhythmic pressure, as though the ground itself had a pulse.

Grim smiled faintly. "Of course I didn't. Want has always been stronger than need."

He lifted his chin, studying Daniel.

"You felt it, didn't you? The shift. The Meadow tugging at you."

Grim's expression softened briefly into something resembling regret. "She used to tug at me, too."

Daniel's stomach tightened. "You knew it was changing."

"I knew you were changing, Daniel," Grim replied. "Disturbing old patterns. Breaking things without understanding why they were built." He stepped forward slowly, his movements unhurried and deliberate. "You visited the Meadow."

Daniel hesitated for only a second. "Yes."

"And you think it chose you?" Grim asked softly. "The Meadow doesn't choose, Daniel. This was your destiny from the day you were born."

Daniel's pulse quickened. "Maybe it's time something changed."

Grim's gaze narrowed. "Change isn't always liberation. You'll find most often, change is just another pretty prison wrapped up in a shiny new bow."

He raised one hand slightly, palm upward, like he was offering something invisible. "This doesn't have to continue. I'm offering you mercy."

Daniel narrowed his eyes. "Mercy?"

Grim nodded slowly. "Give me Alice. She owes a debt older than your memories. Step aside, and I'll let the rest scatter. No more violence. No more suffering."

Daniel was ashamed for considering the offer, even for a second, but he pushed the thought away with a determined shake of his head. "I won't trade someone else's life for safety."

Grim's hand lowered, disappointment flickering in his expression. "Then someone you love will suffer. That's the balance of things, Daniel. Actions and consequences."

Daniel stared back, unflinching. "I'm done playing your games."

Grim tilted his head, considering Daniel carefully, his confidence momentarily uncertain. "If you're not playing mine, whose game do you think you're playing?"

Under Daniel's feet, the ground rumbled.

Grim heard it too, and the mask slipped. For the first time, he appeared genuinely afraid. It was brief—a blink, a quick tightening around the eyes—but Daniel saw it clearly.

Grim straightened slowly. "Be careful," he warned softly, composure restored. "Awakening things you don't fully understand rarely ends well. You're opening doors that should stay closed. And you won't like what steps through."

And just as quietly as he had arrived, Grim stepped backward and vanished into the lingering smoke, leaving Daniel standing amid the ruins, the Hollow's pulse steady beneath him.

The moment Grim vanished, the world stilled, frozen in time and space.

He turned because something had stirred behind him. A thin groan. A scrape of wood shifting.

The Misfit lay curled in a nest of cloaks and ash, skin gray and glistening with fever. His breath came shallow and strained.

The boy blinked up at him. "You... came back."

Daniel knelt beside him, careful not to disturb the worst of the wounds. "You're safe now," he said quietly. "I've got you."

The Misfit stirred, eyes fluttering half-open. "No," he rasped. "Not safe. Not anymore."

Daniel leaned closer. "Can you tell me your name?"

The boy blinked slowly, as if it took effort to remember. "Eban."

Daniel nodded. "Eban. You're going to be okay."

Eban's gaze drifted toward him, wide with frightened awe. "He was afraid," he whispered. "Grim. After whatever you did."

"I didn't do anything," Daniel said.

A dry sound escaped Eban's throat, maybe a laugh, perhaps a cough. "Exactly. You stopped playing by the rules. It's what scares him. He built this place on rules. Obedience. If they break..."

Daniel looked down at his hands. The Hollow pulsed faintly beneath his skin.

"I don't even know what I'm breaking."

"That... might be why it's working." Eban struggled to get the words out.

Daniel reached out, steadying him as another tremor passed through his frame. "I'm sorry."

"Don't be," Eban murmured. "Just finish it."

His eyes drifted shut in exhaustion. Daniel stayed a moment longer, then stood. Grief wrapped around him like a shroud. But underneath, rage flared to life.

From the smoke, another figure stepped forward. Daniel spun around, tense—but it was Alice, soot-smudged, hair wind-tangled, but composed. She crossed her arms and leaned against a half-burned post, watching Daniel with a wary, knowing expression.

"You shouldn't be here alone," she said.

Daniel stared at her, pulse still raw from the confrontation. "You knew Grim would come."

"I suspected."

"You could've warned me."

"You wouldn't have listened. What would you have done differently?" she asked, voice even. "Really?"

He said nothing because she was right.

"He said you owe him something," Daniel muttered. "A debt."

Alice stared at the wreckage.

"Alice? I know this must be hard for you to talk about. But I need to understand. Please. What does Grim have over you?"

She turned back to face him, again. He could see her pain reflected there in her eyes. In the way her mouth trembled to keep from crying.

"I do owe him something," she said, her voice distant. "But not in the way he tells it. I never meant to hurt any soul. That's not who I am. But he found ways to twist the truth and threaten the ones I loved. I didn't know how to tell him no. Now, he holds it over my head. That debt I owe? It can never be paid off. Not while Grim is in control."

Daniel's mind reeled. He knew Alice to be loyal, fierce, and protective. Sometimes distant. But never cruel. Never complicit.

"Once, I was called Elaren," she continued. "And there's more to it. More that I'll tell you when the time is right, but not now. Right now, we need to stay focused. You'll need to trust me."

"Okay. I can respect that," he said with some reluctance. "But that still doesn't answer what Grim has on you."

"I once possessed powerful magic before the Hollow stripped it from me. Grim used what little I had left as a bargaining tool. I helped shape the Hollow when it was still young."

Daniel stared at her, speechless, and tried to make sense of her words. He was sure he had misunderstood. "You built this place?"

"No. Not exactly. I helped contain something even worse than Grim himself. Or so I thought. But the Hollow became a prison. And Grim became its warden."

Daniel didn't know what to make of this new revelation. He reminded himself of his promise not to judge. He knew Alice for who she really was. He knew the burden she had been carrying for decades with no way to escape her debt to Grim, and no way to reconcile her guilt. This wasn't her fault.

Daniel looked down at his hands, at the soot clinging to his skin. "He said I'm changing things."

"You are," she said. "But not because you're stronger. Or chosen. It's so much simpler." She met his eyes. "The Hollow was never meant to hold you."

"What do you mean?"

"Your soul bends the rules just by being here," she said quietly. "You were born tied to something older than this place. The Meadow didn't choose you. It grew with you. That's why the Hollow reacts to you. That's why Grim is afraid. You have always been a part of the Meadow."

He felt the faint thrum, deep in the earth's core, responding to her words.

"I didn't ask for this," Daniel said, though he spoke the words with less conviction. He was losing confidence in himself.

"No one does," Alice replied. "Well, no one except Grim."

He swallowed. "What am I supposed to do?"

Her voice softened. "Be the one story that doesn't have an unhappy ending. Grim built this place to trap pain. You have the power to change that. Your compassion. Your love. Your mercy. And the weapons that the Hollow provided."

Well, shit. It all made sense now. He wasn't the hero. He wasn't the weapon. He was the author of the rewritten story of the Hollow.

But what was he supposed to do with this knowledge? Sit around and accept it? Of fucking course not! He had to figure out how to turn this into a weapon.

A groan erupted from the rubble behind them, snapping Daniel back into motion.

Daniel felt the ground roll beneath his boots, a subtle tremor, not threatening but announcing its presence. He glanced at Alice, who was looking downward, her expression tense.

"What was that?" he asked quietly.

She hesitated, listening carefully. "It's begun. Whatever's been asleep is waking now. Grim was right about one thing: you're opening doors. But what's behind them isn't his to control."

Behind them, Eban stirred in his sleep. A tiny sound escaped his throat. One hand twitched against the ground, fingers curling in the ash as though pulled by some macabre puppeteer. Movements too deliberate for mere dreams. Alice placed a steady hand on his arm.

Daniel turned, watching the boy settle again, though his expression now held something troubled. Dreaming—or touched by whatever was waking.

Alice placed a reassuring hand on Daniel's arm. "We'll face what's coming. Together."

Daniel nodded, unwavering. "Together." And beneath their feet, the Hollow echoed softly, as though in approval.

21

The Promise
of Later

The ruins still smoldered.

Daniel stood where the Misfits' camp had been, ash settling on his shoulders like gray snow. The smoke had thinned since his confrontation with Grim, but the stench lingered. The smell of metal and char and broken promises.

Alice moved through the wreckage beside him, silent. She had been quiet since Grim vanished, since she had revealed the truth about her past. She carried herself differently now that he knew her truth. A burden had been lifted from her shoulders.

They found a small, pixie-looking woman pinned beneath a fallen beam near what had once been a triage area. Lya. She had never drawn much attention—quiet hands, steady when others faltered. During the attack, she had stayed with the wounded, refusing to run when things turned bad.

Daniel dropped to his knees beside her, hands already reaching for the debris. "I've got you," he said, voice rough. "Hold on."

But when he tried to lift the beam, Lya laid her hand on his arm. Her touch was steady despite her injuries.

"Don't waste your strength," she whispered, her eyes searching his. "It's too late for me."

Daniel's chest tightened. "No, it's not. I can—"

"Listen." Her voice was fading, but her gaze held his. "She needs you."

The words shocked him. "Who?"

But Lya's eyes were already losing focus, seeing something beyond the wreckage. "Don't leave her alone," she breathed.

Then her hand slipped from his wrist, and she was gone.

Daniel stared down at her still form, grief and guilt twisting in his stomach. Another life lost. Another person he couldn't save.

The world lurched.

Bright light.

Too bright. Bleached into nothingness.

It seared Daniel's vision as he fell through it. No sound, no body, no sense of direction. Only a pull. A force without name or mercy dragging him backward through the soft membrane of memory until—

White walls. The smell of disinfectants. The steady beep of machines.

Daniel stood in a hospital room, staring at a bed where his mother lay dying.

She was so small. When had his mother become this fragile bird of a woman, dwarfed by machines that beeped with mechanical indifference? The Elizabeth in his memory filled doorways, commanded rooms with her laughter. This paper-thin version, with skin stretched over delicate bones, lips tinged blue beneath the oxygen cannula, looked as if she might dissolve if a draft moved through the room.

His knees buckled. He caught himself against the doorframe, fingers digging into painted metal until his knuckles went white. The smell hit him then, antiseptic layered over something sweeter and more terrible. The scent of a body slowly surrendering.

Tubes snaked from her arms like translucent vines, feeding her a cocktail of chemicals that kept her tethered to a world she was already half-gone from. Her chest rose and fell in stuttering rhythms, each breath a small victory that sounded like defeat.

But around her neck, catching the fluorescent light, hung a small silver key on a delicate chain that once held a locket. It was old, ornate, with intricate spirals carved into its surface. Even here, even fading, she had kept it close.

"Mom," Daniel whispered.

She turned her head just a fraction, as if she had heard him. Her eyes remained closed, but her lips parted, moving soundlessly around shapes that might have been his name. She spoke so faintly he almost missed it. "Daniel? Where are you, sweetheart?"

Sweetheart. She'd called him that when he was small, when scraped knees needed kissing and monsters lived under beds. Now the word fell from her lips like a prayer, like a lifeline cast into dark water.

He reached for her hand, but his palm met empty air where her fingers should have been. The sensation was worse than pain. It was nothingness, the complete absence of the warmth he craved. He tried again, but his hand found only cool hospital sheets and the phantom weight of connection that would never come.

"I'm trying to come home," he whispered to the space between them, though he knew she couldn't hear him. "I'm trying so hard."

Her eyes fluttered open, staring at the ceiling. "I keep dreaming about you," she murmured, her fingers touching the key at her throat. "But you're always just out of reach."

A sob cracked open his chest. He pressed his forehead to the edge of the bed, the vinyl biting into his skin.

"I didn't leave you," he whispered. "I didn't forget."

Her breathing faltered. A skip in the rhythm that made Daniel's world tilt. The steady rise and fall of her chest stuttered, paused, then resumed with a wheeze that sounded like surrender.

No. Not yet.

"Please," he prayed, pressing closer to the bed rail until the metal bit into his palms. "Don't go. Not yet."

The heart monitor's beeping grew erratic. A missed beat. Another. The green line on the screen jumped and dipped like a bird with a broken wing.

Then, slowly, she turned her head again. This time her eyes found him.

Not the unfocused stare from before. These eyes *saw* him. Recognition flared in their depths. Brief but unmistakable. For one impossible moment, the veil between worlds thinned to nothing.

"I'm so proud of you," she said, her voice gaining strength as if his presence was feeding her somehow. "But please... come home. Before it's too late."

His heart seized. She could see him. She knew he was lost somewhere she couldn't follow.

I will," he promised, desperate to make her believe it. "I'm coming, I swear I'm..."

But the room was already wavering at the edges, reality growing thin as tissue paper. The beeping of machines grew distant, muffled, as if heard through water. Alarms began to sound.

"Please don't give up," Daniel begged, but his voice sounded hollow now, echoing from somewhere far away. "I promise I'm coming."

The room was gone, dissolved back into gray mist and broken stone.

He was back in the ruins, still kneeling beside Lya's body.

Alice stood a few feet away, watching him with concern. "Daniel?"

He blinked, the vision still clinging to the edges of his sight. "I saw her," he said, voice hoarse. "My mother. She was..." He swallowed hard. "She's dying."

Alice knelt beside him, close enough that he could feel the warmth radiating from her skin. "Tell me."

The words came slowly at first, then in a rush. He told her about the hospital room, about his mother's pale face and labored breathing. About how she seemed to be fading away, caught between worlds.

"Even there," he said, his voice barely above a whisper, "even dying, she was still wearing this old key around her neck. This silver thing with spirals carved into it. She kept touching it, like it was…" He struggled for the words. "Like it was important."

Alice went very still.

Daniel looked up, catching the change in her expression. The color had drained from her face, leaving her pale as a ghost. Her lips parted slightly, as if she had frozen mid-thought.

"Alice?" he said softly. "What is it?"

She didn't answer right away. Instead, her hand drifted to her own throat. Her fingers traced the hollow of her collarbone where a chain might have rested, the gesture achingly familiar, like muscle memory.

When she met his eyes again, there was something vulnerable in her gaze, a mixture of loss and grief.

"The key," she said, controlling her tone. "Can you describe it again?"

Daniel studied her face, noting the way she held herself, bracing for what was to come. "It was silver, with these intricate spirals carved into the metal. Old, but polished. Why?"

Her vacant eyes stared into memory. Her hands clenched into fists at her sides and uncurled again. "I…" She started to speak, then stopped, her jaw working, churning on her words. "It's probably nothing."

By the way she said it, so quick, so dismissive, it was apparent she was keeping more secrets.

"Alice." He leaned closer, close enough to see the fine lines around her eyes, the way her lips parted slightly when she was thinking. "Don't do that. Don't just leave me wondering like that."

She turned to face him, but there was no other sign she was aware of his words.

"That key means something to you," he continued, his voice gentle but unwavering. "I can see it written all over your face. Please. What aren't you telling me?"

She looked at him then, really looked at him, and something sparked between them. The ruins, the ash, the death—it all seemed to fade into the background. There was only her face in the gray light, only the space between them that felt charged with possibility.

"There are things," she said quietly, "about my past. About what I helped build here." Her eyes searched his, looking for permission to continue. "Things I haven't told you because…"

She trailed off, but her gaze never wavered. In the silence, Daniel could hear his own pulse beating, could feel the pull of her like gravity.

"Then tell me now."

The words came out rougher than he intended, weighted by everything he couldn't say. She was so close he could see the gold flecks scattered through her eyes like stars, could feel the warmth of her breath against his skin.

"Daniel…" His name on her lips was like a prayer. Reverent. Pleading.

"I trust you," he said, and the truth of it surprised him. After everything, the lies, the secrets, the careful walls she kept between them, he still trusted her completely.

Something broke in her expression. Surprise. Relief. A fragility so unlike her. Her hand rose slowly, hesitating, then came to rest against his cheek. Her touch was warm, genuine, anchoring him in a way nothing had since entering the Hollow.

"You shouldn't," she whispered, but there was no conviction in it. They sounded like words she was obligated to say.

He leaned into her touch, his own hand covering hers where it rested against his cheeks. "Too late."

The space between them disappeared by degrees. Her eyes fluttered closed, dark lashes casting shadows against her pale skin. He felt the heat radiating from her, smelled the faint scent of wildflowers that still clung to her despite the ash and smoke enveloping them.

Their foreheads touched, a gentle collision that sent electricity racing down his spine. Their noses brushed. The softest whisper of contact. Her breath mingled with his, warm and sweet. And for one perfect moment, the world held its breath—

A sound cut across the ruins. Sharp and deliberate. Footsteps on broken stone.

They sprang apart, the spell shattered. Alice's hand fell from his face, taking her warmth with it. She was already pulling back. Already rebuilding the walls he had just watched crumble.

"We should go," she said, her voice husky and unsteady. She refused to meet his eyes. "It's not safe here."

The distance between them grew by miles, cold and unbridgeable. Daniel could still feel the ghost of her touch on his skin, could still taste the possibility of what had almost been.

Daniel stood slowly, his pulse still thundering in his ears—but now for an entirely different reason than fear. "Alice..."

"Later," she said, and though her tone tried for dismissal, something softer threaded through it. "When we're somewhere safe. When we have time."

He nodded, even though every part of him wanted to pull her back, to reclaim what the footsteps had stolen. Instead, he followed her through the wreckage, stepping carefully around Lya's still form, carrying both the mystery of the key and the phantom warmth of Alice's touch.

Behind them, the ash continued to fall like gray snow, burying their footprints, erasing the evidence of what had almost been.

But some things couldn't be buried so easily.

The feeling lingered, electric and fragile and impossibly real. The promise of later hung between them like a bridge waiting to be crossed.

And for the first time in a very long time, Daniel let himself feel hope.

22

The Weight of Silence

They found privacy behind the ruins of the old Rook.

The tower itself was crowded now, Misfits sleeping in corners, the wounded laid out on makeshift cots, every echo carrying another voice or another need. But behind it, where the stone wall had collapsed outward decades ago, a narrow alcove remained. Half-shaded, half-buried under fallen blocks. Hidden from the camp but still within reach.

Alice led them there wordlessly, slipping between the broken stones as if she had walked this path a hundred times. Daniel followed, ducking beneath a leaning slab of masonry until the murmurs of the Misfits faded behind them.

The little hollow was barely the size of a bedroom, open to the gray sky above and shielded on three sides by fractured stone. A sliver of the Hollow's endless expanse was visible through a split in the wall, just enough to feel private, not enough to draw attention.

Daniel settled beside the gap, letting the quiet fold around them. The silence between them felt different now—charged with possibility and memory of almost-touches.

"Is this safe enough?" he asked.

Alice nodded but didn't sit. She paced the small space like a caged thing, her nervous energy radiating in waves. "For now."

"Alice." He stood, catching her hand as she passed. "We said later. It's later."

She stopped, her fingers tightening around his for just a moment before pulling away. "I know."

She turned to face him, and he could see the conflict in her eyes—want warring with fear, hope tangled up with something that looked like guilt.

"What you said before," she began, voice soft. "About trusting me. You shouldn't say things like that so easily."

"Why not?"

"Because trust is dangerous here. Because people who trust me tend to get hurt." She wrapped her arms around herself, a barrier he recognized. "Because I'm not who you think I am."

Daniel stepped closer, slowly, like approaching a wounded animal. "You're Alice. That's all I need to know."

"You already know my real name," she said quietly. "Elaren. And everything that comes with it. I helped shape this place. I helped trap countless souls in Grim's web, and I—"

"Stop." He reached for her face, cupping her cheek gently. "I don't care what you did before I knew you. I care about who you are now."

Her breath caught. "Daniel..."

"You've been trying to fix it ever since, haven't you? Everything you've done since I've known you—helping the Misfits, defying Grim, protecting me, you've been trying to make it right."

Tears gathered in her eyes. "It's not enough. It'll never be enough."

"Maybe not," he said softly. "But it's enough for me."

Alice's eyes closed, and for a moment she just stood there, trembling on the edge of something she'd been fighting. When she opened them again, they were bright with unshed tears.

"Daniel..." she whispered, but it wasn't a protest this time. It was surrender.

The space between them disappeared. This time, there were no footsteps to interrupt them, no sounds of danger. Just Alice's gasp as he leaned down, just the flutter of her lashes against her cheeks as her eyes closed.

Their lips met softly at first, a gentle brush. Daniel pulled back just enough to look at her, to give her a chance to change her mind. But Alice's eyes remained closed, her face tilted up toward his, lips parted slightly as if waiting.

He kissed her again, deeper this time, and she responded with a soft sound that sent warmth racing through his chest. Her hands came up to rest against his shoulders, fingers curling into the fabric of his shirt as if anchoring herself.

They moved together slowly, carefully, learning each other. The taste of her, the way she sighed against his mouth, the careful exploration of lips and breath, and the space between heartbeats. Time stretched, suspended in the gray light filtering through the broken walls.

When she finally melted into him fully, her hands fisting in his shirt to pull him closer, it felt like a choice made rather than a moment stolen. She tasted like hope and sorrow and something undeniably her, and Daniel felt like he was drowning in the best possible way.

When they finally broke apart, both breathing hard, Alice rested her forehead against his chest.

"This is a terrible idea," she said, breathless.

"Probably," he agreed, pressing a kiss to the top of her head. "I don't care."

She pulled back to look at him, and for a moment, her walls were completely down. He could see everything: the fear, the hope, the way she was falling just as hard as he was.

The air around them rippled with a familiar tug that made his chest tight.

"No," he said, recognizing the pull of the Meadow. "Not now."

But Alice stepped back, understanding immediately. "Go," she said. "She's calling you."

"Alice…"

"Go," she repeated, but gentler this time. "I'll be here when you get back."

The world folded, and Daniel fell through.

The Meadow was different this time.

More solid. More real. The grass beneath his feet felt substantial, and the air carried the scent of wildflowers instead of ash and sorrow. Golden light filtered through a sky that actually looked like sky.

Elizabeth sat by a stream that babbled softly over smooth stones, her form solid and present. She looked up as he approached, and her smile was radiant, alive.

"Daniel," she said, rising to embrace him.

This time, when she wrapped her arms around him, he could feel her—warm and genuine and unmistakably his mother. He buried his face in her shoulder and finally let himself cry.

"I'm so sorry," he sobbed. "I'm sorry I left you. I'm sorry I couldn't save you."

"Shh," she murmured, stroking his hair like she had when he was small. "None of this is your fault, sweetheart. None of it."

They sat together by the stream, her hand in his, and for a while neither of them spoke. The water moved peacefully over the stones, and Daniel could almost forget they were in a place between worlds.

"How are you here?" he finally asked. "Like this, I mean. So solid."

Elizabeth's fingers moved to the key at her throat, the silver catching the golden light. "I think it's this," she said. "I found it in a creek, not so different from this one. Back when I first slipped into this place. Before I understood where I was."

Daniel studied the key more closely now that he could see it clearly. The spirals carved into its surface seemed to ripple in the light, almost alive.

"It felt important," Elizabeth continued. "Special. Like it was meant for me to find, and I've been wearing it ever since."

"Do you know what it opens?"

She shook her head. "I'm not sure it opens anything, exactly. But it… connects things. I can feel it sometimes, like a bridge between here and there. Between who I was and who I'm becoming."

Daniel's chest tightened. "You're not becoming anything. You're still you. You're still my mom."

Elizabeth smiled sadly. "I am. But I'm also something else now. Something in between." She squeezed his hand. "And that's okay, Daniel. I've made my peace with it."

"I haven't."

"I know." She turned to face him fully. "But you need to. Because holding onto me is hurting us both. You're keeping me tethered when I should be free to choose, and you're binding yourself to something you can't control."

Tears blurred his vision. "I don't know how to let go."

"The same way you do everything else," she said gently. "With love. With courage. With the faith that some things are bigger than our fear of losing them."

The stream babbled beside them, peaceful and eternal. Elizabeth stood, still holding his hand.

"I need to tell you something," she said. "About the key, about why I really think I found it."

Daniel rose beside her, waiting.

"I think it was meant for you," she said. "Not to keep, but to understand. There are doors in this place, Daniel. Doors that have been locked for so long, everyone's forgotten they exist. But you… You're the kind of soul that makes doors remember how to open."

Before he could ask what she meant, she leaned forward and kissed his forehead.

"I love you," she whispered. "More than words. More than worlds. And I'll find a way to tell you again, someday, when you need to hear it most."

The Meadow began to fade around the edges.

"Mom..."

"Let me go, sweetheart," she said, already becoming translucent. "Let me go so I can choose to come back."

And then she was gone, leaving only the echo of her words and the scent of wildflowers in the wind.

Daniel returned to the Rook to find Alice standing by the window, her back rigid with tension. The murmurs of the Misfits drifted faintly from the tower's interior, distant but constant.

"How long was I gone?" he asked.

"An hour," she said without turning around. "Maybe more."

He moved toward her, still reeling from his conversation with Elizabeth. "Alice, she told me about the key—"

"I know what she told you." Alice's voice was flat, distant. "I felt it. The Meadow... It's changing. Because of you."

"What do you mean?"

She finally turned, and the look in her eyes made his heart sink. The walls were back up, higher than ever.

"You're not just visiting there anymore, Daniel. You're changing it. The Meadow was a fixed point. Neutral. Safe. Now it's bending around you, and that's what scares me."

"Alice..."

"The Meadow was balanced. It belonged to no one, served no agenda. But now..." She shook her head. "Now it's becoming an extension of you. Of your will. Your desires."

Daniel felt something cold settle in his stomach. "What are you saying?"

"I'm saying that maybe Grim was right about one thing. Maybe you are too dangerous to be left unchecked."

The words knocked him off balance. "You don't mean that."

But the way she looked at him—wary, guarded, almost afraid—suggested that maybe she did.

"I need time to think," she said, moving toward the tower's entrance. "About what this means. About what you may be unleashing."

"Alice, wait..."

But she was already gone, leaving Daniel alone with her words ringing in his ears and the memory of his mother's goodbye.

He sank against the wall, pulling his knees to his chest. In the space of an hour, he had gained something precious and lost something else entirely. The key around his mother's neck had felt like a gift, a connection to something larger. But Alice's reaction made it feel like a curse.

Outside, the Hollow hummed with its usual restless energy, indifferent to his pain. Daniel closed his eyes and tried to make sense of what Elizabeth had told him about doors and keys and choices.

But all he could think about was the fear in Alice's eyes, and the way she had looked at him like he was becoming something she didn't recognize.

Maybe he was.

And maybe that should terrify him more than it did.

23

The Weight of Centuries

The flames in the Sanctum burned low.

Grim sat motionless on his throne of onyx, shadows gathering at his feet in pools of absolute darkness. Firelight carved hollows beneath his cheekbones, casting his eye sockets into caverns. The wavering illumination painted the chamber walls with shapes that writhed and twisted. Faces perhaps, or hands reaching from stone, the memory of humanity etched into the very architecture.

His pale fingers gripped the armrest, knuckles jutting like broken glass beneath skin that had forgotten warmth centuries ago.

He could feel the boy out there—Daniel—stumbling through revelations, making choices, loving people he would inevitably lose. The familiar ache of recognition twisted in the vacant cavity where his heart had once beaten.

You think you're different, he thought, the words echoing in the vast emptiness of his mind. *You think your love will somehow be pure enough to avoid corruption.*

The flames guttered, and memory unfurled in the gloom.

Candles. Dozens of them.

They lined the stone chamber like fallen stars, their light wavering against frost-laced walls, wax pooling in pale rivulets on the cold stone floor. The air was thick with the scent of iron, a bouquet of spilled blood, and the deeper reek of grave earth and rotting hope.

Outside, the plague had claimed the city. Screams echoed through narrow streets. Pyres burned in the squares, consuming the dead by the cartload. Inside this hidden sanctuary, the world had narrowed to a single man and his impossible choice.

Elias Blackthorne knelt before a stone altar, his physician's robes heavy with ash and failure. His hands—once steady enough to stitch life back into the dying—trembled as they cradled a vial of crimson fluid. The liquid pulsed with its own rhythm, like a second heart that refused to surrender.

Behind him, footsteps approached. Hesitant. Afraid.

"Elias." Renwick's voice cracked on the name. His young apprentice stood in the doorway, face gaunt from weeks of horror, clutching a leather-bound tome like armor. "Please. This isn't medicine anymore."

Elias didn't turn. Couldn't. If he looked at Renwick, he might see the boy he had once taught to set bones and brew healing draughts. Might remember the oaths they had both sworn. Might remember the man he once was.

"Medicine failed them." The act of speaking scraped his raw throat. He had screamed himself hoarse these past weeks, raging at God and death and his own helpless hands. "Every prayer, every remedy, every desperate hour I spent trying to pull them back from the edge. And still..." His grip tightened on the vial. "Still, I held my daughter while she burned with fever. Still, I watched the light go out of my wife's eyes. And I could do nothing."

Renwick stepped closer to his mentor, his voice gentle but firm. "Master..."

"Don't." Elias' voice turned to ice. "Don't call me that. I failed them. Failed everyone who trusted me to save what couldn't be saved. I've

walked down this dark path and dragged you along with me for my own selfish reasons."

"You didn't fail them." Renwick struggled to keep his tone patient, knowing the slightest hint of accusation would set his mentor off on another tirade. They had been practicing this dance for weeks. Elias would dash right up to the fringe of the precipice, prepared to plunge, while Renwick would pull his mentor back from the edge.

"You're the most skilled healer in the city. You saved hundreds..."

"Hundreds." Elias' laugh was bitter, broken. *"And yet, the only two who mattered slipped through my fingers like water."* He finally turned, and Renwick couldn't hide his shock at what he saw. Elias' eyes had sunken deep into his skull, ringed with shadow. His cheeks were hollow; his skin was waxy. He looked like a man already half-dead. *"This won't bring them back."*

"Then why?"

"I know it won't bring them back." The admission tore something in his chest. *"But it will mean another father will never need to lose what I lost. Another husband will never need to hold his wife's hand as she drowns in her own blood, begging him to save her with skills that mean nothing against death itself."*

Renwick stepped closer, desperation bleeding into his careful composure. *"At what cost, Elias? This path leads to nowhere good. You know this. The man who taught me would know this."*

"The man who taught you is dead." Elias turned back to the altar. *"He died with them."*

He placed the vial on the altar with reverent care. The liquid inside had darkened during his vigil—red veined with black, pulsing with its own terrible life.

"They called me healer," he continued, voice dropping to a whisper. *"They knelt beside deathbeds and begged me to offer comfort, as if comfort were a cure. But I will be more than that. I will make death itself kneel."*

"Elias, please..."

But Elias was already uncorking the vial.

The moment the seal broke, the temperature plummeted so fast that frost bloomed across the stone walls like an infection. Shadows erupted from the walls, pouring out of them like blood from cracks that hadn't existed moments before. The candles extinguished themselves one by one, snuffed by winds that had no source. The air grew thick, viscous, choking them with the taste of copper and grave dirt.

Elias lifted the vial and poured the crimson liquid onto the altar.

The world screamed. Stone cracked. Time rippled. Reality bent until it snapped, and through the rupture came something vast and hungry and without mercy.

"Who dares disturb the balance?" The voice invaded their minds, bypassing ears entirely. Ancient, vast, speaking in frequencies that made their bones ache.

Elias dropped to his knees, but his voice cut through the chaos with steady purpose. "I seek dominion over death. I offer my soul to save all others from this suffering."

Laughter echoed from the void—cold, endless, without mercy.

"Foolish mortal. You seek to rule what cannot be tamed. Very well. You shall have your dominion... and carry its burden until time itself ends."

The vial shattered. The altar split down its center. Shadows rushed inward, a tide of living darkness, and Elias opened his arms to welcome them.

Renwick's scream tore through the chamber as the force hurled him against the wall, bones cracking, book splintering beneath him. But Elias did not scream.

He welcomed the darkness as it stripped away his name, his face, his precious humanity. He let it hollow him out and fill the empty spaces with something ancient and terrible. His love for his family became fuel for the transformation, burning away everything soft and mortal until only purpose remained.

When the darkness receded, the altar was gone. The candles lay in pools of cold wax. Frost traced the walls like veins of ice.

In the center of the chamber stood a figure wearing Elias Blackthorne's face, but it was no longer Elias Blackthorne. His eyes had become pale mirrors reflecting nothing. His skin stretched over bones that seemed carved from winter itself.

He looked at his transformed hands, flexing fingers that could now touch the space between life and death.

"So it begins," he said, and his voice carried the finality of closing graves. Grim had been born.

The past retreated, leaving Grim alone with his thoughts.

He sat in the present-day silence of his Sanctum, centuries of regret settling around his shoulders like a familiar cloak. The fire crackled softly, and he wondered—not for the first time—if Elias would have made the same choice knowing what he knew now.

Probably.

Love, he had learned, was the most dangerous force in any realm. It drove souls to impossible choices, made them willing to sacrifice everything for the mere possibility of protecting what they cherished most.

And Daniel... Daniel was drowning in that same love. For his mother. For Alice. For the scattered souls he thought he could save.

"You think you're different," Grim murmured to the empty chamber. "You think your love will somehow be pure enough to avoid corruption."

Water dripped somewhere in the darkness below, each drop marking time he could never reclaim. *Drip.* A decade of solitude. *Drip.* A century of regret. The sound had been his only companion through the endless nights, more faithful than any friend, more constant than memory itself.

He counted sometimes—a thousand drops, ten thousand— until the numbers lost meaning and became just another form of torment. Each one was a small funeral for moments that would never come again. Each one a reminder that while the world above moved forward, he remained frozen in the amber of his own making.

Grim closed his eyes and let the loneliness wash over him like a tide. In the space between one drop and the next, he could almost remember what it felt like to be human. To hope. To love without the knowledge that love was just another word for loss.

Drip.

The moment passed. The memory faded. And still the water fell, marking time in the realm where time meant nothing, for a soul who had traded everything for the power to save no one at all.

Grim's pale eyes lifted toward the shadows.

Old magic was stirring in the deep places of the Hollow. Powers that had been sleeping since before Elias Blackthorne ever knelt before that altar. The boy's presence, his growing power, his refusal to accept the rules, it was waking things that should have stayed buried.

"We shall see," Grim whispered.

Above him, a raven circled the Keep's highest spire, its wings cutting through the perpetual gray like a scythe through grain. It cried once—sharp, clear, final.

And in that cry, Grim heard an echo of his own transformation. The sound of love forging the chains that bind a soul. The sound of hope curdling to anguish.

24

The Breach
Begins

The Hollow had grown colder overnight. Not weather-cold, but the bone-deep chill of condemned prisoners counting down to dawn. The kind that started in your gut and spread until your teeth wanted to chatter, no matter how close you sat to the flames.

Around the dying fire, the Misfits sat in tense silence—seven souls who had chosen to follow a boy into what might be their final battle. The flames guttered low, surrendering ground to mist that crept closer with each dying ember. Even the crackling was muted, as if the fire understood the weight of what tomorrow would bring.

The air tasted like smoke and metal, that copper tang that clung to the back of the throat when fear had been a companion for too long. Nobody had eaten much of the evening meal. It was hard to swallow when stomachs felt like they were trying to crawl up through the ribs.

Daniel sat with the Talon resting beside him. The weapon lay quiet tonight, but its presence weighed on him like stones in his chest. Beside it lay the ledger Kess had carried out of the Bastion, edges still blackened with soot.

"This isn't going to work, is it?" he said finally.

His voice was raw, honest. He didn't want false comfort. He wanted someone else to voice the doubt eating at his insides.

"We're walking into a fight we can't win."

Betsy looked up from mending a tear in her shawl. "You don't know that. You've done more in a few weeks than the rest of us managed in years. Grim's not invincible."

Digger snorted from where he leaned against a tree. "He's close enough. We've all seen what happens to people who get too close to him. The ones who vanish. The ones who come back different."

Alice sat wrapped in her coat, staring into the flames. She hadn't spoken much since they had finalized the plan, but Daniel could see the fear in her eyes.

"I'm not saying we shouldn't try," Daniel said, rubbing his face. "I just can't shake the feeling we're already in checkmate. That he's five moves ahead while we're still figuring out the rules."

"Probably is," Digger said. "But that's the thing about monsters. They don't expect you to punch back. They expect fear. They expect you to kneel."

Daniel laughed bitterly. "What if there's nothing to punch? What if this whole system is built to swallow resistance?"

"Fear's part of the game. But if Grim were truly invincible, he wouldn't need threats. He wouldn't need the ledger. But he doesn't rest. He spies. He schemes. He's not a god—he's a man who forgot how to die."

"And what if we're wrong?" Alice cut through their planning. "What if we make everything worse? There's more evil here than just Grim. And Grim has managed to keep that evil at bay. We don't know what his defeat could mean to our worlds."

No one had an easy answer. Daniel looked around at the faces lit by firelight—worn, worried, but still here. Still willing to follow him into the dark.

"Then we find meaning in our battle. Figure out what we're each fighting for," he said finally. "If we're going to fall, we fall fighting."

The fire cracked, sending sparks into the air. Something changed among them. A kind of grim solidarity. And most importantly, trust.

Betsy resumed her mending. Digger closed his eyes and leaned back against his tree. Alice turned to watch the shadows, but her shoulders had relaxed slightly.

Daniel closed the ledger and tried not to think about what tomorrow would bring.

Later, when the fire had burned down to coal, Digger's voice cut through the quiet.

"There's something you need to understand about Grim."

Daniel looked up. In the dim light, Digger's face looked older, more worn than usual.

"He wasn't always what he is now."

Betsy sighed, setting down her needle. "It's true. He wasn't born into this. Grim… his real name was Elias. He was human. Just like us."

Daniel remembered this from Tate's stories about Grim. Elias. It sounded so ordinary. So human.

"What happened to him?" Daniel asked, wondering if either could shed more light on Grim's history than he already knew.

Digger pulled out his flask, took a long drink, then stared into the dying flames. "He was a healer who lost his family during a plague. He made a deal with the previous Reaper, thinking he could outsmart the system—that if he held the power, no one else would have to suffer."

"He got what he asked for," Betsy said. "Power over death. But the Hollow doesn't give anything freely. It took something from him. His humanity."

Daniel stared at the ledger. "So, he thought he was saving people. But he became the thing that trapped them here."

"Grief does that," Betsy said quietly. "If you let it dig deep enough, it becomes its own kind of prison."

Daniel tried to picture Grim as just a man—someone with love and loss and desperate hope. But the image kept sliding away, twisting back into shadow and cruelty.

"Am I supposed to feel sorry for him?" he asked.

"No," Betsy said firmly. "But you should understand him because you're standing in the same storm he once faced. And you think you're nothing alike. But you are. You both wanted to save someone. You both broke rules to do it. You both carry power that wasn't meant to be."

"He became a monster," Daniel said.

"So could you," Digger replied, not unkindly.

The words felt like a mirror being held up to Daniel's face. He swallowed hard. "Is there anything left of him? Of who he was?"

"Sometimes," Betsy said. "When he's quiet. When he's not performing, that's when you can see the man he used to be."

Digger shook his head. "That's when he's most dangerous. The man he was is the one who thought this was mercy. The monster's easier to fight."

Daniel closed his eyes, thinking of his mother's face. Of the grief that had driven him this far. Of the power growing under his skin.

"I won't become him," he said.

Betsy didn't smile. "Then remember what made him fall. It wasn't the power itself. It was the certainty that he was right."

"And if I forget?"

"We'll remind you," she said.

The fire crackled once more and settled into silence.

Sleep wouldn't come. Daniel sat apart from the others, back against a stone outcrop that leeched warmth from his body. The mist curled around his body, exploring with tentacles of gray vapor sliding between his fingers, testing his resolve with phantom touches that made his skin crawl.

The Hollow pulsed around him tonight, alive in a way that felt almost human. He could feel it watching him. Wanting. Every shadow danced to the music of the night creatures. Every sound magnified, setting his nerves on edge.

He heard a voice, soft and familiar, drifting from the depths of the mist like a lullaby sung in a graveyard.

"Daniel..."

His blood turned to ice water. Through the gray veil, a figure emerged. His mother's skin held the waxy pallor of a corpse, and when she moved, she left no footprints in the ash. Her eyes were too bright, too knowing, reflecting light with no source.

"Mom?"

She reached toward him with a lopsided smirk that was meant to resemble a smile. But it was too wide, and her lips stretched until they cracked at the corners. "You can't save me, sweetheart." The endearment dripped from her mouth like poison.

"Yes, I can. I found you. I remembered..."

"You're already lost." Her voice fractured, harmonizing with itself in impossible ways. "Just like him. Just like all the others who thought love could conquer death."

Her hand reached for his cheek, fingers elongating as they moved closer. The moment her skin touched his, frost spread across his face, burning with cold so intense it felt like fire.

The horror began in earnest when her features melted, peeling away in strips, and revealing a creature underneath that had never been human. Her eyes bled to black, pupils expanding until they swallowed her face. Her mouth stretched wider and wider, unhinging like a snake's, filled with teeth that belonged in nightmares.

"You'll fail them all," she hissed through that impossible maw. "And when you do, you'll come crawling back to join us."

Daniel jerked backward, gasping. The false mother collapsed in wisps of vapor, her laughter echoing even as her form dissolved. And from the mist stepped another figure.

Grim materialized from the swirling night foam, manifesting as if the Hollow had beckoned him and had opened its secret portal for him alone to step through.

But not as Daniel had seen him before. This version was taller, wrapped in living shadow, his face hidden behind a veil of darkness. When he spoke, his voice came from everywhere at once, reverberating through Daniel's bones, through the stone beneath him, through the very air.

"She's right, you know."

Daniel struggled to his feet. "I'm not you."

Grim laughed—a sound like ice cracking. "Oh, but you are. You dream of saving everyone while knowing you're not strong enough. You ache to be the hero while drowning in your own inadequacy. You carry guilt you didn't earn and wield power you can't control."

He began to circle Daniel like a predator. "You touched the Talon and it sang for you. You opened the ledger and it showed you its secrets." His voice dropped to a whisper that filled the entire space. "That thrill you felt when you struck down my lieutenant. Don't pretend you didn't feel the rush of absolute power flowing through your veins. You *craved* it."

The memory surged over him like a wave of acid. The cracking of bones. The tearing of flesh. The lieutenant's eyes widening in shock before the light died. The way the world had gone perfectly still around that moment of absolute destruction. And underneath it all, buried so deep he had refused to acknowledge it, the surge of savage satisfaction when the blade found its mark.

Daniel's stomach lurched, bile rising in his throat. His hands shook as the truth clawed its way to the surface.

"I hated it." He choked on his hollow words.

Grim stepped closer, close enough that Daniel could smell the grave earth that clung to him. "Did you? Or did you hate yourself for loving it?

Grim's laugh was soft, intimate, like a lover sharing a secret. "You think you are here by accident? You were born broken, Daniel.

Fractured in all the right places for power to seep in. That's why the Talon recognized you. That's why death bends to your will. You're perfect for what's coming."

His voice became a caress, poisonous and knowing. "You're exactly what this realm has been waiting for."

Daniel fell to his knees, clutching the Talon to his chest as if it could anchor him to sanity. The weapon was warm, genuine, but Grim's words burrowed deeper than comfort could reach. He tried to speak but couldn't find the words.

Grim knelt before him, close enough that Daniel could see his own reflection trapped in those pale, merciless eyes. "You'll see. When the moment comes—and it will come—you'll choose power over mercy because it's easier. Because it works." His smile was gentle, almost paternal. "Because you're already exactly like me."

The Talon flared against Daniel's chest, sudden warmth flooding through him like sunlight breaking through storm clouds. The light pushed back against Grim's presence, creating a small sanctuary in the nightmare.

But Grim only smiled wider as he dissolved back into the mist. "You're already mine, young reaper. You just don't know it yet."

And then he was gone, leaving Daniel alone with his doubts in the suffocating quiet.

He stayed on his knees for a long time, clutching the Talon like a lifeline while his chest rose and fell in jagged rhythms. The weapon's warmth couldn't chase away the ice that had settled in his marrow, couldn't silence Grim's voice replaying in his mind.

You're already exactly like me.

The words circled his mind like vultures, picking at every doubt he'd tried to bury. Had he enjoyed killing the lieutenant? He had felt exhilaration when he saved his mother. He had been surprised to find he killed so easily without remorse, but pleasure?

Daniel pressed his forehead against the cold stone, trying to ground himself in something real, something solid. But even the rock felt treacherous now, part of a realm that had already claimed him.

When he finally stood, his legs trembled like a newborn colt's. The camp glowed faintly through the mist, and for a moment, he almost couldn't force himself to return. How could he look at their faces, knowing what Grim had shown him about himself?

By the time Daniel returned to the makeshift camp, the fire had been coaxed back to life. Around it, the others sat in quiet preparation—Betsy mending a tear in her coat with precise stitches, Digger cleaning his blade with methodical strokes, Alice sorting through her pack for the third time that night.

No one asked where he had been. But every eye tracked his movement as he emerged from the mist.

Betsy was the first to look up. She saw his pale face, the fine tremor in his hands, the way he clutched the Talon. Without a word, she set down her pack and shifted closer to the fire, patting the ground beside her.

"Sit," she said, an order wrapped in maternal concern.

Alice looked up from her pack, her hand suspended mid-search. She had seen that look before, in her own reflection after particularly dark dreams.

Daniel dropped to the ground beside Betsy. The Talon lay across his knees, its weight both comforting and accusatory. For a long moment, the only sound was the fire's gentle crackling and the gentle swish of Betsy's needle passing through fabric.

"I saw him," Daniel said. "He came to me. In the mist."

The needle stopped moving. Digger's blade stilled against the whetstone. But no one looked directly at him. An unspoken understanding that some confessions required space to bloom.

"He showed me my mother. Told me I couldn't save her. That I was already lost, just like him." Daniel's voice was barely above a whisper. "Said I belonged to him. That the Hollow had chosen me because I was already broken."

Betsy set down her work and turned to him. "Maybe you are broken. Most of us are. But that doesn't mean you're a lost cause, yet."

"What if I could be?"

Betsy snorted. "Daniel, I've spent decades watching people become monsters. Trust me, the ones who worry about it usually don't." She poked at the fire with a stick. "It's the ones who stop asking that question you gotta watch out for."

Alice set her pack aside. "He gets in your head. Makes you doubt everything you know about yourself." Her voice carried the wisdom of experience. "But I've seen you fight, Daniel. I've seen you choose mercy when killing would be easier. That's not who Grim is."

She paused, the firelight catching the clasp still between her fingers. "Empathy without boundaries isn't compassion. It's complicity. Remember that when the time comes."

Daniel felt the knot in his chest loosen. These people had seen him broken, had watched him wield power that terrified him, had heard him confess his darkest fears. And still they sat beside him, solid and unwavering.

"We go to the fortress," he said, and for the first time tonight, his voice was clear and unshakable. "And we make it count."

Betsy smiled, her teeth glowing in the firelight. "Then let's plan what hurts the most."

Digger's grin was the first genuine expression Daniel had seen from him all week. "Now we're speaking my language."

They pulled closer around the fire, speaking in hushed tones about routes and timing, about how to use the ledger and Grim's defenses. Daniel found himself at the center not as a leader giving orders, but as part of a conspiracy of hope against impossible odds. He listened and asked questions as they drew maps in the dirt.

This wasn't desperation masquerading as courage. This was resolve, cold and certain as winter steel.

Eventually, the others drifted away to rest or make final preparations. Daniel stayed by the dying fire, the Talon beside him, both keeping silent vigil.

The night had grown so quiet he could hear his own heartbeat when a rustle above made him look up. A raven descended through the canopy with barely a sound, its wings cutting through the air like black silk. It landed just beyond the firelight and stepped forward, dropping something into the coals.

A single black feather.

It should have curled and crumbled in the heat. Instead, it glowed softly among the embers.

The raven held Daniel's gaze, and in those obsidian eyes he saw depths that stretched back to the first stories ever told. It turned and vanished into the mist as if it had never been there at all.

Daniel stared at the feather. A message from forces beyond his understanding. A reminder that ancient powers had taken notice of their small rebellion.

He didn't reach for it. Instead, he whispered to the night air, "We finish this."

The feather pulsed once with gentle light, and Daniel felt his fear hardened into steel-edged purpose.

Tomorrow, they would face Grim in his stronghold. Some of them might not survive. But tonight, they had each other and a plan. It would have to be enough.

25

Into the Keep

A lice moved carefully through the dying light, exhaustion so profound her bones ached. She'd been sitting alone at the edge of camp, trying to prepare herself for tomorrow, trying to find some last reserve of strength. But the silence had become unbearable.

Daniel looked up as her shadow fell across the coals. Without a word, she sank beside him, close enough that their shoulders touched. The simple contact seemed to drain some of the tension from her frame.

"I couldn't stay away," she said.

Daniel shifted, opening his arm, and Alice leaned into him. Her head found the hollow of his shoulder, fitting there like she'd been made for that exact space. They sat in silence, watching the coals glow red in the darkness.

"I keep thinking about tomorrow," she whispered against his chest. "After the fighting. What happens if we don't all make it back?"

Daniel's arm tightened around her. "We will."

"You can't know that."

"No," he admitted. "But I can choose to believe it."

Alice closed her eyes, listening to his heartbeat. Steady. Real. "I'm not ready to lose this," she said. "Whatever this is between us. I'm not ready to lose you."

Daniel pressed his cheek against her hair. "You won't."

"You don't know what he's capable of," Alice whispered. "I've seen what Grim does to the people who challenge him. How he breaks them." Her fingers curled into his shirt. "You're walking straight into his stronghold, Daniel. You're going to face him directly."

"We all are."

"But you're the one he wants. You're the one he'll focus on." Her voice caught. "What if I can't protect you? What if all of us together still isn't enough?"

Daniel pulled back just enough to look at her face in the coal's red glow. "Alice…"

"I need you to live through this," she said fiercely. "I need to know that even if everything goes wrong, you make it out."

Alice reached into her pocket and pulled out a small, delicate crescent carved from bone, polished smooth by countless touches. She pressed it into Daniel's palm, her fingers brushing his.

"What is it?" Daniel asked, feeling the unexpected warmth of the charm.

Alice's voice trembled, vulnerability leaking through cracks in her composure. "Something my sister gave me, before everything broke apart. She said it would bring luck."

His thumb brushed the polished surface, thoughtful. "Did it?"

Her lips curved faintly, humorless, bitter. "She died two weeks later."

The confession lingered between them, raw, exposed. Daniel winced, words catching in his throat. "Alice, I—"

"She said luck wasn't real," Alice interrupted, gaze fixed now on the coals in the fire pit. "That it's just another way of saying you tried, even though you knew you had lost."

Daniel closed his fingers around the charm, feeling the soft edges press against his skin, the crescent fitting into his palm as it had always belonged there. He met her eyes once more, emotion brimming beneath careful restraint. "Then why give it to me?"

She looked up at him, and in the glow of the coals, he could see tears threatening at the edges of her eyes. "Because if we lose…

I don't want to regret holding something back." She cleared the emotion from her throat. "Because maybe luck isn't about winning. Maybe it's about having something worth fighting for."

Daniel understood—the depth of the admission, the vulnerability it cost her. He nodded, slipping the cord around his neck. The charm settled against his chest, just over his heartbeat—warm, grounding him in this moment of trust.

"Alice," he said, voice steady despite the ache it carried, "thank you."

Her expression softened. A fleeting openness, masked again behind familiar composure. "Don't thank me yet. Just... try to come back."

She stood and faded back into the shadows. Daniel stayed by the coals, aware of the cold space where her shoulder had lain against his skin. The charm pulsed with her body heat, and he understood that fear could forge bonds as strong as any other force out there.

He had no illusions about luck or fate. But this token—small, fragile, heavy with love and loss—felt real in a way few things did anymore.

And as the mist drifted around him, he whispered into the silence. "Thank you."

The fading light answered in silence, and he closed his eyes, feeling—for the first time—ready for whatever came next.

The night held steady, suspended as if captured within glass. It had ceased deepening, choosing instead to remain trapped within a twilight hush, stretched over the clearing like gossamer woven from threads of memory and anticipation. The fire burned low. The glow of the hot coals seeped outward, painting the clearing in a muted warmth.

He found Betsy sitting beneath a gnarled tree. She seemed small beneath it, cocooned within her heavy coat, cupping a chipped enamel mug. She looked up as he approached, her eyes bright in the darkness. She didn't raise her head as he settled beside her, knees bending, hands dangling near his sides.

"Can't sleep?" Her voice was quiet, threadbare, frayed at the edges.

"No. Too much to think about."

She patted the ground beside her. "Sit. Before you go charging off to save the world." He nodded, understanding what she meant.

Daniel settled beside her, grateful for the companionship. Betsy reached into the folds of her coat, withdrawing a small cloth bundle. She placed it in his hands, eyes lifting to meet his, weary yet steady.

"Open it," she said.

Daniel's fingers shook as he unfolded the cloth. Inside was a stone—smooth, river-worn, with spirals carved deep into its surface. It was warm to the touch.

"What is it?"

"They call it an anchor-stone," Betsy explained. "It holds onto things when they're too heavy to carry. Memories, feelings, all that weight we pile up inside ourselves. When you're ready, or when someone else needs it more, you can pass it on."

Daniel traced the spirals with his thumb. "Whose memories?"

Betsy's expression grew distant. "A man I used to know. Lost his family and couldn't find a way to live with it. Instead of letting the grief run its course, he tried to fight it off. Make it go away." She paused. "Grief's like a river. You can let it flow through you, or you can try to dam it up. But dammed water always finds a way to break free."

"Elias," Daniel said quietly.

Betsy added another log to the fire and wiped her hands on her tunic. "I knew him before he became what he is now. Before grief twisted him up inside. He was good people, a healer who'd give you the shirt off his back. Loved his family somethin' fierce." She paused, watching the sparks fade. "But he carried that love like it was gonna crush him. Every person he couldn't save, every loss, he took it all personal. And when he lost the ones that mattered most…" She shook her head. "Well. You see what it did to him."

Daniel looked down at the stone. "And this?"

"A reminder," Betsy said, leaning back against the trunk of the dying tree. "Love is a funny thing. It can build you up or tear you down, depending on what you do with it. Elias loved so hard it ate him alive. But that don't mean love's the problem. It's what you let it turn into."

He closed his palm around the anchor-stone, feeling its energy through his skin. "Thank you."

"Don't thank me yet," she said. "Just remember—when push comes to shove, you listen to your heart. Don't let the hurt make your choices for you."

She squeezed his shoulder once, then stood and walked back toward the others, leaving Daniel alone with the depth of her wisdom and the warmth of the stone in his hand.

He gazed at its smooth surface. He wondered about Elias, about his grief, about kindness twisted into cruelty. How love, left unspoken or misunderstood, could become its own monster.

And beneath the quiet night, holding the anchor-stone close, Daniel made a promise to himself.

He promised that if grief were meant to bloom, he would let it. That he would carry love with care—no matter how it might wound.

The light ebbed into shadow, but the stone's warmth lingered in his palm, quiet reassurance and burden all at once.

He wandered into the mist without meaning to, drawn by a yearning nestled in the marrow, an ache that pulled him forward.

He hadn't intended to go far, yet each step carried him deeper into the shrouded night, the world behind him fading into silence. Trees loomed, their shapes blurred, indistinct, softened edges bleeding into shadow, like smudges of charcoal drawn by an uncertain hand. The air thickened, woven from sighs and echoes of things long gone.

"Daniel..."

The sound reached him, achingly tender. He turned, afraid to breathe, hope and disbelief twisting in his chest.

Elizabeth stood outlined in silver-edged mist, barefoot. The hem of her hospital gown barely touched the grass. Her hair cascaded like river weeds, luminous and ethereal. Her eyes found his at once, and in that moment, everything else ceased to exist.

"You're not supposed to be here," Daniel said, his voice cracking.

She smiled sadly. "Neither are you."

His heart stilled, pain and understanding mingling beneath his ribs. He stepped closer, yet the distance between them remained unchanged, as though the Hollow itself held them apart in mercy or cruelty.

"You're supposed to be back," he whispered, voice breaking beneath the truth he could barely accept. "I let you go—I let you go. I chose the Hollow."

"You did, sweetheart. And I went back. Mostly. But a part of me... some part couldn't stay away. I had to see you one more time."

Daniel felt tears pricking his eyes. "Am I hurting you—holding you here?"

Elizabeth stepped closer, each movement graceful. "No, my sweet boy," she whispered, voice certain. "This time I chose to come back. I couldn't leave without seeing you again."

He gasped, pain and gratitude threading through him. "Why?"

"Because you're about to face something dark," she said, eyes tender, steady, luminous in the gloom. "Daniel, remember who you are. You're the boy who sat with that hurt bird for hours, even when it kept trying to bite you. You knew it was acting out of fear, not out of spite. That's your heart. Don't let this power change it."

Daniel shook his head, desperation in his voice. "I know why—I know what happens if I fail..."

"Not because you want to defeat him," she interrupted, stepping closer, gaze holding his. "But because you want to save people. That's what this was always about for you, Daniel. Protecting the ones you love. Don't let anger make you forget that."

He rubbed the anchor-stone and closed his eyes as if praying for wisdom. "I don't know if I remember anymore."

"Yes, you do, sweetheart," she said, her voice clear with maternal certainty. "I can see it in you still, even if it hurts to look."

He opened his eyes, his thumb still tracing the stone's surface. "I'm losing parts of myself. I can feel it. The Hollow takes pieces every time I step closer."

"Then don't let it," she said fiercely. "Hold onto who you are, Daniel. Hold onto that boy with the bird."

"I don't know how."

Elizabeth's eyes were filled with love and pain. "Oh, my sweet boy. You saved me once. When I was drowning in my own darkness, you were my light. You can do it again."

Daniel let his tears fall, unashamed. "I'm afraid," he wept, feeling once again like that little boy he had so long ago left behind. He thought about all the things left unsaid. Thought about the times, even when he was at his worst, his mom was always there to make him feel loved and whole again.

Elizabeth's gaze softened, radiant as starlight. "I know you are. That's not a bad thing."

"I miss you," he whispered, words vulnerable, aching.

"I know that too," she whispered, love shimmering in her eyes. "But you're not alone. You're surrounded by souls who love you. Who will do anything for you. There's strength in that. And know that I am so very proud of you. I always have been."

"You were there, weren't you? In the shelter. The rafters. You watched." Daniel said.

"Of course I did. I just didn't know if I belonged there anymore," she said, touching his face tenderly.

His heart clenched, grief blooming, painful in its beauty. He wanted to reach out, to touch her, to hold her.

"I love you," he whispered, the truth spilling forth, vulnerable.

She smiled, luminous, beautiful—love reflected in each softened line. "I love you too, Daniel. Nothing will ever change that."

Her form began to shimmer, edges fading, dissolving into mist and memory. "I have to go now," she whispered, voice bittersweet. "But promise me something."

"Anything," he said.

She leaned forward, words urgent, trembling. "If it comes down to choosing, Daniel—please choose mercy. Even if it costs everything."

"Mercy for who?" he asked, grief catching in his throat.

She didn't answer—only smiled, gentle sorrow edged with radiant love. Her form dissolved, fading back into mist, back into ache and memory.

"Mom," he whispered, grief spilling from him, "don't go—please—"

But she was already fading, dissolving into mist, leaving behind echoes of warmth, love, ache. Daniel stood trembling, grief pouring from him—a breaking—sacred and quiet.

He closed his eyes, her presence lingering within every heartbeat.

"I'll choose mercy," he whispered, the promise given, aching. "I promise."

"I love you, Mom," he whispered to the empty air.

The fortress rose from the earth like a wound that had never healed.

It wasn't built, it was grown, conjured up from stone and shadow and centuries of accumulated pain. Spirals covered its surface, glowing faintly in the perpetual gray light of the Hollow. It looked less like a building and more like a scar on reality itself.

Daniel stood at the tree line with the others, staring up at the impossible structure. The air here was different, thicker, more oppressive. Even the mist seemed reluctant to get too close.

"Well," Digger said quietly. "There it is."

"It's smaller than I expected," Alice murmured.

"It's not the size that matters," Betsy said. "It's what's inside."

Daniel felt the Talon pulse against his back; the ledger grew cold against his ribs. The anchor-stone warmed in his hand, and Alice's charm seemed to hum with nervous energy. All these tokens of trust and memory, weighing him down and holding him up at the same time.

"Ready?" he asked, though he knew none of them were.

They crossed the barren ground in silence, the Keep's malevolence closing in with each step. The air grew thinner, harder to pull into their lungs. Daniel felt his head begin to pound, a low throb that matched his heartbeat. Beside him, Alice pressed a hand to her stomach, fighting down rising nausea. Even Digger's steady pace faltered slightly, his breathing becoming labored.

With each step, the world behind them seemed to fade a little more. The trees grew indistinct. The path they had followed blurred and vanished. By the time they reached the fortress entrance, there was nothing left behind them but empty gray—and the sick certainty that the building itself was trying to drive them away.

The doors opened without a sound.

Beyond lay darkness, a hungry void that seemed to breathe with anticipation, tasting their fear and finding it sweet. It didn't just fill the space; it devoured it, leaving nothing but an endless throat waiting to swallow them whole.

Daniel stepped across the threshold first, his jaw set with grim determination. Alice followed without hesitation, her hand briefly brushing his shoulder, a final touch of connection before whatever came next. Betsy crossed with quiet dignity, murmuring something under her breath that might have been a prayer or a curse. Digger came last, pausing for just a beat at the entrance, his eyes scanning the darkness one final time before he stepped into the void with them.

Behind them, the doors sealed shut with a finality that echoed in their bones.

No way back. Only forward.

And from somewhere deep in the Keep came a sound—soft, delighted, pleased.

Laughter.

Daniel drew the Talon, its blade catching what little light filtered down from above. The weapon felt eager in his hands, ready for what was coming.

"Let's finish this," he said.

The Keep breathed around them, and somewhere in its depths, Grim waited.

26

The Price of Peace

The moment they entered Grim's dark stronghold, Daniel felt a vast and patient presence, watching from the shadows between the twisted columns.

Alice and Betsy followed him deeper into the chamber. Even their presence could not warm the space. They moved without speaking, their steps careful. Each footfall echoed through the halls, and they feared the sound would give them away.

The ground rumbled beneath their feet. Daniel paused, his heart quickening with dread.

Grim materialized from the gloom on the walls, a figure of wafting smoke and whispered torment. Threads of grief gathered around him, trailing along the floor like the edges of mourning cloth frayed by time.

Daniel recognized that look in Grim's eyes: grief sharpened to an unbearable edge, pain worn down until it had become armor.

"Bold," Grim murmured, his voice a rasp of stone against stone, "to enter this place with your false courage."

Daniel reached for the Talon at his back, the hilt warm beneath his palm, stirring like a long-held purpose finally rising to consciousness. He eased it free, the curve catching in dim light.

"I didn't come to chat, Grim," Daniel replied, the words shaped with care. "I came to lay something to rest."

Grim's smile stretched across his rippling features. He stepped closer, the chamber sighing beneath his passing. Shapes folded around him, faces forming from darkness—eyes closed, mouths parted, trapped in silent sorrow.

"You speak of rest," Grim said, voice almost gentle. "But do you even know what I am?"

Daniel's breathing slowed, his heart hammering beneath his ribs. He watched those faces move through Grim's form—souls woven into shadow. They watched, their grief a hum beneath Grim's voice.

"You believe the ledger binds them?" Grim asked, voice mocking. "That the Talon might unmake what I've become?"

He lifted a hand, and chains shimmered in shadow behind him—delicate, threaded of silken grief and regret.

"You're no Reaper," Grim continued, stepping forward. "You're a boy tangled in threads stretching back to the roots of time, reaching for an ending you don't fully understand. An ending you'll soon regret."

His voice filled the halls, thick and relentless like war drums pounding through hollow logs. Alice panicked beside Daniel. She had seen this very moment reflected in dreams. The scene before them shifted: the distortion no longer circled Grim, but curled around Daniel instead, insistent yet subtle.

Betsy's fingers tightened on the cloth bundle at her belt, pale knuckles betraying the tension she hid beneath years of trained steadiness.

Daniel felt the tension in his shoulders. He met Grim's eyes and saw what he had only sensed before: a reflection, not an enemy: familiar sorrow, unspoken grief, loss.

"I don't need to rewrite your story," Daniel said, voice edged with sorrow and resolve. "I only need to let it end."

Grim lifted his hand, and the scythe unfurled from shadow, as though it had always been there, waiting. Its edge curved in strange patterns—intricate whorls and sharp edges, and it hummed in a deep, mournful tone.

Grim's eyes closed for just a moment, grief loosening its grip. When he opened them again, they carried a long-awaited relief.

"Then come," Grim whispered, beckoning. "Lay us both to rest."

Daniel stepped forward, heart aching. He carried no promise of victory, no guarantee of peace. Only the certainty that this grief needed its ending. And his promise to show mercy.

He held the Talon, warm beneath his fingertips. The Keep watched.

"Fear made me silent," Daniel said softly. "Love taught me to speak."

And as he raised the weapon, the chamber sighed—an exhale, a release. The first breath of peace it had ever known.

The scythe met the earth like the last stroke of a pen, signing away lingering hope.

A declaration. A seal upon fate itself.

Beneath Daniel's feet, the ground fractured into red-veined helices, splitting open in meaningless patterns. They bled light that soaked the chamber in a bruised red glow, exposing every crack, every scar. Nothing could hide from it. Not even him.

He felt it more than he heard it, low and steady, thrumming behind his eyes, threading through his ribs like wire drawn tight. It coiled around his chest, not loud, but inescapable.

The screams belonged to no living throat. They rose from beneath the Keep, fractured, ancient voices tearing from hollow stone. Agony climbed with them, frantic and shapeless.

Souls spilled upward through the fissures, dozens swelling into hundreds. Dark chains bound them—glistening threads spun from sorrow and loss, from grief that had taken on weight and shape.

They surged like floodwater through cracked earth, filling the chamber with soundless cries. Faces blurred by waiting, bodies twisted by years of absence and ache.

These were not warriors. They were reflections of emotions. Warnings carved in pain.

Daniel staggered, fighting a wave of nausea triggered by the rising chaos. The Talon vibrated in his grip; desperate clarity cut through the storm twisting in his chest.

Beside him, Betsy jerked to a stop, every muscle drawn tight, eyes wide with horror. Alice moved swiftly, blades drawn, her gaze burning through the dimness with fierce, protective defiance.

Above them, Grim rose, lifted by the anguish churning below, arms spread wide—a conductor of pain, orchestrating torment with practiced grace.

"You thought to spare them?" Grim's voice cut through the chamber, edged with contempt, not triumph, bitter as rust. "You believed mercy could mend what eternity itself refused to heal?"

A soul lunged, its mouth stretched in a silent scream. Daniel reacted without thinking, raising the Talon. The weapon pulsed, halting the soul as though pressing against an open wound, staunching its bleeding. Recognition flickered deep within its hollow eyes, sparking briefly before chains dragged it away, swallowed again by the swelling tide.

Grief buckled his knees and cinched tight across his chest. He dropped to one knee, the chamber spinning. It filled with whispers and the rustle of forgotten names. Every soul he had ever seen in the ledger pressed against his ribs.

The Talon's warmth faded beneath his skin, its presence growing brittle. Uncertain.

Release it, whispered from deep inside. Persuasive. *It's easier to let go.*

Behind him came a sudden cry—piercing, desperate, choked off. Followed by the dragging rasp of chains. Daniel turned, heart slamming against ribs too fragile for such violence.

Betsy's eyes widened, meeting his in one shattered heartbeat before chains tightened around her ankles, pulling her toward a fissure yawning wide, crimson light rising to embrace her like open palms.

Alice screamed her name, voice fracturing as she broke formation, steel slashing against silhouettes that yielded but never parted.

Daniel reached desperately—

Too late.

The chains pulled Betsy down, her final gaze fixed on his—unblaming, achingly gentle—as the shades swallowed her back into memory.

Before Daniel could rise, another soul struck him. It passed through with cruel ease—its touch an emptiness cold enough to burn—leaving behind a hollow scraped raw, a wound that could not be filled. Grief dulled past sorrow into a numbness that stole even the shape of pain.

He collapsed again, the Talon slipping from his grip.

It skittered across the stone and came to rest at Grim's feet.

Grim knelt, reaching, fingertips brushing the smooth hilt. He recoiled, pain flaring in eyes gone dark with old, unhealed hurt.

The Talon pulsed, its surface unblemished yet defiant.

Daniel watched. And understood.

It recognized Grim. Not as master or enemy. A sorrow it had held before.

Grim rose, eyes narrowed. His voice edged with disappointment. "You still think victory matters here—that this ends with you standing?"

Daniel couldn't speak. His body faltered beneath devastation, lungs fighting for air that wouldn't come. But behind his closed eyes, a memory stirred, small and warm as a hand against his chest.

Elizabeth's face, luminous beneath hospital light. Her smile, quiet bravery shaping each line. Her touch, fingers reaching out even though she knew he would forget.

A vow whispered into darkness, memory brushing gently across the aching strings of his heart. The love she had given him—unconditional, fierce—stirred to life inside his chest.

The Talon pulsed again, glowing now, waiting at Grim's feet. Daniel didn't yet rise but hope inside him bloomed—fragile but unyielding.

He would not stay fallen.

Grim's figure was haloed by souls who gathered behind him, silent witnesses to their mourning. Daniel's fingers curled against rock, ribs tightening around the ache that would not break him.

Defiance, not victory. Mercy, not vengeance. Accountability, not complicity.

He would rise again because he had promised. Promised someone who believed he could.

And the Talon waited, glowing like a beacon in the dark, ready for the hand that would lift it once more.

The Talon pulsed with the ache of memory.

Daniel didn't feel himself collapse, but he witnessed the surrender. The world peeled away like old bark under careful fingers, exposing raw, wounded truth beneath its skin.

He fell through that opening into memory itself, deep and old, layered in silence, waiting for someone brave enough, or foolish enough, to find it.

And there he was, in a room.

Small. Cramped. Lit by candles whose flames fought to stay alive, their glow casting shadows that stretched and writhed. Daniel choked on the air thick with bitter herbs, stale sorrow, and beneath it all, a sweetness long since soured.

Beyond the walls came muffled, distant cries, tolling bells, rasping coughs—a storm of sound and suffering.

Inside, silence ruled, broken only by the scrape of desperate breathing.

A man knelt, his robes heavy with soot, blood, and grief so thick it had become substance, dripping from his fingertips like ink from a quill. He hovered above an altar, hands shaking, holding a small vial that shimmered in the candlelight. Its crimson contents pulsed with life.

Daniel knew him instantly by the ache radiating from his bowed shoulders. By the way his fingers clenched so tightly they nearly burst.

Elias Blackthorne.

Grief poured from Elias like an open wound. Upon the altar lay a braid of golden hair, delicate and soft as down, a child's faded ribbon, and a tarnished ring. Objects gathered and placed with reverence and desperation.

His voice scraped against the silence, ragged. "Let it be enough. Let me trade what remains."

The door creaked behind him, opening to reveal another figure— young, pale, a leather-bound book clutched to his chest like armor that might shield him.

Renwick. Youthful, unscarred by the Hollow's touch, eyes wide with fear.

"Elias," he whispered, voice breaking. "Stop. Please."

Elias did not turn. His gaze fixed upon the altar; eyes shadowed beneath grief and guilt woven through each line of his face. "You think I don't know she's gone? That they both are?"

Renwick's words were woven with sorrow. "Then why do this? Why won't you let them rest?"

Elias lifted the vial, uncorking it, pouring its contents into the cracked basin before him. The crimson liquid hissed, whispering as it touched stone, staining it, spreading like ink through water.

"Because grief is currency," Elias murmured, his voice aching beneath its calm. "And I have saved enough sorrow to buy them peace."

He spoke words Daniel did not recognize, syllables edged in pain, felt instead of heard. Each one bruised beneath his skin.

The candles dimmed. Their flames turned black as soot. The space folded inward.

Then, a formless voice emerged. *Who disturbs the balance?*

Elias sank to his knees, his voice vulnerable, broken open by longing and loss.

"Let me carry their burden," he begged. "Let me gather the grief they cannot bear. I will bind their pain to myself. I will pay any price."

The voice replied with indifference made tender by ancient sorrow. *Then carry what they could not, Elias Blackthorne. Hold their grief as your own, until it holds you instead.*

A shadow descended, weaving into Elias's form. Wrath joined blood. Guilt became breath. Grief stitched through bone.

Elias's scream was deep, resonating through the cold stone chamber.

And when he rose, he rose transformed, no longer Elias Blackthorne, but a figure shaped irrevocably from darkness itself.

A Reaper.

Now—

The Sanctum returned, reality swathing Daniel like a cloak drawn across anxious shoulders.

Grim stood, swaying, smoke spilling from parted lips, eyes wide, fractured with anguish. "I only meant to save them."

There was pain in his voice. Regret.

"You didn't save them." Daniel tightened his grip around the Talon, but not as preparation to fight. "You made them prisoners to your pain."

When Grim met Daniel's eyes, the fury was gone. In its place sat the quiet devastation of a man seeing his mistakes clearly for the first time.

And somewhere deep within the Sanctum, a single chain began to fracture.

Daniel rose, the hair on the back of his neck prickling. The Talon glowed in his grip, steady as a hand laid against a grieving heart. It became a witness, not a blade of war, pulsing like a heartbeat that had nearly forgotten its own rhythm, now remembering what it was to rest again.

At the chamber's far edge, Grim stood in shadow, smoke billowing around him. His scythe lay broken, half-melted, surrendered upon the stone like a sacrifice.

Where the shattered weapon lay, something else stirred. Threads of shadow and pale light lifted in the chilled air. The scythe did not vanish; it unmade itself, waiting for the next hand that the Hollow would choose.

His eyes held bewilderment. Not rage, but a grief held just beneath the surface.

The Misfit warriors watched in amazement. Witness to a victory they thought could never be.

One shape stirred at the edge of Daniel's vision. Small and familiar, a woman's silhouette, radiant. Her presence vibrated through the crumbling chamber.

Mom.

Or the memory of her. She neither spoke nor cried. Her eyes found Daniel's, and in those eyes was held a love deeper than words.

Her presence there steadied him. Gave him the courage to do what had to come next.

Daniel stepped forward, each footfall unhurried and deliberate. The Talon shimmered. It opened multiple pathways toward freedom for the trapped souls, inviting them to find their way to the path meant for them. It guided without threat. Nudged without invoking fear.

"You were never meant to be trapped here like this," Daniel whispered, voice shaping each word thoughtfully. "You belong to yourselves alone. To your own destinies. This is not what death was meant to be."

At Elizabeth's wrist, the phantom chain that imprisoned her soul to this place pulsed once and broke, as if made of frost touched by morning warmth. She drifted forward, her soul free to return to her body, radiant, her eyes shining with gratitude and peace.

Grim's howl cut the air, panic bleeding through his voice. "You don't understand. You can't hold them all—"

Daniel watched him come undone. The Talon beside him still shimmered with a deep golden glow.

"I'm not holding them," he said softly. "I'm letting them go."

Another chain broke, releasing a soul, followed by another, and another. Each snap resonating throughout the chamber, each sound a sigh of relief.

The fortress began to hum with a deep, resonant tone of gratitude and relief, as long-bound souls had finally been set free.

Alice stood frozen beside him, her voice a reverent whisper. "He's doing it. The Hollow hears him."

And it was.

The walls pulsed, alive. The Keep exhaled, welcoming a long overdue change, grief finally permitted to become memory instead of a chain.

Daniel moved forward, stepping toward the center, toward the heart of all things sorrowful and bound.

The Talon ascended, held by quiet promise and resolve, the certainty of someone who knew grief's shape intimately and chose to let it go.

And the Hollow itself paused, waiting as the world changed beneath Daniel's touch.

The first soul reached out. A woman, hollow-eyed and hesitant, her hair drifting like smoke around shoulders bowed by centuries of waiting. Her hand hovered near the chain at her wrist, nervous. Unsure if this was a trick of some kind.

Daniel met her gaze. No words passed between them. He nodded. Once. The chain broke with a tight metallic click.

Grim staggered, gasping, smoke seeping from deep phantom wounds. His voice cracked under the strain of desperation he could no longer mask.

Daniel moved toward the pedestal; the half-burned ledger still clutched in his hand. He laid it on the stone, feeling it pulse beneath his palm, a heart encased in shadow, pounding louder with every soul set free.

The Talon guided him. A sculptor's chisel. A precise tool carving truth from illusion. He lowered the blade, tracing a single deliberate helix across the surface. The mark burned slowly, cutting a line of molten gold, unbinding but not destroying.

The ledger buckled beneath the Talon's blade. Light seeped from its cuts.

Names flowed out, radiant scripts suspended briefly before vanishing. Each was a life reclaimed. A story released. The chamber filled with a gentle brilliance, darkness driven back.

Grim fell to his knees, arms enfolding his chest, agony etched into every line of his face. "You think you've found peace," he rasped. "But you've mistaken destruction for salvation. Without this, the Hollow consumes itself."

Daniel turned toward him, the Talon glowing at his side. Its light touched his face, revealing no triumph, only a quiet, aching sorrow. He saw the fear in Grim's eyes. The fear that had held him to this place for centuries. The fear of not knowing what comes after. The fear that held him to his curse even after the grief had worn thin.

"Then let it fall," Daniel said, his voice steady but despondent. "Let all that was cruel and unjust burn away. Let something gentler rise from its ashes."

The last chain snapped, resonating like the final note of a lament. The freed souls rose like embers caught in an upward draft, drifting beyond the reach of sorrow.

And the ledger fell silent, the stronghold crumpling beneath Daniel's feet with quiet surrender.

For the first time in memory, the Hollow knew what it meant to be empty, open, ready for a future built from something other than grief.

Chains fractured, turning to rust and memory before fading into motes of golden dust. The stone walls, etched deep with spirals and sigils, lines of fracture spreading like the slow unfurling of petals at dawn.

Overhead, the ceiling arched and buckled, sighing downward, as though surrendering into a long-awaited sleep. Stone warped, yielding beneath the quiet dignity of acceptance, gracefully folding history into layers of dust and remembrance.

From the ledger's core, a soft radiance spilled—a warmth delicate as candlelight, brushing across closed eyelids before waking. Daniel stepped back as the ledger split open. Not pages, but wings, unfolded into ash, fluttering once, then dissolving into memory.

The souls rose, one by one. Then dozens. Then countless more. They ascended, curls of golden mist spiraling outward. No longer lost spirits, carried by unseen currents toward long-denied horizons. Chains fell behind them, discarded like chrysalises abandoned in metamorphosis.

No cries pierced the silence. No voices spoke of gratitude or vengeance. Only reverence filled the chamber. Each soul became an ember, rising skyward. Sparks lifting from an ancient fire now extinguished, scattering into realms unseen.

And amid the luminous dispersal, one figure lingered—a silhouette shaped from soft-edged memory.

Mom.

She drifted in quiet stillness, her form wavering slightly at the edge of vision. She turned slowly, her gaze meeting Daniel's across the fading distance—as heart to heart, not as ghost to living. Her eyes, deep with sorrow yet alight with serenity, held his for a fleeting moment.

She smiled, a gentle curve of lips familiar and heartbreaking, soft as sunlight passing through cloud cover. And with that quiet smile, she dissolved, her form woven into the light that now filled the chamber, beyond grief's reach, beyond longing's ache.

The ledger's ashes settled into a dusty mound. The Talon dimmed, its glow fading into solemn stillness, its edges dulled. Its purpose fulfilled.

And Grim—

Grim wept.

He collapsed onto the floor, no longer wreathed in shadow. No longer the monstrous reflection. He lay as a man now, shoulders hunched, hands pale and human against the cracked stone. His features were deeply lined with sorrow and regret, no longer distorted by darkness.

Elias Blackthorne looked up through smoke-blurred eyes. Human eyes. Eyes filled with a familiar ache.

"Did it hurt?" he rasped, voice raw as stone scraped bare.

Daniel knelt beside him, offering presence without benefit of comfort—truth, not pity.

"Yes," Daniel said quietly. The admission settled between them, heavy yet gentle.

Elias let out a faint, broken sound, or perhaps a sob softened by relief. "Good," he murmured, eyes closing carefully. "Then you did it right."

His chest rose once more. Shuddered. Then stilled. The lines of suffering relaxed from his face. Elias released the long-held breath of centuries, and finally, the Reaper passed on, unchained, free to rest.

The Hollow shivered around them, quaking beneath a quiet recognition of its own ending. Walls creaked as the Keep drew nearer to collapse. With no master, it was no longer needed in this world. Mist seeped through widening cracks, carrying whispers of remembrance and release.

"We have to go—now," Alice's voice cut through the quiet. Urgent.

She grabbed Daniel's arm, her grip firm, grounding him in this moment of ending.

He rose, recognizing the gravity of what had happened. His gaze drifted once more to the ledger's resting place, now nothing more than dust and fading embers. At his feet lay the Talon, still and silent, its purpose spent, its edge dulled by the gentle finality of mercy granted, not vengeance taken.

He did not lift it again.

He left it where it lay, a symbol, now quiet, of stories completed and burdens laid aside. Then, with each step resonating through the collapsing chamber, he turned away and began to run.

Stone folded behind him; the fortress surrendered itself piece by piece into gentle ruin, history closing in like a book returned to fine powder. Yet as he fled, Daniel felt a sort of resolve rather than fear or panic. A deep knowing that this place, once cruel, would bloom again in time, gentler things would take root where pain had long been planted.

As they broke through mist and shadow into clearer air, above and beyond the veil of the Hollow's lingering sorrow, a single raven called out, a cry resonant and clear, echoing through sky washed clean by endings.

A benediction, not a warning.

Its voice carried over fading stone and settling dust, sanctifying the ruin behind them, honoring the peace yet ahead. Daniel paused briefly, marveling at the purity of the sound. A solemn farewell from something wiser, older, and now finally free.

He left the rubble of the fortress behind, stepping into an uncertain future, emptied of chains, burdened only by promise.

And as the raven's cry faded, the Hollow behind him released a final, grateful sigh, folding itself away into memory.

Far beyond the Hollow's reach, something old stirred.

As Daniel's unbinding rippled through the planes, a hairline fracture opened in the seam between worlds. And through that crack, a raven-shaped shadow slipped into the divine realm. Silent. Unseen. And ancient.

27

Where We
Say Goodbye

aniel stood where the Keep had collapsed, dust still settling around his boots. The air tasted different now—cleaner, though still tinged with ash and memory. The oppressive weight that had hung over this place for centuries was gone, leaving behind something fragile and uncertain.

Alice walked beside him, her face drawn with exhaustion and grief: the space where Betsy should have been felt hollow, a reminder of what their victory had cost. The surviving Misfits gathered in somber quietude. There were too few of them, Daniel thought, but still here. Still breathing.

"It's too quiet." Alice lowered her voice to suit the spirit of the moment.

Daniel nodded. The Hollow's usual groans and whispers had ceased. Even the mist seemed less aggressive, drifting rather than pressing. It was peaceful in a way that felt almost foreign.

Around them, shapes emerged from the shadows, the last of Grim's creatures, the twisted things that had once prowled these gray lands. But they moved differently now. Drifted peacefully. Without hunger or rage.

One of them—massive and crumbling—dragged itself toward the center, ribs visible beneath sagging skin. It paused in front of Daniel, breath ragged and shallow. Its head tilted, slow and uncertain, as though waiting to be told what to do.

Daniel didn't reach for a weapon. He simply watched it with understanding and sympathy. He understood what it meant to be lost.

The creature blinked, if that was what it could be called. Without a sound or a struggle, it folded inward. It simply unraveled—like smoke caught in a breeze.

Its body dissolved into motes and light, drifting upward in small spirals before vanishing into the white clouds of the new Hollow's sky.

Another followed. Then another. They came forward in ones and twos. Some crawling. Some limping. Some upright, wobbling with effort. None of them spoke. None of them resisted. They simply let go.

One by one, they disintegrated. Their bodies faded. Their forms came undone. The pain that had shaped them no longer held its form, and without it, they ceased to be.

Alice stepped beside him, her presence solid and steady. When she spoke, her voice no longer held its signature edge. "They weren't evil."

Daniel nodded once. "They were just lost. Like all of us were."

There was one creature left. It crouched in the shadow of a broken stone, skeletal and shivering. Its skin hung in peeling folds, like scorched parchment. Its single remaining eye searched the empty expanse like it was waiting for someone to call it home.

Daniel approached it slowly. As he drew near, the creature flinched—but did not flee. It looked up at him. Its mouth opened, but no sound came from it.

For the briefest moment, Daniel saw something in its eyes. Recognition. A child's fear. A man's failure. A need so raw and blinding it had calcified into hatred.

He knelt, but the creature didn't move.

"I know what you came from," he said. "And I'm sorry." He lowered his hand. Open. Empty.

The creature stared at his hand for a long time. Trembling, it leaned forward. Its head brushed against his palm like a wounded animal leaning into warmth it barely remembered. And in that touch—brief, feather-light—it dissolved. Quiet as moonlight.

Daniel remained still, hand suspended in the air, tears tracking silently down his face. He wasn't sure when he had started to cry. The tears weren't hot. They came like the Hollow's mist—slow, inevitable, without anger. Grief without urgency. Love that no longer had a place to land.

Alice placed her hand on his shoulder. The others gathered quietly around them. Survivors. Witnesses. None of them spoke. There was nothing left to say.

A faint scent, reminiscent of spring flowers, wafted on the gentle wind. Daniel swiveled toward the source.

She stood at the edge of the clearing, barely more than a silhouette against the mist. Her hair moved gently in the breeze, and her hands hung at her sides, clearly shaking and confused.

Daniel's heart nearly stopped. It was her eyes first. That storm-gray depth he had carried in memory, in dreams. Eyes that had watched him sleep, laughed with him at the kitchen sink, gone wide in fear the day everything fell apart.

She looked older than he remembered. Worn by time and worry. A face shaped by love, by grief, by the years neither of them got to share.

"Daniel..." she whispered.

His knees nearly gave out. He blinked hard, but she didn't vanish. She was there—truly there. He could see the lines at the corners of her mouth, the faint freckle near her jaw, the way her lower lip always trembled when she tried not to cry.

"I thought I had lost you," she said.

He found his voice, but barely. "You didn't, Mom. I'm still here."

She stepped closer, her arms twitching at her sides, unsure whether to reach for him or protect herself from what this might be. Daniel didn't move. He was afraid that if he did, the illusion would break.

But she didn't blur at the edges. She only came forward, one step at a time, until they stood within reach of one another.

"You're taller," she said, her voice fraying at the edges.

He smiled—barely. "You're not."

A breath of laughter slipped out of her, cracked and wet. She lifted a hand slowly, gave him time to stop her. He didn't.

Her palm came to rest against his cheek. Warm. Real. The dam inside him broke.

Daniel turned his face into her hand and closed his eyes, every part of him trembling. She smelled faintly of lavender and of something maternal and safe, aching with memory.

"I didn't get to say goodbye," she whispered.

"You don't have to."

His hand covered hers where it touched his skin. He opened his eyes. They glistened with his tears, unashamed.

"I can't stay," she said.

"I know."

They stood like that for a moment—held in the stillness between reunion and farewell. Words were sparse, but they weren't needed when the message between mother and son was felt more than words could convey.

"There's something I need you to do," he said, remembering a vital promise made so long ago.

Her brows furrowed, hesitating a second. "Anything."

His throat tightened, but he pressed on. "There's a girl. Ava. She might be there. Near you. Watching over you. And I won't get to tell her this myself."

Her face crumpled with understanding.

"I want her to know that she's brave," he continued. "That she was always brave. Even when I wasn't. And that I'm so proud of her for finding her way."

She nodded, tears slipping freely now. She took both his hands in hers. "I will," she said. "I'll find her. I'll tell her everything."

Daniel leaned forward, resting his forehead against hers. Their breath mingled—one final, steadying moment.

"And I'm proud of you," she said.

He let the words settle. Let them fill every hollow place inside him.

"I love you," he said. "I never stopped. Even when I told you something different. I always loved you."

The light around her began to swell—not in a rush, not like some cruel wind ripping her away. It was gentle. Reluctant. Like the world was trying to let her go as softly as it could.

"And I love you, my sweet angel. I'll love you forever and always."

Daniel didn't fight it. He watched her fade. Watched her rise as if the Hollow itself was lifting her, piece by piece, into the place she belonged.

And just before she vanished, she smiled—a promise she would always be there when he needed her.

Then she was gone.

The place where she had stood glowed, the stone warmed by her presence. Daniel looked down, shudders coursing through him.

A storm of regret and longing churned within him, each heartbeat a painful reminder of words left unsaid and moments lost to time.

He didn't cry. Not this time.

But he knelt and placed a hand where hers had been.

And for the first time since entering the Hollow, he whispered not to the dead, or to the damned, or to the dark.

He whispered to the living.

"Find your way back."

And far away—beyond the veil, beyond the Hollow, beyond the limits of shadow and sleep—a mother stirred in a hospital bed.

Elizabeth's eyes fluttered open, her hand instinctively reaching across the narrow space between beds. Her fingers found Daniel's—still warm, still real, still connected to the rhythmic beeping of machines that had become the soundtrack of her vigil.

She had been dreaming. Or remembering. The boundary between the two had blurred during these long weeks of sitting beside him, watching his chest rise and fall with mechanical precision while his mind wandered into realms she couldn't follow.

But he was different now. She could feel it, subtle as the moment between seasons. The quality of light filtering through the hospital blinds had changed, grown softer, more golden. The antiseptic smell had faded. Even the constant hum of machinery felt muted, distant.

"Daniel?" she whispered, squeezing his hand.

His breathing had changed. Slower. Deeper. Not labored, but peaceful. Like settling into sleep after a long, arduous journey.

Elizabeth sat up straighter, her heart beginning to race. "Daniel, can you hear me?"

The monitors continued their steady rhythm, but she could sense him pulling away. Not his body—that remained warm beneath her touch. Something that had been holding on by the thinnest of threads. His mind.

"I know you're far away," she whispered, leaning closer. "I know you've found somewhere else. Somewhere important." She let her tears fall without shame.

His face was serene. The worry lines that had appeared over the past year had smoothed away. He looked like her little boy again, the one who used to climb into her bed during thunderstorms and fall asleep against her shoulder.

"It's okay," she said, though her voice cracked on the words. "If you need to go... It's okay."

The machines began to change their tune. Subtle at first, a slight irregularity in the heart monitor, a dip in the oxygen readings.

Elizabeth felt it before she heard it, the way a mother knows when her child is about to wake from a nightmare.

But this wasn't waking. This was the opposite.

"Mrs. Donnelly?" A nurse appeared at the doorway, alerted by some change in the monitors.

Elizabeth didn't look away from Daniel's face. "I think... I think it's time."

The nurse moved quickly to check the readings, but Elizabeth already knew what she would find. The numbers were dropping steadily, peacefully. Not the chaotic crash of a body fighting to live, but the gentle ebbing of a soul that had made its choice.

More staff arrived—doctors, additional nurses, people with urgent voices and quick hands. They spoke about medications, procedures, and options.

"No," Elizabeth said quietly, and the authority in her voice stopped them all. "Don't. Please."

"Mrs. Donnelly, we can still..."

"He's not coming back." The words came from somewhere deep, from a place that knew truths beyond medical charts and protocols. "He's already gone where he needs to be."

She looked down at their joined hands. His was still warm, but she could feel life flowing out of it like water through cupped palms.

Nestled between their fingers was something she hadn't noticed before, a small, smooth stone etched with a spiral. Betsy's anchor-stone.

As Elizabeth touched it, a memory not her own shimmered at the edge of her awareness: laughter in the Meadow, a girl with kind eyes, a promise made in chains.

The stone pulsed once, then stilled.

"I love you," she whispered, bringing his hand to her lips. "Whatever you've become, wherever you are... I love you."

The heart monitor's beeping slowed. Steadied, and then faded.

Elizabeth closed her eyes and felt the moment it happened—not just the flatline on the machines, but the cutting of an invisible cord, the final severing of ties that had bound his soul to this world.

The alarms sounded, but they were distant. Unimportant.

In the sudden quiet of her heart, Elizabeth understood. This wasn't death. This was her son's rebirth.

Her little boy had become something else entirely. Something the machines couldn't measure, something the world of hospitals and medicine couldn't contain.

"Time of death," someone said behind her. "3:17 AM."

But Elizabeth was already standing, already moving toward the window where dawn was beginning to paint the sky in shades of gold and silver.

Somewhere beyond the veil, beyond the Hollow, beyond the limits of shadow and sleep, her son had work to do.

And for the first time since this all began, she smiled.

The Hollow settled. The last winds died. The gray thinned at the edges like dawn behind clouds. The ground beneath their feet no longer quaked. It held them.

Daniel rose, stiff as an old man. The creatures were gone. The name Grim no longer echoed. The Hollow had stopped torturing.

And for the first time in its long, haunted life, it rested.

Daniel turned toward the others. Alice met his gaze, her nod slight but steady.

Behind them, the path stretched forward, uncertain, unmarked.

"We go?" someone asked softly.

Daniel looked ahead. There were no signs. No prophecy. Just space enough to begin again.

"Yes," he said.

They walked together. Not as fugitives. Not as soldiers. But as survivors with hearts still beating, even if bruised.

The Hollow did not roar.

It exhaled.

As they moved deeper into the transformed landscape, Daniel felt the magnitude of what was to come settling over him. The scythe formed in his grip, shaping itself to him as though it had been waiting for a hand to claim it. The weight settled, solid and sure. It was nothing like the weapon Grim had carried.

Around them, more souls began to emerge from the mist, freed from their chains but uncertain of their path.

He stopped, turning to face them. The survivors gathered beside him—Alice, the remaining Misfits, and dozens of liberated souls who looked to him with a mixture of hope and fear.

"You're all free now," Daniel said, his voice carrying across the assembled crowd. "The chains are broken, and you have a choice."

The souls drifted, their forms flickering faintly. "What choice?" one asked, doubtful.

"To move on," Daniel said, gesturing toward the horizon where soft light now glowed. "Or to stay. Help me rebuild this place into something better. A place of transition, not torment."

A few souls immediately stepped forward, determination in their glowing eyes. "We'll stay," said a tall man with a weathered face. "We've seen what this place was. If there's a chance to make it right, we'll take it."

Others hesitated, their gazes darting between the distant light and Daniel. Finally, a young woman spoke, her voice soft but resolute. "I want to go home. I want peace."

Daniel nodded. "There's no wrong choice. Go if you're ready. Stay if you feel called. Either way, you're free."

One by one, souls stepped forward to make their decisions. Some dissolved into gentle light, drifting toward the horizon like fireflies carried on a warm breeze. Others moved closer to Daniel, their presence a quiet pledge of allegiance.

As the crowd thinned, Alice approached him, arms crossed tightly over her chest. "You're really staying, aren't you?"

Daniel nodded. 'I have to."

Her jaw tightened, and she looked away. "I hate this place," she muttered. "But if anyone can make it less awful, it's you."

He chuckled softly. "Not exactly a glowing endorsement."

Alice's lips twitched into the barest hint of a smile. "Don't let it go to your head."

The scythe pulsed in his hand, its weight both comforting and daunting. As he tightened his grip, the ground beneath him rumbled gently. The Hollow began to reshape itself, the jagged, oppressive structures softening into something less hostile. Paths of soft light stretched into the mist, leading toward hope rather than despair.

A single raven landed on a nearby stone, watching him with its unblinking gaze. Daniel met its eyes, his resolve hardening.

"This is just the beginning," he murmured. The raven cawed softly, as if in agreement.

Around him, the remaining souls—those who had chosen to stay—watched silently, their faces carrying uncertainty and cautious hope. Daniel turned to them, his voice firm despite the exhaustion weighing on him.

"We rebuild. Together. This place has taken enough from all of us. It's time to give something back."

A murmur of agreement rippled through the crowd, and for the first time in what felt like an eternity, Daniel saw a flicker of genuine hope in their eyes.

He took his first step as Hollow's new guardian, the scythe glowing faintly in his grasp, ready to face whatever came next.

28

The New Reaper

The Hollow had changed.

Its once-jagged terrain had softened beneath Daniel's presence. The mist curled gently, no longer pressing in like a weight, but drifting as if the Hollow, at last, could let go.

Daniel stood at the edge of the great black river; the scythe balanced across his palms. Its weight felt more solid. Steadier. No longer resisting him.

The raven perched on a nearby stone, watching him with ageless, ink-dark eyes that never blinked.

"You're still here," Daniel murmured. A faint smile tugged at one corner of his mouth.

The raven cawed softly, tilting its head, not in warning, but perhaps in approval.

Daniel looked down at the river's surface. His reflection shimmered—faint, fractured—but present. "I wasn't sure I could make it," he admitted, voice low. Not to the raven. Not even to himself. He was speaking to the Hollow.

The scythe shimmered faintly in answer, the runes along its edge pulsing.

The Hollow wasn't healed. But it was listening.

A faint sound drifted through the mist. A low bark carried on the shifting air. Daniel lifted his head, half expecting to see the black hound at the tree line. Maybe Wolfie was still out there, showing the lost their way home.

A light appeared in the distance, glinting through the mist like a flame fighting the wind. Daniel turned toward it, the raven taking flight and settling onto his shoulder with a rustle of feathers.

"Someone's lost,' he said quietly.

He walked.

His feet sank into the terrain with each step—less hostile now, more yielding. The light grew stronger as he approached, resolving into the shape of a soul. Frail. Flickering. Curled into itself like a frightened child.

Daniel knelt before it, setting the scythe aside.

"Hey," he said gently. "It's okay. You're not alone."

The soul flinched. "I don't know where to go," it whispered. Its voice was ghostly and fading. "I'm afraid."

Daniel nodded slowly. "I know. I was, too."

The soul looked up. Its eyes were hollow but searching.

"You don't have to stay here," Daniel said. "Let me help."

"Are you the Reaper?" the soul asked.

Daniel paused. "I am. But not the one from the fairy tales you've heard."

A long silence. Then, slowly, the soul reached out. Its hand faded in and out but solidified as it touched his.

He pulled it upright, and the raven gave a low, steady cry. A path shimmered behind them, lit by moonlight that no longer hides in the Hollow.

"Follow the light," Daniel whispered. "It'll take you where you need to go."

The soul lingered. Its shape wavered with uncertainty. Then, softly, "Thank you."

It stepped into the light and was gone.

Far away, in the too-bright hush of an empty hospital room, Elizabeth sat in the chair she'd occupied for weeks. The machines were silent now, unplugged and wheeled away three days ago. But she couldn't bring herself to leave. Not yet.

It had been three days since the machines went quiet. Since Daniel had finally let go and become something else entirely. Elizabeth still came to sit in the empty room, unable to fully accept that he was gone.

She had fallen asleep, forehead pressed to the edge of the mattress. And in the liminal drift between waking and dreams, she saw him. Not as he was three days ago. Not small and pale and quiet in a hospital bed. But very much alive, and older.

He stood in mist, cloaked in quiet, his eyes faintly aglow. Not from some form of possession. But of freedom.

"Daniel?" she whispered in the dream. Her voice cracked on the name.

He turned toward her. Smiled gently.

"I'm here, Mom," he said.

And though she couldn't touch him, she felt the warmth of his hand in hers.

She awoke with a soft gasp. The room was silent again—just the ticking of machines and the dim flicker of morning light. Her hands folded empty in her lap.

"I know you're still with me," she whispered aloud. "I'll never stop believing that."

Down the hall, other machines continued their fragile rhythm— other patients, other vigils. The sounds of the hospital ward carried on, steady and faint.

But she smiled anyway.

A soft knock at the doorframe made her look up. A young woman stood there. She was in her early twenties, with dark hair and kind eyes that held the particular exhaustion of someone who had fought her own battles with the space between worlds.

"Mrs. Donnelly?" the woman said quietly. "I'm Ava."

Elizabeth felt a strange flutter of recognition, though she was sure they had never met. "Ava?" The name sparked something: a memory from the dream, Daniel's urgent request.

"Your son... he helped me find my way home. I promised him I would watch over the people he loves." Ava stepped closer, her presence somehow both gentle and solid. "I've been keeping vigil, three doors down, since I woke up."

Elizabeth's heart swelled. This was the girl Daniel had asked her to find. "He wanted me to tell you something," she said, her voice thick with emotion. "He wanted you to know that you're brave. That you were always brave. Even when he wasn't."

Ava's eyes filled with tears. "He said that?"

"And that he's so proud of you for finding your way." Elizabeth reached out and took the young woman's hand. "He couldn't tell you himself, but he needed you to know."

Ava squeezed her fingers gently. "Thank you for telling me. And Mrs. Donnelly? He's not gone. He's exactly where he needs to be, doing exactly what he was meant to do."

Elizabeth nodded, finally understanding. Her son had become something beyond what hospitals could measure, beyond what this world could contain.

And this brave young woman would help her remember that love transcends every boundary.

Back in the Hollow, Daniel stood at the river's edge again. The soul was gone, but the solemnity of the moment lingered—soft and solemn, like the last note of a song.

The raven leapt from his shoulder and landed in front of him. Its form shimmered, feathers rippling like smoke in moonlight. For a moment, it seemed larger—more than a raven, less than a god. A presence cloaked in wings. And when it looked at Daniel, it wasn't as a creature looks at its master. It was the look of an equal.

Its wings spread, black and iridescent. Its gaze never wavered.

Daniel inhaled the Hollow's new stillness and exhaled slowly, tension easing from his body.

The scythe thrummed softly in his grip.

The ground around him shifted. The jagged terrain softened further, the river's black waters clearing just enough to show glimpses of light beneath. The shadows retreated, not banished, but at rest.

This place was still the Hollow. But it no longer felt like a prison. It felt like a passage. It felt more like home than anywhere else he remembered.

He turned slowly to face the horizon. Mist writhed at his feet, curling gently like smoke from a candle just extinguished. And there—in the far distance—a soft glow had begun to rise. Not warm like the world he had left behind. Not cold like the world he had endured.

Just present and full of possibilities.

Daniel tightened his grip on the scythe.

"This is just the beginning," he whispered.

The raven cawed once, sharp and clear.

Then it spread its wings.

And together, they stepped forward into the fading light.

The End

Whispers After the Hollow

The door is still there.
But it no longer watches.
It waits. Quietly.
As if it already knows what comes next.

Mist drifts through its frame like breath
exhaled at the end of a long story.

There are no more screams behind it. Only
silence. And the hush of remembering.

Daniel stands on the far side now. No longer
lost. No longer afraid. But changed.

The Hollow breathes. And this time, it does not resist him.

PRELUDE TO

The Twilight of Vraskel

Beyond the fading Hollow, the breach shivered—its seam of light thinning to a razor-fine fissure between worlds.
On the other side lay the Divine Realm: black-sand plains swept by cold wind, basalt cliffs rising like broken teeth, and temples carved from midnight stone.

The raven-shaped shadow stepped through.
Its wings unfurled, vast and silent, blotting out the pale horizon as it took its first breath of stolen air.

And deep in the heart of that land, where old runes slept beneath ice and ash, something ancient stirred in answer.

Twilight was coming.

COMING NEXT

The Twilight of Vraskel

Long ago, the gods cast Vraskel into the depths of the Hollow.
They thought his fall would end an age of terror.

They were wrong.
When Daniel's unbinding tears open a fracture between realms, something ancient slips through—a shadow shaped like a raven, carrying twilight on its wings. The divine realm of Dyrhala trembles as temples crack, omens burn, and whispers of a fallen god spread like sickness through its sacred halls.

Exiled and half-forgotten, Elaren is summoned home—called to face the twilight she once helped prevent.
But Vraskel is no longer merely fallen.

He is rising.
He is hungry.
And twilight follows in his wake.

The Twilight of Vraskel
Book Two of the Hollow Prison Series
Coming soon

T.M. ROCHE

The Hollow is only the beginning...

If you'd like to know when new stories rise from the Hollow's depths — to glimpse the shadows that linger beyond these pages and discover what worlds I'm conjuring next — join me at:

DragAndFlyPress.com

From there, you'll also find links to my author pages, social spaces, and exclusive extras

Your support keeps these stories alive.

If this book spoke to you, please consider leaving a review. Even a few words make an *underworld* of difference.

Acknowledgments

This story was not shaped in solitude.

To my beta readers—Megan, Paul, Will, and Jane—whose eyes found both the cracks and the hidden treasures. Your honesty and patience carried this book farther than I could have managed alone.

To my editor and proofreader, Chris Knight of The Deliberate Page, whose careful attention caught every whisper (literally) between the lines. You gave this haunting tale the polish it needed to truly take flight.

To Tamara Cribley of The Deliberate Page, my dear friend and tireless supporter, who not only guided me as a formatter and coach but also cheered me on when I needed it most. This book would not have crossed the finish line without you.

To my husband, Rob, for enduring late nights and long silences when the Hollow claimed my attention more than it should.

And to every reader who turns these pages: you give stories their true voice. This book belongs to you as much as it does to me.

About the Author

TM Roche grew up in a tiny valley in rural Pennsylvania, where stories of ghosts and things that go bump in the night were more common than pumpkin pie in the fall. That sense of wonder has woven itself into the dark fantasies she now writes.

Today, she is an editor and storyteller, publishes through Drag & Fly Press, and believes the best tales linger long after the last page is turned. When not conjuring the Hollow and its haunted depths, she can often be found exploring quiet cemeteries, hidden trails, and other forgotten places near her home in Colorado, gathering echoes for future tales.